SPECIAL MESSAGE TO READERS

THE ULVERSCROFT FOUNDATION
(Registered UK charity number 264873)

Established in 1972 to provide funds for research, diagnosis and treatment of eye diseases.

Examples of major projects funded by the Ulverscroft Foundation are:-

- The Children's Eye Unit at Moorfelds Eye Hospital, London
- The Ulverscroft Children's Eye Unit at Great Ormond Street Hospital for Sick Children
- Funding research into eye diseases and treatment at the Department of Ophthalmology, University of Leicester
- The Ulverscroft Vision Research Group, Institute of Child Health
- Twin operating theatres at the Western Ophthalmic Hospital, London
- The Chair of Ophthalmology at the Royal Australian College of Ophthalmologists

You can help further the work of the Foundation by making a donation or leaving a legacy. Every contribution is gratefully received. If you would like to help support the Foundation or require further information, please contact:

THE ULVERSCROFT FOUNDATION
The Green, Bradgate Road, Anstey
Leicester LE7 7FU, England
Tel: (0116) 236 4325

website: www.ulverscroft-foundation.org.uk

0060311703

D1615054

THE ORPHAN TWINS

London, 1910. Lily is ten years old when she realises her grandmother, a washerwoman in the backstreets of London's Bermondsey, is seriously ill. She's determined to do what she can to help and keep her grandmother's illness a secret — even from her beloved twin, Artie.

When tragedy strikes and the twins are faced with the prospect of a workhouse or an orphanage, a benefactor offers to take Artie in and educate him. All Artie's needs will be taken care of — but the gentleman has no use for a girl. The twins never thought they'd lose each other.

As the orphan twins grow up and take different paths, their new lives are beyond anything they could have imagined. Will they ever find a way to be together again?

LESLEY EAMES

THE ORPHAN TWINS

Complete and Unabridged

MAGNA
Leicester

First published in Great Britain in 2020 by
Aria
an imprint of Head of Zeus
London

First Ulverscroft Edition
published 2021
by arrangement with
Head of Zeus
London

A catalogue record for this book is available from the British Library.

ISBN 978–0–7505–4876–2

Published by
Ulverscroft Limited
Anstey, Leicestershire

Printed and bound in Great Britain by
TJ Books Ltd., Padstow, Cornwall

This book is printed on acid-free paper

For my beautiful daughters,
Olivia and Isobel,
who bring joy to my world.

1

Bermondsey, London

January 1910

Lily entered the yard from the alley that ran behind the shabby little terraced house that was home. Seeing Gran at the kitchen window, she raised a hand in a wave only to realise that Gran was hunched over the sink in what looked very much like pain, her eyes screwed shut and her lips clamped tightly together.

Lily's steps came to a halt as she was torn between rushing to darling Gran's aid and allowing Gran her pride because Maggie Tomkins would hate to be caught out in what she was likely to consider weakness. Standing watching for a moment, Lily hoped Gran had simply stubbed her toe or received a minor burn from a hot iron. Despite that hope, the memory of Mum doubled up and coughing blood caused a chill to rise up Lily's spine.

'Cor, Lil! Dunno where it came from but it was a whopper!' Artie burst into the yard behind her, having paused to inspect a caterpillar he'd noticed in the alley.

The noise roused Gran who looked up and straightened with a guilty air as though she'd been caught out in wrongdoing. Always hungry, Artie rushed into the kitchen for his dinner. Lily fol-

1

lowed, but slowly. Thoughtfully.

'Are you home for your dinners already?' Gran said, wiping sweat from her forehead. 'I wouldn't have stood idle if I'd realised the time. But it's hot in here with all this ironing and there's only so much heat a body can take before she needs to catch her breath.'

She waved round the room at all the shirts she'd ironed. Two irons sat in the hearth warming up for the next lot.

Had she really only been catching her breath? Being a washerwoman was certainly back-breaking work. But Gran was pale instead of flushed and could easily have opened the door or window to let in a blast of freezing winter air if she'd needed to cool down.

Lily looked back at the shirts and wondered if there were actually fewer of them than normal. If Gran was ill, it stood to reason that she'd be unable to work as hard.

'Let's get some food inside you,' Gran said.

'I'll fetch it,' Lily offered quickly. 'You put your feet up.'

'Put my feet up when there's work wants doing?' Gran laughed, but Lily persisted.

'Just for a minute or two. I've been sitting down at school all morning. I need to move around.'

'Maybe I will sit down,' Gran finally conceded. 'But not for long.'

To Lily's relief, Gran pulled out a chair that was tucked under the small kitchen table and sat. Lily moved to the cupboard where food was kept along with plates, cups and cutlery. Inside she found a loaf on a wooden board which she carried to the table together with a knife before returning to the cupboard in search of something to put on the bread.

Artie loved the meat paste that came in round white pots but it had been a long time since they'd had any of that. Sometimes there was cheese but not today.

There was butter but not much of it so Lily reached for the jam pot instead. Gran had made the jam from the blackberries Lily and Artie had gathered from any stray bush they'd been able to find in the autumn months but the jar was already half-empty and there weren't any more. Less work meant less money coming in, of course, and that meant emptier cupboards.

Gran had been ill only twice before as far as Lily could remember. The first time, they'd all had upset stomachs and spent the day dashing outside to the privy. Gran had blamed a piece of mutton she'd cooked in a stew. 'I'll give that butcher a piece of my mind,' she'd threatened, and as soon as she was well enough she'd marched into his shop to tell him what had happened.

''Course that mutton was off,' she'd insisted when he'd argued. 'You must have let it sit in the window too long.'

'I didn't!'

Gran had simply crossed her arms and waited.

'Look, I'm not saying you're right,' the butcher had finally said, looking round at his other customers as though fearing they might take themselves and their custom elsewhere. 'But I can see you're out of sorts so, just to show I'm a man who likes to help his customers, I'll make you a gift of a nice

3

string of sausages.'

'I'll take some bacon too,' Gran told him. 'And the same again next week.'

Gran was afraid of no one but there'd been no free sausages or bacon the second time she'd been ill because there'd been no one to blame for her bad chest. The only wonder was that her chest hadn't been bad more often considering they lived in a house that spent its days filled with steam and its evenings with the steam turning to drips downs walls and windows. Sometimes the drips turned to ice.

Lily decided to say nothing of her suspicions for the moment, seeing as Gran obviously didn't want to worry them. Lily didn't want Artie worried either. But she'd watch Gran carefully from now on and help as much as she could.

She cut a thick slice of bread for Artie as he was always so hungry. 'Gran?' Lily invited.

'I'll have mine later.'

Would she, though? Probably not, if food were in short supply. Lily was tempted to go without eating too but Gran would know then that she'd given the game away about being unwell. Her pride would be hurt as Gran liked her grandchildren to be both well-fed and well-shod. No running around in bare feet in all weathers for them. Artie would realise something was wrong as well.

Reluctantly Lily cut a slice of bread for herself but made it a thin one. She spread jam liberally on Artie's slice but added little more than a dab to her own.

She picked her slice up quickly to hide the

4

lack of jam but Artie had already noticed. 'I've got more jam than you,' he pointed out. He was a sweet boy who liked to be fair.

'You've got more growing to do,' Lily told him, hoping a little good-natured teasing would distract him from the jam before Gran noticed it too.

Artie pulled a face. It was a sore point with him that Lily should be just thirty minutes older yet a whole two inches taller. 'You a girl and all,' he often complained.

Lily took after their father and Gran, being straight and slender with the near-black hair and blue eyes common among people from the Irish homeland Gran had left as a child – though Gran's hair was white all over now. Artie was more like their gentle mother – small and soft with honey-coloured eyes and toffee-coloured hair.

'Just wait until we're eleven,' Artie said now. 'I'll catch you up and leave you behind.'

'We'll see,' Lily said, smiling, and she was glad to see Artie tuck into his bread with every sign of having forgotten his extra jam. 'School was good this morning,' she said, changing the subject before he remembered it. 'Miss Fielding said she was pleased with my handwriting.'

'You always write a nice hand,' Gran said.

'Davie was sick in my class.' Artie grinned.

Lily looked at Gran and they both rolled their eyes. Boys laughed at the oddest things. 'Poor Davie,' Gran said.

'He said he felt better afterwards. I think he did it on purpose because Mr Simpson has new shoes and — '

'I think we've heard enough of Davie,' Gran

5

said. 'You'll put us off our dinners.'

Talk of Davie's indisposition hadn't put Artie off his dinner. He crammed his bread into his mouth and ate it hungrily. Lily ate hers more slowly then lifted the kettle onto the fire to save the cost of lighting the gas on the stove. It was a rare day when there wasn't a fire in the kitchen hearth. Gran boiled most of the washing water on the stove in the big copper but the fire was used for extra water as well as for heating the irons and drying the washing, especially at this time of year when it could hang on the lines in the yard all day and still come in damp.

Gran looked out of the window where sheets billowed on the washing line like sails. 'I'd better fetch that lot in,' she said, hands flat to the table as she levered herself out of her chair.

To Lily's eyes it seemed to require more effort than usual. Lily waited until Gran was outside then got up to return the loaf and jam to the cupboard. With her back to Artie so he couldn't see what she was doing, she reached for the old tea caddy in which Gran kept their money. It felt worryingly light.

Replacing it, Lily took out cups and a small jug of milk. The rest of the milk was kept in the front parlour where it was cooler. They used their tea leaves three times before they gave them to Harold Finnegan on Grace Street to use on his allotment in return for occasional vegetables or rhubarb. It was a day for new leaves but Lily used the old ones again. There wasn't much life left in them but hopefully Gran wouldn't notice the tea was weak.

'Any buttons to sew back on?' Lily asked, as

6

Gran returned with her arms full of washing.

Gran's sight wasn't what it had once been so sewing was a job Lily took on gladly.

'A few. There's a fallen hem that needs mending too.'

Artie drank his tea then wandered back outside to see if any of his friends were playing in the alley. Lily set to work with the sewing, glancing in Gran's direction occasionally and noting the lines that cut crevasses into the ageing face. Gran was definitely under the weather but everyone felt under the weather sometimes and usually they got well again.

Not always, though. Dad had dropped dead unexpectedly due to a sudden bleed on his brain. Within a year Ma had fallen ill. Tuberculosis, the doctor had called it, though everyone else had called it consumption. Arrangements had been made for her to go to a sanatorium at the seaside where the air was cleaner but she'd been taken off by pneumonia before she could get there.

The cold lick of dread was back in Lily's stomach. 'Why don't I stay at home this afternoon and help with the laundry?' she offered.

'And miss school? You'll have one of those inspectors down on me for keeping you away from your book learning.'

'We aren't doing book learning this afternoon.' More was the pity because Lily loved it. 'We're doing sewing and you've taught me all I need to know about that.'

'You're a quick one, that's for sure. Your dad always said so.'

Lily remembered overhearing Dad saying

7

exactly that and adding, 'I wish Artie were half as quick. It doesn't seem fair that a girl should have more brains than a boy when it's Artie who'll have to put food on the table when he's older.'

Gran had pointed out that, as a widow, she'd been putting food on her own table for years as did countless other woman.

'I know,' Dad had admitted. 'But let's hope Lily finds a decent man to make her life easier than ours. No one's quicker at working out pounds, shillings and pence than Lil, and if she can work in one of those smart shops up West she might be in the way of meeting someone. But Artie...'

'The boy'll catch up. Lily'll see to that.'

'You're right there.'

'I just want Lily and Artie to be happy,' Mum had said, and Lily had imagined both Dad and Gran smiling fondly because Mum had been a tender-hearted, domestic soul of neither education nor ambition.

She'd been perfectly content to stay at home and make a little money sewing for others though that sort of work paid only a fraction of a man's wage. Lily understood that work like Pa's job of loading and unloading ships down on the docks needed a man's strength. But women's work took a different sort of skill and it didn't seem fair that it should pay so much less. After all, where would men be if their clothes fell apart for want of a timely stitch or if they had nothing hot to eat on a winter's night?

To Lily's way of thinking, people were like pieces of jigsaw puzzles. They came in different shapes and sizes but all of them were needed to make the puzzle complete.

Not that Dad had particularly enjoyed his job. 'All that lifting, pulling and pushing wears a body out,' he'd said another time. 'But I didn't have much schooling so I'm not fit for anything else. I've seen how schooling can raise some men up to better jobs so I hope you'll pay attention to yours, Artie.'

'I'll try, Dad.'

Artie was no dunce but he had some silly boys in his class and, despite his good intentions, he wasn't above being silly himself. Looking back, Lily sometimes wondered if Dad would be with them still if his work hadn't put so much strain on his body. She didn't want the same thing happening to Artie and, in any case, she wanted her brother to have a choice about how he made his living so she was glad to do what she could to help him.

Luckily, they had some wonderful books that Dad had bought for them from the second-hand shop. Dad hadn't been much of a reader – he'd stumbled over long words — but he'd wanted Artie to read well and had known how much pleasure books gave to Lily too. On his last Christmas he'd come home with Rudyard Kipling's *Just So Stories* and they'd had great fun imitating the animals in the stories. Dad had loved to laugh.

Lily finished Gran's sewing then went into the alley to call Artie. 'What?' he asked, running up to her.

'I thought you might do a few sums before we go back to school.'

Artie looked back at his pals longingly, but he

9

was too nice-natured to argue.

Back in the kitchen Lily fetched a scrap of paper from the box in which they kept old envelopes and anything else that had a spare bit of space for writing.

She wrote out some simple sums to warm up his brain and, while he worked through them, picked up the three-legged wooden dolly, plunged it into a tub full of washing, and twisted it this way and that to stir the clothes and — hopefully — shift the dirt from them.

There didn't appear to be much soap in the water today. Gran was never wasteful but she took pride in her work and didn't usually skimp on soap, soda and starch. Was the lack of soap another sign that money was especially tight at the moment?

Coming in from the yard after putting some sheets through the mangle, Gran peered into the tub regretfully. 'Better grate a few more flakes in,' she said, not managing to hide her disappointment over the fact that they were needed.

Lily rubbed the block of soap against the grater to send a tiny cascade of flakes into the water then got back to work with the dolly. When Artie had finished the easy sums, she set him a harder one. 'How much would it cost to feed a family of six for a month if they all have an egg for breakfast and eggs cost a penny each?'

'Eggs for breakfast!' Artie eyes lit up at the thought of it.

'Pay attention to your lessons and maybe one day you can have eggs for breakfast,' Lily said.

She waited for him to ask a vital question. 'Which month, Lil?' he finally said. 'Some months

10

have more days in them than others.'

Lily beamed. 'Let's say July.'

'Thirty-one days, then.'

He sucked on the end of the pencil then worked out that six eggs a day for thirty-one days meant one hundred and eighty-six eggs. At one penny each the cost was fifteen shillings and sixpence.

'All that money!' Artie said.

'More than many a man earns for a full day's work,' Gran pointed out, and Lily supposed it was more than Gran earned for several days' work.

'Which is why we don't have eggs for breakfast,' Lily told Artie. 'Not yet anyway.'

She set him another question to answer while she worked the dolly again but soon it was time to return to school. 'You're a lucky boy, having a sister who's willing to spend time helping you,' Gran told Artie.

'I know.' Artie gave Lily a quick hug. 'You're the best, Lil,' he said, then ran out to the alley.

Lily lingered at the door, searching Gran's beloved face for signs of pain. 'Are you sure I can't — '

'I'll manage fine,' Gran said. 'You can't preach schooling to Artie then not go to school yourself.' She shook a tea cloth at Lily. 'Off with you.'

Lily hesitated for a moment longer then followed Artie. But she spent the afternoon worrying and as soon as the bell rang to announce that school was over she left by the girls' door and ran to find Artie who sauntered out of the boys' door with two of his pals.

'I'm going straight home,' Lily told him.

'Shall I come?'

'No, it's all right.' She didn't want him wondering why she was even keener to help Gran than usual. Besides, she knew he wanted to take a turn with the marbles his friend, Davie, had been given by a seaman uncle.

Lily found Gran folding sheets. 'I'll do the deliveries,' Lily offered.

'Wouldn't you rather play out after being cooped-up in school?'

'I don't think my friends are playing out today.' Lily hadn't actually asked them.

'Well, I won't deny it'll be a help if you do take the deliveries round,' Gran said.

Together they consulted the lists Gran had drawn up using words when she knew them and just letters and symbols when she wasn't sure. They wrapped the clean washing in much-used brown paper and tied them with much-used string.

'I'm charging Frank Baines a bit less seeing as he's been laid off with those leg ulcers,' Gran explained. 'The same goes for the Bennetts seeing as the old lady needs medicines. Don't let on, though. They've got their pride.'

Lily put some of the packages into the large bag they used for deliveries. 'I'll be back for more soon,' she told Gran, and set off to deliver the clean washing across their corner of Bermondsey, waiting for the brown paper and string to be returned to her, and collecting the money that was due.

It was counted out very carefully indeed by young Mrs Bennett who even handled farthings as though she'd have preferred not to let them go, but living in upstairs rooms with little space for drying her own washing meant she had no choice

12

but to use a washerwoman. 'How's old Mrs Bennett?' Lily asked.

'No change, but we don't expect one. Not for the better, anyway.'

Lily smiled sympathetically. 'Have you got any more washing for Gran?'

'Over there.' Mrs Bennett indicated a sack.

Lily took a bundle of handwritten labels from her pocket, found the one that bore the Bennett name and popped it into the sack. 'Bye, then,' she said, then walked round to the next customer.

She knocked on Mr Baines's door but only as a warning. Opening the door herself, she popped her head round it. 'Only me, Mr Baines. Can I come in?'

'You can.' He was sitting in his chair with his ulcerated legs up on a stool.

'Shall I put the washing away for you? It's no bother.'

'You're a good girl, Lily Tomkins.'

Afterwards, he nodded at the table. 'Money's there.'

There was a small pile of coins. 'Thanks, Mr Baines.'

'That orange is for you too.'

'For me?' An orange was a treat indeed.

'All the way from Spain,' Mr Baines said.

'Don't you want it for yourself?'

'Can't say as my stomach does well on oranges. You take it.'

'Thank you! I'll see you next week and I hope your legs feel better.'

She finished the first round of deliveries and collections then went home for the next lot. 'Aren't

13

you going to eat it?' Gran asked, when Lily flourished the orange.

'By myself?' As if Lily would do that! 'We can share it after our dinner.'

Gran cooked their proper dinner at the end of the day to keep the smell of it away from the laundry. Today she made a stew of potatoes, carrots and onions.

They never ate meat more than once or twice a week as it cost too much but, thinking about it, Lily realised it had been more than a week since they'd last had meat.

'Lily's got a treat for you later,' Gran told Artie.

His eyes brightened. 'A treat?'

'An orange,' Lily told him. 'From Mr Baines.'

Artie didn't need to be told he had to eat his stew first. He was gobbling it up.

Lily was enormously relieved when Gran poured a small bowl of stew for herself and ate it. Hopefully, it meant she was already on the mend.

But when Lily lay in bed that night she heard Gran groan as she came up the stairs to go to her own bed. Gran's footsteps were slow and laboured, and she heaved a great sigh when she reached the tiny landing that separated her room from the one Lily shared with Artie. Lily closed her eyes and pretended to be asleep when Gran came in to kiss them goodnight. There was a rustle of sheets and blankets as Gran tucked the sleeping Artie in, then Lily felt Gran's lips on her own head. With another sigh Gran left them alone.

Lily let a long time pass then got up, wincing at the icy feel of the worn linoleum floor covering beneath her feet. She tiptoed outside Gran's

14

room, listened for the sound of regular breathing then opened the door. Moonlight was beaming through a gap in the curtains, lighting up Gran's face where she lay against the pillow. It was a wrinkled but beautiful face in Lily's eyes. Creeping forward, Lily placed a gentle kiss on the creased skin. 'Love you, Gran,' she whispered, then glided back to bed.

Hopefully, Gran would get better quickly but today had brought home to Lily how very precarious their situation was. Sooner or later Gran might need a doctor and she wouldn't want to go to a poor hospital or anything like that in case the people in charge decided she wasn't well enough to look after children.

That might mean Lily and Artie were sent to the workhouse or some distant orphanage.

But seeing a doctor outside a hospital cost money, and with rent to pay, coal to buy and three mouths to feed Gran had never been able to set money aside for emergencies. Might Lily find a way of earning enough money to save a little emergency fund? It wouldn't be easy. Helping Gran with the laundry and shopping already took up much of Lily's time, and missing school would not only get Gran into trouble but also start Artie worrying about what was going on.

Perhaps Lily could run errands for other people alongside running errands for Gran. She wouldn't earn much – a few pennies here and there – but they'd mount up over time. It had to be worth trying.

2

'How much would this errand cost?' Mr Higgins asked, when Lily took his washing round and announced that she was running errands for people.

'Just a halfpenny,' Lily told him. None of their neighbours were rich so she knew she was unlikely to get any business if she asked for more. 'I can fetch things like cigarettes and milk or shoes from the cobbler. Or I can post letters.

You know you can trust me. I'm Maggie Tomkins's granddaughter, after all.'

'Hmm.' He gave her a long look as she stood before his chair, hands clasped behind her back. 'All right. You can fetch me ten Woodbines from Welby's. Be quick about it or I might think you've gone off with my money.'

He gave her two shillings. Lily raced to the corner shop, bought the cigarettes and raced back to hand them to Mr Higgins along with his change which he counted carefully. 'You haven't taken your halfpenny,' he pointed out.

'I thought I should wait for you to give it to me.'

He pushed a halfpenny across the table and Lily picked it up. 'Thanks. Maybe I'll call tomorrow and see if you have any more errands for me.'

'I'm not promising I'll have any.'

'I can ask, though, can't I?'

'I suppose you can. Knock on the window and I'll beckon you in if I need you.'

Lily took the halfpenny home and wrapped it in

16

an old sock. By the end of the first week she had seven halfpennies in there — three from Mr Higgins, two from his neighbour, Mrs Platt, and two from Mr Wright across the road.

Gran seemed no worse but neither did she seem any better. She was eating little and looked terribly tired in unguarded moments. She also looked deeply relieved for all the help Lily was giving but she fired up one afternoon when she and Lily were alone and Lily asked, 'Feeling all right, Gran?'

''Course I am!' Gran insisted.

Lily regretted asking the question because Gran got up and busied herself instead of resting for a moment over a cup of tea. Lily was sure Gran still wasn't back to her old self, but some illnesses took a while to pass and Lily hoped Gran's was one of them.

Even so, she made it known to her customers that she was available for errand-running in the mornings too. It meant getting up very early to fill the copper and set it to boil, put washing in the dolly tub or the old tin bath to soak, mix starch, scrub grubby collars and cuffs, and eat breakfast too, moving quickly while trying to look as though she wasn't rushing at all.

She encouraged Artie to leave for school sooner than was really needed by suggesting he'd like to play with his pals then, as soon as he'd joined them, she'd say, 'Don't be late,' and hasten away as though going to see her own friends, Gertie and Ruth. In reality she'd race off to get her errands done before running back to school in time for the starting bell.

By the end of the second week the money in the

sock totalled eightpence. By the end of the third week there was a shilling and thruppence.

Gran still wasn't better. No matter how hard she was trying to hide it, the signs were there. Less washing was coming in and yet Gran was behind with it.

There were occasional creases in ironing that used to be perfect, little food in the house and Gran herself seemed... smaller somehow. Not the vigorous Maggie Tomkins of old.

For all that she was trying to leave Gran her pride, Lily couldn't help speaking out again when she caught Gran's worn hands rubbing her middle as though trying to soothe pain. 'I wish you'd tell me if you have a belly ache.'

'Only a bit of wind, Lil.'

It was more serious than wind. Lily was certain now. She wished she knew how much it would cost for Gran to see a doctor, but asking any of their neighbours would arouse their suspicions about why she wanted to know and word might get back to Gran. Perhaps when Lily had three shillings in the sock she'd speak to Gran about seeing someone.

In the meantime, money was tighter than ever. It didn't help that the weather was so bad, one rainy day being succeeded by another and making it impossible to get anything dry without piling coals onto the fire.

'Urgh!' Artie said, as he stepped into a puddle in the alley as they walked home for their dinner one day.

He lifted a foot to inspect his shoe. 'I've got a hole.'

'I'll plug it up with something when we get home,' Lily told him. 'Don't mention it to Gran.'

'Why not? She can get it mended.'

'Mr Groves has died. Until Gran finds someone else to wash for, there's less money coming in,' Lily told him.

Gran had washed for Mr Groves for years but the loss of his money was only a small part of the problem. There was no need for Artie to know that, though.

'How long will I have to wait?' Artie asked.

'I don't know. Just try to be patient.'

Artie grinned, always seeing the sunny side of things. 'At least I've got one dry foot.'

Gran had draped washing all around the house, including on the backs of the chairs so they sat on the floor to eat their dinner of bread and dripping.

Sunday dawned more brightly but Gran was looking grey. Thinking she might rest if left alone in the house, Lily suggested that Artie might like to come with her to see the ships down at the docks.

They walked past St Mary Magdalen Church and the dreaded workhouse on their way to Tower Bridge where they stopped by the river. On the opposite bank stood the Tower of London with its grey stone walls and a tower at each corner. Lily was always saddened by the sight of it because she felt sorry for all the people who'd been imprisoned there over the years. Artie found it gruesomely fascinating because some of those prisoners had had their heads chopped off.

There were wharfs to the east and west but it felt natural to turn their heads east towards Butler's Wharf where Dad had worked. Beyond it were more wharfs as far as the eye could see — Coventry, Landells, West's, Mesnard's...

Still more wharfs were clustered around St Saviour's Duck, the thin finger of water that stretched south of the Thames. Some of the wharfs had ships in, bringing foods such as tea, sugar, grain and spices as well as rubber. 'I'd like to sail on a ship one day,' Artie said.

Whatever he decided about his future, the more education Artie had, the higher he was likely to rise. 'If a ship has to sail for 2,386 miles on its journey, how many miles does it have to sail to reach the halfway mark?' Lily asked.

Artie thought about it. 'One thousand one hundred and ninety-three,' he finally said.

Lily was about to tell him he was right when someone else said, 'Well done, boy.'

Turning, Lily saw a man standing behind them. A tall, thin, white-haired man who was undoubtedly a gentleman judging from his fine clothes and crisp voice.

'How many miles does it have to sail to complete three quarters of the journey?' he asked.

Lily worked the answer out quickly. One thousand seven hundred and eighty-nine miles. Eighty-nine and a half to be accurate. But it was Artie the man had asked. Artie had closed his eyes in concentration and Lily willed him to get the answer right.

'One thousand seven hundred and eighty-nine miles,' Artie said.

'Plus?' the man prompted.

'Another half a mile.'

20

'Very good. I like to see a boy who can use his brain.'

'My sister helps me,' Artie pointed out.

'Females are useful for teaching children elementary reading, writing and arithmetic. But the male needs a more thorough education if he's to make his way in the world. What else do you know? The capital of France perhaps?'

Artie looked momentarily panicked but Lily sent him a steadying nod and he answered uncertainly, 'Paris, sir?'

'Correct. And what about literature? Do you enjoy reading?'

'Stories? Oh, yes, sir.'

'Do you have a favourite book?'

' *Just So Stories*. I like reading about the animals.'

'You have the book at home?'

'Yes, sir. Our dad got it for us.'

'He is a great reader, perhaps?'

'No, sir. He didn't have much schooling but he wanted schooling for us.'

'He sounds like a sensible man. But am I to understand he's no longer living?'

'Not for the past four years.'

'You live with your mother?'

'With our gran, sir. Our mum died too. Three years ago.'

'My condolences. But forgive me. I haven't introduced myself. My name is Crispin Alderton. I am a schoolmaster. A headmaster in fact. Newly retired.'

'Arthur Tomkins, sir,' Artie told him. 'This is my sister, Lily.'

21

'What age are you, Arthur?'

'Ten, sir.'

'You go to school?'

''Course. The inspectors would be after me if I didn't.'

'Quite. Well, keep up your education, Arthur, and perhaps I'll ask you more questions another time. Your address is … '

'Jessy Street. Number twelve.'

'And where might Jessy Street be?'

'Bermondsey, sir.'

Mr Alderton nodded. 'Good day to you, Arthur, and … erm … ' He waved a vague hand in Lily's direction.

'Her name's Lily,' Artie said.

Mr Alderton's narrow lips twitched in what appeared to be a smile, and with that he sauntered away.

'Well done for getting the answers right,' Lily told Artie.

'You'd have got them right faster.'

They walked on but dark grey clouds were blowing in and Lily's thoughts were returning to Gran anyway. 'Time for home,' Lily said.

The rain held off as they walked back to Jessy Street and Lily was glad to see Davie playing marbles in the alley because Artie ran to join him. It meant he wouldn't see Gran if she were sleeping. Neither would his bouncing energy startle her awake.

The kitchen was empty when Lily entered. Sunday or not, there was ironing to be done so Lily put the irons in the fire to heat. She moved quietly but heard Gran coming downstairs. 'I was tidying a

22

drawer,' Gran said, but her silvery hair was messy and Lily guessed she'd been lying down instead.

Lily's heart twisted painfully. She'd never seen darling Gran look so ... bewildered. 'I'll make some tea,' Lily said, hoping to squeeze a little more life out of the tea leaves in the pot. Gran began to inspect a bundle of washing, separating anything that needed a button or a stitch. At least it was a job she could do sitting at the table. She looked up at a sudden rattle on the window panes. 'More rain!'

A moment later Artie rushed in. 'Close the door!' Lily urged, not wanting Gran to catch a chill from the draught.

He closed the door and came to sit at the table. 'We met a strange man when we were out,' he told Gran.

'He wasn't strange exactly,' Lily said hastily, seeing Gran frown. 'He just heard me asking Artie questions — arithmetic questions — and asked some questions of his own. He was impressed that Artie knew the answers.'

'So he should have been. You're a clever boy,' Gran approved.

'I'm not as clever as Lily.'

'But neither are you a dunce.'

'The man spoke funny,' Artie said. 'Like a gent, I mean. He said he used to be a schoolmaster but I expect it was at a school for rich boys.'

'Rich or poor, it's important to get some schooling while you can,' Gran said.

While you can? Did that mean Gran thought things were changing for them all? Lily's stomach gave a sickly lurch.

Lily went about her errand-running with an extra sense of urgency the next day and was delighted when afternoon came and Mr Higgs from around the corner gave her threepence instead of just a halfpenny. 'One good turn deserves another,' he said, referring to the way Lily had cleaned and bandaged the finger he'd cut on Saturday when he'd dropped a milk bottle and been careless picking up the broken glass.

The money in the sock reached almost three shillings. Gran had been sick for a whole month now so clearly needed help with getting better. Surely three shillings would be enough for a deposit for the doctor — if doctors took deposits.

Lily never had the chance to find out because she entered the yard to hear loud voices coming through the open kitchen door. 'You know I'm good for the money. I've never been short before,' Gran was protesting.

'But you're short now, Mrs Tomkins. And it's now what matters.'

Lily hastened to the door and saw that Gran's visitor was the rent collector.

'I just need more time,' Gran said, and there was a desperation in her voice that Lily had never heard before.

Lily stepped into the kitchen and closed the door to stop Gran's personal business from being overheard by all their neighbours. It signalled to Gran that Lily wasn't only present but had also realised what was going on. Poor Gran looked stricken.

24

The rent collector, Mr Jones, simply looked irritated. He stuck out his chin as though to show that the presence of a child wouldn't stop him from doing whatever he planned to do.

'How much short are you, Gran?' Lily asked.

'One and six,' Mr Jones said, leaving Lily in no doubt that he wouldn't take a penny less.

'Wait there.'

She ran upstairs and counted out coins from the sock. 'One and six,' she said, returning downstairs and handing them over.

There were lots of coins — pennies, halfpennies and even farthings. Mr Jones put them on the table and counted them out. 'One and six,' he confirmed. 'Well, Mrs Tomkins, I'll bid you good day. But don't forget I'll be back next week.'

When another week's rent would be due.

Mr Jones nodded and left them. Lily looked at Gran, waiting for her to speak.

Gran took a moment then swallowed. 'Thanks for helping, Lil, but where did you get all that money?'

'I've been running errands.'

'Saving for books, I suppose.'

'Saving for you to see a doctor. Please don't tell me you're not sick, Gran. It's been weeks.'

Gran's mouth opened as though to insist that she was fine but she must have realised there was no point in pretending anymore. She sighed, pulled out a chair and sat down heavily. 'I haven't been so good,' she admitted.

'Then you need to see a doctor.'

Gran shook her head.

'I'll earn the money, even if it means missing

25

school. You know I'm not learning anything new there, and — '

'I've already seen a doctor, Lil.'

Lily blinked. 'What did he say? Has he given you medicine to make you better?'

The kitchen door burst open and Artie ran in. 'I'm starving,' he announced.

'Then let's see if we can spare you a bit a bread to be going on with,' Gran said, getting up.

Lily chewed on her lip but didn't protest. She and Gran were both keen to protect Artie. They wouldn't be able to talk properly until he'd gone to bed, but that was hours away. The waiting was going to be awful.

3

Lily lay in bed, listening as Artie's breathing grew slower and deeper. 'S'my turn,' he murmured, and Lily guessed he was dreaming about Davie's marbles.

She slid from between the covers, stuffed her feet into the shoes she'd left ready and wrapped a spare blanket round her shoulders. Creeping to the door, she left the room and went downstairs.

Gran was sitting at the table waiting for her. She looked grave and Lily felt a flutter of dread. 'What's the doctor going to do to help?' she asked, sitting opposite Gran.

'There's something inside me that shouldn't be there, Lil. A growth.'

Lily's shiver owed nothing to the chill that had crept into the room with the dying of the fire. 'Can't the doctor make it go away? Or take it out?'

'No, Lil.'

'So what's going to happen?'

Gran's silence gave Lily her answer. 'Oh, Gran!'

Lily got up to wrap her arms around Gran and be hugged in return. Sobs rose up from deep inside Lily's soul and she wept against Gran's shoulder as Gran's worn but well-loved hand stroked comfort into her hair. 'There, there, my love. There, there.'

Lily had no idea how much time passed but eventually her body was exhausted and her sobs turned to shuddery breaths.

27

'Dry your eyes, Lil. We've got a lot to talk about,' Gran said, passing her a handkerchief.

More tears welled in Lily's eyes but Gran needed her to be sensible now. Lily wiped her face and blew her nose. 'Good girl,' Gran said, and waited for Lily to return to her seat.

How long? That was the question Lily wanted to ask. But it felt too cruel. Too stark.

Too terrifying.

'Now then,' Gran began. 'I'll keep going for as long as I can but we have to face facts, Lil. I'll be lucky to last a year.'

Lily felt as though her heart were being stabbed with ice.

'You know what'll come afterwards?' Gran asked.

'The workhouse,' Lily said.

'It's the last thing I want but you needn't despair. You might not have to stay in the workhouse itself because you may be boarded out with a family, but if you're too old for that once you turn eleven, you could be sent to one of those training schools I've heard about. Even the workhouse is better these days.

Whatever happens, you'll have a roof over your heads and food in your bellies.

And remember, in another few years you'll be able to work and make your own futures.'

'But boys and girls are kept apart in the workhouse, aren't they?'

'There's no stopping that but, like I say, it won't be forever.'

Would Artie lose his spirit, though? Would he lose his hope for a better future because he feared

28

his life would always be tainted by having been in the workhouse or some other institution? Worse still, would he fall into bad ways with bad people and give up on learning?

Lily pulled her thoughts in for Gran's sake. 'Artie and I will manage,' she said. 'But what about you?' The thought of Gran being in pain was unbearable.

'I'm off my food and I get tired,' Gran admitted.

'Your belly hurts?'

Gran looked ready to deny it only to realise it was too late for that.

'Sometimes. And sometimes I need the privy in a rush. But I don't need to take to my bed yet. I can still work.'

'You can't do as much as you used to.' That was obvious. 'You need me to help with the laundry and earn money in other ways or we won't be able to pay the rent.' Neither would they be able to pay for medicine if Gran's pain got worse.

'You're a good girl, Lil, but you need to go to school. It's the law.'

'I'll go to school often enough to stop us getting into trouble.' But she'd invent a sickness of her own when she needed to stay home.

'Your dad wanted both of you to stay at school until you were fourteen,' Gran said, shaking her head as though she was letting him down.

'You can't help being ill,' Lily pointed out.

'True enough, but I dread leaving you with no one looking out for you. Except that I hope you'll look out for each other.'

''Course we will, Gran.'

29

'No one must know I'm ill,' Gran said. 'Not until it's impossible to hide.'

'I understand.' They couldn't take the risk of rumours reaching the ears of someone in authority who might decide to interfere and break the family up before it was absolutely necessary. This time together was precious, to be protected at all costs. And people might stop sending their washing if they suspected Gran was ill.

'About Artie,' Gran said then.

'We should hold off telling him as long as we can,' Lily replied.

Gran nodded. 'I'm sorry the burden's all on you, Lil. But you're strong.'

Lily didn't feel strong. She felt like weeping again. But she'd have to find the strength from somewhere because she couldn't let Gran down.

4

'It isn't like you to miss school,' Miss Fielding said, after calling Lily to the front of the class.

'I felt sick,' Lily explained. 'Lots of people are sick at the moment. Agnes, Ida … '

'I was hoping you'd win a prize for perfect attendance.'

Lily had been hoping the same thing. The prize would have been a book which she'd have loved but right now she had to give all of her attention to keeping the family going.

'Is all well at home?' Miss Fielding asked.

Lily faked an expression of puzzlement as though she couldn't understand why Miss Fielding should suspect all might *not* be well. 'Yes, Miss.'

She hated lying, though, particularly to someone she liked and admired.

'You're an excellent pupil, Lily. I hope you'll come to me if you need help.'

'Thank you, Miss.'

Yesterday had in fact been the first time Lily had missed school as she was trying to fit the work into the time before and after school as well as her dinner break. These days she was always the first to get up so she could light the fire, make a start on the washing and prepare bread and tea for their breakfasts.

Sometimes she'd tackle a little sewing and ironing too.

31

She woke Gran in time for her to make her way downstairs slowly and only then called Artie who gave no sign of realising that Lily was doing the work Gran used to do. Luckily, another of his friends, Sidney, had been given some marbles and, keen to spend time outdoors taking a turn with them, Artie never noticed how busy Lily was. Neither did he see past the show of good cheer Gran put on in front of him.

Despite all her efforts, the work had fallen behind and she'd taken a day off school to catch up. Artie had believed her when she'd pretended to be ill. He'd given her a hug and said, 'Poor Lil. You'll hate missing school.'

Would Miss Fielding believe her too?

'Very well, Lily. You'd better sit down so we can get on with the lesson,' Miss Fielding said.

Relieved, Lily returned to the others.

Strangely, despite all her running around she wasn't tired exactly. She felt as though a strange electric current were running through her and igniting her body with energy. But there were times when sleep suddenly ambushed her. One day she'd been sitting at the kitchen table waiting for the irons to heat in the fire only to be jolted awake as Artie burst through the back gate. Another day, it had only been a sneeze from someone in the class that had stopped her from nodding off as Ida Banfree stumbled through a reading in class. There'd also been some nights when she'd fallen asleep so quickly she hadn't remembered getting into bed.

'You're doing too much,' Gran had protested after two weeks had passed.

Denying it, Lily had changed the subject. 'We'll be in March next week, Gran.'

Spring was always welcome in the Tomkins household. It meant the days were growing longer and milder. Washing was easier to dry and they needed fewer coals on the fire.

Miss Fielding said nothing more that day and Lily made sure to attend school on the day that followed. She was running between errands after school when she heard someone calling, 'Little girl!'

She skidded to a halt and turned, unsure if the call had been directed at her but keen to take any opportunity of earning a halfpenny or two. Seeing a tall, thin man some way behind her, memory stirred. Of course. The gentleman they'd seen by Tower Bridge some weeks ago.

She walked towards him, trying to remember his name. Mr Allman? No, not Allman. Alderton.

'Good afternoon,' he said.

Lily nodded. 'Mr Alderton.'

'I've looked out some books that I thought might interest your brother.' He held out a small stack of books tied together with string.

How kind of him! 'Thank you,' Lily said. 'He'll look after them, I promise.'

'Perhaps I might call in a week or two to learn how he's getting on with them? You live at twelve Jessy Street, I think your brother said.'

'Just around the corner,' Lily confirmed, though she thought Mr Alderton would get a shock if he did call. The Tomkins home was a tiny terraced house built of soot-blackened brick that opened straight onto the pavement at the front.

'Good day to you,' he said, inclining his head.

'Good day to you too,' Lily echoed.

She watched him walk away then ran off to complete her errands, holding the heavy books under her arm.

'What's this?' Gran asked, when Lily arrived home and put them on the table.

Lily reminded her of the man they'd met at the docks some weeks before.

'He remembered Artie?' Gran asked. 'Heavens.'

'Blimey,' Artie said, when he saw the books.

'You'd better wash your hands before you touch them,' Gran told him.

The parcel contained five books. The largest was *Drummond's Atlas for Children*. As Artie flipped through it, Lily saw maps of continents and countries.

'That'll be useful,' she said.

The second was *A Boy's History of England* and the third *Elementary Mathematics*. Artie pulled a face over that one. 'I won't understand a word of this unless you help me, Lil.'

'I'm not sure I'll understand it either, but I'll help if I can.'

The fourth was *Flora and Fauna of the British Isles*. 'What's flora and fauna?' Artie asked.

Lily opened the book and looked through the pages. 'Plants and animals, by the look of it.'

'I like this one,' Artie said, picking up a story book which had a picture of a toad dressed in a hat and coat on the cover.

It was called *The Wind in the Willows* and Artie read the opening lines out loud. ' The Mole had been working very hard all the morning, spring-cleaning his little home. First with brooms, then with dusters; then on ladders and steps and chairs, with a brush and a pail of whitewash; till he had dust in his throat and eyes, and splashes of whitewash all over his black fur, and an aching back and weary arms. Yes, I like this one.'

'You'll have to look at all of them or Mr Alderton might be offended,' Lily said.

'Is he really coming to visit?'

'He'll have to visit if he wants his books back.'

'Lord knows what a gentleman will make of me,' Gran said.

'You're good enough for anyone,' Lily insisted. 'If Mr Alderton turns his nose up at you, he's a fool.'

* * *

Mr Alderton came ten days later. Hearing a knock on the front door, Lily guessed the caller might be him because everyone else came through the back yard. The front door led straight into the small front parlour. 'Come in,' Lily invited.

The room looked even smaller with Mr Alderton inside it because, even though he was thin, he was also tall and slightly stooping. There wasn't much in the way of furniture – just one shabby armchair and one plain wooden chair placed either side of an empty fireplace with a small, scuffed table nearby and a cupboard to one side. It was in this cupboard that the books were kept in an effort to keep them dry from the steam and dampness of the washing.

'Sit down,' Lily said. 'I'll fetch my grandmother.'

35

She ran upstairs to Gran's room. Gran had been lying down but must have heard Mr Alderton arrive because Lily found her sitting up in bed. 'Is it — '

'Mr Alderton,' Lily confirmed.

Gran rubbed her cheeks to give them some colour. Lily noticed the laudanum bottle within reach on the window ledge. This must be one of Gran's bad days because now that laudanum could only be bought with a doctor's prescription, Gran was eking out her old supply. 'We don't need to trouble the doctor yet,' she'd said.

'Shall I tell Mr Alderton you have a headache?' Lily asked. Gran's face looked as white as her hair.

'No need for that. Just give me a minute or two.'

Lily returned downstairs. She had no idea what went on in the houses of ladies and gentlemen but in Jessy Street the friends and neighbours who called were offered tea. Lily offered it to Mr Alderton.

'Thank you. Is Arthur at home?'

'He's out but I'll call him in.'

Lily put the kettle on the kitchen fire and went out to the alley to call Artie.

His eyes widened when she told him Mr Alderton was here. 'Blimey, Lil. I hope he doesn't ask me lots of questions.'

'Just do your best if he does. You need to wash your hands and face before you see him.'

Back in the kitchen she gave him warm water, soap and a scrap of old towel.

'Don't forget your nails and behind your ears,' she said, whispering in case Mr Alderton overheard.

36

Warming the teapot, Lily decided weak tea was a poor way of repaying his kindness in lending the books so put fresh leaves in the pot. She also poured a little milk into Gran's green pottery jug and put a small amount of precious sugar into her green pottery bowl. Gran was proud of having a jug and bowl that matched.

She came downstairs as Lily and Artie were carrying in the tea. She'd combed her hair but still looked dazed. Mr Alderton stood up politely as Lily introduced Gran. Then he sat back down on the armchair while Gran took the wooden chair.

Lily poured a cup of tea for each of them, feeling relieved when Mr Alderton declined the last of their sugar.

'It was kind of you to lend books to my grandson,' Gran said.

'How have you been enjoying them?' he asked Artie.

'I like *The Wind in the Willows* best,' Artie said, fetching the books from the cupboard.

Lily nudged him and he added, 'Sir.'

'What about the atlas?'

'I like that too. We've been finding different places on the maps.'

'May I?' Mr Alderton reached for the atlas and opened it. 'Can you identify Persia for me?'

Artie gulped then stood at Mr Alderton's shoulder, peering at a map.

It was upside down to Lily but Persia wasn't hard to find.

'It's … um … It's …' Artie's finger hovered. He looked at Lily who signalled him to move his finger forward and he breathed out thankfully as he spotted Persia. 'There, sir.'

Mr Alderton turned a page. 'The West Indies?' he asked.

This was easier for Artie. He also knew the answers to Mr Alderton's questions about the goods that came from both the West Indies and the East Indies. Sugar, spices, rubber ... Artie had seen them being unloaded at the docks.

Mr Alderton invited him to read out loud from the history book then said, 'That will do for now.'

He drank some tea, his expression thoughtful. 'I was headmaster in a boys' school for many years,' he finally said. 'That was a fee-paying school for boys in comfortable circumstances. However, I have long felt that education is vital to raise other boys out of poverty and to benefit society in all sorts of ways. Having retired and found myself somewhat under-employed, I have decided I might do something towards putting my ideas about education into practice. I'm unable to do anything on a grand scale but if I can help even one boy I shall feel ... useful again.'

He paused for a moment to be sure Gran was following then continued. 'I wonder if Arthur might be that boy? He's intelligent and I'm impressed with the fact that he's taken the trouble of looking at the books I provided. That shows application. Diligence. No boy can advance in life without diligence, can he?'

'No,' Gran agreed uncertainly.

'What I have in mind is that Arthur should come to me for additional study, perhaps on Saturday afternoons? My housekeeper, Mrs Lawley, will take good care of him.'

Artie sent Lily a horrified look. Saturday afternoons were for marbles, exploring the docks, seeing what the tide had brought to the riverbanks, and playing football. Lily answered with a look that bade him to be still. Mr Alderton was offering him a wonderful opportunity.

The elderly man fished a small silver box out of his pocket, extracted a card and passed it to Gran. 'My address in Hampstead.'

Lily had an idea that Hampstead was a good way from Bermondsey but Mr Alderton had thought of that. 'I suggest Arthur travels to me by bicycle.'

'I don't have a bicycle,' Artie pointed out.

'Fortunately, I'm able to arrange the loan of one through my cousin. He's a canon at Southwark Cathedral and can vouch for my bona fides if you have any concerns about the arrangement. I'd been visiting him when I first met Arthur and I'm on my way to visit him now. Shall I expect Arthur on Saturday? At one o'clock?'

Gran looked at Lily who nodded keenly.

'Yes,' Gran said. 'Artie's a good lad and we appreciate your kindness.'

'Excellent. I shall arrange for the bicycle to be delivered soon.'

Mr Alderton rose. Lily showed him to the door and closed it after him, turning back to Artie. 'I know you're going to say you get enough book learning at school and at home with me, but this sort of chance could change your life.'

'I like my life,' Artie argued. 'I like my Saturday afternoons.'

'You won't be ten years old forever. You've got to think of your future.'

'Listen to your sister,' Gran urged. 'She's more brains than me.'

Lily was grateful to have Gran on her side because that meant Gran was on Artie's side too — if you looked at the whole of his life and not just his Saturday afternoons of fun. Would Artie understand that, though? He was being offered a golden opportunity — one Lily would have treasured – but would he let it slip through his fingers?

5

Artie was happier when a young clergyman from the cathedral delivered the bicycle along with a letter from the canon assuring Gran that Mr Alderton was a trusted and respected teacher with a conscientious housekeeper who'd take care of Artie. The bicycle wasn't new but no one else in Jessy Street had one, not counting Peter Shaw who rode a bicycle with a basket on the front when he made deliveries for the grocer.

Artie had never ridden a bicycle before but was keen to learn. 'I'm going to try now,' he said.

'Remember it doesn't actually belong to you,' Lily said.

'I'll take care of it.'

An hour later he called her out to watch him ride up and down Jessy Street.

'Very good,' Lily praised.

The bike was undamaged but there was a graze on one of Artie's knees.

'Everyone falls off a few times when they're learning,' he said airily, and Lily hid a smile.

'You should let me wash that before it turns nasty.'

He rode the bicycle to the back alley, brought it into the yard and came into the kitchen. 'Sid and Davie have asked for rides,' he said.

'Oh, Artie! '

'It's all right. I've told them the bike belongs to someone else.'

'I hope it won't stop them from letting you take a turn with their marbles.'

''Course not. Sid and Davie aren't mean.'

A map with directions to Hampstead had been delivered too. Lily went over it with Artie several times to be sure he knew where he was going.

* * *

He spent Saturday morning out with his pals. 'Don't go far,' Lily warned. 'I'll call when you need to get ready for Mr Alderton's but I haven't time to go looking for you.'

'I'll stay close,' Artie promised, but would he remember if one of his pals suggested going to the river or searching for bits and pieces they could use to make a cart on wheels? Lily wondered yet again if she were doing the right thing in keeping Gran's illness secret from him. He might take Mr Alderton's lessons more seriously if he knew things were desperate, but it felt cruel to worry him sooner than was necessary. Besides, if he knew nothing, he couldn't let anything slip accidentally.

Fortunately, Artie was at the bottom of the alley when Lily called him though she saw his shoulders slump as he realised his playing time was over.

'You need to wash and have something to eat. I've cut two slices of bread for you. Eat one now and I'll wrap the other for you to take to eat later. Mr Alderton's going to teach you, not feed you.'

Afterwards she inspected him for signs of grubbiness. Satisfied that he was as smart as his raggedy trousers, shirt and shoes allowed — one shoe still with a hole in the sole — she joined him in the yard as he wheeled the bicycle into the alley.

'Watch out for cars and carts!' she called.

Gran had come out to wave him off too, but she was obviously tired. 'Go and lie down,' Lily said. 'Artie won't be back for hours so you can have a proper rest.'

'There's all this washing to finish.'

'It won't take two of us.'

'Perhaps I will have a little rest,' Gran said. 'But then I'll be down to help.'

Three hours passed before she reappeared. 'You should have woken me, Lil. It isn't fair that you're doing all the work.'

'I don't mind. I'm going to make some deliveries and see if anyone wants errands running now.'

Lily had already made up the parcels of washing. She put them into the big delivery bag and went out, passing Janet Flynn who lived at number sixteen.

'How's your gran?' Mrs Flynn asked. 'I haven't seen her out and about in weeks.'

Lily forced a smile. 'You know Gran. Always working.'

'No one could call Maggie Tomkins a slacker,' Mrs Flynn agreed. 'Three mouths to feed and no man bringing in a wage packet. It's hard.'

'That's why I'm helping.' Lily patted the bag so Mrs Flynn would understand she couldn't stand chatting for long.

'Tell Maggie I asked after her. Maybe I'll pop in for a cuppa one day soon. While I can.' Mrs Flynn rubbed her belly. She already had six children and Lily supposed a seventh must be on the way.

Smiling again, Lily hastened on. Gran had never

43

been one for gossip, having neither time to waste nor a liking for talking behind people's backs. But she'd never hesitated to help anyone in need and was known for her kindness far beyond Jessy Street. Perhaps it had been a mistake to encourage Gran to rest indoors so much if people were beginning to wonder about her. Might Gran walk to the corner shop one day next week just to get her face seen?

Lily picked up a few errands as she delivered and collected washing, each halfpenny earned being sorely needed if they were to manage next week's rent.

She also bought carrots and potatoes cheaply as the greengrocer would be closed on the morrow.

Artie returned at six and sat down at the table to get his breath back after the long cycle ride. 'Cor blimey, Lil, you won't believe what I've got to tell you about Mr Alderton's house. It's five floors high, just for one old man. And one woman who isn't quite as old. Mrs Lawley. She keeps house for him.'

Lily was relieved to see that, far from looking miserable, Artie looked like a boy who'd had an adventure.

'Imagine having someone to make your meals, look after your clothes and clean the house as well,' Artie said.

Lily looked at Gran and they both burst out laughing. 'Haven't you got people to make your meals, look after your clothes and clean the house where you live?'

Gran asked.

'Eh?' Artie was puzzled but only for a moment.

44

His expression turned wry.

'All right. I know you two look after me.'

'It's my job to look after you,' Gran said. 'But I hope you don't take Lily for granted.'

'I don't,' Artie assured them, but then he frowned. 'Do you think I don't help enough?'

'It's more important for you to get an education so you can help Lily when you're older,' Gran said.

'It's a shame you can't have lessons from Mr Alderton, Lil,' Artie said.

Lily smiled but it was rather a stiff smile. She didn't begrudge Artie his opportunity at all but she couldn't help feeling just a little envious. She would have cherished a chance to learn more than the school could teach her.

'It's a shame all right,' Gran agreed. 'But seeing as she can't have lessons, you've got to learn enough for the pair of you.'

'Was it easy to find the house?' Lily asked.

'I got a bit lost on the way but I asked a policeman for directions like you said I should, so I wasn't late. Mrs Lawley let me in. I think she feared I was going to be a rough boy with no manners because she was strict at first. Not very friendly.

She told me to leave the bicycle in the front garden and be sure to wipe my feet on the mat. Then she took me upstairs to a room at the back of the house. You'd have loved it, Lil. It was filled with books and there was a huge desk by the window where Mr Alderton sat.'

'What books did you see?' How thrilling to be surrounded by so much knowledge and adventure. Beautiful illustrations too, perhaps.

45

'I knew you'd ask, but I couldn't stand staring at them when Mr Alderton was waiting. I'll try to look next time.'

Lily was glad to hear there'd be a next time. It meant Artie had done well.

'Mr Alderton had questions ready for me,' Artie went on. 'He said he needed to find out what I already knew before he could plan lessons. I don't think I got even half the sums right nor half the questions about kings, queens and wars but he didn't seem surprised. When I'd answered as many questions as I could he let me have a rest and Mrs Lawley brought a tray in.'

Artie's eyes brightened at the memory. 'It wasn't just tea for Mr Alderton and a glass of milk for me but cake as well. Three types! Mr Alderton didn't eat any — no wonder he's so thin — but he let me try all three kinds. I had a slice of what he called farmhouse fruitcake first. It was so tasty! Then I had a slice of cake which had jam in the middle. Something to do with the old queen ...'

'Victoria sponge?' Gran suggested.

'That was it. The last cake tasted spicy and I was told it was ginger. I wanted to bring some back for you two but didn't like to ask even though Mrs Lawley was friendlier by then.'

'Quite right,' Gran said, 'though it's a shame Lily couldn't have cake.'

'Mr Alderton sent me into the garden to do what he called running the cake off, then he got me doing something called reading comprehension. That was hard too as it was all about different kinds of words. I've never heard of things like adjectives before. The last thing I had to do was

46

write a story. You'd have written an amazing story, Lil. I wrote about a boy finding an old clay pipe by the river. It wasn't really a story because it was about me finding that broken pipe last year, but Mr Alderton didn't seem to mind. After that he said he'd see me next week and sent me home. He gave me more books to read, though.'

Artie picked up an old brown satchel and put it on the table then took out three books.

Lily picked one up: *The Call of the Wild.* 'It's about a dog,' Artie told her.

'This one's *Peter Pan*. It's about a boy who doesn't grow up though I don't see how you can stop yourself from growing up. This one looks the best. *Tarzan of the Apes.* It's about a man who lives with monkeys in the jungle.'

'Mr Alderton's a kind man,' Lily said.

'He says it's important for boys to read. I don't know why he doesn't think it's important for girls to read.'

'Men can be clever in some ways and stupid in others,' Gran said. 'It's all very well thinking girls will get wed but not all girls get asked. Even if a girl does get wed she can be left a widow. Look at me. Still, Lily's got you to look out for her, hasn't she?'

''Course she has,' Artie grinned.

Smiling back at him, Lily got up to stir the stew she'd made.

* * *

She started reading *Peter Pan* that night but it was hard to see the words in what remained of the firelight and lighting the gas would cost money

47

they couldn't afford. Besides, it would be foolish to read late into the evening when she had to be up early.

Lily didn't forget her idea of taking Gran out so she could be seen by their neighbours. Returning from school for dinner on the following Monday, Lily was pleased when Gran announced, 'I'm having a good day.'

'If you rest this afternoon, you might be up to doing some deliveries with me later,' Lily suggested. 'We don't want people beginning to wonder why you're staying indoors.'

'I'll be up to it,' Gran insisted, and Lily returned from afternoon school to find Gran had pinned her hair into a low bun at the back of her neck and brushed her drab brown coat.

Lily packed the bag with the three deliveries that were closest to home. 'Lean on me if it helps,' she said as they stepped outside, but Gran was already waving to Janet Flynn who was taking a breather out in the alley.

'Haven't seen you out and about in a while,' Mrs Flynn said.

'I've had plenty to do indoors. Besides, I'm not the sort of fool who won't make the most of having young legs willing to run the errands.' Gran nodded at Lily's legs.

'She's a good girl, your Lil. Who knows? Maybe I'll have a girl this time.'

Mrs Flynn patted her belly. 'I wouldn't be without my six boys, but a girl ... '

'Here's hoping,' Gran said.

She squeezed Mrs Flynn's arm and walked on to Mr Beeton's house. 'It's been a while since I last saw you, Maggie,' he said, welcoming them inside.

'I've got Lily here to do my running around these days.'

'Young legs,' he agreed. 'Shall I put the kettle on?' Mr Beeton was a widower and lonely.

'Why not?' Gran said, sitting down.

Lily took out his parcel and unwrapped it while they waited for the kettle to boil. 'This week's washing is over there,' Mr Beeton said, nodding to the corner where a small pile of shirts and under-clothes sat.

Lily put them into a sack. 'Do you have any errands that need running?' she asked.

'You could fetch me some tobacco and a tin of shoe polish. Oh, and a rabbit if the butcher's got one. I've a hankering for rabbit stew tonight.' He handed her some money and Lily raced off, call-ing first at two of his neighbours in the hope of picking up more errands and being rewarded with a commission to buy margarine and fish paste for Mr Webb.

Gran got to her feet on Lily's return. 'Thanks for the tea, Bert. It went down a treat.'

Mr Beeton paid Gran for the washing and gave a penny to Lily instead of just a halfpenny. 'See-ing as you had to go to two shops for me. Are you saving for something special?'

Gran tensed but Lily smiled. 'I like books,' she told him, which was true even if it wasn't the real answer to his question. Lily's pennies would go in the old tea caddy along with Gran's money.

They made another two deliveries, Gran being welcomed warmly, then called in at the corner shop so more people could see her out and about. There were several women inside and all of them looked pleased to see Gran who laughed and spoke her mind with the forthrightness of old. 'You tell your Reg he'll be getting a piece of my mind if I hear he's supped his wages away down at the Ship and Anchor again,' she advised newly-wed Mrs Linnet. 'Reg needs to grow up and start acting like a man.'

It was good to see Gran so respected and liked. She turned to the shopkeeper.

'I'll take a tin of corned beef, please.'

She paid over the money then turned back to the other customers. 'Better get on. Our Artie will be wanting his tea and you know what hungry lads are like.'

Lily hoped she was the only one to notice that Gran's face had turned the colour of the feathery ash that lay in the hearth after the fire had died down.

'Lean on me,' Lily urged when they got outside, and Gran needed no second invitation.

Her coat had fitted properly once, filled out by her strong shoulders and finishing above her ankles. Now it looked like someone else's coat, trailing in the dirt.

'I won't pretend I'm not glad to get home,' Gran said, sinking into a chair the moment they arrived.

'Have you got some pain?' Lily asked.

'The pain's not so bad, but I feel as weak as a newborn babe.'

'Rest for a while. I'll do those other deliveries then make the supper.'

'Pass that sack of washing then.'

Lily passed her Mr Beeton's sack. Not because Gran intended to do anything with it, but so she'd look busy if Artie came in.

Lily put the remaining parcels in the bag then went out, managing to earn another halfpenny as well as to collect money due to Gran. She tipped it all into the old tea caddy, got some washing soaking and started on a supper of potatoes, cabbage and half of the tin of corned beef.

The other half went onto a plate which she placed in the cupboard under the stairs to keep cool and fresh for tomorrow's supper. She was mashing the potatoes and corned beef when Artie came in, but she stepped aside to let Gran dish it up as usual. Artie ate every scrap of his share, suspecting nothing when Gran said she'd keep hers warm in the oven while she fetched washing in from the yard. Only after he'd gone back out to play did Gran attempt to eat. She managed little but at least Artie hadn't noticed that her appetite was poor.

'You won't have to go out again for a while now you've been seen,' Lily assured her.

★ ★ ★

Two weeks passed. Three weeks. Artie appeared to be getting on well at Mr Alderton's. He still cast regretful looks at his pals when he was separated from them on Saturdays but his only complaint had come after his second visit when he'd returned home with a satchel of books which he'd thumped

51

onto the table in outrage. 'Mr Alderton wants me to do more book learning at home! Every day!

Even when I've been to school! He calls it prep and says that boys at smart schools do it to help them get on.'

Lily had felt irritation building. Why couldn't Artie understand how lucky he was? But she'd pushed the feeling down again. Artie only wanted to be like his friends and perhaps it was tiredness that was making her bad-tempered. A touch of envy too. 'I've been setting you extra sums and spellings for years,' she'd pointed out.

'Yes, but — '

'I'll help,' she'd promised, suspecting he was actually afraid of being unable to cope. 'If I can,' she'd added under her breath as it occurred to her that, without Mr Alderton explaining things to her, she might not be able to cope either.

'Good cake today?' Gran had asked, giving Artie's thoughts a happier turn, and he'd told them about a cake which had a scattering of nuts on top.

'Mrs Lawley let me have two slices,' he'd said.

Lily wasn't surprised that Artie had won Mr Alderton's housekeeper round. He was a sweet-natured boy.

Luckily, Lily had mastered the sums Mr Alderton had set so far, whether they were fractions, long division or sums involving pounds, shillings and pence.

She'd had to spend time looking at the English grammar book Mr Alderton had supplied before she understood what was meant by different types of words, but once they were fixed in her head

52

they stayed there and she was able to help Artie to remember them too.

Lily used his afternoons with Mr Alderton to try to catch up on washing that couldn't be managed in the week but she still missed another two days of school, much to Miss Fielding's disappointment. Much to Lily's disappointment too, though she assured Gran she'd missed nothing important.

Another week went by then Lily took Gran to the corner shop again only to fear she'd made a mistake after hearing one neighbour remarking to another, 'Maggie Tomkins is looking peaky.'

Lily butted in with, 'She just needs the sun on her face.'

Mrs Flynn called in for a cup of tea too and gave Lily a searching look when she left. 'Everything all right?'

'Everything's fine,' Lily insisted, though Gran was wilting from the strain of pretending to be well.

'There's something about visitors that wears a body out,' she said.

Between Mrs Flynn and the people in the shop it couldn't be too long before gossip started circulating about Gran's health. Lily had hoped for many more months with Gran but she couldn't escape the fact that Gran was fading fast.

Lily didn't regret keeping Gran's illness a secret from Artie so far, but he'd have to be told about it soon because it would be awful if he learned the truth from someone else. She'd let him enjoy their birthday first, though. May was only two weeks away, after all.

Their birthday fell on a Saturday this year.

'Don't think I'm complaining, but do I still have to go to Mr Alderton's?' Artie asked.

'People still have to go to school or work when it's their birthdays,' Lily reminded him.

'I suppose that's true. And I'll get cake at Mr Alderton's which is fitting for a birthday, isn't it?'

Gran usually made a cake for them but this year Lily had other ideas. 'Why don't we have a pudding instead seeing as Artie's already getting cake?' she suggested to Gran.

She'd been saving sugar for a suet pudding with golden syrup. Maybe custard too if she could manage the extra milk. There was a tense moment in the week when Janet Flynn called in again, rubbing her now visibly pregnant belly and saying, 'I'll take a little sugar in my tea, if that's all right? I need it with the boys driving me mad at home and this one giving me a kicking from inside.'

To Lily's relief, Mrs Flynn had left enough sugar for the pudding but her eyes had watched Gran suspiciously and been thoughtful when they'd rested on Lily.

Artie was delighted with the pudding. 'It's even better than Mrs Lawley's cake,' he declared. High praise indeed.

Lily had set aside a penny and bought sweets for Artie — his favourite barley sugars. She didn't expect anything in return but Artie gave her a collection of small pebbles he'd found on the riverbank. They were made from white, blue and brown glass worn smooth by years of having been dragged this way and that along the riverbed as the tide moved in and out. 'I hope you think they're pretty,' he said.

'I do think they're pretty.' Lily smiled as she

54

touched a blue pebble.

Neither of them expected anything from Gran this year but she'd made a handkerchief for each of them out of an old sheet and even embroidered their initials in one of the corners. Gran had learned embroidery years before when in domestic service but rarely embroidered these days. Lily had to swallow hard when she thought of Gran going to the trouble of making gifts when she was feeling so unwell.

'We can't have you going to Mr Alderton's with just a rag in your pocket,' Gran told Artie. 'And it'll be nice for you to take a decent handkerchief to school, Lily.'

'I'll make a point of using mine in front of Mr Alderton so he knows I've been brought up proper,' Artie said.

One more week, Lily decided. One more week and she'd tell Artie about Gran.

Before the week was over their vicar called, arriving just as Lily returned from school. She was itching to get started on the ironing and errands but stayed indoors to make him a cup of tea and help Gran if his questions became too probing.

'It's been quite a while since I last saw you in church, Mrs Tomkins,' he began.

'That's because I have to work,' Gran told him.

'There are other days for work.'

'There are. And I work on those days too. But there's only so much washing a body can peg out at a time when their house and yard are as small as mine. Besides, doesn't it say in the Bible that the Sabbath was made for man, not man for the Sabbath? I think God prefers me to put food in

55

my grandchildren's mouths than parade about in Sunday finery to please those who think being seen in a building is more important.'

Lily hid a smile. This was Gran at her finest.

'I take your point, Mrs Tomkins, but —'

'A body can pray while she's ironing in her kitchen just as well as on her knees in a pew.'

The vicar smiled faintly. 'I hope the children will keep up their attendance at Sunday School.'

'I hope so too but we'll have to see.'

'They won't want to miss the Sunday School tea.'

The tea was a feast of sandwiches and cake eaten in the church hall. There were games too, and books were presented to those with perfect attendance. Lily had already missed several Sunday mornings because of helping Gran. Artie had missed some Sundays too.

'The tea is a grand affair all right,' Gran conceded. 'But sometimes hard choices have to be made. Young Artie is taking extra lessons, you know. He has extra book learning between those lessons too.'

'Lily can still come t—'

'Lily helps Artie. It's the Christian way to help each other, isn't it, Vicar?'

'Talking of helping,' Lily intervened, 'you said you were going to put those shirts in water to soak, Gran. Shall I do it for you?'

'Yes, please, Lil.'

The vicar took the hint, drank his tea quickly and got up. 'Thank you for your hospitality, Mrs Tomkins. I hope to see you and the children at church soon, but if you need any assistance in the meantime, I hope you'll ask for it. If your health should take a turn for the worse, for instance, or —'

'Thank you, Vicar.' Gran walked past him and opened the door.

When he'd gone her shoulders drooped and she sat back down. 'A good man, that one, but a tiring one,' she declared.

They didn't talk about what he'd said. Lily suspected he'd heard rumours about Maggie Tomkins looking peaky and Gran probably suspected the same.

They could put off telling Artie what was happening no longer. He had to be told today.

It turned out that he didn't need to be told anything. They were eating their supper that night when Lily noticed him staring at Gran intently. He turned to Lily, saying nothing but questioning her with his eyes. *Gran's ill, isn't she?*

6

They didn't talk until they went to bed. Then Artie cried and Lily cried with him.

'You should have told me before,' he sobbed.

'And made you unhappy sooner?'

'She's really going to die?'

'We need to be brave for Gran's sake, Artie.'

'But if she saw a doctor ... '

'She's seen one.'

'You guessed something was wrong a long time ago, didn't you?'

'A while ago,' Lily admitted.

'That's because you're clever. I didn't guess until now because I'm stupid.'

'No, you're not.'

'I must be. She's got so thin and... *small*, and I didn't notice.'

'That's what Gran wanted.'

'Do other people know?'

'I think they're starting to wonder. But we need to stop them from wondering.

If people think Gran can't look after us anymore, they might send us to be looked after somewhere else.'

Artie's eyes widened. 'The workhouse?'

'Or some sort of orphanage. Either way, we'll not only be separated from Gran but from each other too.'

'I don't want to be apart from either of you.'

'That's why we need to keep Gran's illness a

58

secret — so we can stay together for as long as we can.'

'How will we manage?'

'I'm already doing a lot of the washing and running errands to bring some money in.'

Artie made a disgusted sound but the disgust was directed at himself. 'All I've been doing is playing out and seeing Mr Alderton. But I'm going to start helping now. I may not be any good at ironing but I can run errands for you. I'll tell Mr Alderton I need to stop having lessons.'

'No, Artie. Mr Alderton's your best chance of getting an education.'

'I'll have to stop seeing him anyway after ... after ...'

'Even if you can only see him for a little while longer, it'll help.'

Artie thought about it. 'How much longer do you think?' he asked, wincing at what amounted to a question about how long Gran might live.

'I don't know. However long it is, we've got to make every minute count.'

Artie nodded miserably. 'I'll be up early with you tomorrow,' he said.

'Better get some sleep, then.'

Lily tucked his blankets around him and kissed his forehead. Getting into her own bed, she lay on her back and stared sightlessly into the darkness. She heard Artie roll over and begin to sob into his pillow. Tears rolled from her eyes too but she kept her crying silent, hoping Artie would soon exhaust himself into slumber. She was glad when his breathing slowed to shuddering jerks and finally to the deep snuffles of sleep but it was a while before she slept.

* * *

He was still sleeping when Lily got up in the morning and she hadn't the heart to wake him quite so early. She had the fire going, one lot of washing heating in the big copper on the stove and another lot of washing soaking in the dolly tub before she woke him. For a moment he looked peaceful but then memory returned and his expression turned stricken. Lily thought he might be about to cry again but there was a danger of Gran hearing so she gave him a bracing pat on the shoulder. 'You said you wanted to help.'

'I do.'

He joined her in the kitchen, hair still tousled from his pillow. 'Where shall I start?'

'Work the dolly in that tub,' Lilly said. 'Try not to wet your hands because they'll get chapped.'

He looked at Lily's hands — reddened and sore — and shook his head as though he still couldn't believe he'd been too blind to notice before.

He picked up the wooden dolly and used it to stir the washing. After a while she asked him to take some clean washing outside and squeeze it through the mangle before she hung it on the clothes line. He wasn't quick, but she couldn't fault him for willingness.

After a while she took a cup of tea up to Gran. 'Artie knows,' Lily said.

'He guessed, I suppose. I don't need a mirror to tell me I'm not looking good.'

'How are you feeling?'

'There's a bit of life left in me yet, Lil. I'll be down in a minute to talk to the boy before he goes to school.'

Artie burst into tears the moment Gran appeared. She folded him into her arms and let him sob against her wasted chest.

Lily slipped out to run errands then raced to school in time to see Artie arriving. His eyes were red and his step was heavy. 'I'm sorry I didn't help with the errands,' he said.

'You can help later. You needed to be with Gran this morning.'

He nodded and his face crumpled. 'I can't believe she's — '

'Not here, Artie.' Other children were in earshot. 'Meet me at dinnertime.'

'Oi, Artie!' It was Davie calling. 'Why weren't you at the corner?'

They usually walked to school together.

'Got soap in my eyes,' Artie said, pointing to the redness and impressing Lily with his quick thinking.

They moved towards the boys' entrance, but just before they reached it Artie turned and sent Lily a look that was full of secret sorrow.

They met again at dinnertime. 'I don't mind if you want to play with Davie,' Lily told him.

'I want to help.'

Lily was relieved to hear it because it meant she could concentrate on washing and ironing. 'Knock on Mr Higgins's window and he'll tell you if he wants anything fetching today,' she told Artie. 'Old Mrs Piper has a bag of pineapple chunks on Thursdays. I'll give you the money and she'll pay you back. Saves going to her house twice. Mr Franks wants his dog walking but only for a few minutes as it's getting wobbly. Miss Smith might have letters to post. Always ask if they know anyone else who wants an errand running then plan the best way of doing things to save time. Come home and have some dinner first, though.'

They both hugged Gran tightly on their return. Then Lily cut bread and spread dripping over it, and they ate it quickly, Gran sitting nearby and saying she couldn't face food just at the moment.

Lily was tempted not to return to school for the afternoon but Gran insisted though they got home to find her struggling to lift a basket of washing. Gran's strength was fading with frightening speed. 'Let me take that,' Lily said.

With Artie's help she made parcels of the washing that was ready for delivery and sent him off after explaining how much money was due for each parcel and urging him to try to pick up more washing and errands. Gran had managed very little work that day so Lily got down to some washing while he was out.

'All done,' Artie said, tipping coins into the old tea caddy on his return. 'Only three errands but that man at number twenty-three says he wants some shopping done tomorrow.'

Artie paused then added, 'I could get round faster on the bicycle.'

'Sadly, it isn't your bicycle,' Lily reminded him. Mr Alderton hadn't said anything about Artie using it for anything except his Saturday lessons. 'Did your friends miss you today?'

'I told them I still had sore eyes.'

'I should pretend Mr Alderton's keeping you busy if anyone asks tomorrow,' Lily suggested, though that wouldn't explain why Artie was suddenly rushing about running errands. 'Or you can say you're earning money to buy something.'

'A bike of my own?'

'Good idea.' Lily hesitated, looking at Artie's wan face, then said, 'Why don't you go out now? I'm sure you'll find Davie or someone else who wants to kick a ball around.'

'What are you going to do?'

'Get dinner ready.' Seeing Artie was about to protest that it wouldn't be fair if he played while she worked, Lily added, 'But I'll sit down and read afterwards.'

She was glad when he came in later looking a little less pale but he struggled with the lesson Mr Alderton had set for him, rubbing his eyes with tiredness.

'Sorry, Lil. My brain isn't working tonight.'

The next morning she let Artie sleep until it was almost his usual time for getting up. 'I said I'd help,' he protested.

'It's no good getting up early if it stops you from doing your lessons,' Lily pointed out.

'But — '

'The lessons are more important.'

'I'm still going to help later,' he insisted, and he worked so hard that Lily couldn't help kissing him and telling him he was a good boy.

'I'm eleven!' he protested. 'The same age as you.'

'Thirty minutes younger,' Lily pointed out, and he scowled. Artie was still two inches shorter.

Artie was triumphant when he returned from Mr Alderton's on Saturday. 'Mr Alderton says I can use the bike for errand running!'

'You told him about Gran?' Lily was appalled.

'He said he understands I need to help. Riding the bike won't take as much out of me as running. I can go further too, so there might be more people who —

What's wrong, Lil?'

'Nothing, I hope.'

'Do you think he might get us taken away from Gran?' Artie looked worried now.

'Did he say he would?'

'No. But he didn't say he wouldn't.'

'Did he say he'd see you next Saturday?'

'Yes, and he set more lessons for me to do at home.'

'That's a good sign,' Lily said, not liking to see Artie looking anxious.

He brightened suddenly. 'I just told him Gran was poorly. I didn't say *how* poorly. He might think she'll get better.'

'Let's hope so.'

It wasn't only the possibility of Mr Alderton reporting them to the authorities that was troubling Lily. It was also the possibility that he might decide it wasn't worth his while teaching a boy who'd soon be in the workhouse. But Lily didn't want Artie to feel bad so she smiled and praised him for getting permission to use the bicycle.

Mr Alderton said nothing to suggest he was having second thoughts about Artie over the following weeks, and there was no doubt that the bicycle helped Artie to run more errands. Every halfpenny counted more than ever because Gran was hardly managing to work at all. Lily had taken an afternoon off school, having feigned a stomach-ache in the morning, and was pegging out sheets in the yard when a voice demanded, 'Why aren't you at school?'

Lily's head whipped around. Janet Flynn had stepped in from the alley.

'I've got an upset tummy,' Lily told her.

'Upset tummy, my eye. Your gran's badly, ain't she?'

Lily hesitated.

'You've done a grand job of keeping things together, Lily Tomkins, but now you need help.'

'We're fine,' Lily insisted, frightened now.

'I don't mean help from nosy parkers who'll take you and Artie away. That happened to a cousin of mine when her man died. She and the kids went into the workhouse and for years they only saw each other for a few minutes on Sundays. I was just a girl then and couldn't help, but it was terrible for poor Sally. No. What I mean is help from me and others who think well of your gran and can keep their mouths shut about what's going on.'

Was such a thing possible?

'I'm not saying we can take a lot of weight off your shoulders,' Mrs Flynn cautioned. 'But we can start by fitting some of your gran's washing in with our own then see what else we can do. Don't think of it as charity. Your gran would be the first to help us if the tables were turned.'

'Thank you,' Lily said, not knowing what else to say.

'I'll step in and say hello to Maggie, if that's all

66

right?'

Mrs Flynn didn't wait for an answer but walked into the house. When she returned a short time later her face was grave. Living alongside Gran made it hard to spot small daily changes in how she looked but Janet Flynn hadn't seen Gran in two or three weeks and the small changes had obviously added up.

'I'll talk to the other women about the washing,' she said, then left muttering something that sounded like, 'After all, it won't be for long.'

Lily sat down on the doorstep, touched by their neighbour's kindness but wanting to cry at those final words. Her throat felt so tight she could barely breathe but she heard Gran calling her and fought the feelings down.

'Be a love and run up for the bottle, will you, Lil?'

Lily went upstairs for Gran's bottle of laudanum and saw it was almost empty.

Maybe Lily could ask Mrs Flynn if she knew where more might be bought without the need for a doctor's prescription for, despite all their efforts, they were struggling to buy food and fuel as well as to pay the rent.

Mrs Flynn called again later as Lily was bringing in the sheets that had been hanging in the yard. 'There's four of us to help with the washing — Ada Baker, Tilly Fosse, Bessie Tench and me. Ada can't take much because she's already washing for her Aggie's family, and Tilly hasn't got much drying space, but we'll do what we can.'

They went inside and made up a sack for each woman and Lily wrote two lists of what each sack contained — one copy for herself and one for the women.

'You'd better draw pictures too,' Mrs Flynn recommended. 'Ada's reading is pretty good but the rest of us don't get on with it so well.'

When the sacks and lists were ready, she headed back into the yard. 'Here's hoping for decent drying weather,' she said.

She reached the gate that led into the alley and paused, digging in her pocket for some coins. 'Here,' she said. 'We can't take away that growth inside your gran but we can try to take away the worst of the pain. I got up a bit of a collection so you can get something from the doctor.'

Lily was touched beyond words but anxious too. The more people who knew Gran was ill, the more likely it was that people like the vicar and teachers at school would hear and report the situation to the authorities. Even the doctor himself might take it into his head to interfere and separate the family.

'I didn't ask anyone who might blab,' Mrs Flynn assured her. 'Let me know when the doctor comes. I'll come round too and if you call me Auntie Janet in front of him he won't know you're coping with Maggie on your own.'

Just as they'd hoped, the doctor assumed Mrs Flynn was part of the family.

The help given by their neighbours was a godsend but Lily and Artie were still working hard. Too hard for Gran's peace of mind, though there was nothing to be done about it. 'In another few weeks it'll be the school holidays,' Lily said.

'Things'll get easier then.'

In the meantime they simply knuckled down to the work.

* * *

Lily was rushing home from school one day when she saw a familiar figure in the distance. A tall, thin, stooping figure. Mr Alderton. Oh, no. Was he intending to call to say he'd realised how ill Gran must be and had decided he'd be wasting his time by continuing to teach Artie? Not only would that be a terrible blow to Artie's prospects, it would also mean giving back the bicycle and how would Artie manage so many errands then? Those errands were the difference between paying the rent or not.

She broke into a run, taking a short cut down an alley to reach Jessy Street sooner. Gran was sitting in the kitchen, wrapped up in a blanket and with her hair looking like a dandelion clock that would scatter at the first breath of a breeze. 'Mr Alderton's coming,' Lily told her.

'Oh, Lordy.' Gran shifted forward as though to heave her weakened body to her feet.

'Don't,' Lily urged. If Mr Alderton intended to cut Artie off, it didn't matter a jot if he saw Gran in the kitchen rather than the parlour.

Besides, there wasn't time for Gran to tidy herself because a knock sounded on the front door.

Lily went to open it. 'Good afternoon, Mr Alderton.' That was how her teacher always greeted people.

'Good afternoon. Might I have a word with Mrs Tomkins?'

69

'Yes, but you'll have to see her in the kitchen. She isn't well.'

'So I have heard.'

He looked bewildered by the state of the kitchen as there was washing and ironing everywhere — hanging from the drying rack attached to the ceiling, draped over another drying rack that stood on the floor, piled up on the table and soaking in both the dolly tub and the bath tub. Lily pulled a chair away from the table and invited him to sit then stood at Gran's shoulder protectively.

'Arthur has told me you're unwell,' he began. 'Might I enquire as to your prospects for recovery? It isn't my wish to be indelicate or intrusive but Arthur was distracted the last time he came to me. Tearful.'

'I'll speak plainly,' Gran told him. 'I've no chance of recovery. But I hope this doesn't mean you'll give up on our boy.'

'What will become of Arthur?'

'There's no family or anyone else to take him and Lily in. They're good people round here despite how it might look to those on the outside, but the harsh fact is that none of them has the space nor the money for my two. So it'll be the workhouse or some sort of orphanage.'

'That makes it all the more important for Artie to learn as much as he can now,' Lily burst in.

'It would certainly be a shame to interrupt his progress,' Mr Alderton said. 'I have a proposal for you to consider, Mrs Tomkins. I suggest Arthur should come to me instead of the workhouse or an orphanage.'

Gran frowned. 'I don't follow.'

70

'I suggest that he comes to live in my house. My housekeeper will see to his physical well-being while I attend to his mind. My intention is for Arthur to be able to earn a better living for himself than will otherwise be the case. I can ask Mrs Lawley who keeps house for me to call on you to reassure you that good care will be taken of the boy.'

'That's as may be, but what about Lily here?'

Mr Alderton looked puzzled. 'I don't understand your meaning, Mrs Tomkins.'

'Are you offering a home to Lily as well?'

Clearly, the thought hadn't crossed his mind. 'I know nothing of girls and their needs,' he said, leaving Lily in no doubt that he had no interest in learning about them. 'Your granddaughter looks a useful sort of girl. Doubtless, with training from an appropriate institution, she will find a place in the world.'

'You think I should let them be torn apart so Artie goes to your house — a grand place from what I've heard — and poor Lily goes to the workhouse? No, Mr Alderton. Your offer is kindly meant, I'm sure, but it's out of the question.

Lily and Artie will be everything to each other after I'm gone.'

'My offer is a fine opportunity for Arthur. Must he miss out on an advantage because his sister can't share in it?'

Oh, heavens. The thought of being separated from Artie as well as from Gran was terrible. Lily felt it scoop a hollow deep inside her. But she had to think of Artie.

'No,' Lily said. 'He mustn't miss out on it.'

71

Gran turned to her in appalled surprise. 'Think what you're saying, Lil.'

'I *am* thinking. Getting an education is Artie's best chance of making something of himself.'

'But you won't see each other. Artie will be in Hampstead and you'll be ...

We don't know where you'll be, but it won't be Hampstead.'

'Boys and girls are kept apart in the workhouse anyway. Probably in orphanages too,' Lily argued. She looked at Mr Alderton. 'Would you let Artie write to me? Perhaps even visit?'

'If Arthur wishes it.'

Gran was still shaking her head.

Mr Alderton rose to his feet. 'It isn't a decision lightly to be made, perhaps. I shall leave you to think it over, Mrs Tomkins. Believe me when I say that Arthur's entire life could be changed for the better.'

Lily was still reeling from the thought of separation but she rallied herself to remember her manners. 'You won't stay for a cup of tea?'

'Thank you, but no.'

She saw him to the door then returned to Gran who was bristling with indignation and something else Lily only gradually realised was helplessness. 'I wish I could live longer, Lil. Not for my sake but for yours and Artie's. If I could manage just a few more years I could see you both making your ways in the world. God would get no complaint from me if he wanted to call me home then, but to call me now...'

Lily kissed Gran's cheek. 'You know it's a fine chance for Artie.'

72

'What's a fine chance for me?' Artie came through the back door.

'Let's get the work done and we can talk later,' Lily said

'But — '

'People are waiting for their errands to be run.' She didn't want him getting too upset to be of help.

He looked as though he wanted to argue but he clamped his lips together and nodded.

It was after supper when Lily told him about Mr Alderton's suggestion. 'Is he mad?' Artie demanded. 'I can't leave you, Lil. I *won't* leave you.'

'You must, Artie.'

'Gran?' he appealed. 'Lil's gone mad too.'

'No, she hasn't.' Gran's voice was quiet now. Flat with defeat. 'I don't like it any more than you, but it's too good a chance to pass up.'

'What sort of a brother would I be if I let my sister go to the workhouse while I lived like a prince in a fairy tale?'

'The sort of brother who'll work hard so he can help his sister in the future,' Gran told him. 'The sort of brother who'll build a better life for her as well as for himself.'

'That'll take years. I can't be apart from Lil for years.'

'We'd be apart most of the time in the workhouse or orphanage,' Lily pointed out. 'Mr Alderton says you can write to me and visit me too.'

'It won't be the same.'

'Everything's changing whether we like it or not,' Gran said. 'If I've got to die, I'd rather go knowing you have a chance to do more than scrimp and save all your life.'

'I won't leave Lily.'

'Oh, yes, you will,' Lily said. 'Stop being so selfish.'

'Selfish?' Artie's eyes were wide. Hurt too.

Lily regretted having pained him but she was tired and her heart felt as though it were falling to pieces, shedding joy the way a tree shed its leaves in autumn.

'Gran needs peace of mind and so do I. It won't be possible for me to help you if we're separated in a workhouse or orphanage so it'll be a weight off my mind to know you're getting an education.'

'Yes,' Gran agreed, 'and an education means you'll be better able to help Lily once you're old enough to earn a living.'

'I hadn't thought of it like that,' Artie admitted sadly.

'So you'll tell Mr Anderson you accept his offer?' Gran said. 'His *kind* offer?'

'Yes.' Artie agreed.

'Tell him to send his housekeeper to me like he promised. I can't have you going to just anyone.'

Gran patted Lily's hand because she'd have no choice about where she was sent.

'I'll miss you, Lil,' Artie said, when they went up to bed that night.

'I'll miss you too.' She'd shed private tears about it. 'But in another few years we'll be together again. Not just for a visit. For always.'

'It might be sooner than you think.'

'Oh?' Lily saw fear in his eyes.

'Mr Alderton might think I'm a dunce when I

haven't got you to help me.'

Lily wrapped an arm around his shoulder and pulled him close. 'I might get to answers a bit quicker than you, but you'll get to them your-self soon enough if you keep trying. Mr Alderton doesn't complain when he teaches you on Satur-days, does he?'

'Sometimes he sighs or taps his fingers when I'm slow.'

'He wouldn't have asked you to learn from him every day if he thought you were stupid.'

Artie shrugged and Lily realised he was crying again.

She felt tears pooling in her own eyes but blinked them away. 'Let's not think about being apart. Let's just make the most of the time we still have together.'

But time moved with horrifying speed.

Mr Alderton's housekeeper visited and Gran pronounced Mrs Lawley to be a sensible woman. 'A little strict, maybe, but that's no bad thing for keeping a boy on the straight and narrow. She keeps a decent table too, from what she told me. Artie shan't starve in her care.'

Mrs Flynn and her team of neighbours called in often and did what they could to help.

Soon other neighbours were calling in as word gradually leaked out about Maggie Tomkins being on her way out of the world. Their own vicar was among them and Lily was glad Janet Flynn was in the house to fend off questions about how they were coping.

She was even gladder when he produced a small bag of coins which he explained came from his parish hardship fund. Reluctant as though Gran was to accept charity — Lily too — the fact was that they needed help with the rent and for another visit from the doctor, especially as fewer customers were sending their washing now they knew Gran was ill.

With Artie due to go to Mr Alderton's Lily insisted he should keep up his school attendance but her own fell off as Gran could no longer be left alone.

'Please don't tell anyone,' Lily pleaded, when her teacher confronted her and Lily finally had to admit the truth. 'It isn't going to be for much longer. School finishes for the holidays soon anyway, and it isn't as though I'm behind with my learning.'

Miss Fielding looked torn between sympathy and duty. 'I can't make any promises,' she said, but the term duly ended and no one had intervened.

It was a relief no longer to have to juggle school with caring for Gran but the long summer days felt strangely unreal when things at home couldn't have been bleaker. No one mentioned how they'd cope when school started again in September because no one thought Gran would still be with them.

It was the end of August when Gran called Lily and Artie to her side. 'I want to talk about my funeral,' she said. 'You've probably heard about people paying a few pennies a week to the insurance man so they can have a decent burial. I've never been able to manage that so it'll be a pauper's funeral for me, same as it was for your mum

76

and dad. You need to know that it doesn't matter at all. We went on loving your mum and dad without having a headstone to visit and I know you'll go on loving me.'

'We will,' Lily assured her and Artie nodded, clearly too choked to speak.

'I know you'll go on loving each other too so maybe I'm being an old fool in wanting promises, but will you give me them anyway? Promises to love and look after each other always?'

'Yes, Gran,' Lily said. 'I promise.'

'Artie?'

'I promise too.'

'Then I can rest easy.'

There was only one more thing that needed to be done and it was Janet Flynn who suggested it to Lily. 'I've been asking questions and you can turn up at the workhouse any day but it's usual to get a ticket from the Relieving Officer first. Why don't I see him with you?'

The Officer was a thin man with a hooked nose who asked questions about Lily's name, age and circumstances. It was truly terrible when Mrs Flynn confirmed that Gran had no more than a day or two to live though the Officer nodded with the air of a man who'd heard many desperate stories and grown used to them. He wrote out a ticket for Lily to show when she arrived at the workhouse. Unable to bear to look at such stark proof of Gran's approaching death, Lily put it straight into her pocket.

Gran fell into a deep sleep the following evening. Mrs Flynn sat downstairs while Lily and Artie sat at Gran's bedside with blankets around their shoulders.

The house was quiet, the only sounds being Gran's breathing and occasional footsteps passing down Jessy Street. The footsteps grew fewer as the evening advanced and ceased as midnight came and went. Then it was quiet enough for just the mournful chiming of a distant clock to reach them.

In time Artie's head and shoulders drooped. Lily eased them onto the bed and let him sleep. The clock chimed two o'clock and Lily sat on, holding one of the thin, papery hands that had loved and cared for her all her life.

Gran's breathing finally stopped. Lily kissed Gran's forehead then sank down beside Artie to sob her grief as the clock chimed again. It was three o'clock in the morning. Their old lives were over. Their new lives had begun.

8

Mrs Flynn insisted that Lily and Artie should stay in her crowded little house on the nights that followed Gran's death though it meant that some of her own children had to sleep on the floor. She also helped Lily and Artie to pack up the few things they wanted to keep such as a small packet of family photos, some of the pottery Gran had loved, samples of her embroidery, the wedding rings of Gran and Mum, and the family's collection of books. Mr Alderton's housekeeper came and took the boxes to Hampstead in a taxi.

Mrs Flynn also organised a sale of Gran's remaining possessions, inviting the neighbours to make offers before the landlord came to take back the house.

'They're Maggie's things, remember,' she told them. 'Maggie was quick to help us so you can be quick to help her little ones. That includes you, Doris Lokes.'

Doris was a skinflint who'd cheat her own mother to save a farthing.

The sale raised little, but even a few shillings were better than nothing.

Lily bought a small posy of flowers to lay on the ground where Gran and other paupers were buried. She also bought paper, envelopes and stamps so she and Artie would be able to write to each other. The rest of the money she gave to Artie so

79

he wouldn't arrive at Mr Alderton's house completely penniless.

Artie was to ride the bicycle to Hampstead. He wheeled it out to the alley but burst into tears. Lily took him into her arms and couldn't stop her own tears from falling but eventually she eased them apart. 'Be brave and make Gran proud,' she said.

'I'll try.'

He got on his bike and rode off, leaving Lily with no idea when she might see him again. Lily's throat felt so tight she couldn't swallow.

'Go for a walk, Lil,' Mrs Flynn suggested, and Lily nodded.

She walked up to the river for what she suspected might be her last look at it for quite some time. The workhouse wasn't prison, but it still took away a person's freedom. Lily would have to be strong if she were to survive it without having her spirit crushed. She was sure she *would* survive it, but the fight back against grief would have to wait. Just now the grief was overwhelming.

She was glad when it began to rain because the water streaming down her face hid her tears. She stared at the river — sludgy in colour and pockmarked by falling raindrops. It was as though even the sky was mourning Gran.

Lily had never felt so low in all her life than when she retraced her steps to Jessy Street. Her head hurt and her body seemed drained of all energy. 'Aw, Lily,' Mrs Flynn said when she saw her. 'I wish I could take you in but — '

'You haven't the room. Don't feel badly about it. You were a good friend to Gran and you've been

80

a good friend to Artie and me.'

With a neighbour minding her own children, Mrs Flynn insisted on accompanying Lily to the workhouse.

'I'll say goodbye here,' Lily said, when they reached the door. 'You need to get home to the children.'

'You'll come and see me if you get the chance?'

'I will,' Lily promised.

'I wish I could say I'd write but I'm not so good with writing.'

'It doesn't matter. I'll be getting letters from Artie.'

''Course you will,' Mrs Flynn agreed, but a flicker of something like doubt passed across her face.

Lily was about to assure her that Mr Alderton had agreed to Artie writing and visiting when she realised that their neighbour's doubts ran deeper than that. Did Janet think that Artie would grow apart from Lily, out of sight gradually becoming out of mind?

If so, she was wrong. Artie's life might be going in a different direction for a while, but that didn't mean the ties that bound him to Lily were weakening. Artie was her twin, as close as close could be, and that wouldn't change just because they had a few miles between them. Even so Lily felt jangled up inside.

Forcing a smile, she hugged her old neighbour then knocked on the door, waving Janet off as she waited for her knock to be answered.

Someone — Lily supposed he was some sort of porter — let her in, required her to stand waiting

81

for a moment, then beckoned her to follow him to an office.

'New girl, Mr Simms, sir,' he said to the thin man who sat inside at a desk.

Mr Simms held out a hand for Lily's ticket then asked her a number of questions which she answered in a daze. She *would* keep her faith in Artie. She would.

She waited for the questions to stop then said, 'I have a brother, sir. He has ...'

Oh, what was the word? Benefactor. That was it. 'He has a benefactor, sir.'

'Benefactor?'

'A gentleman who's taken him in to give him an education. My brother is going to write to me here. May I write back? Artie will send the stamp and everything.'

'You may,' Mr Simms said. 'If he really does write to you.' He too made it sound doubtful.

'Artie *will* write to me, sir. I know he will.'

Mr Simms looked unconvinced but disinclined to argue. 'The education you'll receive here will be basic. But it will teach you to be useful so you can provide for yourself one day.'

'Yes, sir. Thank you, sir.'

She wanted to ask him if she'd be moved on somewhere — to a school, perhaps — but a Matron arrived to take her elsewhere and Mr Simms looked irritated when he saw Lily hadn't moved.

The Matron led her away to be bathed and examined by the Medical Officer.

It was embarrassing to be stripped, poked and prodded, but Lily kept her chin tilted proudly,

82

glad that no fault was found with her health and no lice were found in her hair.

She listened with only half an ear as she was told about rules and routines. Up at six to wash, dress, clean shoes and make beds ... Prayers and religious instruction ... Breakfast ... Lessons ... Dinner ... Domestic lessons ... Supper ...

More domestic lessons ... More prayers ... Bed ... Church on Sundays ... One bath each week ...

Lily managed to ask about a school but the Matron knew nothing about that.

'The sooner you settle down here the better,' she advised.

Lily had every intention of seizing whatever opportunities the workhouse offered but a few days of coming to terms with her situation were what she needed first. Injured animals could retreat to their dens to lick their wounds. Lily would retreat in her head.

She was taken to the dining hall where people were sitting on long bench seats behind long tables. All the girls sat together and Lily was nudged onto a bench beside another girl of around her own age who stared at her momentarily but said nothing. Supper comprised bread, cheese and milk. Lily wasn't hungry but, judging from the way everyone else tore into the rations, she supposed that if she missed a meal now there'd be little chance of making up for it another time.

Besides, it wouldn't do to let her body weaken so she forced the food down.

Afterwards, there was a lesson in sewing but years of helping Gran with repairs had already made Lily a quick and neat seamstress. Prayers followed, then bed, a narrow iron-framed bed in a long room full of identical beds. Some girls seemed to be in such low spirits that they took no notice of Lily or anyone else. But a few curious looks were sent her way together with an actual smile from the girl in the next bed. 'I'm Kathleen,' the girl said.

'Lily.'

'It's hard on your first day, isn't it?'

'Have you been here long?'

'A month. But I won't be here for much longer. My ma's in the women's ward but we'll both be out when Pa gets back from sea. He's a sailor.'

Lucky Kathleen, having a family and freedom beckoning. Lily's attention was caught by two girls further down the room.

'Mary and Martha,' Annie told her. 'They're twins.'

Lucky Mary and Martha too, having each other close. Lily wondered what Artie was doing. What he was thinking. Feeling. How many weeks or even months would pass before she saw him again?

Her throat tightened and she swallowed hard. 'Goodnight, Kathleen,' she said, getting into bed and curling up small. It was the only way she could be private.

She kept her crying silent, not wanting to disturb anyone else, but other girls cried at different times of the night. Were they missing loved ones too? Or simply hating their lives here?

Lily must have dozed eventually because she was woken with what felt like brutal haste and given no chance to find her bearings before she had to get up.

She hoped Artie had managed more rest. He needed a sharp brain for his lessons.

Lily's morning routine moved along briskly. Kathleen sat next to her at breakfast which was watery porridge. Again Lily forced herself to eat it as there was no alternative. Was Artie finally getting the breakfast egg he craved?

'Schoolroom next,' Kathleen told her, and Lily forced her own brain to sharpen a little.

She might be licking her wounds but she wasn't going to let any chance for learning slip by. She went to the classroom eagerly but soon realised she was unlikely to learn anything at all here. She'd been lucky in having a father who encouraged her to read and a teacher who encouraged her to attempt harder work but here all the children of Lily's age were given the same work, and none of it was challenging.

Looking around, Lily saw that some girls were struggling while others were simply staring into space. No one asked for harder work and neither was it offered. Disappointment settled on her like the silent fall of soot from a chimney.

They moved into the girls' playground after dinner. It was a small space but at least it was open to the sky. Martha and Mary were there and the sight of them walking arm in arm gave Lily another pang of longing for Artie's company.

The afternoon lessons were sewing and knitting, then the girls had to take part in cleaning their sections of the workhouse. 'No cutting corners,' they were instructed as they dusted, swept and scrubbed.

Lily went to bed feeling bleak at the thought of

wasting almost three years here. She summoned the memory of Gran's beloved face into her mind and imagined what Gran would say to her now. 'Don't give up, Lil. Three years isn't forever and before you know it you and Artie will both be out in the world. Then you can be reunited.'

The thought of never seeing Gran again made tears spill over. Lily turned into her pillow to weep in silence.

She woke the next morning determined to count her blessings and hoping Kathleen might be one of them. But the day brought change. The matron beckoned Kathleen forward and spoke to her. From the radiant smile that burst out on Kathleen's face Lily guessed that her father had returned from his travels to claim his wife and daughter. Lily had time only to wish Kathleen good luck.

Without her, Lily felt even bleaker but the following day the Matron had news for her too. 'You're moving.'

'Moving?'

'A place has come up at Booth's Cottage Schools.'

'Do all workhouse orphans go there?'

'Not as far as I know.'

A school was surely good news but there was a complication. 'I have a brother who's going to write to me here. Will he be told where I've gone?'

'Mr Simms will inform any next of kin.'

Was Artie Lily's next of kin even though he was a child? Lily couldn't ask because the matron had already moved away, frowning with bad temper as her tongue ripped into another girl who was chewing her hair.

Nothing more was said about moving. When morning came Lily began to go about her day as usual until the matron bustled up. 'What do you think you're doing? Didn't I say you were moving?'

There was no point in explaining that no one had told Lily *when* she'd be moving.

'Don't keep Miss Huxtable waiting.'

Miss Huxtable? Lily opened her mouth to ask who she was and also to seek reassurance about Artie but the matron cut her off. 'Hurry yourself, girl.'

Lily was sent down to the hall where she'd first entered. A boy of around her age was already there, looking small and shrunken. Was he going to the school too? Lily hastened to the porter to ask about Artie but the man's attention turned to a woman who bustled into the hall in coat and hat. She was a big woman with a face that reminded Lily of a bad-tempered bulldog. 'Cart's 'ere, Miss 'Uxtable,' he told her.

'Thank you, Smith,' she said, then glared at Lily and the boy. 'Don't dawdle.'

She swept outside, Lily and the boy following. 'Please,' Lily said. 'I need to be sure my brother knows where I'm going.'

'Mr Simms will inform next of kin.'

'Artie isn't grown up yet. Does that make a difference?'

The question flummoxed the woman but she tightened her mouth. Clearly, she wasn't the sort of person to admit when she didn't know the answer to a question.

87

'Please,' Lily said again, 'If I could just ask at —'

'It isn't for children to ask questions. Now, get in the cart or you'll make us late.'

Swallowing down her frustration, Lily climbed up and sat on a narrow bench seat beside the boy, the space for their legs being limited by stacks of empty vegetable baskets. Grunting from the effort, Miss Huxtable climbed up to sit on the opposite bench and the cart lurched away. Lily turned to the boy. 'Hello. I'm Lily.'

She didn't get to know his name because Miss Huxtable barked, 'Hush over there.'

The boy slumped down with his mouth open, snuffling noises coming from his nose. He was a sad specimen with no fight in him, but pity for him and anger with Miss Huxtable re-lit the flame of fight in Lily.

It was daunting to think of the years that lay ahead but school might be an improvement on the workhouse and Artie was bound to find out her address eventually, even if he had to bang on the workhouse door to demand why she'd hadn't replied to the letters he'd surely write. Mr Alderton might even intervene on Artie's behalf, not wanting his pupil to be too upset to concentrate.

Lost in thought, Lily was roused by Miss Huxtable suddenly urging them to climb down from the cart and be quick about it. Had they arrived already? They were still in London and all was bustle but Lily didn't have a chance to take her bearings because Miss Huxtable strode off into what Lily realised was a train station. 'The Sevenoaks train?' Miss Huxtable asked a porter.

He pointed and Miss Huxtable set off in the

direction indicated, Lily hastening after her before running back to fetch the boy who was staring around in wonder as steam hissed into the air and whistles blew to announce departures or arrivals.

Lily had only travelled by train once when Mum and Dad had taken her and Artie to Folkestone for the day but she guessed this boy had never travelled anywhere.

They walked along a platform then boarded the Sevenoaks train, a fearsome, metal beast breathing out steam like a dragon breathed out fire. Miss Huxtable walked along the corridor then opened the door to a compartment which had two bench seats facing each other. She sat on one bench, spreading her skirts as though settling in for some time. Lily and the boy sat on the other.

Lily had an idea Sevenoaks was in Kent to the south-east of London. Some of their neighbours had gone to Kent to pick hops for beer-making in the summer months but Gran had always been too busy with washing to spare the time.

A whistle blew and the train pulled off slowly, gradually gathering speed as they shuffled through the city then reached bursts of countryside interspersed with towns and villages. Were Booth's Cottage Schools in the countryside? Lily had only ever lived in Bermondsey. She'd been happy there among people she loved but it might be nice to exchange terraces for trees. On the other hand, the further she was from London, the harder it might be for Artie to visit.

It began to rain, raindrops slashing across the windows then trickling down them in wobbly tears. Miss Huxtable made tut-tutting sounds

89

when they reached Sevenoaks and stood outside the station looking for someone who didn't appear to be there. She put up her umbrella but left Lily and the boy to stand with the rain gradually making rats' tails of their hair.

'At last!' Miss Huxtable muttered as a cart appeared, but a glower grew on her face when she saw it was uncovered. 'You're late!' she hissed at the driver but he gave no sign of caring.

They climbed onto the cart and sat on narrow benches again. Miss Huxtable drew her skirts beneath the shelter of her umbrella but once again Lily and the boy were left uncovered. The cart set off and Miss Huxtable dug in her bag for a cloth which she opened to reveal two slices of dry bread and two small pieces of cheese. 'Here,' she said, offering them to Lily and then the boy.

Another dig into her bag resulted in a second cloth which she opened to reveal a pie. It had to be cold by now but it smelt appetisingly of meat and gravy. Miss Huxtable tucked into it with obvious pleasure and, after a moment, Lily and the boy ate their much less appealing bread and cheese.

It was September but the rain was chilly. Lily pulled the collar of her coat up to stop the rain from trickling down her neck. The boy simply sat and shivered, his nose growing pinker while his fingers darkened to raw purple. Lily wished she had something to put over him but couldn't see even a sack to use.

In time there were fewer people and houses but more fields. Some had horses grazing in them while crops were growing in others.

The rain stopped and the air tasted cleaner. It

tingled on Lily's tongue and brought new smells to her nose — smells that she imagined came from the earth and all the greenery.

She was surprised when the cart turned between tall gateposts because they looked rather grand for orphans but a sign on the grass verge beside them announced that this was indeed Booth's Cottage Schools. There was more writing underneath in smaller letters and Lily turned to read it as they passed: *Founded and maintained by the Booth's Charitable Trust.*

They hadn't gone far before the drive split into two. The carter took the right-hand fork, coming to a halt outside a house which was large by Lily's standards and seemed to be one of several houses fronting the drive. 'Out,' Mrs Huxtable instructed Lily.

The boy looked unsure if he should get down too. 'Not you,' Miss Huxtable told him, irritably.

Lily climbed down and Miss Huxtable followed, grunting again. A woman emerged from the house and spent a minute or two in conversation with Miss Huxtable while Lily looked around. The house was fairly new and called *Nightingale* according to a sign over the big wooden door. It had a large porch with a pointed roof and windows on each side of it. There were more windows on the upstairs floor and still more windows in the attics. The house faced a green with trees in the middle. Beyond them Lily caught glimpses of more buildings. Were they the boys' houses?

Miss Huxtable huffed and puffed her way back into the cart. 'Behave yourself,' she told Lily by way of farewell.

91

The cart returned along the drive, presumably to take the boy to the boys' area.

'I'm Mrs Henderson,' the woman said. 'You can call me Mother.'

Lily was taken aback by that, especially as Mrs Henderson didn't look particularly motherly. She was a thin, nervous woman. Following her up the steps and through the door, Lily found herself in a wide hall which had several doors opening off each side as well as a staircase leading upwards. Of the two doors closest to Lily, one was shut but the other was ajar, giving her a glimpse of two long tables with bench seats. The dining room?

'This way,' Mrs Henderson said, leading the way further down the hall where she knocked on another door. A male voice bade her enter. Mrs Henderson beckoned to Lily to follow.

This room contained a sofa and two chairs arranged around a hearth. A desk stood near the window and a man sat behind it, neat and trim as far as Lily could judge. 'The new girl, dear,' Mrs Henderson said. 'Lily Tomkins.'

Standing, he walked around the desk and looked down at Lily. 'I'm Mr Henderson but you can call me Father. Mrs Henderson and I are the foster parents of Nightingale House though I work in the administration offices during the day. I'm the bursar of Booth's.'

'Yes, sir. Thank you, sir,' Lily said, though she wasn't sure what a bursar was. Something to do with money and accounts?

'You're a fortunate girl to be sent here instead of being kept in the workhouse,' he continued. 'I hope you'll show your gratitude by becoming a useful member of the household and learning skills that will allow you to make your own living in the world when you're older.'

'I will, sir. Thank you, sir.'

Nodding, he returned to his chair and Lily followed Mrs Henderson back into the hall. There was another door opposite but it was closed. So too was a further door at the end of the hall which Lily supposed led to the kitchen as she could smell cooking.

'We rise at six,' Mrs Henderson told her, starting up the stairs. 'We encourage usefulness instead of idleness so we all have jobs to do.'

'Yes, Mrs — Mother.'

Mrs Henderson opened a bedroom door and Lily counted twelve narrow beds inside it.

Where were the other children? Either they were extremely quiet or they were out of the house.

'You'll sleep here,' Mrs Henderson told her, pointing to one of the beds near the door. 'It's your responsibility to make the bed each morning and I won't have sloppiness.'

Returning to the landing, Mrs Henderson entered a large room which proved to contain three small cubicles for bathing. She turned the taps on in one of the baths and looked Lily up and down as though assessing her size. 'I'll fetch your uniform,' she said. 'Get undressed, child.'

Once again Lily felt self-conscious being naked in front of a stranger and having her hair inspected for lice. She was given a towel and a uniform of a dark red dress, white pinafore and boots that weren't new but were in better condition than her own boots. She was also given a drawstring bag which contained soap, hairbrush and comb. 'They're all marked with a number that's personal to you. Fix that number in your head and don't take anything that has a different number.'

'No, Mother.'

Lily got into the bath and washed.

'Hurry now,' Mrs Henderson urged, as chattering voices suddenly burst into the house downstairs.

Lily dried and dressed herself quickly then followed Mrs Henderson back to the dining room. Silence fell as Mrs Henderson entered. 'We have a new girl today,' she announced. 'Lily Tomkins.'

Faces of all shapes and sizes turned in Lily's direction. There were far more than twelve girls here. Clearly, Lily's bedroom was only one of several.

Mrs Henderson signalled Lily to sit on the nearest bench. Mr Henderson swept in and the girls all stood as he and his wife walked to the top table.

'Sit,' he instructed, and they all sat down again.

Four older girls brought in the food and Lily was pleased to see that it was much better than workhouse fare — sausages with boiled potatoes, carrots and green beans. Gravy too.

Mr Henderson led them in a prayer then the girls tucked into the meal. Lily glanced around as she ate but cautiously, not wanting to be caught staring. She counted thirty-six girls' heads including her own. Some of the girls looked younger than Lily and some looked older. It would take time to get to know them all but a few of the girls stood out for her.

One was the prettiest girl Lily had ever seen,

a golden-haired fairy with bright blue eyes and soft, pink cheeks. Another was a tall, strong-looking girl with red hair that looked to be as stiff and wiry as the bristles on a scrubbing brush. A third girl was biting her nails while a fourth was sniffing from a head cold. A fifth girl had sharp, dark eyes and a mean little mouth. Lily decided to keep her distance from that girl.

The sausages were followed by tapioca pudding. Afterwards, everyone stood to attention as Mr Henderson walked out. 'Half an hour of recreation for those of you who aren't on clearing duties,' Mrs Henderson announced.

The bigger girls began to stack the dishes and cutlery onto trays, presumably to return them to the kitchen. Not having been allocated a duty, Lily went into the hall then waited to see where the other girls went.

Some moved down the hall to the door opposite the Hendersons' room.

Following, Lily saw rows of numbered hooks with coats hanging on them. She wondered if one of them would be for her but, glancing back, she saw that the door opposite the dining room had been opened and decided to return along the hall to investigate.

She found a large room containing tables, chairs and — oh, bliss! — shelves of books and games. Chess, draughts, dominoes ... Some of the girls took the draughts and sat at a table to play. Others took books but Lily soon realised they were simply trying to look busy if one of the Hendersons came in because the books were ignored in favour of chatting.

Lily walked to the bookcase. *A Child's Book of Sermons* was the first in a row of similar books. Then there were history books, a child's atlas, the same *Flora and Fauna of the British Isles* book that Mr Alderton had loaned to Artie, *Household Tasks for Children*, *A Child's Instruction in Sewing and Mending*, *The Life of Florence Nightingale* (was the house named after her?) and a shelf of story books. Some of them were familiar – *The Wind in the Willows* and *Just So Stories* being among them – but others were new. *Little Lord Fauntleroy*, *The Children of the New Forest*...

Lily took *Little Lord Fauntleroy* off the shelf and carried it to the wooden bench that had been built under the bay window. Lily had every intention of trying to make friends once she was feeling stronger but it wouldn't hurt to get to know the girls from a distance first.

The pretty girl had a sizeable group sitting around her. She was like a princess holding court because the others seemed to be hanging on her every word. They included the sharp-eyed girl who looked proud to be sitting at the fairy princess's right hand. Lily was too far away to hear what was being said, but it seemed to involve a lot of whispering behind hands and laughter.

The recreation time was soon over. Lily returned her book to the shelf and joined the flow of girls heading for the door, soon discovering that it was time for chores. Lily's job was to clean the bathrooms and she was relieved when Mrs Henderson found no fault with her work though other girls were chastised for poor floor-sweeping and leaving smears on brass door handles.

96

Tea was two slices of bread and margarine. A cup of cocoa too. Another period of recreation followed then the girls settled to sewing or knitting while Mr Henderson read to them from *A Child's Book of Sermons*. Lily was required to sew buttons onto boys' shirts in place of buttons that had fallen off. She hoped the boy from the cart was settling in well.

Eight o'clock was bedtime. Lily lay in the darkness, sifting through her first impressions of the school and the people in it. She'd heard names being mentioned in the conversations that had gone on around her. Rose, Agnes and Ivy were the names of the pretty girl, the sharp-eyed girl and another girl who'd sat on Rose's other side. The red-haired girl was called Elsie. There were other names — Ann, Mary, Hannah, Edna, Jean — but Lily couldn't fix faces to them yet.

Gran's face came into her mind together with Artie's. Lily had got through the day without crying but now she turned into her pillow and wept again.

She felt dull-witted with tiredness the following morning but got up, ate her porridge, found a coat waiting for her and joined the other girls as they walked to the school building which she learned was used by the girls in the mornings and the boys in the afternoons. Rallying her energies, Lily told herself that the lessons here were bound to be better than at the workhouse where children were coming and going all the time.

The schoolroom itself was a high-ceilinged hall filled with rows of wooden desks with benches behind them. There were portraits of King George and Queen Mary on one wall together with a decorative plaque announcing once again that the school owed its existence to the Booth's Charitable Trust. There was a large map of the world between the windows on the opposite wall.

Unsure where to go, Lily waited as the younger children headed for the front rows while the eldest headed for the rows at the back. A teacher finally directed Lily to one of the middle rows.

There were two teachers. Miss Lee gave her attention to the younger girls.

Miss Jones taught the girls of Lily's age and older. Each teacher had a blackboard on an easel, Miss Lee's being at the front and Miss Jones's being halfway down the hall so it could be seen by all the girls in her class.

Lily was given a copybook, pencil and pen with instructions to take good care of them. Miss Jones didn't mention what would happen if Lily failed to take care of them but left her in no doubt that the punishment would be severe. Not that Lily had any intention of incurring it. She'd only ever had a slate before and, being keen to learn, was equally keen to look after her things.

The school day began with a hymn — 'Praise my soul, the King of Heaven' — and a prayer. Then Miss Jones announced that her girls would start with spellings. She wrote two columns of words on the blackboard, directing her middle girls to learn the words in the first column and her older girls to learn the words in the second column.

Lily already knew how to spell the words she was supposed to learn — *train, cart, ticket* and so on. She knew how to spell the words the other girls were learning too – *carriage, journey, passenger*... Even so, she recited each letter of the easy words as Miss Jones pointed to them with her stick. ' *T-r-a-i-n* ...'

Eventually, Miss Jones rubbed the words off the board and began asking individual girls to spell the words out loud. One girl was asked to spell *ticket*. 'T-i-k,' she began, only to stop when Miss Jones frowned.

'You.' Miss Jones pointed to Lily who spelt it correctly but quietly, not wanting anyone to think she was showing off.

Spelling was followed by dictation, maps, times tables and arithmetic, all of which were easy to Lily. But she wouldn't despair. Here she had books to read and who knew? If she proved herself a good and attentive pupil, maybe her teacher would be willing to set her harder work, even if Lily had to do it in her own time outside of regular lessons.

A dinner of stew followed by suet pudding with jam awaited them back at the cottage. It was much better than anything else Lily had eaten recently, not just at the workhouse but at home too because money had been so tight.

Afterwards she went into the recreation room, hoping to read a few pages of *Little Lord Fauntleroy* then spend a little time outside but the room fell silent as she entered. Lily stopped in her tracks, surprised and confused, then her gaze came to rest on Rose, the dainty fairy.

There was nothing fairy-like about her expression now. She was glowering at Lily and so were her followers. She held Lily's gaze for a moment then lifted her nose and made a great show of turning away as though Lily were a disgusting slug.

Bewildered and upset, Lily walked to the bookcase but *Little Lord Fauntleroy* wasn't there. Looking around, she saw that the sharp-eyed girl, Agnes, was pretending to read it, a challenging sneer on her face.

Lily headed outside to lean against the cottage wall and try to work out what she'd done to earn such hostility. Another girl walked up and leaned beside her. It was tall, big-boned Elsie with the red hair. 'You've put Rose's hackles up,' she remarked.

'I don't see how.'

'You're clever. Rose likes to be the clever one. You made a fool of Agnes too.'

Lily didn't understand.

'You spelt *ticket* right after Agnes had got it wrong.'

With Agnes sitting behind her, Lily hadn't seen which girl had made the error.

'Someone had to spell it right!' Lily protested.

'Someone in Rose's group. Or Rose herself.'

Lily was appalled. 'Rose is really that mean?'

'She's a lot meaner than that. Look after yourself, new girl.' Elsie straightened and walked unhurriedly away.

How on earth was Lily going to learn anything if she had to hold herself back all the time? Loneliness rushed over her. If only Artie would write to her soon.

9

Lily realised she had two choices. She could try to make friends with Rose and her group by saying sorry and being careful not to outshine them again, or she could ignore them and go her own way, putting up with their meanness as best she could. The possibility of three years of friendlessness was daunting but Lily still chose to go her own way. How else could she learn anything and stop herself from becoming as nasty as they were? And how else would she stand any chance of keeping up with Artie?

Not that she *could* keep up with him exactly. With Mr Alderton teaching him that was probably impossible. But she didn't want to fall so far behind that her ignorance raised a barrier between them.

Lily kept to herself all through the following day, desperately unhappy but vowing not to give in to self-pity because Gran would have hated that. She attended her lessons, ate the food she was offered and carried out her chores without even attempting to make friends though she didn't let her manners slip.

She thanked the girls who brought in the meals, returned a dropped handkerchief to its owner, and stood back to let another girl go through a door ahead of her.

Little Lord Fauntleroy was missing from the shelf again at recreation time but Lily didn't bother looking around to see which of Rose's cronies had taken it.

Instead she began to read *Life of the Saints* because she guessed it was the sort of book that Rose and her cronies would find horribly dull. It was amusing to think of one of them having to pretend to read it so as to deprive Lily of the book.

Sure enough *Life of the Saints* was gone when Lily went to the shelf the following day. Seeing Ivy sighing over it, Lily smiled and took *The Wind in the Willows* instead though she'd read it before.

The day felt long and lonely. Painful, too, when her arm was pinched as she came out of school. Lily couldn't be sure who'd pinched her, but Agnes was nearby and Lily saw her talking to Rose afterwards as though reporting what she'd done.

But there were worse burdens than loneliness and Lily had the comfort of knowing that Artie was getting a better start in life. Besides, she'd already survived three days here and who knew? In time Rose and her cronies might grow bored of tormenting her.

The Wind in the Willows, *Little Lord Fauntleroy* and *Life of the Saints* were all missing the following afternoon. Hiding her misery, Lily took *A History of English Kings and Queens* to the window seat.

Someone slid onto the seat beside her. Red-haired Elsie Davenport. 'You wanted this one, didn't you?'

She was holding out *Little Lord Fauntleroy*.

'I got to it before Rose and her gang,' Elsie added.

'That was kind.' Lily took the book.

Elsie grinned. 'Rose needs to know that she can't have everything her own way.'

Lily glanced at the pretty girl who was looking furious. 'I hope she won't be mean to you for helping me.'

'It doesn't bother me if she is. Agnes pinched me once and I threatened to sit on her if she did it again.'

The thought of it made Lily smile.

'I've been watching you,' Elsie said then.

'Watching me?'

'You stand up to Rose. I like that.'

'So do I.' Another girl came and sat on Lily's other side. 'I'm Phyllis Beckett.'

Phyllis was a slender, dark-haired girl who wore glasses. Seen from a distance, there was nothing remarkable about her appearance but now she was close Lily could see intelligence and humour in Phyllis's grey eyes. 'Looks like the princess isn't happy today,' Phyllis remarked.

'She doesn't like me,' Lily admitted.

'She likes you even less now we're talking to you. But that's her hard luck, eh, Elsie?'

'Yup,' Elsie agreed.

The thought of having Elsie and Phyllis on her side gave Lily a warm glow.

She was happy to set her book aside to talk to them. Like Lily, both girls were orphans from London. Elsie had been at Booth's for almost two years and Phyllis for nearly as long.

'My dad delivered coal,' Elsie said. 'He had a cart and a horse called Dobbin. A dear old thing. The day after Dad died Dobbin just crumpled up in the yard and died too.'

'There was no one else to look after you?' Lily asked.

'I lost my mum when I was five and my only brother when I was six. Frank was two years younger than me. Dad had called the business Davenport & Son because he hoped to take Frank in with him. After Frank had gone, Dad talked about calling it Davenport and Daughter instead because I always helped him to load the sacks onto the cart and looked after Dobbin too. Maybe that's why I'm so big.'

'It was influenza that took my parents,' Phyllis said. 'My aunt might still be alive but she moved to America before I was born and stopped writing. My dad used to work in a brewery but both he and my mother were great readers who believed in a better world with education and opportunities for everyone. I believe in that too, especially education and opportunities for girls.'

'Me too,' Lily said.

It was her turn to share her story. She told them about Mum, Dad and Gran, and the chance her brother had been given to make something of himself.

'It must be hard to be stuck here when he's in a smart house in Hampstead,' Elsie suggested.

'Never mind the grand house,' Phyllis said. 'He's got a chance for the sort of education we'll never have.'

'It isn't all about books and learning,' Elsie persisted. 'If Artie's raised by a gentleman, won't that turn him into a gentleman too?'

'Artie will never be so much of a gentleman that he looks down on me,' Lily insisted. 'He isn't just

104

my brother. He's my twin.'

Despite their smiles Lily could see that both girls had doubts. Oh, heavens.

Phyllis's concerns mirrored Lily's own but did Elsie have a point too? Artie surely had too good a heart ever to sneer at his sister, but might the day come when he was secretly embarrassed by her lack of social polish as well as her lack of education? Lily felt cold suddenly.

But, no. She wouldn't allow such fears to take root in her mind. She had to keep her faith in her twin.

10

Lily worked hard at hiding her feelings on the days when Mrs Henderson handed out letters, determined to deprive Rose of the satisfaction of seeing her disappointment when no letter came from Artie. Not that Rose could crow about receiving letters herself. Only a few children received occasional letters from distant family members or old neighbours and Rose wasn't among them.

Elsie and Phyllis weren't among them either so Lily tried to copy their bored expressions as the more fortunate children were called out.

Then, three weeks after her arrival, Lily's name was called. A thrill of excitement passed through her and she took her letter with trembling fingers.

'Thank you, Mrs — Mother.'

Lily carried the precious letter to the window seat and sat down to read it.

Dearest Lil,

I hardly know where to begin as I've never written a letter before.
What I most want to tell you is that I miss you every day and every night. Especially every night becos you are not here for me to tell you about the day. I'm very glad you are not in the workhouse anymore. I hope you are all right at Booth's and have good food to eat.

I am all right at Mr Alderton's house. I don't know how it is becos he doesn't shout but he has a way of looking at me and waiting for me to pay attention that scares me a bit. Not that he is unkind so don't worry about me. Lessons are hard without you helping but I'm doing my best even if Mr Alderton sometimes thinks I'm slow. I have time to play in between lessons and I have made friends with a cat that lives on one side of us and a dog that lives on the other side. I'm allowed to take the dog for walks sometimes. I'm also well fed. I don't know how this is either but I eat until my belly is so full I think I won't be able to eat again for hours but somehow I soon start feeling hungry. Mrs Lawley says it's becos I'm a growing boy.

Well, Lil, I hope you are happy if it is possible to be happy with all that has happened. I miss Gran horribly and I'm sure you do too. Please write back soon.

Your loving Artie x

The letter made Lily want to laugh and to cry too. She missed Artie so! But she was glad he was coping.

'He's fine,' she said, looking up at Elsie and Phyllis.

Over Phyllis's shoulder, Lily saw Rose glaring at her with a hatred born of jealousy. Lily had received a letter that brought her joy. Rose had received nothing.

Oh, dear. Lily didn't flaunt her letter. She simply put it in the pocket of her pinafore, touching it every now and then to feel the warmth of Artie's love. She wrote back to reassure him that she was well, writing mostly about her new friends but also reporting that she wasn't the only clever girl in school because he'd know that she longed to be with girls who enjoyed learning.

Phyllis was even faster than Lily at adding and subtracting columns of pounds, shillings and pence. She could divide and multiply them easily too. 'It's the only thing I'm good at, though,' she was quick to say.

'You might be able to get work in a shop instead of going into service,' Lily encouraged. It troubled her that every girl from Booth's was expected to go into service.

'Perhaps it's because we can live in,' Phyllis suggested, and Lily realised it was probably true.

They'd be fourteen when they were sent out into the world to earn their livings. Not many jobs apart from domestic service came with accommodation attached, and not many landladies were likely to want lodgers who were quite so young.

'We needn't be in service forever,' Lily pointed out. 'We can make our own decisions when we're older.'

'I'm no good at anything,' Elsie said. 'Unless you count hauling heavy baskets and digging in gardens.'

Elsie was a godsend when it came to carrying baskets of wet washing outside to dry on the washing line when on laundry duty, and also when it came to working in the vegetable patch where Booth's grew much of its own food.

She grinned. 'I'll be hopeless in service. Imagine me washing fancy china and glasses.' She held up her hands to show how much bigger they were than Lily's or Phyllis's. 'I should have been born a man. Then I could have worked heaving coal like my dad with a nice horse like Dobbin to help.'

'Your strength will make you useful wherever you work,' Lily told her. 'Besides, you're clever in your own way because you're wise.'

'Wise? Me? You're having a laugh.'

'No, I'm not. You see the truth in people.'

'Get away with you.' Elsie pulled a face but Lily meant every word.

She kept Artie's letter under her pillow at night and carried it in her pocket during the day.

Until the morning came when she returned from the bathroom and lifted her pillow to find the letter wasn't there. Had it slipped down the bed or under it?

Lily pulled back the covers and got to her knees to survey the floor but it wasn't to be found.

'Lost something?' Elsie asked.

'My letter.'

'Humph!' Elsie said. 'I think we all know who took it. Leave this to me.'

Elsie waited until the other girls were heading downstairs before she stepped across Rose's path. 'Give it back,' she said.

'I don't know what you're talking about. '

Elsie rolled her eyes. 'Are you going to be boring about it?'

Rose flushed. 'I'm not boring.'

'You're horribly boring. Now give it back or—'

'I don't have Lily's rotten letter!'

109

'How would you know I meant Lily's letter if you hadn't taken it?'

'I... I heard you talking about it.'

'Liar.'

You're a bully, Elsie Davenport. I'm going to report you to Mother.'

'Mrs Henderson isn't your mother or mine. I wonder what your mother would think of the way you've turned out? Do you think she'd be proud of you? I don't.'

'Let me pass.' Rose looked around desperately. 'Agnes, fetch Mother now.'

'Do that,' Elsie approved. 'In the meantime, let me tell you about something you might not have noticed, Rose. I'm a clumsy sort of girl, not good with delicate things like sewing. The scissors slip in my big hands and sometimes they cut off more than I intend. If your hair happens to swing in my direction, I might—'

'I'm going to tell Mother you're making threats.'

'Threats? Did you hear me make threats, Phyllis?'

'No,' Phyllis said, 'and I've been standing here all the time.'

'We're going downstairs now,' Elsie said. 'If you put the letter back, we won't need to talk about it again. But we're all getting tired of your nastiness, Rose. You've still got Agnes and Ivy for friends but the other girls haven't been paying you much attention recently. Haven't you noticed?'

Lily hadn't noticed, but now that she thought about it, she realised Elsie was right.

Rose's group had shrunk while more girls were friendly to Lily, Elsie and Phyllis.

By evening Artie's letter was back under Lily's pillow.

* * *

A month passed before Lily received another letter. She was delighted to see he'd learned to spell *because* and even more delighted to hear that he'd cycled over to see their old Jessy Street neighbours.

> *I knew you'd like news of them. Mrs Flynn has had her baby. Another boy but I forget his name. I saw Davie too. I hoped it would be just like it used to be when we played together but it wasn't. Davie said I'd started speaking like a toff and my suit must have cost more than his dad earned in a week. I told him I was still the same old Artie but I don't think he believed me. He made me feel awkward so I didn't stay long.*

> *I don't know if I'll be able to go over there again anyway. Mr Alderton said he was surprised I hadn't chosen somewhere more educational to go. A church or a palace or something like that. So I suppose I'll have to keep to those sorts of places for a while.*

> *Of course, the person I most want to see is you, Lil. I'm glad to hear you have friends in that place. It makes me feel better to know you're not too unhappy and to hear that you have roast meat and a nice pudding on Sundays. Mrs Lawley makes jam roll too. It's one of my favourites.*

111

Poor Artie. The advantages weren't all stacked on his side because Lily had friends on hers. Hoping he wasn't horribly lonely, she wrote back and reconciled herself to another wait of several weeks before she received Artie's next letter.

But four weeks passed, and no letter came. Mr Alderton had tried to steer Artie away from visiting old neighbours. Perhaps he was trying to steer him away from Lily too in case staying in touch with his humble beginnings held Artie back from both his education and his transformation into a gentleman.

It became hard to stay cheerful. One Saturday Mrs Henderson required Lily to deliver a note to the foster mother of Fry House which was two cottages away.

She was walking back, fighting the worry that gnawed inside her when her eyes were caught by movement further along the drive. It was a boy on a bicycle.

A jolt of excitement shot through Lily. She hardly dared to hope ... But soon it was beyond doubt. 'Artie!' She waved an arm and ran to meet him only to come to a halt as doubts crowded in and a strange shyness overcame her.

Three months had passed since she'd last seen him. Artie's clothes were new and smart. Even the way he held himself was different as though he'd left the urchin behind and was taking on the look of a boy who'd turn into a man in a few years' time. He'd grown too. Filled out a little. Narrowed the gap between their heights.

'You came,' she finally said.

''Course I did.'

He grinned then and Lily felt lightheaded with relief. So far at least he remained her Artie despite the outward changes.

He got off the bicycle and lowered it to the grass verge then caught hold of Lily in a hug. She threw her arms around his neck. 'It's so good to see you!'

'I'd have come before but I have lessons on Saturday mornings and Sunday School on Sundays. I had to wait for a holiday.'

'You didn't come all the way on the bicycle?'

'Hardly. I cycled to the station, caught the train to Sevenoaks and cycled from there. It still took me almost three hours to get here but it's worth it to see you, Lil. It's all right for me to visit, isn't it?'

Visits were rare but happened occasionally. 'I'll tell Mrs Henderson you're here and then we can have a cosy chat.'

Artie picked his bicycle up and they walked back to Nightingale House.

'Visits are usually arranged in advance,' Mrs Henderson pointed out, as Artie waited outside. 'But he's here now so you can take him into the recreation room.'

'Might we walk around the garden for a while?'

'If you wish, but keep to the girls' side.'

'Thank you, Mother.'

Lily was eager for her friends to meet Artie but she wanted him all to herself for a while first. They propped the bicycle against the cottage wall and set off arm in arm back along the drive where they were unlikely to be disturbed. It was December and cold but Lily didn't mind that.

'Tell me what it's like at Mr Alderton's,' she

urged. 'Do you spend all your time with him?'

'I have lessons and meals with him except for extras like cake which I have with Mrs Lawley as Mr Alderton doesn't eat between meals. We have our dinner in the evenings and something called luncheon in the middle of the day. Mr Alderton doesn't like talking during meals which is a good thing as I wouldn't know what to say to him.'

'He isn't friendly?'

'He doesn't smile much and he never tells jokes.'

'Oh, dear.'

'He's just one of those people we never really get to know. But it was kind of him to take me in, and Mrs Lawley makes up for him being a bit … far away in his thoughts.'

'You're not unhappy?'

'I miss you but I like Mrs Lawley and I love playing with the neighbours' dog and cat. I know I'm lucky to be getting an education too.'

'Tell me about your lessons.'

As well as English grammar he was learning algebra, arithmetic, science, history and geography.

'That's wonderful,' Lily told him, though it dismayed her to think how little she was learning.

She understood what Davie meant about Artie's speech because Mr Alderton was knocking the urchin out of him there too. Not that he'd spoken all that sloppily before and neither did Lily because being brought up reading books had taught them about the letters that went into words. The fear that he might be leaving her behind sent a chill into Lily's stomach but Gran hadn't been a stupid person despite what she called her lack of book learning. Surely Lily could teach herself things from books once she was out in the world?

'What about you?' Artie eventually asked.

She told him something of her life at Booth's but said nothing about her lessons because she didn't want him to feel bad. She focused on telling him about Elsie and Phyllis instead.

'We're like two halves of a whole,' Artie said. 'I have an education. You have friends.'

'Come and meet them.'

They returned to Nightingale House and sat in the recreation room. Lily was delighted to see that Artie, Elsie and Phyllis liked each other on sight. 'It makes me feel better knowing Lil has friends like you,' Artie told them.

He'd brought in a bag that had been strapped to his bicycle. 'Mr Alderton is giving me what he calls an allowance,' he said. 'A sixpence every Saturday. I've been able to buy more paper and stamps for you, Lil.' He took them out of the bag and passed them to her.

'I also bought these ... ' He reached in again for a small paper bag. 'Sugar mice,' he explained. 'One for each of you.'

Elsie looked as pleased as if he were giving her the Crown Jewels. 'I haven't had a sugar mouse in years.'

She licked the top of the mouse's head and closed her eyes to enjoy the sweetness. 'Mmm.'

Phyllis took the tiniest nibble out of her mouse. 'I'm going to save the rest for later.'

'Me too,' Lily said, overwhelmed by Artie's kindness in thinking not just of her but also of her friends. 'But you shouldn't have spent so much money. Between the stamps, the sugar mice and your train fare you can't have much left.'

'I wanted to give you a treat, Lil. It makes me happy. Besides, I promised Gran to look after you, didn't I?' He paused then added, 'I still miss her dreadfully.'

'So do I.'

They were quiet for a moment then Lily rallied and introduced Artie to a few of the other girls.

They all looked pleased to meet him except for Rose, Agnes and Ivy who sent scowls Artie's way. 'Who are they?' he asked.

'People who don't matter,' Lily told him.

'They aren't mean to you?'

'They're mean to everyone. We don't let them bother us.'

'We can deal with those witches, make no mistake,' Elsie assured him.

Artie didn't stay for much longer as the daylight was fading already. 'It's a long journey back and Mr Alderton doesn't like lateness,' he explained.

Lily walked out with him and they hugged for a long time before he got back on the bicycle. 'I'll write,' he promised.

She ran down the drive beside him for a while then stood waving. The drive curved. Artie paused to wave back then pedalled out of sight.

Lily had no idea when she'd see him again. She realised she was crying and wiped tears from her eyes only for more tears to flow.

It was some time before she felt calm enough to return to Nightingale House where Phyllis and Elsie waited. Phyllis gave her a comforting squeeze and Elsie gave her a nudge of understanding. Breathing deeply, Lily reminded herself that she needed to take a leaf out of Gran's book and be brave. She still had blessings to count and the best of them was that Artie had proved himself to be the loving twin he'd always been.

A lot could happen in the years of separation that lay ahead of them, but Lily wouldn't go inviting troubles in prematurely.

11

Lily was touched when Artie sent her a book for Christmas as she knew he must have saved hard to buy it. He also sent a tin of toffees for her to share with her friends. Included in the parcel was a letter in which he told Lily that his journey home from Booth's had turned into a disaster.

I got a puncture and had to walk most of the way to Sevenoaks. I missed the train I planned to catch and arrived in London late. It was even later by the time I got to Hampstead. Mr Alderton and Mrs Lawley were about to ask the police to start looking for me. I didn't like worrying them but it was worth all the walking to see you, Lil. I don't think Mr Alderton will like me visiting again while the evenings are so dark, though, but spring isn't so far away.

Meanwhile I hope you'll have a nice Christmas. It'll be our first Christmas apart. I'll miss you and Gran too.

Lily had no gift to send in return but wrote a story called *Artie's Adventures at the Bottom of the Sea* and sent that instead. It was a silly story in which Artie met fish, seals, whales and even a mermaid but she hoped it would make him smile.

Writing a story for Artie gave Lily the idea of writing stories for Elsie and Phyllis too. Elsie's story involved her in saving a group of children from a bridge collapse because she was the only person strong enough to carry them over the mountains before a storm struck. Phyllis's story had her leading the fight for votes for women and being fêted as a heroine when she finally succeeded.

Elsie and Phyllis were so thrilled with their stories that they made Lily read them out loud one evening as they sat around a toasty fire in the recreation room.

Lily was surprised to look up and see that everyone was listening except for Rose, Agnes and Ivy who were talking among themselves rather louder than necessary, presumably hoping to thwart the storytelling. It didn't work, especially after Elsie told them to shush and there was a murmur of agreement from other girls.

The idea of making small gifts for each other took hold. Mr and Mrs Henderson allowed the girls to make paper chains to decorate the recreation room and Lily was cutting paper when she decided to attempt a paper angel too.

Liking the result, she made a red-haired angel for Elsie, a dark-haired angel for Phyllis and angels for all the other girls in the house. 'Would you like one?' she asked Rose, but the pretty girl only curled her lip.

Agnes and Ivy curled their lips too.

'Please yourselves,' Lily told them. It was their misfortune if they wanted no part of the fun.

Other girls made paper angels and doves for each other too.

'I'm not even going to try making angels or doves,' Elsie said. 'With my big hands I'd probably cut their heads off.'

'I'm no good at that sort of thing either,' Phyllis said. 'I'm offering a different sort of gift — help with arithmetic to anyone who wants it. You don't need help, Lily, so I've got this for you.'

It was a spray of holly bound up with trailing ivy.

'It's beautiful,' Lily assured her.

'Elsie let me sit on her shoulders so I could reach the holly with the best berries on, so it's from her as well.'

'Carrying Phyllis gave me an idea for what I can offer as gifts,' Elsie said. 'Piggy-back rides.'

She was serious. Big and strong, Elsie duly gave piggy-back rides in the grounds, out of sight of the Hendersons who thought girls should behave with decorum. She set up a route from one tree to another and back again, running as fast as she could and jumping over a dip in the ground. Lily had never heard so much laughter though it puzzled Mrs Henderson to see the girls looking flushed and dishevelled.

Artie wrote monthly now his allowance meant he didn't have to ration stamps.

One day he wrote that Mr Alderton was taking on another pupil and for a moment Lily was alarmed. Did that mean he was disappointed in Artie? But no.

Reading on, Lily learned that this new boy went to school but his parents wanted him to have extra coaching to ensure he'd pass an examination for something called public school. Artie considered it strange to call a school public when as far as he could work out it was private and cost a lot of money.

Artie was looking forward to having another boy around though that didn't mean he was lonely.

He enjoyed cycling around London by himself when he had time free. He'd seen the Royal parks, Buckingham Palace, the Houses of Parliament, Westminster Abbey, St Paul's Cathedral, the Bank of England, the Mayor's Mansion House... He fancied seeing the animals in London Zoo soon.

Lily spent a lot of time on the letters she wrote to him. Artie always had something new to tell her — something he'd learned or something he'd seen — but there was little variety in Lily's life as she never left Booth's. Neither did she hear much of what was going on outside it. Even in Jessy Street she'd known something of the world through neighbours, the ships at the docks, the newspaper boys calling out news ...

Lily wasn't the only one who found it frustrating. Phyllis also fretted at being so excluded from the world. 'I haven't seen a newspaper since I came here,' she complained. 'And to think I used to stand at my dad's shoulder reading all about governments and laws, and the women who are fighting to get the vote.'

Lily was reduced to writing about small incidents that she hoped might amuse him, and the comings and goings at Booth's as girls left to go into service and new girls arrived to take their places. Few new girls joined Rose's group which had shrunk to just three and become no more than a minor irritation.

Despite the restrictions of life at Booth's, Lily had moments of happiness and hoped Mum, Dad and Gran would feel proud of how she was coping. But she also had moments when worry got the better of her wish to stay cheerful.

121

One day she laid all of Artie's letters across her bed. She was proud of the way he'd proved the doubters wrong and kept in touch with her. She was also proud of how neat his handwriting had become and how his words flowed better too. Yet the letters showed that he was striding ahead in life while she was stuck in limbo.

She'd been right to believe Artie would stay in touch with her. She trusted his tender heart to keep caring about her too because, in addition to his letters, he sometimes sent picture postcards and once he sent another book which must have cost him several of his weekly sixpences. But between his lessons and the people he was meeting she couldn't help fearing that the differences in their lives were ever-widening.

It didn't help that months passed without another visit from him. It wasn't until Easter when the daylight hours were longer that Artie came to Booth's again, this time having written to warn Lily to expect him.

She posted herself outside Nightingale House to wait for him and her heart thrilled when she saw him riding the bicycle along the drive. But she didn't break into a run this time. She walked towards him instead, realising she was even more nervous than on the last occasion he'd visited. On that occasion they'd been apart for three months. Now they'd been living apart for more than six months and the changes in Artie might run deeper.

Relief rushed through her when she saw him smile but the nervousness didn't entirely fade. Coming to a halt, he held out his arms in invitation. Oh, to heck with all the doubts. Lily needed to trust him.

Quickening her pace, she threw her arms around him. 'It's so good to see you, Artie.'

'You too, Lil. I believe I'm as tall as you now.'

Lily stepped back and saw that he was grinning. She saw that he was right too.

He really was as tall as her. Lily didn't mind that at all. It was the possibility that he might outgrow her in other ways that bothered her.

'I haven't finished growing yet,' she teased. 'I might have a growth spurt and leave you behind.'

They spent time talking alone and Artie told her about Charles, the boy who was being coached by Mr Alderton. 'He's older than me but a nice chap.'

Nice chap? Lily supposed he'd picked up that way of talking from Charles.

'We play cricket in the garden sometimes. I was hopeless when I started but Charles has taught me how to hold the bat and how to throw the ball too.

Actually, it's called bowling, not throwing.'

'I'm glad you have a friend,' Lily said.

'I don't see a lot of Charles but he comes on Saturday afternoons and after school on Tuesdays. I thought he might … you know. Look down on me. But he doesn't. As I said, he's a —'

'Nice chap,' Lily finished, thinking that, if Artie were destined to become a gentleman, it hadn't happened quite yet.

Not for a moment did she wish him to feel awkward in the company of boys like Charles. But it was comforting to think that the awkwardness Artie felt now might help him to understand her feelings should he become a gentleman in the future.

'Mr Alderton wants me to start learning Latin,' he told her.

'Latin?'

'An old language that people have mostly stopped using. I don't see the point, but Mr Alderton seems keen so I'd better give it a go. What about you, though? What's your news?'

There was little to report apart from the day to day ups and downs of life at Booth's. 'Come and see Elsie and Phyllis,' she said, after a while.

'Heavens, who's this fine young gentleman?' Elsie joked.

Artie kissed her cheek and Phyllis's cheek then held up a paper bag. 'More sugar mice,' he said, then held up a second bag. 'Oranges too.'

Elsie eyes shone. 'It's been years since I had an orange.'

Watching Artie with her friends, Lily felt another burst of pride in him. He was kind and good-humoured, and Lily tried to hug every moment close because she knew more months would pass before she saw him again.

May came and, like Christmas, they had to spend their twelfth birthdays apart.

Mrs Lawley made a cake for me, Mr Alderton gave me a pen and I loved the funny story you wrote for me, Artie wrote. *Did you have a nice birthday, Lil?*

Lily had been wished, 'Many happy returns of the day,' by Mrs Henderson, though with so many girls at Booth's birthdays were common and nothing special was done to mark them. But Artie had sent her a notebook with a picture of

Tower Bridge on the front while Elsie and Phyllis had made her a posy of greenery from the garden. She wrote in glowing terms of her pleasure in both gifts.

★ ★ ★

Soon Lily had been at Booth's for a whole year. Artie visited again in a new suit of clothes, having outgrown the first suit. He was taller than Lily now and his confidence had grown in proportion to his height. His friend Charles had gone off to his public school but two more boys were to come to Mr Alderton for coaching. *Roland and Edmund,* he wrote a few weeks later. *Both seem to be nice chaps. They like to play cricket too. Rolo and Edmund both say I'm a decent bowler so Charles must have taught me well.*

Lily was glad for him though she was still troubled by the thought of him outgrowing her in more ways than height. But on his next visit she began to wonder if, beneath his smiles and laughter, something was troubling him too.

'What's wrong?' she asked.

'Nothing.'

Lily pulled a disbelieving face

Artie sighed. 'Mr Alderton is thinking of putting me in for an examination for a public school in another year or so.'

'Just out of interest, do you mean? You don't have the money actually to go to one of those schools.'

'He says he'll pay if I pass.'

Lily's eyes widened. 'How kind of him! But do

125

you want to go to one of those schools?'

'Honestly, Lil? I don't know.'

Lily realised that, despite the polish he was acquiring, he still wasn't quite confident enough to brazen out any attempt to make the humbleness of his beginnings in Jessy Street count against him. Not yet anyway. 'Are you worried you won't fit in because the other boys will turn their noses up at you?'

'Charles, Roland and Edmund are nice enough but the others ... who knows?'

Lily's heart swelled. 'Now you listen to me, Arthur Tomkins. You might come from Jessy Street, but you're as good as anybody. It isn't how much money a person has that matters. It isn't how they speak or what they wear. It's what's in their hearts.' Something she should remember herself when she next felt insecure about the way her life was lagging behind Artie's.

'You're right,' he agreed, but clearly he doubted that everyone thought the same. 'It wouldn't be so bad if I could go home at the end of each day but these schools are boarding schools. You live there for months until the holidays come.' Which meant there'd be no escape if the other boys were cruel.

Lily felt for him. 'You shouldn't be worrying about any of this. It won't be for another year and a lot can happen in twelve months. Mr Alderton might decide not to put you in for the examination after all, or you might sit it but not get through. If that's the case you've no need to feel bad about letting Mr Alderton down because he knows you've had to struggle through life more than other boys. Or you might decide you'd like

126

to try that sort of school anyway. Worrying about it now is a waste of time. Remember what Gran used to say about worrying?'

'It's like inviting troubles into your home and making guests of them when they might have walked straight past.'

'Exactly.'

Artie's expression turned wistful. 'I still miss Gran badly. Mum and Dad too.'

'So do I. But they're with us in our hearts and in all the things they taught us.'

He smiled. 'Dearest, Lil. You always talk sense. I'm lucky, having you for my sister.'

He couldn't have said anything to make her happier.

'If you were sitting the examination, you'd pass it easily,' Artie said, but times had changed. He'd learned things Lily had no chance of learning at Booth's because she'd never managed to persuade her teacher to set more challenging lessons. Lily wouldn't even know where to start in an examination.

Not for anything did she want to hold Artie back but, despite all she'd said about people's hearts being more important than anything else, the thought of him at a smart boarding school gnawed at the edges of Lily's own confidence.

She tried to practise what Gran had preached about inviting troubles in, but found that all she could do was fight the uncertainty and wait to see what happened.

12

A year later Artie sat the examination and came to Booth's to tell Lily the result.

'Well?' she asked, ready to comfort him if he'd failed, especially if he felt bad about disappointing Mr Alderton.

'I passed,' Artie told her. 'I'm going to a school called Camfordleigh in Norfolk.'

'I'm so proud of you, Artie.' It was true but as Lily wrapped him in a hug, she couldn't stop her confidence from trembling a little. 'Mr Alderton must be delighted.'

'He is. He's going to pay for everything – the fees, my uniform, my train fares… He's going to increase my allowance too. Roland and Edmund are going to different schools so I won't know anyone at Camfordleigh, but you've made good friends here, Lil. I hope I'll make good friends there.'

He was nervous. Lily could see it in the way he swallowed after he spoke.

'Just be your big-hearted self, Artie.'

He smiled but she wondered if he thought she didn't understand the world of boys' schools. Perhaps she didn't. It made her feel even more cut off from the world. 'You'll write to me often?' she said.

'As often as I can,' he promised. He paused then said, 'I wrote to Davie about his brother but I never got a letter back.'

The older brother of his former Jessy Street friend had gone down with the *Titanic*, having worked in the engine room. Lily had only heard of the scale of the disaster because Artie had told her about it in a letter. In the Sunday church service at Booth's they'd been asked to pray for the souls of those lost at sea but hadn't been told any details.

'Davie might have been too upset to write back,' Lily suggested, though she thought it more likely that Davie either feared his own letter-writing skills were poor or felt that the friendship had fallen into the gap between their different lives.

It was another reminder of the difference between Lily's world and Artie's but, beyond the pang of concern she felt, Lily refused to dwell on it while he was with her. Every moment in Artie's company was to be treasured.

She'd never asked Artie for anything before but she'd asked him to bring a newspaper today and she read it hungrily after he'd gone, sharing it with Elsie and Phyllis. They read that there was to be a Board of Trade enquiry into the sinking of the *Titanic*, that England would be sending a team to compete in the Olympic Games in Stockholm, that there'd been a fire in a mill in Yorkshire and that a woman had flown an aeroplane across the English Channel.

It was the first newspaper they'd seen in ages as Lily's request to look at Mr Henderson's daily newspaper after he'd finished with it had met with a refusal.

'Your energies will be better directed if you concentrate on learning skills that will enable you to

129

earn a living. Accepting one's place in the world is vital to contentment,' he'd said.

But why did her place in the world have to be confined to domestic service?

And what was wrong with knowing about the world anyway?

Phyllis was growing increasingly frustrated too. Mr Henderson overheard her talking about the suffragettes one day and took her to task for it. 'Those women are an abomination!' he told her.

'Stuffy old fool,' Phyllis called him afterwards.

She took to trying to exercise her mind in other ways. 'Ask me a question,' she sometimes begged, and Lily or Elsie would come back with, 'If each person eats four ounces of carrots and carrots cost tuppence per pound, how much will it cost to feed thirty-seven people?' or, 'If a person's wage is one hundred pounds per year, how much will that person earn if she works for just thirty-nine weeks?'

Phyllis loved working sums out in her head and was almost always right. Lily reached the right answers too, but not quite as quickly. She was better at ideas and words.

'I'm no good with figures *or* words,' Elsie would say. 'You two are the clever ones.'

Lily and Phyllis insisted it wasn't true. All-seeing Elsie was clever in a different way though she could never believe it.

Being the eldest by several months, Elsie would leave Booth's at Easter while Lily and Phyllis would stay until summer. Elsie was gloomy about the prospect of leaving.

'Booth's isn't paradise but it's probably better

than what comes next. For me, anyway. You two have brains and gentle hands so you'll be able to work your way up from the kitchen. I'll be stuck peeling spuds forever.'

'You mustn't think like that,' Lily urged. 'You have a lot to offer.'

'Lily's right,' Phyllis agreed. 'You're honest, hardworking, strong … '

Elsie only shrugged.

Lily's own views on leaving Booth's were mixed. It would be a step towards independence and being reunited with Artie in years to come. For all her doubts about the different directions their lives were taking Lily still hoped that one day they'd live together again or at least live close by, seeing each other often. But leaving Booth's also meant parting from her friends and that made her sad.

'We might have to be in service for a while, but we can do whatever we like when we're older,' Lily pointed out. 'Once we're sixteen we can try to find better jobs, preferably together.'

Rose walked past at that point, turning away from them as though they were insects.

'She's probably thinking her looks will get her through life but she's wrong,' Elsie observed.

'Why do you say that?' Phyllis asked.

'Haven't you noticed how some people are pretty as children but grow out of it? Rose is one of them.'

Lily looked at Rose and realised Elsie had a point. Rose's hair wasn't as fair these days. Neither were her features as dainty. She was still attractive, but far less likely to turn heads. It was

131

typical of Elsie to have seen it before anyone else.

'Rose is growing out of her looks but you're growing into yours, Lily,' Elsie said then.

'Me?' Lily laughed. 'Maybe you're not so wise after all.'

'Elsie's right,' Phyllis said. 'You're as skinny as a railing but your face is lovely and you're ... graceful, I suppose is the word. Dark hair, blue eyes, pink cheeks ... You're like Snow White in the fairy tale.'

'You're mad,' Lily told them. 'Both of you.'

'If you're putting us into fairy tales, you'd better make me the giant at the top of Jack's beanstalk,' Elsie said.

'Who can I be?' Phyllis asked.

'Dick Whittington,' Elsie decided. 'You can go to London and make your fortune then I can come and live in your smart house and never have to peel a spud for as long as I live.'

Phyllis smiled. 'What would you like to do instead of peeling spuds?'

'I don't know, but I'll have to think of something. It isn't as though I'm ever going to get married.'

'Why not?'

'Look at me. I'm bigger than most men already and besides, I'm not ... What's the word, Lily? It means quiet and obedient.'

'Docile?'

'That's the one.'

'You might find a man who doesn't want a docile wife,' Lily suggested, but Elsie only pulled a face.

'I don't suppose I'll get married either,' Phyllis said. 'There can't be many men who'll put up with a wife who's prepared to chain herself to railings to campaign for women's votes. What about you, Lily?'

'Who knows? I want to make something of myself when I'm older and I'd hate to be stuck with a man who tried to stop me.'

Lily still had no clear idea of what she wanted to do with her life but she hoped to find something that would give her a sense of satisfaction. She wanted it to come from her own efforts too. Gran might have expected Artie to support his sister once he became a man but Lily knew she'd prefer independence to being a drain on her brother's purse.

Artie went to Camfordleigh in the autumn. Lily couldn't help worrying about him and longed for a letter.

Two weeks passed before he finally wrote to her.

Dearest Lily,

Sorry I haven't written before but I've been hoping to have something good to tell you. Unfortunately, this isn't an easy place for a boy like me. Most of the boys have been to what they call prep schools which I understand are boarding schools for younger boys so they're used to sleeping in dormitories and sharing lessons with so many other boys. I'm not, and it feels strange to have nowhere to go if I want to be by myself for a while.

We've been put into houses which are named after old boys who were at the school years ago. I'm in Irving House. Each house competes against the others to be best in all sorts of things. The boys take it very seriously and some of them boast about how many points they won for the houses at their prep schools. I didn't go to a prep school so I have nothing to say about points and houses.

The boys seem to speak a different language too. They use words like quad for the big yard between the buildings and tuck for the sweets and chocolate they bring from home or buy from the little shop here.
They also call their mums and dads the mater and the pater, and talk about their people instead of their families. Everyone here is known by their surname so I'm Tomkins. It feels odd to me but no one else seems to mind.

Have I made any friends? Not yet. I think the other boys know I'm different from them and I haven't found a way to fit in. Not that they're all awful. I like some of them, especially one called Fordyce, but others aren't nice at all. There's a small boy called Simons who started out crying a lot because he was homesick. Some of the boys began mocking him and calling him Snivelling Simons. Before you ask, yes, I did try to be kind to Simons but he's found another friend now. They both like Latin and chess, and I've no interest in either.

I won't pretend I haven't felt like crying myself, especially when some of the nastier boys thought it was a great joke to fill my shoes with water, but I've managed to hold back so no one calls me Tearful Tomkins.

Write back to me soon, Lil. I miss you so much!

Your loving Artie x

Poor Artie! Lily's heart ached for him. She wrote back straight away to try to boost his spirits and a week later she received a reply.

Dearest Lil,

It was such a relief when your letter came. I'd been feeling terribly lonely but it made me feel better to know you were thinking of me and wishing me well.

Things have started to change for me. It began when new boys like me had to run what's called a cross country race over fields and through woods. I suppose all the hours I've spent on the bicycle paid off because I won the race easily. Winning got me noticed, and boys — even the Head of House – started saying things like, Tomkins could be useful.

Then the Head of House took me onto the field to see what I could do with a cricket ball even though the cricket season has finished and he called me a Good Chap . I'm also learning a sport called rugby that involves a lot of running, and I seem to be pretty good at that too.

So all in all I'm finding my feet here. I don't think I'm ever going to be one of the cleverer chaps but I don't appear to be completely dim. It's a big relief, I can tell you, sis.

135

It was a big relief to Lily too.

After his awkward beginning Artie seemed to settle down well, judging from his letters. He made friends, including Fordyce, who was another talented rugby player, Clements, who was another runner, and Britton, who was hopeless at sports but a decent chap who shared their dorm. Lily supposed that dorm meant dormitory.

She had little hope of seeing him at Christmas as Mr Alderton would doubtless consider the daylight hours too short for safe bicycling to and from Hampstead. Artie spent Christmas with Mr Alderton as usual then went to Fordyce's house for a week.

It's an amazing house in the Hertfordshire countryside with seven bedrooms and lots of other rooms too. His parents are a bit vague but nice. They left us to do what we liked most of the time. His grandfather has built a model railway in the attic and it's wonderful. We spent a lot of time up there and also cycled to St Albans which has both a cathedral and old Roman walls.

Lily was delighted that Artie had enjoyed his holiday though the contrast between his world and hers seemed to be growing ever stronger.

It wasn't until his school term ended just before Easter that she saw him again.

Lily was used to seeing changes in him but she'd never seen him looking so tall and self-assured. He'd brought another newspaper, a book and two tins of sweets. 'He's going to be a charmer, your brother,' Elsie said.

Lily agreed. Artie had the loveliest smile.

136

He was friendly and open too, asking questions about life at Booth's and answering questions about Camfordleigh. But as Lily waved him off at the end of his visit she reflected on the one question she hadn't asked. Had he told his friends that he had a sister in a children's home? A sister who'd soon become a servant? She'd been too afraid of how he might answer.

★ ★ ★

Time at Booth's had often dragged but it had picked up pace over their last year and the arrival of Easter meant it was time for Elsie to leave. 'I'm not going to cry,' she insisted, only to burst into floods of tears as she hugged Lily and Phyllis goodbye.

She'd been placed in a household in Chislehurst, just far enough away to make it difficult for her to return to Booth's on a visit. 'But I'll write,' she promised.

She wrote a couple of weeks later.

I'm one of three servants here. There's a cook, a maid and me. As expected, I haven't been let loose near the china. I lay the fires and sweep the grates. I haul coal in from the shed and put it into shuttles. I scrub floors. Also as expected, I peel a lot of spuds. Carrots too. Apples, pears, onions...You name it, I peel it.

I also do reaching. That means lifting things down from high shelves and cupboards and putting things up. 'Reach this for me, Elsie,' and, 'Reach that for me, Elsie,' rings out morning, noon and night. I even hear it in my dreams. Still, beggars can't be choosers.

Write and let me know your news and here's hoping you'll be given places close to mine so we can see each other during our time off. Not long now. Time flies when you're having fun. And even when you're not.

With love from your friend, Elsie, who misses you x

Lily was missing Elsie too and so was Phyllis. *We can't wait to see you again,* they both wrote.

Summer came and it was time for Lily and Phyllis to go out into service.

'Nervous?' Artie asked, home from school and managing to squeeze in a visit.

'A little. But I'll work hard so I hope I'll do well.'

'I hate the fact that you have to work when I don't.' He shook his head regretfully.

'Don't think I've forgotten what Gran said about helping you when I'm older.

It's what I want too.'

'I'm not made for idleness, Artie.'

'I know. But even so... You'll write and let me know how you get on?'

'Of course I will. But please don't worry about me.'

Phyllis was going to the household of a Mr and Mrs Purvis in Sevenoaks, Lily to a Mr and Mrs Everett of number six Beeches Mansions, five miles away from Phyllis in Drayford.

Despite the narrowness of life at Booth's, Lily was deeply grateful for the care she'd received and made sure the Hendersons and her teacher knew it. Now she was stepping back out into the world but she was still far from free. And who knew what she'd have to face as the very lowest of domestic servants?

13

Beeches Mansions weren't mansions at all but tall houses of four storeys, starting with basements and rising to attics. The housekeeper, Mrs Tibbs, was a small, harassed woman who looked Lily up and down and said, 'Hmm. I hope you're stronger than you look.'

Clearly, she'd have preferred a big girl like Elsie. Lily decided to mention that in her next letter to her friend. For now Lily could only draw herself up tall. 'I'm strong,' she said.

'Rules,' Mrs Tibbs announced then. 'We're up at six to lay the fires and boil the water. I cook but you'll need to help. A woman comes in to do heavy cleaning and laundry sometimes but not often. Mostly it's down to me so you'll need to help with that too.'

Lily said nothing, not having been invited to comment.

'The Master has his breakfast in the dining room at seven-thirty before he leaves for his office in London so there's no time for dawdling. The mistress has a breakfast tray in her room. Sometimes she has her luncheon in her room too.

Fancies herself delicate, does the mistress.'

Lily sensed that Mrs Tibbs was no great admirer of the Everetts.

'Dinner is served in the dining room at eight sharp. Guests are rare but I get extra help in if the family's entertaining. If the mistress agrees, that is. Mostly, it's you and me does all the work, including attending the mistress and her fancies. This isn't a job for a slacker. Any questions? If not, I'll get you kitted out and — '

'Time off?' Lily said.

'You haven't even hung your coat up and you're talking about time away?'

Clearly, Mrs Tibbs was unimpressed.

'I'll work hard,' Lily promised. 'But I'd like to know when I'll have time off so I can see my friends.'

'No gentleman friends allowed,' Mrs Tibbs told her.

'My friends are girls, but I have a brother too.'

'No visitors allowed either. I'll do my best about the time off but this house doesn't have a dozen servants to cover for each other and the mistress isn't keen on keeping to a schedule for half days and holiday. It doesn't suit her fancies. I hope you're not the whining sort, like the last girl.'

'I don't think I'm a whiner.'

'Come along then. I'll show you where you'll sleep.'

Mrs Tibbs led the way upstairs. 'Back stairs for us. Move quietly, speak only when spoken to and never get in the way of your betters,' she instructed.

She was breathing heavily when they reached the attics. 'This is yours.' She opened the door to a small room with a sloping ceiling that contained an iron-framed bed, a small cupboard, a bedside table and a plain wooden chair. 'I'm next door. Chamber pots are under the beds and it's your job to take out the slops each morning. There's a bathroom for the family but it isn't for us to use.'

She picked up two black dresses that were lying across the bed. 'I can see one of these is going to be too short. The other will be too wide but there's nothing to be done about that and it won't show so badly with an apron over the top. There's a spare dress this size in the cupboard along with two spare aprons and caps. Take care of them and keep them clean as you won't be getting more. Hurry along and change, then come back downstairs.'

The dress swamped Lily but the white apron did indeed help to disguise the poor fit. She brushed her hair, pinned it at the nape of her neck then fastened the cap on top.

The housekeeper nodded approval when Lily returned to the kitchen. 'You look clean and neat enough. That's something. Now then, I — '

She broke off, sighing as a bell rang. 'The mistress,' she announced. 'I'll see what she wants. You start peeling those potatoes.'

Spud-peeling. Lily would write to Elsie about that too.

* * *

Mrs Tibbs often sighed in the days that followed, usually because of what she called Madame's fancies. Lily didn't get to meet Mrs Everett for several days and even then only met her by chance. Mrs Everett had been resting all morning but a telephone call had revived her enough to demand luncheon in the dining room before going out. 'The mistress has left the dining room in a mess,' Mrs Tibbs complained afterwards. 'It was bad enough her dropping the fish without grinding it into the carpet with her shoe. Give me a hand clearing it up, will you?'

Lily was carrying a cloth and bucket of water towards the dining room when Mrs Everett returned unexpectedly. 'Oh, heck,' Mrs Tibbs muttered.

Lily stood with her head down respectfully.

'I forgot a magazine I promised to a friend,' Mrs Everett told Mrs Tibbs. 'I need you to fetch it. And did I mention that I spilt cold cream on my dressing table? You'll need to wipe it up and go out for more. Or send Minnie here.' She waved a gloved hand in Lily's direction.

'This is Lily, Madame. Minnie left a year ago and then we had Ada. Lily is the new girl.'

'So many girls! I can't be expected to remember them all. Well, Lily, I trust you'll make yourself useful.'

Lily looked up into her mistress's face. Mrs Everett was approaching fifty and might have been handsome without the petulant expression and the bright red lipstick that had leaked into the wrinkles around her discontented mouth. 'I'll do my best, Madame,' Lily said.

Mrs Tibbs fetched the magazine then opened the door for Mrs Everett who moved down the steps to a car that was waiting outside. 'Don't expect her to remember your name,' Mrs Tibbs said.

Lily smiled but wondered why so many girls passed through these doors only to move on elsewhere. Within a couple of weeks she had her answer. There was simply too much work. Mrs

Everett appeared to think she had a ladies' maid and a host of other servants at her disposal. Time and again she rang the bell for Mrs Tibbs to go and draw curtains, iron a dress, shop for hair pins, polish shoes, collect stockings, sew on buttons, post letters, clear up spillages and run a hundred other errands inside and outside the house.

It didn't help that the master was a stickler for mealtimes and tidiness. Mr Everett was a thin-bodied, thin-haired man to whom smiles were alien. Poor Mrs Tibbs was run ragged and was often in discomfort due to the bad veins in her legs.

'You must let me help more,' Lily said.

'You do enough for your six shillings a week, but I'd be grateful if you'd iron Mrs Everett's dress and take it up to her. My legs need a sit-down before I go up those stairs again.'

Lily often waited on Mrs Everett after that though it didn't mean that the mistress remembered her name. Mrs Everett called her simply, 'Girl.'

Lily also began to wait on Mr Everett in the dining room. 'Did he say anything about me?' she asked Mrs Tibbs after the first time.

'No, but take that as a compliment. If he hadn't liked the way you did things, I'd have heard about it, make no mistake.'

Time off was tricky due to Mrs Everett's unpredictability. It wasn't possible to find a day when Lily could see both of her friends together but over the weeks that followed she managed to see Phyllis on one afternoon and Elsie on another.

Phyllis was working in a bigger household but had got into trouble in her first week. 'Some of the staff were sick so I was sent out to do some shopping. Mrs Pascoe, the housekeeper, had told me which shops she used but I looked around and managed to get the shopping cheaper. I thought she'd be pleased but she accused me of not knowing my place and trying to make her look bad. I don't like her enough to suck up and try to put things right so I'm keeping myself to myself.'

'It sounds miserable,' Lily said.

'At least there's a second-hand bookshop nearby and the owner lets me borrow books for a penny each.'

Elsie was simply bored. 'I spend the day reaching this, reaching that, peeling, scrubbing...'

Despite her heavy workload, Lily decided she was in a better situation than her friends because she'd settled into a comfortable relationship with Hilda Tibbs. 'I reckon I struck lucky with you, dear,' Hilda told her when they were taking a precious break over a cup of tea. 'You're a hard worker, and careful too. And you never whine.'

'Have you worked for the Everetts for long?' Lily asked.

'Fifteen years.'

'You've always worked in service?'

'I fancied working in a dress shop when I was young but I needed a place to live and service was a way of getting it.'

'You didn't try for shop work when you were older?'

'I didn't think they'd want me, to be honest.'

She'd lost her confidence, Lily guessed. 'Was Mr Tibbs in service too?'

'Bless you, dear. There is no Mr Tibbs. Never has been. Calling myself Mrs Tibbs is about respect, do you see? I'd like to say I had my chance of marriage when I was younger but it wouldn't be true. I was never pretty like you, Lily. You may look like a strong wind could blow you over, but you have a lovely face and you move like one of them ballet dancers. Not that I've seen a ballet dancer, but I can picture one.'

'Fifteen years is a long time to be in a job. Especially a difficult one.'

'I suppose I haven't been able to face the upheaval of finding something else.'

'You intend to work here forever?'

Hilda laughed. 'For a few more years anyway. Then I want to retire and live with my sister. Marion is a housekeeper in Bromley. We're saving up to buy a little house together in Hastings. That's what keeps me going. The thought of a little house by the sea.'

'I hope you get it soon,' Lily said.

Hilda deserved some happiness. Lily felt both affection and admiration for her but she also thought there was something a little sad about Hilda's life. Not because of the work she did – Lily wouldn't turn up her nose at any sort of honest work — but because Hilda had lacked the confidence to pursue her dream.

Instead she'd settled for second best and pinned her happiness on what might be just a few short years by the seaside if she and her sister lived long enough to enjoy them.

Lily didn't want to settle for a second-best life and pin her hopes on a future that might never happen. She wanted to enjoy her work and feel she was achieving something with it, however small. At fourteen there was nothing she could do about it yet, but she vowed to take care that her confidence in her power to change her life didn't seep away as Hilda's had done.

Affection for Hilda made Lily answer questions eagerly when an inspector from Booth's came to check on her. Yes, the conditions were good. Yes, she was well fed and well treated. Yes, she had time off and received her wages on time.

No, she had no complaints.

The inspection had made Mrs Tibbs nervous. 'Thank you, dear,' she said, after the inspector had left. 'It was good of you to stretch the truth like that, especially about the time off. I wish I could make your time off regular.'

'I know you do your best.'

The Everetts told Hilda that they'd be home for Christmas. Hilda broke the news to Lily. 'It's going to be a lot of work so I'm afraid there won't be time off for us. I hope you weren't hoping to go away?'

'I wasn't.' Lily had nowhere to go. 'I'd like to see my brother and friends at some point over the festivities, though.'

'I'd like to see my sister,' Hilda sighed.

* * *

The Everetts' son and daughter-in-law came for Christmas. 'You're certainly an improvement on the last girl,' Ralph Everett said, coming down to dinner earlier than expected to help himself to a glass of whisky in the dining room where Lily was setting the table. 'What's your name?'

Lily disliked everything about him from his oil-slicked hair and knowing eyes to the arrogant leer of his mouth. 'Lily, sir.'

'Pretty name for a pretty girl, what?'

Lily didn't answer but headed for the door. Unfortunately, he was standing in her way. 'Excuse me, sir.'

He took a very small step to the side and it was only because Lily was so slender that she managed to slip by without touching him. 'I'll see you later, Lily,' he said, breathing whisky fumes over her.

Shuddering, Lily fled to the kitchen.

'Oh, dear,' Hilda said, seeing her face. 'Mr Ralph?'

'Horrible man.'

'He didn't ...'

'No. But the way he looked at me and spoke to me...'

Hilda sighed. 'I used to wish I was pretty but being plain meant I never had to put up with that sort of nonsense. Don't worry. I'll do the waiting-on if you help in here.'

'There's too much waiting-on for one person,' Lily said, concerned about Hilda's bad veins. 'I'll just keep my distance from him.'

'All right, but let me know if it becomes too much.'

Lily kept out of Ralph's way, gliding quietly about the house and listening out for him so she could slip away unseen if there was any chance of meeting him alone. He continued to look at

148

her when she served meals but Mr Everett proved an unexpected ally in giving his son a sharp look when Ralph leered at Lily one evening. Lily supposed he didn't approve of his son showing an interest in a servant.

'Phew,' Hilda said, when the working day was over. 'Time to put our feet up.'

It was time for their own Christmas celebration too, such as it was. Lily had bought lemon verbena soaps for Hilda. 'Bless you, dear. They're lovely,' she said. 'I hope you won't be disappointed by my gift to you.'

The gift was a pair of black stockings. 'Just what I need,' Lily assured her.

The Everetts went off unexpectedly two days after Christmas, intending to be away for more than a week. Artie had sent Lily another book for Christmas.

She'd sent him a small drawing of the River Thames she'd found in a bookshop.

It's to remind you of home when you're away, *she'd written.*

But she hadn't seen Artie since starting work and neither had she seen much of her friends. 'Do you think I might have some time off now?' she asked Hilda.

'I think we should both have some time off. I'm going to invite Marion to visit. I know she can't stay here but she sometimes stays in a guest house on Webster Road. Why don't you ask your brother and friends to visit too? I know I said we're not allowed visitors but we've been run ragged these last weeks. In fact, we're run ragged most of the time thanks to Madame's fancies so we're entitled to a visitor or two. We can entertain them down here.'

After a flurry of letter-writing, it was all settled. Marion Tibbs would stay at the guest house for two nights, Artie would stay for one night and, after much counting of pennies, Elsie and Phyllis decided to stay for one night too.

Marion Tibbs came first. Lily found her to be calmer than her sister but just as nice. 'Hilda writes often and always tells me what a delight you are, Lily,' Marion said. 'I can see she's right and it's a weight off my mind to know she has you with her. Poor Hilda has had to work far too hard over the years.'

Artie arrived next. 'Heavens!' Hilda declared. 'I wasn't expecting … Heavens!'

She went on to praise Artie's handsome appearance, his kind eyes, perfect manners and charming smile but she was obviously a little in awe of him at first.

'He speaks better than the Master,' she whispered to Lily. 'Who'd have thought… Well!'

Who'd have thought what? That a servant like Lily could have a brother who'd pass as one of their so-called betters? But no. Lily wasn't going to let doubts about their future paths spoil the fact that they were together now.

When Elsie and Phyllis arrived the party began with a delicious meal cooked by the Tibbs sisters and sherry Marion had been given by her employer. 'Just a sip for you young ones,' she said.

There were paper hats and party games — charades and consequences — then they all raised their glasses to count down to the New Year.

150

'Happy 1914!'

Lily didn't see Elsie and Phyllis the following morning as they both had to return to work early but she had a long walk with Artie before he left. 'I'm glad you're with a nice person like Mrs Tibbs but I hate you working so hard while I don't work at all,' he said again.

'You *are* working,' Lily insisted. 'You're getting an education.'

Curiosity over what he'd told his friends about her niggled at the back of her mind but once again she held her tongue. People could be cruel and Lily understood how Artie might have to put on an act in order to survive bullying and sneers. Even so she'd be hurt if she learned he'd glossed over her situation because he was embarrassed by her and perhaps even a little ashamed of her.

Artie would feel bad about admitting it too. Perhaps it was best for both of them to steer clear of the subject.

A new year had begun. It was a time for optimism. Lily would turn fifteen this year and sixteen the next. Then she'd be able to make her own choices about her life.

14

'Letter for you,' Hilda said, smiling.

Lily felt the usual burst of pleasure when she saw Artie's handwriting on the envelope.

'Sit down and read it,' Hilda suggested. 'You deserve five minutes to yourself after rushing round all morning.'

Lily sat the kitchen table and opened the letter. Artie had won a cross-country race against a rival school which meant Camfordleigh had been awarded something called the Benfield Shield for the first time in seven years.

Camfordleigh also had a new headmaster after the retirement of the previous man. Mr Avery was modern in his outlook, and had brought in two younger teachers, including Mr Burrows who taught Artie history.

Lessons aren't just about kings and queens of old anymore. They're about recent times. Mr Burrows has also set up the News Society which is a club where we read newspapers and talk about things that are happening in the world. He says that the school may be buried in the countryside but we should still have knowledge of the rest of the world. Mr Burrows has become my favourite teacher.

Fordyce has chipped a tooth. He told Matron he did it tripping up a stair but actually he was sliding down a banister...

152

Lily was pleased that Artie sounded happy. There was nothing new in her own life but she was trying to read as much as possible. 'I don't see why you shouldn't borrow the Everetts' books as they never read them,' Mrs Tibbs had said. 'Just spread the other books out to cover the gaps in the shelves.'

Lily also read the newspapers Mr Everett tossed into the wastepaper basket after his breakfast, reporting to Mrs Tibbs on odd stories about people and items for sale. Mrs Tibbs shook her head in wonder at some of them. 'A contraption to straighten noses? Fancy!'

Lily told her about West End shows and London picture houses too. Mrs Tibbs had once been to a revue but she'd never been to the cinema. 'Moving pictures don't sound natural. I think they might make me feel seasick,' she said.

Lily longed to see a moving picture and hoped to persuade Elsie or Phyllis to go to the cinema with her one day. Not that Lily was spending her wages freely.

While she had no intention of falling into Mrs Tibbs's trap of saving for a time far in the distance at the expense of enjoying what life had to offer now, the future Lily had in mind was less than two years away. Having a little money behind her would be very helpful indeed when she moved on from Beeches Mansions.

Hopefully, she'd find work in London so she'd be nearer to Artie during his school holidays. Elsie and Phyllis were keen to go to London too, Elsie being bored in her job and Phyllis actually loathing hers ... Phyllis's housekeeper had turned even

153

nastier after she'd caught Phyllis reading about the suffragettes.

'Disgraceful women who should know better,' the housekeeper had raged.

Phyllis wasn't actually sure she approved of the way the suffragettes had escalated their campaign to window-smashing. She worried that it might be seen as vandalism instead of the acts of thinking people who deserved the vote, but she wasn't going to admit that to her housekeeper. 'I think they're wonderful,' she said.

'Wonderful? When they're causing trouble and trying to turn everything what's natural upside down? Women are better off at home instead of meddling in men's matters and stirring up discontent.'

'I'd like to join them one day.'

'Then you'll be saying goodbye to your job here. Suffragettes, indeed!'

Phyllis couldn't wait to say goodbye to her job. Lily would be glad to leave the Everetts too, though she felt regret at the thought of leaving Hilda.

'I've never had the knack of making friends,' Hilda had told her. 'Chatting to people doesn't come naturally to me. I don't know what to say and if I open my mouth, my words come out sharp. But it's different with you, Lily. You make me feel comfortable. You may be forty years younger than me, but you're a true friend.'

Lily had hugged her. 'You're a great friend to me too.'

At Easter Lily saw Artie only once before he left London to accompany Mr Alderton on a tour

of English cathedrals. 'It'll be interesting to see places like York and Durham which I've never visited before but I don't suppose I'll have as much fun as Fordyce, who's sailing around the Isle of Wight, or Mr Burrows, who's travelling around Europe by train. He's the history teacher I mentioned. He's very interested in the politics over there and feels he should go there now in case there's trouble later.'

'Trouble?'

'Kaiser Bill and his sabre-rattling,' Artie explained.

'That's been going on for years.' Even back in Bermondsey Lily had seen children fighting with toy swords as they pretended to be the Kaiser.

'Mr Burrows thinks Germany is spoiling for a fight. But don't worry, Lil. He's not suggesting it's going to happen soon, and Britain might not get involved anyway. He just thinks he should see Europe while he can. My holiday won't be half as exciting but at least I won't be scrubbing floors like you.'

Artie's guilt was taking hold again. 'Send me a postcard,' Lily said, to give the conversation a more cheerful turn.

He sent her three postcards from his travels and Lily treasured them.

When Artie next wrote he was at school again and playing cricket but trying to work for his end of term examinations.

I won't be able to look Mr Alderton in the face if I flunk them. I hope to see more of you when I'm back in London for the summer. Perhaps we could even manage a day out together.

155

A day out together sounded blissful. Lily received another postcard in early July as Artie's school term neared its end.

Did you read about the assassination of the Austrian Archduke? Mr Burrows has suggested we read newspapers over the summer so we know how Austria-Hungary reacts but I heard another teacher tell him it was ridiculous to be concerned about the consequences of tragic events happening miles away in a country most of us have never even heard of. Have you heard of Bosnia-Herzegovina, Lil? I expect you have as you've always been clever.

Lily had a vague idea that Bosnia was between Austria-Hungary and Greece but looked it up in the Everetts' atlas to be sure. It did indeed seem to be very far from Britain.

Weeks passed and Artie returned to London after spending a few days with Fordyce. He travelled down to see her, flushed with heat because the summer was proving to be glorious. 'I passed all of the examinations, thank goodness,' he told her. 'I wasn't bottom of the class but I was a long way from the top. I hope Mr Alderton isn't disappointed in me.'

'Has he said he's disappointed?'

'No, but ... I don't know, Lil. I can't help wondering if he'd have preferred to sponsor a boy with a more academic turn of mind.'

'You weren't top of the class in your first year and he didn't mind that,' Lily pointed out.

'I expect he made allowances for me being a

little behind the other boys when I started at the school, but I've been there for two years now and I can't helping wondering if he hoped I'd catch up and even overtake some boys.'

'I remember him saying he just wanted to give you a better chance than you'd have without his help. You may not become a university professor or write complicated books, but you'll still find better work than you would have done in Bermondsey, and you'll have some choice about what you do. Really, Artie. Stop worrying and enjoy the holiday.'

He smiled. 'You've always been sensible, Lil. I'm definitely going to treat you to a day out soon. Mr Alderton has suggested I tutor some younger boys over the holidays so I'll be earning a little money of my own.'

Artie's wobbles gave Lily a sense of perspective about her own concerns.

Everyone lacked confidence about something and so far her concerns about her bond with Artie weakening had come to nothing. They'd been separated for almost four years now and Artie was as loving as ever. Maybe she should cling to that thought instead of fearing what the future might bring.

Hilda was all for Lily having the time off. 'I'm going to insist on it,' she promised, but was spared the bother of having to ask the Everetts because they went away for a week.

Artie took Lily to Folkestone on the train. It was the first time Lily had seen the sea since Mum and Dad had brought them to Folkestone years ago. 'It's vast,' Lily said, staring out at the expanse

157

of blue-green water. 'The air tastes different here. Cleaner and saltier.'

The sounds were different too — the cawing of gulls instead of gentle birdsong, the soft swish of waves instead of lumbering cars and carts.

'It's peaceful,' she remarked. 'Europe's troubles feel as far away as the moon.'

'Have I told you that Fordyce's eldest brother and two of his cousins are in the army?' Artie asked. 'The whole family is pretty tense about the situation.'

'Will it come to war, do you think?'

'Germany seems to want a fight and is using the assassination situation to urge Austria to start one. That's what Mr Burrows believes, and why would Germany turn down Britain's proposal for a peace conference if it wasn't true?'

'Is Mr Burrows writing to you?'

'Me and some of the other boys in the News Society.'

'I pity Fordyce's family and all the others who'll have to fight if Britain gets dragged into it. I'm glad you're too young to go to war.'

Artie smiled. 'Don't worry, Lil. I'm safe and perhaps the trouble will blow over after all.'

But by early August Britain was at war and before the month was over Fordyce's eldest brother was dead.

15

Out shopping to save Hilda's legs, Lily paused to stare at the poster that had been pasted to a red pillar box.

Your King and Country need you. A Call to Arms. An addition of 100,000 men to His Majesty's Regular Army is immediately necessary in the present grave National Emergency. Lord Kitchener is confident that this appeal will be at once responded to by all those who have the safety of our Empire at heart.

The poster went on to describe the terms of service. Only medically fit men between the ages of nineteen and thirty of at least five feet three inches in height and with a chest measurement of at least thirty-four inches were required.

Married men and widowers with children could apply and would receive a separation allowance for their families.

Service would last for the duration of the war and the men who enlisted would be discharged with all convenient speed, if they so desired, the moment the war was over. Men who wished to join could attend any military barrack or obtain the address of a recruiting office from the Post Office.

There was no need for the men of Drayton

to make enquiries of the Post Office, because a recruiting officer had come to town. Lily watched as a group of young men approached the steps of the town hall where the officer had set up.

They were grinning and jostling each other. 'Lost your backbone, Bert?' Lily heard one say.

'Mother'll kill me if I enlist.'

'A man shouldn't be afraid of his mother! Come on, Bert. It'll be a lark.'

'Oh, all right.'

Bert joined his friends as they climbed up the steps and Lily walked on, wondering what his mother would say when he got home and told her what he'd done.

Not all mothers were against their sons enlisting. Some actually boasted of having sons who'd answered the call for volunteers. They bought Union Jack flags and displayed them in their windows, sometimes alongside pictures of their menfolk in khaki uniforms. If the men were lucky enough to have uniforms, that was. There was currently a shortage.

'My George is having to parade up and down the training camp in his own clothes. His trousers and coat are getting ruined,' Lily heard one mother complaining.

'At least he's being paid thruppence a day for wearing them,' another mother said. 'They gave my Alec someone else's old clothes to save paying him to wear his own. He says they make him look like a proper ragamuffin. There aren't enough rifles either so they have to pretend they're carrying them. Still, I expect it won't be long before they're kitted out properly.'

'Let's hope it won't be for nothing because it might all be over before our lads get to the fighting.'

'Over by Christmas, they say.'

★ ★ ★

But there was no sign of an end to the war by Christmas.

The Everetts stayed at home for both Christmas and New Year so there was no party in the kitchen for Lily and Hilda. They toasted 1915 with a cup of tea instead.

Ralph Everett and his petulant wife had come to stay but Lily dealt with his leering advances easily. 'Just being friendly,' he said, running his hand over her slender hip as she set the table in the dining room.

'I'm sure your parents will be pleased to hear how friendly you're being,' Lily told him. 'So will your wife.'

He snatched his hand away and glowered but Lily didn't care. Nor did she care when he spilt coffee deliberately to cause her more work. His moody resentment was a small price to pay for staying unmolested.

Lily saw Artie only once over the Christmas holiday. 'It's getting harder to cycle in London these days,' he told her. 'They're worried about German airships so they've banned the sort of signs that light up and other lights have to be dimmed. They've even smeared the streetlamps with dark paint. I could barely see to pay my fare last time I travelled on a bus.'

'Do you think the Germans really will attack from the air?'

'They've already used Zeppelins to drop bombs across the Channel,' Artie said. 'I expect it's only a matter of time before they use them here.'

Lily was appalled when, only weeks later, the first bomb fell in Norfolk, the county where Artie's school was based. *But nowhere near it,* Artie wrote to reassure her.

Mrs Everett had begun the year in a bad mood that didn't shift in the weeks that followed. Lily heard her talking on the telephone one day. 'Everyone has grown so dull! I go up to town and see men walking about in dreary brown uniforms. I pick up a newspaper and it's full of the war. I can't even meet my friends for a leisurely luncheon or tea because some of them are rushing to roll bandages or learn how to mop fevered brows. Tell me something delicious, Marjorie. Tell me some gossip.'

Artie was as interested in the war as Mrs Everett was bored by it.

Winter isn't a good time for fighting according to Mr Burrows. Terrible weather and too much mud. The horses and cannons become bogged down in it and so do the men. Come the spring there'll be more action and then we'll see what's what. Fordyce is trying to put a brave face on things – a chap has to do that here – but sometimes he's angry and sometimes he just goes off by himself for a while. You'd advise me to be patient with him, wouldn't you?

162

She would.

Lily met Artie in London one day during his Easter holidays when the Everetts were away in Tunbridge Wells. It was her first time back in London since leaving all those years ago. They walked past Buckingham Palace then through St James's Park and along Piccadilly before Artie treated her to ham and eggs in a Lyon's Tea Rooms. She saw many men in khaki but was too busy hoping they'd stay safe to worry about their dreariness.

'Some of the Camfordleigh old boys have visited the school in their uniforms,' Artie told her. 'Most of them were in the OTC.'

'OTC?' Lily queried.

'The school's Officer Training Corps. I'm going to join but don't worry, Lil. I'm still too young for the real army.'

The year wore on and the war made itself felt at home in food shortages and price rises as ships that were bringing in food from overseas were sunk by German submarines. 'Makes me shudder to think of those U-boat things sneaking up on ships and sending those… What do they call them?' Hilda asked.

'Torpedoes.'

'Makes me shudder, it does. As for those flying things … '

'Zeppelins?'

'Imagine one of them flying over while you're asleep in your bed and dropping a bomb on you.' Hilda shook her head.

The Zepellins had reached London now. Seven people had been killed and dozens more injured.

The food shortages continued. 'I told Madame that eggs went up to tuppence each a while ago,' Hilda said. 'Now they're threepence thruppence and the grocer says he shouldn't wonder if they went up to fivepence. Bacon's gone up from tenpence a pound to twice that price, and as for sugar, the grocer says he can get hardly any. The mistress only shakes her head and says war is a ghastly business. She won't give me more money for housekeeping but she always seems to have enough for those creams she puts on her face. She doesn't understand that the shops have long queues either, so a good bit of the working day has to be spent waiting in line.'

'Maybe the Americans will come in on our side now,' Lily suggested, thinking of the sinking of the RMS *Lusitania* with almost two thousand people on board, many of them American civilians.

'Yes, and let's hope they show those nasty Germans what's what.'

But America didn't enter the war. The death and destruction continued, and expectations of an early peace drained away.

Given the cost of eggs and shortage of sugar, Lily didn't expect a cake on her sixteenth birthday but Mrs Tibbs baked one for her anyway, saying, 'I don't see why you should go without because the mistress is mean with money.'

It was a quiet birthday as Artie was at school and neither Elsie nor Phyllis could get over on a visit. But now they were all sixteen they intended to take the train to London when they could get a day off together and start looking for work. Artie was concerned that she'd be putting herself in

164

danger from Zeppelins but Lily was determined and so were the others. She did worry about how she might break the news of her plans to Hilda, though.

Fate took away the necessity. 'That's it,' Hilda said, when eggs had gone up to fourpence. 'I'm going to tell the mistress I can't manage the sort of meals she wants unless she gives me more money.'

Hilda took her bad legs upstairs in umbrage only to return a few minute later, white-faced with shock. 'They're leaving,' she said. 'The master has been promoted so they're moving to Edinburgh. It's all arranged. They even have a buyer for the house.'

'How is that possible?' Lily asked. 'No one's been to see it.'

But then she remembered a man walking around the house with a measuring tape and notebook a few weeks earlier. Mrs Everett had described him as a surveyor who was assessing how the house might be wired for electric lighting in place of gas lamps, but clearly he'd been an estate agent.

She also remembered another day when Mrs Everett had sent Lily on the bus to Chislehurst to find a replacement for a lost button while also sending Hilda all around Drayton to hand deliver invitations to a card party that was later cancelled. That must have been the day the house had been opened to viewing by people interested in buying it.

'When are the Everetts leaving?' Lily wanted to know.

'Next week. They must have been planning this for a while.'

165

'They didn't want us to know in case we left before they did,' Lily guessed.

'That sounds like the Everetts. I'm sorry, dear. We're to stay for an extra week after they've gone to clean the house ready for the new buyers. Mrs Everett thinks she's doing us a huge favour with that extra week though heaven knows where she thinks we're going to live afterwards.'

'What will you do?' Lily asked.

'I'm going to write to Marion and tell her what's happened. We reckoned on working for another couple of years but perhaps we've enough put by for our cottage by the sea as long as it's a small one. We could take a paying guest or two to help put food on the table. But what about you, Lily? Will that Booth's place help you to find work?'

'Not now I'm sixteen.' Lily swallowed down a wave of anxiety. It was one thing to explore what London had to offer when there was no pressure to find work quickly. It was quite another to be forced to find a job urgently or face destitution.

She straightened her shoulders, reminding herself that at least she had a little money put by to fall back on. 'I was hoping to move to London eventually anyway so I can see more of Artie. This just means it'll happen sooner.'

She spent an uneasy night which left her both tired and angry. How dare the Everetts treat them so shabbily?

'I'd like my black shoes taken to the cobbler today,' Mrs Everett told her at breakfast time. 'Tell him I need them back tomorrow.'

'I'll drop them at the cobbler but then I'm going to London,' Lily said. 'You must have been planning your move to Edinburgh for months but you've left Mrs Tibbs and me needing to make urgent plans for our futures.'

'You'll do as you're told, girl. I'm your employer.'

'Not for much longer. You *could* have given us time to make arrangements but you didn't. That means we have to make our arrangements now even if it inconveniences you. If you refuse permission for me to go to London, I'll pack my bags and leave right now, and where will that leave you? In chaos, that's where.'

Mrs Everett's mouth opened and closed but no words emerged.

'I take it I have your permission?' Lily said.

She turned and headed for the door only to pause and look back. 'Oh, and we expect an extra week's wages on top of the money we'll get for staying behind for a week to clean. We'll have it paid in advance and have references written in advance too. I'll write them out then you can copy them and sign them.'

'I've never heard such insolence.'

Lily shrugged. 'Take it or leave it.'

'All right! An extra week's wages.'

'And excellent references for both of us.'

Leaving the room before Mrs Everett exploded and threw something, Lily ran to the kitchen. 'Whatever's happened now?' Hilda asked, seeing Lily's flushed face.

Lily told her about the demands she'd made.

'You never did?'

'We have to stand up for ourselves.'

'You're a slip of a girl, Lily Tomkins, but I reckon you've more courage than a lion. What would you have done if she'd told you to leave?'

'Panicked,' Lily admitted.

She sat down and wrote out two glowing references then took them up to Mrs Everett for copying onto her personal notepaper. Mrs Everett snatched them from Lily's hand without a word.

'I'll come back for them in twenty minutes,' Lily said.

She spent the waiting time writing notes to Elsie and Phyllis, explaining what had happened. I need to find a job and place to live as soon as possible so I'll take whatever I can get to tide me over. Hopefully, you'll be able to join me in London soon.

Mrs Everett handed over the references without a word when Lily returned for them. Lily read them through then said, 'Thank you.'

She posted her notes, dropped Mrs Everett's shoes at the cobbler then caught the train to London, her reference tucked into an envelope inside her bag.

Despite spending her first eleven years in London Lily was familiar with only a small pocket of it. Being alone in the big city now felt daunting. But she braced her shoulders and headed for the underground railway that would take her to the northern parts of the city.

Strongly suspecting that Mr Alderton would prefer to see her fade from Artie's life completely, Lily had decided she shouldn't risk crossing paths with him near his house in Hampstead. She wasn't even sure if Artie himself would welcome the risk of crossing paths with her if he happened to be out with a Camfordleigh friend or one of the boys he coached during the holidays. Lily might feel secure of Artie's love but she was still uncertain about how she might fit into his future life. She took the train to Highbury and Islington instead, thinking that those places were close to Hampstead but not too close.

The *Situations Vacant* pages of a newspaper were probably a good place to start her search for work. Lily bought a newspaper and found a bench where she could sit and read it. There were advertisements for shop workers, seamstresses, clerks, a watchmaker, a gardener, a window cleaner, a hotel porter, and travelling agents for the sale of remedies for the improvement of health, but no accommodation appeared to be offered alongside the jobs.

She turned to the domestic service column. An experienced ladies' maid was wanted. A cook ... A footman ...

Lily set her sights lower on the job of live-in housemaid in Islington. There was an address to which applicants could write but exchanging letters would take time and returning for an interview would cost money.

At the bottom of the page was an advertisement for Mrs Pinkett's Employment Agency, *Specialist in the Placement of Domestic Staff*. Hoping an agency might help her to find work sooner, Lily asked for directions from a passer-by and soon she was sitting opposite a middle-aged woman who wore her ample body like a comfortable cushion. 'This is an excellent reference,' Mrs Pinkett told her.

Lily hid a smile. Of course it was excellent. She'd written it herself.

'So you're a useful sort of girl. But rather young.

'I'm sixteen. I'm in good health and I don't tire easily.'

'A vacancy came in yesterday that might suit if you're available immediately?'

'I have to work two more weeks,' Lily said. She wouldn't leave Hilda to cope alone.

'Pity, but I'm sure we have something else.' She reached into a box on top of her desk. 'It's the war, you see. Girls are starting to turn their noses up at domestic service because they're doing the jobs men used to do before going off to fight. Or they're working in munitions factories. More money, more freedom.'

She pulled out a card. 'This one's promising. Housemaid in a house in Highbury, not far from here.'

'Is it a live-in position?'

'It is. The housekeeper is Mrs Daniels and I know she's seeing applicants today. Let me write a note for her. You can take it straight round.'

'What if she doesn't offer me the position?'

'Come back and I'll see what else I can suggest. Good luck, Miss Tomkins.'

Six Highbury Row was a large, white-painted and rather elegant house though, like others she'd seen, the windows had been criss-crossed with strips of paper to stop the glass from flying about in the event of a Zeppelin attack. Lily paused outside the servants' door, breathed in deeply and knocked.

'Get that, will you, Ruby?' she heard a voice call.

A maid a few years older than Lily opened the door.

'I'm here to see Mrs Daniels,' Lily explained. 'I

170

have a note from Mrs Pinkett.'

Lily was taken to a small room that appeared to belong to the housekeeper, a big, bustling woman. 'I expect hard work from all the staff,' she said. 'We don't carry slackers. I hope you're stronger than you look?'

'I may be slender but I work hard.' Lily told her the sort of things she'd done at Beeches Mansions.

'You're with this Mrs Everett for another two weeks?'

'I promised to stay that long and I wouldn't like to go back on a promise.'

'That's a good attitude. All right. I'll give you a chance.'

Lily was surprised it had been so easy.

'This Mrs Daniels is lucky to have you,' Hilda said, on Lily's return. 'You've made these past two years happier for me than I'd have thought possible.'

Lily wrapped her arms around her friend and they both had a little cry until Hilda laughed. 'Look at us, shedding tears when there's work to be done.'

The following weeks passed quickly. They spent the first week packing up the Everetts' things then the Everetts drove away with the mistress too busy complaining to her husband about a problem with their new Edinburgh house to say goodbye to her staff.

After cleaning the house from top to bottom Lily and Hilda packed their own few things and parted with hugs and more tears. 'Don't forget to let me know how you're getting on,' Hilda urged.

171

'And don't stand for any nonsense in Highbury. You can always come to Marion and me in Hastings. Sea air will be better for you than dirty old London.'

Marion was leaving her job too and the sisters planned to stay in a guest house while they looked for a property to buy. Lily smiled. 'Thank you so much. You've been a true friend.'

Lily knew good fortune had smiled on her in placing her with Hilda. Would she be lucky again?

She found a very different household in Highbury. The Sinclair family had four children still living at home. Victoria and Ellen were sisters of eighteen and nineteen, pretty girls who squabbled about which of them was prettiest and most attractive to men. James was seventeen and away at school most of the time while younger brother Albert attended a day school nearby. Mr Sinclair was something in banking, his wife a frighteningly fashionable lady who lunched, shopped and served on charitable committees.

It was a demanding household but at least there were more staff including a cook, scullery maid, ladies' maid, and two housemaids, including Lily who was junior to Ruby. Lily and Ruby shared a bedroom but their interests were very different, Ruby being just as keen as the Sinclair sisters on fashion and young men.

'You could be a pretty girl if you made more effort, Lily,' Ruby told her. 'You could do something about your figure too. Do you know you can send away for a potion that will increase your bosom?'

'Thanks, but I'm happy with what I have.'

Ruby shook her head despairingly. 'You should get your nose out of books and get a ring on your finger instead. Who knows what's going to happen with this damned war? My friend, Alice, got married only for her man to die of wounds or something gruesome. But at least she got the chance to walk down the aisle and she's getting a widow's pension now.'

'I'll bear it in mind,' Lily said.

She didn't go hunting for a man but she did visit Janet Flynn, the neighbour who'd been so kind when Gran was ill. It felt strange to be back in Jessy Street, so shabby at first sight but with a warm heart beating in its community, and it was lovely to see Janet and her ever-expanding brood. 'Well!' Janet said. 'Haven't you grown into a beauty?'

Lily laughed. She saw prettier girls every day. 'How are you, Janet? How many children have you now?'

'Nine. I would have had ten but little Silas caught the measles and … ' She shrugged sadly. 'I'm glad you're here, Lil, even if it's only to say goodbye. We're off to Liverpool. My Jack's cousin has offered him a job and has a house lined up for us that's twice the size of this one.'

'I wondered about the boxes,' Lily said, realising Janet had been packing. 'I hope you'll be very happy.'

Lily didn't stay long but came away feeling glad that she'd had a chance to thank Janet for her kindness in those dark days.

★ ★ ★

173

With Lily settled in London, Elsie and Phyllis were keen to follow. They had no luck in getting work together but in time Phyllis was taken on as a housemaid in Islington and shortly afterwards Elsie met Lily to tell her she'd been offered a job in the kitchen of a house north of Primrose Hill. 'I know it isn't far from where Artie lives but I won't let on that I know him if I pass him in the street,' she said.

It disturbed Lily to hear someone put into words her own suspicions about how Artie might feel. 'I'll just wink at him,' Elsie added.

Two weeks later all three girls met for an evening walk in the park known as Highbury Fields. The daylight hours were long now. 'You know the first thing my new housekeeper said to me?' Elsie asked.

'Reach that jar down for me?' Phyllis suggested.

'It was a box but yes, that's the gist of it. I reach things and peel things but I'm glad to be here in London.'

'Your housekeeper's nice, though?' Lily wondered.

'She can be a dragon sometimes but at other times she's all right. I just don't think I'm made for domestic service.'

Lily still hungered for something different too though now she was in London and closer to Artie she didn't feel she had to rush to identify what it might be.

Besides, she owed it to her current housekeeper to stick to the job for a few months at least.

Artie came home for the summer and Lily was looking forward to seeing him.

She had something to tell him, though, and wasn't sure how he'd react. 'You remember I wrote to you about Ruby, the housemaid whose bedroom I share?' Lily asked as they walked around Highbury Fields.

'Mad about fashion and men?'

'She's been dismissed because she was caught trying on one of the mistress's dresses.'

'Oh, dear.'

'She wanted to leave anyway to earn more money in a munitions factory but it means I have to do some of her work, including dusting the drawing room photographs. One photograph is of James Sinclair in his school uniform. I've realised it's the same as yours. Camfordleigh uniform.'

'James Sinclair.' Artie gave the name some thought. 'He's older than me. In a different house too. I hardly know him.'

Lily couldn't gauge if the thought of having a sister as a servant in another Camfordleigh boy's home embarrassed him because he'd turned away to look at a dog on the opposite pavement. It was a dachshund, the breed Artie called sausage dogs due to their long bodies and short legs.

'Do you know dachshunds originally came from Germany?' he asked. 'I heard a story about one of the poor creatures being attacked. As if a dog could be responsible for the war!'

Lily had read of other attacks on shops owned by people with German-sounding names, even if those people had lived in Britain for most of their lives. It was madness.

Ever reluctant to force Artie to admit to awkwardness, Lily let the subject of James Sinclair drop.

The Sinclairs had taken a holiday so it wasn't until their return that Lily actually met James. Not that she met him precisely as he didn't acknowledge her existence. 'Arrogant so and so,' Lily muttered under her breath.

She couldn't imagine Artie ignoring anyone that way no matter how uncomfortable the circumstances. He took Lily, Elsie and Phyllis to tea in a nearby café one afternoon and charmed them all. Then just before he was due to return to school he took Lily to Hastings.

The Tibbs sisters had bought a small cottage they were running as a guest house. It had only three bedrooms but the sisters shared one room so paying guests could use the others. Having coached more boys over the holiday Artie insisted on paying for Lily and him to stay overnight despite the sisters telling him no payment was required.

They had a wonderful time, the longest time they'd spent together since circumstances had torn them apart. Mostly they were with the sisters, but they also took a walk along the shingled beach by themselves, admiring the ruins of Hastings Castle to one side of them and the sea to the other. A long pier stretched out into the water and had an ornate pavilion on the end. 'Apparently, it's a theatre,' Lily said.

It was impossible to be unaware of the war as there were soldiers from nearby training camps about. Lily wasn't the only one who noticed them. Walking past two older men, she caught snatches of their conversation.

176

'To think they said the war would be over by Christmas,' one said, shaking his head.

'They just didn't say which Christmas,' his companion pointed out.

Lily looked up at Artie. At sixteen he was tall, handsome and full of promise.

She'd spent years worrying she might lose him to his education and new social circle. Now she had the war to worry about too. It terrified her to think the hostilities might continue long enough to draw him into them.

16

Autumn set in and spirits were mixed. Casualty lists in newspapers made for sombre reading and Artie wrote to say that two more Camfordleigh old boys had been killed, including a cousin of Fordyce. Now she was in London Lily sometimes saw soldiers on the street who'd clearly been badly injured. They had disfigured faces, missing limbs or sightless eyes due to the awful gas attacks she'd read about that not only seared their lungs but turned men blind as well.

Zeppelin raids continued to kill and injure civilians in London and elsewhere too. A bomb even fell near the Lyceum Theatre, killing seventeen people and injuring more. Artie wrote to suggest she leave London but Lily insisted on remaining so as to see more of both Artie and her friends.

She wasn't allowed visitors at Highbury Row. Elsie and Phyllis weren't allowed visitors either so they walked when they could but otherwise met over inexpensive cups of tea in cafés now the days were shorter, colder and wetter.

'Have you seen this?' Phyllis demanded, bursting into a café one day and throwing a newspaper onto the table. 'The Germans have shot a nurse in Belgium. A nurse!'

Lily and Elsie shared the newspaper to read the story of British nurse, Edith Cavell. It was shocking to think of the death by firing squad of a woman who'd only wanted to help others.

'No one is safe in this war,' Elsie said.

They weren't the only ones who were outraged by Nurse Edith's death. More men volunteered to fight and, when he came home for Christmas, Artie reported that his favourite teacher, Mr Burrows, had been among them.

Again there was no Christmas party but Lily, Artie, Elsie and Phyllis met in a tea room near Piccadilly to exchange small gifts and eat fresh eggs. Such a treat these days! 'Hopefully, everyone will get enough to eat now they've appointed a Food Controller,' Phyllis said. 'I've heard that some people are starving, especially out in the countryside.'

There was no get-together to celebrate the New Year either. They all saw 1916 arrive quietly and separately.

For all that men were still volunteering to fight for King and country, there weren't enough of them and Artie hadn't long been back at school when conscription was introduced. Men aged between eighteen and forty-one now had to join-up whether they wanted to or not.

This year Artie would turn seventeen. But there might still be peace long before he reached eighteen.

Reading of so much tragedy in the newspapers revived Lily's wish to make the most of her own life. After all, she'd been at Highbury Row for a decent length of time now. It would be fair to move on — if she could find an opportunity. Lily still wasn't sure what sort of opportunity she wanted, but she did know she didn't want to work as a servant anymore.

On her next afternoon off Lily met with Elsie. It was a cold but dry day so they simply walked for a while as Elsie told her sad news about her housekeeper's nephew. Harold hadn't believed in war and wouldn't fight as a matter of principle. He'd been given numerous white feathers by girls who called him a coward but it wasn't his own death he feared. He just didn't want to bring about anyone else's. Eventually he'd volunteered as a stretcher bearer instead. He was killed within weeks of going to France.

'Harold was her only nephew and she's devastated.'

'I'm sorry,' Lily said. They were approaching Bax's Bakery where they planned to buy penny buns.

There was a queue inside and the baker himself was serving instead of the usual girl.

He was a short, middle-aged man with the sort of drooping face and body that put Lily in mind of a sad-looking bloodhound she'd once seen pictured in a book.

'What can I get you?' he asked, when they finally reached the front of the queue. 'Please don't begin by complaining about the length of time you've had to wait. It couldn't be helped.'

'You're short-staffed?' Lily asked.

'The girl who worked here left to drive an ambulance. Very laudable, but where does that leave the people who want their bread and buns?'

'Are you looking for someone else?'

'I am.' He nodded towards the window and Lily saw he'd put a card up, presumably advertising for help. She'd been too busy talking to Elsie to

180

notice it before.

'Are you interested?' he asked.

'I might be.' Lily was aware of Elsie's surprise but also felt a small stirring of excitement.

'Ahem!' The woman who was waiting behind them coughed impatiently.

'I can see this isn't a good time to talk,' Lily said.

'Come back at closing time and we'll have a chat. Now, what can I sell you?'

Lily bought two buns. Hunched against the chill, she and Elsie ate them sitting in Highbury Fields. 'Do you really want to work in a shop?' Elsie asked.

'That particular shop might be just what I'm looking for.'

'Oh?'

'It's a big shop with room for a few tables and chairs.'

'A café, do you mean?'

'Mmm.'

'The baker only wants someone to serve in the shop.'

'Perhaps he just hasn't seen the shop's potential.'

Elsie laughed. 'Well, if anyone can turn it into a café, it's you, Lily. There's no harm in talking to him, I suppose.'

'None at all.'

'I doubt the job pays much, though. Not enough to cover the lodgings you'll need if you leave service.'

'True enough.' Lily still wanted to speak to the baker.

She returned alone as he was putting a *Closed* sign on the door. He must have been baking since dawn and he looked exhausted.

'Come into the back,' he said, lifting a section of the counter so they could both pass through into the kitchen. It was a large room with a small table and two chairs in the corner. He sat down wearily and ran his hands over his downtrodden face.

'I'm looking for someone to work full-time. Sundays and Wednesday afternoons off. Twelve shillings a week.'

'Is there accommodation?'

'Accommodation?'

'Somewhere to live.'

'It's not that sort of job.' He sighed as though she'd wasted his time.

'What's upstairs?' Lily asked quickly. 'I take it you don't live there?' She'd looked up at the windows as she'd approached and seen that they were curtain-less and dusty.

'There's nothing up there except storage space.'

'I don't need luxury, and if I lived upstairs, it'd be no trouble for me to help in the mornings and close up after you'd gone home. You could knock the rent off my wages.'

'I just want someone to work in the shop.'

Lily swallowed down her disappointment and got to her feet. 'I'm sorry I troubled you. I hope you find someone suitable soon.'

Her smile lasted no longer than the time it took her to reach the street, the depth of her disappointment surprising her. There was nothing special about a job in a bakery, after all. It would have meant long hours on her feet for small reward, with no guarantee that Mr Bax would like her idea for a café area or anything else. But her interest had been sparked, lighting her up inside only for the brightness to be extinguished like a candle.

Walking back to Highbury Row, she paused to look up at the house. Lily knew how to be grateful and she appreciated the food, shelter and small wage she received here. Yet she still craved something new. Not riches or social standing but challenge and satisfaction.

How on earth was she going to find them, though? The amount she could save each week was pitiful and the lack of a home was a serious handicap. But she was a fighter, wasn't she? She'd find a way somehow.

The next time Lily walked past the bakery she saw a girl behind the counter.

The girl looked pert and self-important to Lily, but perhaps that was jealousy talking. Not liking the idea of being resentful, Lily turned her attention to the other shops in the area.

'What are you looking for?' Phyllis asked, as she and Lily were walking together a few days later.

'Opportunity.' Lily told Phyllis about her ideas for the café. 'I want to keep my eyes open in case any other ideas strike me.'

There was a card in the greengrocer's window: *Help wanted. Three days each week.* But Lily couldn't live on part-time wages and no accommodation appeared to come with the job. A baby was crying in the rooms above the shop so presumably the greengrocer lived up there. Besides, Lily couldn't see her way to making her mark on a shop like this.

After two weeks of looking she couldn't see her way to making her mark anywhere close by. Walking back to Highbury Row, she wondered if she should try the centre of London on her next afternoon off.

'Excuse me, but I think that gentleman is trying to catch your attention,' a passing woman told her.

Lily looked round and saw the baker waving to her from his shop. 'Thank you,' she told the woman, then crossed the road to Mr Bax. 'Do you want to speak to me?'

'I do. Are you still looking for work?'

'Perhaps.' The pert girl was nowhere to be seen.

'Come in for another chat.'

He led her to the kitchen table again. 'I got a girl in but she was too full of herself for my liking. We had words and she stormed off in a huff. I got another girl in but she couldn't work out the customers' change.' In other words, he was desperate.

'There's the problem of accommodation,' Lily reminded him.

'Take yourself upstairs and see what you think. But be warned. It's a mess.'

He nodded towards a door and, opening it, Lily found a set of back stairs.

Climbing them, she found four doors on the next floor. Two of them opened into rooms that overlooked the back of the building, one room being larger than the other. Both were stacked randomly with what appeared to be baking supplies — boxes, tins, jars of jam, bottles of preserved fruits, and shallow crates filled with straw that she

184

guessed contained apples, pears or both. There were also a few broken items Mr Bax hadn't got rid of. Clearly, he was a better baker than a house-keeper.

A third door opened to another set of stairs leading downwards, probably into the shop. Clearly these stairs weren't in use because they were piled with boxes, most of which looked empty.

The final door opened to a large room with two windows that overlooked the front of the building. More boxes were stacked in here but Lily felt excitement fizz at the possibilities the room offered. Not that she intended to share those possibilities until she'd proved herself to Mr Bax.

Returning to the back stairs, she climbed higher and found two attic rooms that had been abandoned years ago judging from the cobwebs, dust and grime.

They could stay abandoned as far as Lily was concerned. The rooms on the middle floor were enough to serve her purpose.

'I'm happy to move upstairs,' Lily said, returning to the kitchen. 'Perhaps we could move the stores to the smaller room so I can have the other room at the back.'

'You don't want the big room at the front?'

'Perhaps that could be a sitting-room.'

'You're not faint-hearted, I'll say that for you. You can cook for yourself down here and use the bathroom too, but what about furniture?'

Lily supposed she'd have to use her savings for some basic furnishings, but, before she could speak, Mr Bax continued with, 'I can't afford to buy new so you'll have to pick up what you need second-hand and let me know the cost.'

'That will be fine,' Lily said.

'When can you start?'

'Not for another week. I have to give notice.'

'Fair enough. One week.'

'Can I come before then to clean the rooms?'

'Come whenever you like.'

Lily returned to Highbury Row with exhilaration bubbling in her veins. Her housekeeper was unhappy but philosophical when she heard Lily was leaving. 'I knew what would happen when Mrs Sinclair expected us to do Ruby's work for no extra money. I'll tell her things will only get worse if she doesn't pay fairly.'

Ruby's work had nothing to do with Lily's decision but she kept quiet about that, liking the idea of helping Mrs Daniel and the other staff to win an increase in their wages.

'What will you do if the baker doesn't like the idea of a café?' Phyllis asked, when Lily told her the news.

'I've no intention of suggesting it until I've proved I'm a good worker. If he still doesn't like the idea, at least I'll have had experience of working in a shop and that might be useful when I take my next step.'

'If you do open this café, don't forget Phyllis and I are first in the queue for jobs,' Elsie said.

'I won't.'

'In that case I suppose we'd better help you to turn this dump into some sort of home.'

Lily didn't know how she'd have managed without their help. Together they turned the smallest room into an orderly store room, cleaned up the

186

second room so Lily could sleep in it and cleaned up the big room too. Lily found a bed, a cupboard and a table with four chairs in a second-hand shop and had them delivered on the day she moved in. The table and chairs looked lost in the big room but Lily didn't mind.

She threw herself into work, dressing smartly in a neat black dress, pristine white apron and cap then presenting herself in the kitchen well before her starting time so as to help Mr Bax to carry trays of bread, rolls and baked goods into the shop. She helped him to clear up at the end of the day too.

'You're no slacker,' Mr Bax told her, approvingly. 'You're quick and you've got a good head when it comes to giving change. You always have a smile for the customers too.'

The days became a week. Two weeks. Three …

Easter arrived and Artie came to see Lily's new home. It was impossible for him to hide his worry. 'The last thing I want is to spoil your fun, Lil, but aren't you a little young to be living alone?'

'I'll be seventeen soon. So will you.'

'I don't like the thought of you here by yourself at night.'

'People live in the buildings on both sides,' Lily pointed out. 'I love living here. I have independence. Somewhere to invite you and my friends.'

'Yes, but — '

'Be happy for me, Artie.'

'There's nothing I want more than for you to be happy, Lil. I've had all the advantages and you all the disadvantages. You deserve a chance for a better life, but this place … ' He waved an arm

187

around the big empty room at the front of the building.

'It's perfect,' Lily insisted.

'You don't blame me for worrying? A chap is supposed to look after his sister.'

'I don't blame you at all,' Lily told him.

He still looked unconvinced about Lily's situation. At times Lily had doubts too. What if loneliness *did* set in? Boredom too? And also disappointment if Mr Bax refused to listen to her ideas? Lily pushed the doubts aside, determined to stay hopeful.

She spent some time alone with Artie before he left. 'I've heard that some of the conscripts are sorry specimens,' Artie told her, Fordyce's military family being his source of information. 'But they're being fed and trained so I'm sure there'll be a big push before too long. Maybe even the push that'll bring about peace.'

'Let's hope so.' Lily was fervent.

Artie returned to school and Lily decided it was time to start putting her ideas into action — if Mr Bax allowed them.

The bakery shop had two windows overlooking the street with a door in the middle. One window was much bigger than the other and it was in here that trays of bread and baked goods were displayed to attract the attention of passers-by.

The counter ran from front to back on this side of the shop so it was possible for Lily to reach into the window and take items from the display as well as from the counter and the shelf behind it. The smaller window was on the customer's side of the shop but displayed only a notice giving the shop's opening hours.

One morning Lily asked, 'Do you think I might arrange the windows a little?'

' *Arrange* them?'

'To make the shop look even more appealing.'

'We're selling bread, buns and cakes,' he pointed out as though their nature made them appealing enough.

Lily stood waiting and after a moment he threw up his hands. 'Go ahead with your arranging. But I don't promise to like it.'

She was down very early the next morning, bringing all the things she'd gathered together with this day in mind. She began by placing empty cardboard boxes in the big window, arranging the smaller ones at the front and the taller ones at the back. She covered them with white cloths she'd picked up in a second-hand shop then placed baskets of bread and plates of cakes and pastries on the boxes to create a tiered display. To the side she placed a vase of daffodils.

She put another covered box into the smaller window and placed a pretty china teapot on top, together with a cup and saucer. She arranged another vase of daffodils beside them.

'Come and see,' she invited.

Mr Bax sighed but wiped his floury hands on his apron and came through to the shop. His heavy eyebrows shot up when he saw what she'd done. 'Looks ... fancy,' he said.

But his expression turned thoughtful as two women walked by outside. They were talking but when one of them pointed to the window, they stopped, moved closer for a better look then came inside. 'I usually go to Evans's for my baked goods but this place looks clean and fresh,' the first one told Lily. 'I'll take half a dozen scones, please.'

'I'll take a Victoria sponge,' her companion said.

Mr Bax shook his head, clearly bemused by the ways of women. But, understanding the value of pounds, shillings and pence, he left Lily to her customers.

'We're out of scones,' Lily reported later.

'Out?'

'Sold out.'

He looked at the clock. 'That's early.'

'Isn't it?' Lily agreed, with a private smile.

'All right, I'll admit it,' Mr Bax said at the end of the week. 'There must be something in these fancy displays of yours so it's only fair that I should pay for them. Let me know the cost and I'll refund it. You'll find a little extra something in your pay packet too. Only a little something so don't get excited. It's just my way of saying thank you.'

Lily was delighted. Being repaid the money she'd spent on china and cloths meant she could buy paint for the table and chairs in her sitting room. 'I'm afraid you'll have to sit on the floor,' she told Elsie and Phyllis when they called in to see her one Sunday.

'You've been busy,' Phyllis said, nodding at the furniture as it stood drying on old newspapers.

'Mmm,' Lily agreed.

'You look good on it, though.' Elsie gave Lily one of her shrewd looks.

'I feel good.' Despite the early starts and long days Lily enjoyed working at the bakery far more than she'd enjoyed domestic service. 'I love being able to use my ideas, and the customers are nice too. Most of them anyway. I'm getting to know them.'

'So this is the start of Lily's empire,' Elsie said.

'Hardly an empire. I just hope I can keep the takings up.'

'You will,' Elsie predicted. 'Then you can employ Phyllis and me.'

'Yes, please,' Phyllis said.

Lily laughed. 'Wouldn't that be nice? But it'll take more than a few extra sales to justify more staff.'

At least she could offer her friends a place to meet and eat. On that thought she took them down to the kitchen for a supper of toasted cheese followed by a custard tart that had been left over from the shop.

As the weeks passed she continued with her displays of flowers and also greenery that Mr Bax brought in from home after she learned he had a garden.

He was a widower who lived in the downstairs part of a nearby house and had sole use of a garden in which he grew fruits and rhubarb for use in the bakery as well as potatoes and other vegetables.

'With everything in short supply these days a man has to do what he can to supply his own ingredients. Fruit gives sweetness so saves on sugar and makes it less obvious when I have to use margarine instead of butter,' he'd told her.

He had two older sisters, Beatrice and Betty, who were both unmarried and working as companions-cum-nurses to elderly people. Beatrice was allowed to grow vegetables in her employer's garden while Betty had free rein to pick the apples, pears and plums that grew in the garden of her employer. It was Beatrice and Betty who made much of the bakery and bottled fruits.

'They used to go out picking wild blackberries for jam too but that's got harder since the war started as everyone else is after blackberries too,' he said.

Lily met the Bax sisters when they came to the bakery out of curiosity.

'Bernard's been telling us about the changes you're making,' Beatrice told Lily.

'It all looks so pretty,' Betty approved.

How sweet they were! Their closeness put Lily in mind of the Tibbs sisters, but while Hilda and Marion had different personalities, the Bax women were very much alike in character. Not in appearance, though. Beatrice was tall and thin while Betty was small and round.

'We'll have to come back soon and see what else you're doing,' they said, and Lily took that as her cue to introduce more ideas — special offers for when Mr Bax wanted to use up particular ingredients, and small but free samples of cake or pastries to tempt the customers to buy. She also bought card, ink and paints to make colourful signs to advertise the offers.

She was delighted when Mr Bax totted up each week's takings and pronounced that they were doing well. He gave her another small but welcome bonus on her birthday and also baked a cake which his sisters came to share along with

Elsie and Phyllis.

Lily was seventeen now. So was Artie. Before the war she'd been impatient for him to become an adult so they could be together again. These days she wanted to slow things down because every passing day took him closer to being caught up in the war. If only there could be peace.

Lily's hopes for an end to the fighting rose towards the end of June when Artie wrote to say, *We hear there's a big push going on. The biggest bombardment there's ever been …*

Two days later another letter came from the Tibbs sister. We haven't heard anything ourselves, but people have told us they've heard the guns going off in France, day and night. Thousands and thousands of shells…

'I expect they're trying to destroy the German trenches and the barbed wire that protects them so there won't be much resistance when our boys go over the top,' Mr Bax said.

★ ★ ★

The first day of July was a Saturday. There'd been talk in the shop that morning of guns being heard even in London so Lily went out and stood in Highbury Fields during her break. Was that rumble coming from the war or distant traffic?

It was hard to know but, whether she could hear the guns or not, she prayed that this really was the beginning of the end of the war.

But days passed and there was no news of victory. Instead the casualty lists were longer than ever. Customers looked bewildered and wretched, and one customer — a gentleman — put into words what people were beginning to fear.

'This push along the Somme river. It's a bloody disaster.'

Artie was white-faced when he visited after coming home for the summer holiday. 'Mr Burrows is dead. Killed in action on the first day of battle.'

'Oh, Artie, I'm sorry!'

'He was such a good teacher. Such a good man. Another old boy has died too, and another will be in a wheelchair for the rest of his life.'

Artie was depressed but also angry. 'I wish I were old enough to do my bit,' he fretted.

Lily wished the opposite. She knew it was selfish when others were losing their loved ones but she couldn't help it. 'The best thing you can do right now is to live your life as well as you can.'

It was the best thing she could do too. Men were going through hell to serve King and country. It was important that those left at home should keep things going — thriving, even — so there'd be an England for them to return to. On that thought, she decided to make her next proposal to Mr Bax.

17

'You're hovering,' Mr Bax said, the next day. 'I suppose that means you've got a suggestion to make. What is it? More plates? More flowers?'

'A table and chairs for the shop,' Lily told him.

His heavy eyebrows went up. 'This is a bakery, not a café.'

'Yes, but some customers buy rolls or buns then stand outside to eat them. Why not provide a table and chairs so they can sit down and eat in comfort? There's plenty of room.'

Mr Bax sighed. 'You've got that look in your eyes. The one that says you're not going to give up until I agree.'

'There's no need to go to any expense. I have a table and chairs upstairs we can use. Just to test the idea.'

'Where will you sit of an evening?'

'I'll manage for a while.'

'Go on, then. But I don't want people falling over the furniture then taking me to court because of their injuries.'

Lily smiled. 'You're a treasure.'

He rolled his eyes but Lily knew he was pleased by the description.

He helped her to carry the furniture downstairs. 'I see you've painted it. You've been plotting this for a while.'

'I've been thinking about it,' Lily admitted.

'And you such a slip of a girl.'

Lily was thrilled when one of the first customers of the day asked, 'Is it all right to eat my bun at the table?'

She was even more delighted when a young man came in wearing the blue suit of a convalescent soldier. He looked tired and Lily was glad to be able to offer a place for him to rest for a while. The table was often in use in the days that followed. In fact some customers competed for its use.

Late one morning, four young women rushed in and threw themselves into the chairs. 'Got them!' one of them said triumphantly.

'It's a pity you don't serve tea,' her friend told Lily.

'Isn't it?' Lily said, looking at Mr Bax who was replenishing the bread baskets.

'No tea,' he said at closing time.

'Several people have asked for it. For soup and sandwiches too.'

'It wouldn't be worth the extra work for just a few people and it might mean food going to waste.' That would be a terrible thing when food was scarce.

'What if there were more than a few people? There's room for three tables out there.'

'You've measured up, I suppose.'

For sure she had. 'We can keep the food simple and if it doesn't make a profit we can stop.'

'I don't have more tables.'

'It'll be easy enough to find them and paint them. Don't you want the shop to earn more money?'

'Of course I do. A man has to save for his retirement somehow, especially when he has sisters who are going to depend on him. But it'll be a lot of hard work for small reward.'

Mr Bax held to his view for another week but every time he came into the shop there was at least one person sitting at the table and he overheard more than one asking if tea or hot food were available.

'I hope I'm not going to regret this,' he finally said, 'but if you can pick up furniture cheaply, we'll give it a try.'

Elsie and Phyllis helped Lily to find another two second-hand tables and six chairs then came round to paint them. Lily also bought more china and devised a simple menu of soup, sandwiches and rolls.

The little café was a great success and Lily was thrilled but one day she noticed Mr Bax looking serious. Grave, even. At closing time he called her into the kitchen. 'I'm sorry, but I think I made a mistake, Lily.' His hangdog face was especially sombre.

'Mistake?' Lily was dismayed.

'In allowing you to start up this café. I can see how much it means to you but — '

Before he could finish Elsie called from the shop door. 'Hello? Have I found myself in a ghost shop?'

Phyllis was due in a moment too.

'We'll talk tomorrow,' Mr Bax said.

He reached for his coat and left.

18

Lily slept badly but got up early, hoping to talk to Mr Bax before the shop opened. Frustratingly, trouble with the oven meant that he got behind with the baking and she didn't like to distract him. But he caught up gradually and, shortly before opening time, he looked at his watch. 'Let's have that word, Lily.'

She tried to look calm but feared she was making a bad job of it.

'There's no doubt that you've a good head on your shoulders,' he told her.

'You see possibilities other people would miss and I can see how you'll make a success of a business one day. But I think I was wrong to let you start a little café because I've realised you probably hope to extend it upstairs and give jobs to Elsie and Phyllis. Am I right?'

'I really think it could work.'

'Perhaps it could. But I'm no longer young and I've got retirement in my sights. So have my sisters and they've no pensions to speak of. They're depending on me for support. I rent the rooms where I live now because my wife never fancied living here above the shop but they're not big enough to provide a home for my sisters too. I need to buy somewhere suitable for all three of us and that means selling this place in a year or two. All your hard work would come to nothing, Lily. There's no future here.'

'I see.' Lily swallowed hard.

'I'm sorry to disappoint you.'

'No!' The last thing Lily wanted was for Mr Bax to feel bad when he'd been so kind. 'You're being honest.'

'You need to find a place that offers prospects. I don't want to lose you, but neither do I want to hold you back. If you find somewhere else, I'll be sorry to say goodbye but you'll leave with my blessing.'

He paused then said, 'My wife and I couldn't have children but, if we'd had a daughter, I'd have been proud if she'd turned out like you, Lily.'

She'd never seen him so emotional. Touched beyond words, Lily kissed the drooping cheek. 'You'd have made a wonderful father. I understand completely so please don't feel bad. I'm only seventeen, remember. There's plenty of time for me to find a different opportunity.'

For his sake she smiled and chatted with customers as much as ever but it was terribly hard to hide her disappointment. As soon as Mr Bax left to go home, she allowed herself to cry, hoping to get it out of her system. Afterwards, she dried her eyes, made herself a cup of tea and sat down to think.

First of all, she had to put her disappointment into perspective. Compared to the horrors of war, illness, injury and starvation this blow to her ambition was trivial.

Secondly, she had no actual right to feel disappointed. Mr Bax had never promised her more than the chance to serve his customers in return for a wage.

And thirdly, she really was young with a lifetime of opportunity ahead of her.

Except that she had neither money nor connections to help. But she was Gran's granddaughter, wasn't she? That meant she couldn't just give up.

Exhausted by crying, she was glad to be spending the evening alone. She didn't sleep well again but straightened her shoulders when she studied her wan face in the mirror in the morning. *Make Gran proud and show some backbone.*

She forced smiles all day and faked another one when Elsie came to visit in the evening but Elsie's all-seeing eyes saw straight through it. 'What's up?' she asked, settling in a café chair with the air of someone preparing to hear a long story.

Lily told her what Mr Bax had said and Elsie nodded.

'I thought it might be something like that.'

'Mr Bax has to do what's right for himself and his sisters,' Lily added, eager to be fair to him.

'Just as you've got to do what's right for you,' Elsie agreed. 'So what's that going to be?'

Lily was puzzled.

'You're not just giving up on your dreams?'

'I've every intention of looking for other opportunities but heavens, Elsie, I think I'm allowed a few days off from planning my future. Right now we need to think about food. I made extra soup so there'd be some left for us.'

'What kind of soup?'

'Vegetable.'

'Perfect.'

Lily put it on the stove to warm and cut bread on which Elsie scraped margarine, butter being so

200

precious. 'This can't be the only building in London that's suitable for a café,' Elsie said.

'True.' But Lily couldn't afford to buy a building and imagined no one would rent one to a girl who was still years away from her twenty-first birthday and had no money behind her. Besides, setting up somewhere else would involve buying the pots, pans and utensils that were already available here to say nothing of a working kitchen.

She stirred the soup thoughtfully. 'I might try to get work in an existing café in the hope of rising through the ranks to become the manageress. The experience would be useful, and once I'm a little older a bank might take me more seriously if I ask for a loan.'

Glancing around, she saw Elsie was grinning. 'Why are you smirking?'

'Because I know you'll find a way. Somehow. Is it only running a café that'll make you happy, though?'

'Not necessarily. I had no idea of running a café until I started working here. But I do enjoy it.'

'Perhaps you should keep an open mind about the next opportunity.'

Elsie was right but Lily found nothing suitable advertised in the *Situations Vacant* pages of the newspaper. Neither did she see opportunity beckoning when she walked out in the evenings or on her days off. She even called in on several estate agents and a bank, but she'd been right in thinking no one would rent property or lend money to a young girl.

'There's always munitions work if you want to earn money to put by for the future,' Elsie pointed out. 'You'd have to pay for lodgings but it still might be worth considering.'

'Are you considering it?' Lily asked, because Elsie had obviously been giving it some thought.

'I'm sick of domestic service and so is Phyllis. We won't rush into anything but maybe after the summer … We might be able to find lodgings together.'

Lily agreed to think about it too but it felt like a step sideways instead of forwards. Perhaps even a step backwards, bearing in mind how much she enjoyed working here. Luckily, she was due to go to Hastings with Artie to stay with the Tibbs sisters again. Lily hoped it would boost all of their spirits, especially as the news from the war was heart-breaking.

It was terrible to Lily to see raw grief on the faces of some of the customers.

She knew it was the same for Hilda and Marion whose paying guests included the families of soldiers who were convalescing nearby, some having suffered the most appalling injuries. Artie was still upset about Mr Burrows, of course.

Mr Bax was closing the bakery so he could take his sisters to Brighton for their annual week's holiday so Lily had no need to worry about the shop. She and Artie travelled to Hastings by train. At seventeen and smartly dressed, Artie was an attractive young man even allowing for a sister's partiality. Taller than Lily by a good four inches and much broader in the shoulder, he had a trim figure topped by soft brown hair, kind eyes and a charming smile. Lily couldn't miss the admiring looks that were sent his way but Artie was too

202

modest to notice.

It was a huge relief to Lily that several years of mixing with richer boys at Camfordleigh had left his tender heart intact. He was kind and sunny-natured with everyone, however humble, and looked to be as pleased as Lily to be spending time with Hilda and Marion again.

But beneath his smiles it became clear to Lily that he was troubled. 'You're thinking about the war,' she guessed as they walked along the beach again, Hilda and Marion having insisted that brother and sister should have some private time together.

'This time next year, I'll be out there in the thick of it.'

'The war might be over long before you turn eighteen.' But it might not.

'I'm keen to do my duty,' Artie said. 'Please don't think I'm not. But a chap doesn't really know how he'll behave in battle. A lot of the Camfordleigh boys have family in the forces and I've heard that some soldiers fall into blue funks of fear. Or run away. They shoot deserters, you know. I'd hate to disgrace myself that way. I'd let down Mr Alderton, the school and most of all you.'

He also had to be worried about the prospect of death or injury.

'It's natural to have those worries, Artie.'

'If something happens to me, you'll be alone in the world. That bothers me too.'

'I'll never be alone because I have my friends,' Lily pointed out, hoping to relieve him of that worry at least.

'Have you met any special friends?'

'Elsie and Phyllis are my— Ah. You're asking if I'm walking out with anyone. The answer is no. I've never met anyone who interests me in that way.'

She'd had offers from young men who came into the bakery and invited her to see a show or go out for a drink, but had never felt interested enough to accept.

'Is that a comfort or a worry?' she wondered.

'Both, I suppose. I hate the thought of someone taking advantage of you, especially when you live by yourself. But I do like the thought of there being someone to take care of you.'

'You really don't need to worry about me. You shouldn't worry about yourself either. If the war's still going in another six or nine months, that'll be the time to start thinking about being a part of it. Until then, just enjoy what life has to offer. Like being here in Hastings. Come on. I'll race you to the castle.'

Lily broke into a run and after a moment Artie followed though he was subdued for the rest of the visit. 'Why don't you stay on for a while?' he suggested, the night before he was due to leave to return to London and then to school.

'Please do, Lily. We'd love to have you,' the sisters urged.

Lily agreed to stay on for one more night.

Artie left after breakfast and Lily walked him to the station. 'I know it's impossible to stop worrying sometimes,' she told him as they parted. 'But don't let it run away with your imagination. If I've learned anything growing up, it's that worrying about things that might never happen wastes precious time.'

He smiled and kissed her cheek then passed through the barrier towards his train. Lily waved as the train pulled out of the station then made her way back outside.

Not wanting to add to Artie's troubles, she'd said nothing about her disappointment over the café but now she felt the weight of it returning to press down on her shoulders.

Doubtless realising that Lily would be feeling emotional after parting from Artie, Hilda had urged her not to rush back. Glad to have some time alone, Lily walked around the town and along the seafront. She looked at cafés and other shops too. She even bought a cup of tea in one café, drawn in by curiosity after seeing a card in the window announcing, *Waitress wanted*. It was easy to see why the café was short-staffed because the manageress was a sharp-eyed shrew who bullied her poor waitress mercilessly. Still, there had to be better cafés elsewhere.

Lily returned to the sisters' house. 'I'll make a start on lunch,' Hilda said, but Lily and Marion both put a stop to her efforts to haul herself out of her chair.

Hilda was still suffering with her legs. Life in Hastings suited her happiness but it had done nothing to improve her health as far as Lily could see. Marion was solicitous of her sister too though she also looked tired. She must have seen the concern in Lily's face because as they made the lunch together she said, 'We do try to be careful about the number of guests we take in. Sometimes we give ourselves a break by putting the *No Vacancies* sign in the window.'

Lily was glad to hear it. The sisters were due some rest and relaxation after spending so many years apart doing jobs they didn't particularly like. Perhaps that was how it was for most people and how it would be for Lily too if she let go of her dreams.

'Look after yourselves,' she urged the sisters when she left them the next day.

'You'll write?' Hilda asked.

'We so enjoy your letters,' Marion added.

'I'll write often, and I'll come back to see you just as soon as I can.'

Lily was in a thoughtful mood on her return to London. With several days free before the bakery reopened, she spent hours wandering around London the way she'd wandered around Hastings.

By the time Mr Bax reappeared she'd had an idea.

19

Mr Bax expressed himself delighted by the fudge Lily gave him as a gift from Hastings. She was equally delighted by the box of toffees he gave her as a gift from Brighton and decided to share them with Elsie and Phyllis who never received gifts from anyone except each other.

Lily had no intention of trying to talk to Mr Bax during the busy working day so was happy to chat about their holidays as they prepared the shop for opening.

It was closed for only one week each year but Mr Bax still fretted about whether his regular customers would transfer their loyalties elsewhere.

He looked out from the kitchen several times during the course of the morning and Lily was able to reassure him that business was brisk.

'Evans's Bakery on Mountley Street is all very well but their bread doesn't compare to Bax's,' one customer said.

'My husband missed having Bax's apple cake last week,' said another.

Lily even saw a compliment in the accusing words of one working gentleman who bought a roll to eat at a table. 'I had to eat out in the rain last week,' he glowered.

Towards midday another customer had something different to say. 'I hope it wasn't bad news for them next door.'

'Sorry?' Lily didn't understand.

'I saw a telegram being delivered.'

Oh, dear. Mr and Mrs Solliford who ran the haberdashery shop next door were quiet and private so Lily didn't know them well. But they looked to be of an age to have a son in the forces. Of course, telegrams could bring good news instead of bad, but soon afterwards another customer reported that Mrs Solliford wasn't serving in the shop today because her son had been killed.

A little later still another customer reported that she'd been buying buttons when Mr Solliford had begun to cry. She'd come away and he'd locked the shop door behind her.

Lily waited until the end of the afternoon then, with Mr Bax's permission, took soup and bread to their neighbours, managing to catch a friend of theirs as he was letting himself into their shop. 'So kind,' he said, taking the tray.

'Please pass on our condolences and let us know if there's anything else we can do to help,' Lily said.

She didn't know how she'd cope if she ever received news of Artie's death.

The thought of it made her shudder but she tried to follow her own advice about keeping her imagination and her worries apart.

Mr Bax was waiting for her, his expression particularly doleful. 'Have you decided to leave?' he asked. 'You've been serious behind your smiles today. And I don't think it's because of our neighbours' sad news because you were serious before then.'

Lily sat at a shop table and invited Mr Bax to join her. 'You know I have ambitions.'

'You're a clever girl. It's natural.'

'They're not grand ambitions but I'd like to feel challenged.'

'I understand, Lily. I'll be sorry to lose you but, as I've said before, it wouldn't be fair to hold you back.'

'I haven't actually found a way of moving forward at the present time.'

'You're going to stay for a while longer?' His face lifted in a smile.

'Yes. But I'd like you to reconsider my café suggestion. No, wait!' His face had begun to droop again. 'I don't want to put you under any sort of pressure but please hear me out. I know you plan to retire in a year or two. All I want is a year or two of the café.'

'It wouldn't be worth the cost of setting it up.'

'I can do the painting and decorating, and I know I can pick up tables and chairs cheaply because I've made enquiries. It isn't as if they have to match or be in perfect condition because I'll paint them to fit in with the furniture we've already got.'

'But there's no kitchen up there.'

'I can use the downstairs kitchen and carry things up and down the back stairs so I won't bump into customers.'

'You'd still need a serving station.'

'I thought I could use my bedroom for that. I could sleep in an attic.'

He grimaced at the mention of the grimy attics.

'I could clean it up,' Lily said.

'What about the ... er ... comfort of the customers?' he asked then. 'It wouldn't be practical for them to use the lavatory off the kitchen.'

'Not all cafés have lavatories for customers,' Lily pointed out.

'I suppose that's true.'

'You don't want to risk your retirement money and I understand that,' Lily told him. 'What I have in mind might actually make you some money because the property could fetch more if sold as a going concern with a café as a well as a bakery.'

Mr Bax's mouth opened and then closed, as if this possibility hadn't occurred to him before.

'Even if the buyer didn't want the café, you'd be selling a property that's clean and newly decorated. And the furniture could still be sold separately.'

'I can see that a café could be advantageous to me but you'd have wasted your time.'

'I wouldn't, though. I'd have had a chance to explore whether a café is what I really want for the future and had valuable experience of managing a business. If you let me manage it.'

'I certainly wouldn't have the time to look after it.'

'A buyer might actually want to keep me on. Even if they didn't, the experience could help me to get a similar role somewhere else. Banks and landlords might take me more seriously too, if I were ever in a position to open a business of my own.'

Running the café for even a short time would also help Lily in other ways. By keeping busy, she'd have less time for worrying about Artie. And if she made a success of the venture, Artie might feel proud of her. She could be his equal instead of a poor, unfortunate relation.

Lily didn't mention those reasons to Mr Bax, though. They felt too much like emotional blackmail.

'There'd be other costs,' he said. 'China, silverware, tablecloths … '

'Why don't I put some figures together?' Lily suggested.

'All right, but don't forget to include the costs of food and drink. The extra wages too, because we'd need help to run a café as well as the shop.'

'Thank you!'

'I'm not making any promises.'

'I understand. However my figures turn out, please say no if the café idea doesn't feel right or you just don't want the upheaval. I'll have other chances.'

Lily reported the conversation to Elsie and Phyllis when they came over that evening.

'I knew you'd find a way,' Elsie said, grinning.

'Nothing's settled. I'd hate to put poor Mr Bax under pressure, and I'll never forgive myself if I'm responsible for delaying his retirement or making it poorer.'

Phyllis was as practical as ever. 'All you're doing at this stage is working out a budget. If you want my help, I'll give it gladly. I'd love to use my brain for once.'

'I'll stay out of budgets, but I'll happily scout around for prices,' Elsie said.

'And if the café goes ahead, I'll help with decorating too, including all the high parts. I'm not called Reach-up-Elsie for nothing.'

Lily's long working hours made her grateful for all the help she could get.

Over the next weeks the budget gradually took shape.

She was particularly cautious with estimates of income because who knew how many customers would come to the café or how much they'd spend? The three tables downstairs could accommodate ten people in all. With a mix of tables upstairs, the café would be able to accommodate another thirty. Not all of the tables and chairs would be occupied all of the time, though.

She divided each day into early mornings when customers might buy breakfasts, mid-morning when they might buy tea and cakes, lunchtimes when they might buy more substantial meals, and afternoons when orders were likely to be lighter again.

She totted all her figures up only to stare at them then calculate them again, being even more cautious about estimated income. She also added a figure for unforeseen expenses or price increases. The responsibility still weighed heavily.

'I'm not expecting an answer now,' she assured Mr Bax when she gave him the figures, 'and please don't hesitate to say no.'

'I'll look at them at home,' he said.

She bit back any mention of the café the following day. 'I appreciate your patience,' Mr Bax told her as he left for the evening. 'Just bear with me a little longer.'

'Of course,' Lily said. 'It's a big decision and I don't want you to feel rushed.'

He said nothing the next day either though to be fair he was even busier than usual because plumbers had to come to fix a problem with the

212

water supply.

Waiting was hard.

'At least he's considering the idea properly,' Elsie said.

But Lily wondered if he were merely working out how best to tell her no.

Another day passed with no discussion but the following day he finally invited her to sit down for a talk. 'You've gone to a lot of trouble,' he said.

'Yes, but I don't want you to be influenced by—'

'I've been working on some figures of my own.'

'I see.' Doubtless his figures would show she'd been wildly optimistic in hers.

'My figures are for extra items,' he explained.

Lily frowned. What had she overlooked?

'I thought over what you said about increasing the value of this property. I realised it made sense so I got the plumber in to give me a cost for installing a bathroom in the small store room upstairs.'

'There wasn't a problem with the water supply?'

'That was an excuse to stop you fretting about what he was doing. I know you didn't plan on major changes but it seemed to me that, even if a new owner didn't want a café, he or she might want to live above the shop so turning the small room into a bathroom would be useful. So would a sink and stove in the middle room you suggested using as a serving room. There's plenty of space for them and enough space for storage too if I put shelves in.'

'But it's all too expensive, surely?' Lily asked.

'I think it's worth the investment. But before I say yes to a café I need to know you aren't nursing any secret hopes that I'll change my mind about retiring in a year or two. I don't want to be responsible for all your dreams tumbling down when the property is sold.'

'One year,' Lily assured him. 'Maybe two years, but only if that suits you.'

'Then we have a café to launch. What are you going to call it?'

Lily's mind went blank. 'What about Bax's Café?' she suggested.

'Lily's Café would be better.'

Lily cheeks grew warm. 'Do you really think so?'

'Actually I prefer Lily's Tea Room.'

Lily tested the sound of it on her lips and liked it. A smile broke out, so big that it stretched across her entire face. Leaning forward, she kissed Mr Bax's cheek. 'Thank you so much for this opportunity.'

'It'll benefit both of us, given a lot of hard work and a sprinkling of good luck. But tell me, Lily. We can only take one extra staff member on so who's it going to be? Phyllis or Elsie?'

Oh, heavens.

20

'You should choose Phyllis,' Elsie said. 'She's got a brain as sharp as a tack so she'll have no trouble adding up bills and giving the right change. She'll be amazing at helping to buy supplies at decent prices too.'

'You should choose Elsie,' Phyllis said. 'With the shop to run as well as the café, her energy is exactly what you need.'

'I want both of you,' Lily said.

She felt terrible at having to choose between them because she could see that they both wanted the job and the accommodation that came with it. Whoever was chosen would live up in the attics with Lily, sharing the excitement of a new adventure. Whoever wasn't chosen would be stuck where they were, for the time being at least.

'I'm going to toss a coin and let it choose for me,' Lily said.

She took a halfpenny from her purse. 'Heads for Elsie, tails for Phyllis,' Lily announced.

She threw the coin into the air, caught it on one hand and slapped the other hand over it to keep the coin in place. She glanced at Elsie, who was trying to hide a swallow, and at Phyllis, who was tilting her chin as though bracing herself to be brave.

Lily uncovered the coin. 'Tails,' Elsie said. 'The job is yours, Phyll. You deserve it.'

'Best of three throws,' Phyllis suggested, but

Elsie would have none of it.

'You won fair and square, Phyll,' Elsie insisted, even though her smile didn't quite mask her disappointment. 'I'd still like to help with the café when I can.'

'You're part of Lily's Tea Room even if you can't be paid a wage,' Lily assured her. 'I shan't make promises I can't keep, but I still hope we can work together one day.'

'So do I,' Phyllis agreed.

Without a trace of resentment, Elsie shopped for decorating materials, washed and painted walls and woodwork, cleaned brushes, carried furniture and even helped Phyllis to move in once she'd worked her notice. Elsie also came up trumps with some of the things they needed to fit the café out.

'You've got to come!' she cried, bursting in at the end of a working day to tell them that a guest house near where she worked was closing down. 'They might be selling off furniture and things like that,' she explained. 'We should ask them anyway.'

They all hastened round and found themselves invited in by a fraught young woman who had two children trailing around her ankles and another on the way.

'We're selling everything,' she confirmed. 'A second-hand dealer is coming to take away anything that doesn't sell.'

Not everything was suitable for what Lily had in mind — one table was too big, the chair cushions were too drab and the china looked too institutional — but there were other things that looked very useful indeed.

'How much are you charging?' Phyllis asked.

'We're open to offers.'

Phyllis conferred with Lily and they made an offer for five smaller tables, some chairs, a tall Welsh dresser to go in the tea room, a sideboard for the serving room, cutlery, glasses, and cruet sets.

'That sounds reasonable,' the young woman said. 'Are you interested in bedroom furniture?'

'Only one bed and perhaps a cupboard,' Lily told her.

'You'll be able to collect your things soon, I hope?'

'How soon?' Lily asked.

'Within the next few days. The people who are buying the building want to take possession as soon as possible.'

'We haven't finished decorating yet, but I suppose we can work around the furniture,' Lily said.

'Are you running a guest house too?'

Lily explained about the café and the young woman smiled again. 'It'll please my parents to know their things will be used for a new adventure like that. The guest house is theirs, you see, but my brother lost both of his legs in the fighting in France so they're retiring early to look after him.'

'I'm sorry,' Lily said.

'My husband's serving over there too,' the young woman said, anxiety etched into her face.

'I hope he'll stay safe.'

Tragedy was everywhere. Returning home, Lily saw that their neighbours, the Sollifords, still hadn't reopened their haberdashery shop after their son's death.

They'd gone to stay with family the day after Lily had taken soup around, and she hadn't seen them since.

As ever, tragedy spurred Lily on to make the most of her life. She was delighted when Mr Bax hired a man to collect the things she'd bought from the guest house in his lorry. Once delivered, they added to the chaos in the upstairs rooms but it was worth the inconvenience to have acquired the items at such good prices.

Mr Bax also arranged for his workmen to begin installing the bathroom and kitchen without delay and even helped with the decorating when the bakery was closed. Having begun the venture cautiously, he was throwing himself into it with enthusiasm. For the first weeks Lily and Phyllis snatched sleep among paint cans and ladders. But gradually the café took shape and it was lovely to have a bathroom, kitchen sink and stove upstairs.

Lily wanted the café to be successful from the very first day so she made pretty notices to sit in the small window and on the wall behind the shop counter, announcing, *Opening soon – Lily's Tea Room.* 'I hope you'll come and try it,' she told the customers.

The final Sunday before opening was spent ensuring everything was sparkling clean and ready for use. 'We should take some photographs,' Mr Bax said, lifting a Box Brownie camera from his bag.

'Why don't you change into your uniforms and I'll take the photos?' Elsie offered. 'If you'll show me how the camera works?'

Mr Bax changed into white baker's clothes while

Lily and Phyllis put on black dresses with crisp white aprons and caps. Elsie took photographs of them down in the shop and up in the café.

'You should be in the photographs too,' Lily told her.

'Don't bother about me.'

Lily wanted to bother about her. 'You're part of our team,' she insisted.

'Elsie could pose as a customer,' Phyllis suggested.

Elsie sat at a table and Mr Bax took photographs of her pretending to give an order to Phyllis and being served tea by Lily. Afterwards they all sat down to drink sherry that Mr Bax had brought in as a treat.

Lily sent copies of the photographs to Artie who wrote back to wish them all good luck. Was he proud of her? Lily certainly hoped so.

She sent more copies to the Tibbs sisters who wrote back to say they always knew Lily would go far in life, almost as though she'd become the Queen of England and gone to live in a palace. The letter made Lily smile because the reality was that all she and Phyllis actually had were narrow beds, chests of drawers and hooks for hanging clothes on their doors. With nowhere to sit apart from on their beds, they had to use the tea room in the evenings and cook in the serving room or bakery kitchen.

Those letters arrived several days after the café opened on a Monday morning in mid-October. On that first morning Lily and Phyllis had got up early only to be startled by banging on the shop's front door. It was Elsie. 'Just wanted to wish you all the luck in the world,' she said, breathless from running.

She thrust a card into Lily's hands, a homemade card which featured drawings of cups, saucers, cakes and an odd-looking teapot. 'Couldn't get the spout right,' she explained. 'You know me. My bones are big but there isn't an artistic one among 'em.'

'It's perfect,' Lily and Phyllis assured her.

Inside she'd written, May fortune smile upon Lily's Tea Room and all who sail in her. Oodles of love, Elsie x

She gave Lily and Phyllis clumsy hugs. 'Got to dash,' she said, and raced away.

'I wish she could be with us,' Lily said.

'The more successful we can make this place, the better our chance of being able to give her a job in the future.'

The Bax sisters had also sent a card wishing them the best of good fortune.

Lily displayed the cards on the tea room dresser.

Lily and Phyllis both worked in the downstairs shop when the bakery opened on the understanding that Lily would staff the tea room as soon as any customers headed up there. Within five minutes of opening a man came in. Slouching and down at heel, he looked at the three tables in the shop then slid his gaze to the open door to the now-cleared staircase that led upstairs. 'More tables?' he grunted.

'Lots more.' Smiling a welcome, Lily led him upstairs. 'Where would you like to — '

'Tea and buttered roll,' he said, walking to a table and opening his newspaper.

'Don't fob me off with margarine.'

The tea room looked beautiful, even if Lily said so herself. The walls were white and so were the tables and chairs, but there was colour in the chair cushions and curtains, and in the Michaelmas daisies that stood in small china vases on the tables. More flowers stood on the dresser alongside patterned china plates and books. It was a fresh and deliciously pretty room but its charms were lost on this man.

For a moment Lily felt alarmed as well as disappointed. Had she made a catastrophic error of judgement about the café? It would be terrible if

Her ears picked up the sound of female voices and footsteps on the stairs.

Four middle-aged women came in and stood looking around. 'Well, isn't this nice?' one of them asked, to murmurs of agreement from the others.

Alarm receding, Lily showed them to a table and took their order for tea.

'Those cakes do look tempting!' one of the women said, gazing hungrily towards the cakes which Lily had displayed on glass-domed stands on the dresser.

The women added cakes to their order, despite the earliness of the hour.

More customers made their way upstairs and soon Lily found herself rushed off her feet. At two o'clock Mr Bax took over the shop so Phyllis could take a break, then Phyllis came up to the tea room so Lily could snatch something to eat.

As soon as they closed for the day Lily put the kettle on so they could put their feet up over a cup of tea before tackling the cleaning and preparation for the next day's business. 'It was wonderful to have so many customers but it may have been curiosity that brought some of them in. We can't expect every day to be as busy,' Lily said cautiously.

But the rest of the week *was* just as busy. 'First weeks have novelty value, though,' Lily suggested. 'Next week will give us a better idea of what our regular custom is likely to look like.'

She'd been putting tips into a small bowl. Counting them out, she was pleased to see that they added up to almost seven shillings. She divided them into three equal piles but Mr Bax refused to take a share. 'You girls have earned the tips,' he insisted.

'Why don't we save the tips for our futures?' Lily asked Phyllis.

'Good idea.'

'On second thoughts, why don't we save the first five shillings each week and spend anything left over on treating Elsie to an occasional outing?'

'That's an even better idea.'

By the end of the first month it was clear that the café was set fair to be successful though they'd had to make adjustments with regard to the sugar, as it was in such short supply. Lily had noticed a customer sneaking sugar cubes into a handkerchief so she could take them home. After that, they served only loose sugar and removed the bowls from the tables quickly.

With only three of them running the kitchen, shop and café the workload was heavy but Lily was thrilled by the compliments they received from customers.

'Charming ...'

'Delightful...'

And even, 'Good grub at decent prices.'

Lily and Phyllis took Elsie to see a variety show and they made their way back singing one of the songs. ' *You'll never see me frown, when I'm in London Town ...* '

Beatrice and Betty Bax came to try the tea room and declared it to be delightful, promising to return weekly if they could. With Mr Bax's Michaelmas daisies over for the season, Lily had given the tea room an autumnal feel, using gold, copper and bronze foliage from Mr Bax's garden, and placing vegetables among the leaves — scrubbed carrots, turnips and little pumpkins.

When December came she chose a Christmas theme instead. Mr Bax's neighbours had holly trees – one with dark leaves and another with leaves of pale green and cream. They were happy to donate sprays of both sorts. Lily arranged them with trailing ivy and sprigs of fir, adding red baubles and gold bows here and there. She was thrilled with how pretty the tea room looked.

One day in early December a *For Sale* board went up outside the Sollifords' shop next door. 'I heard they just didn't have the heart to continue after losing their son,' a customer remarked.

Lily pitied them and hoped they'd find peace eventually. No one seemed to know whether the shop would continue to sell haberdashery or something else.

Whatever it sold, Lily hoped it would attract customers to the street.

Another thought struck her. The new owner

223

might have an opening for Elsie.

If she couldn't be employed in the tea room or bakery, the next best thing would be to have her working next door. Mr Bax might even let her move into the bakery attic. He was fond of Elsie and if she could pay him a little rent …

Lily decided to keep her thoughts to herself for the moment, not wanting to raise Elsie's hopes only to have them dashed if the buyer had no need of help.

After setting up the tea room early one morning she paused to look out of the window. It was frosty outside and people were scurrying to work hunched under hats and with thick scarves around their necks. It was the sort of day when hot food should sell well — soup and the new dishes they'd introduced including winter vegetable tart, spicy sausage tart and baked potatoes. Lily was keen to keep the bill of fare interesting while keeping costs low and adapting to the shortage of good quality flour as well as sugar. At least there were fewer food queues these days, even if people were being urged to eat sparingly and waste nothing.

Turning away, she was surprised to see that a customer — a man in his twenties — had already come upstairs and was standing in the doorway. Embarrassment at being caught daydreaming made Lily's face grow warm.

'Good morning. You're our first customer so all tables are free as you can see,' she said, aiming to sound pleasantly efficient, but a glint of amusement in the man's eyes suggested he'd noticed her blush. Frustratingly, that made it harder for her to conquer it.

'Thank you,' he said, smiling.

Moving forward, he headed for a table near the window, putting his gloves down and taking off his coat. He looked around, noticed a coat stand and raised an eyebrow. 'May I?'

He was tall and well-built with glossy, near-black hair and blue eyes. Dark blue eyes that still glinted with humour.

'Certainly.'

He hung his coat up, returned to the table and sat down.

His jacket was blue too — an unusual royal blue — and he wore a loose red cravat in place of a tie. Not that there was anything of the dandy about him. Both jacket and cravat looked soft with age, as though he wore them only for comfort.

Lily let him settle as she brought scones from the serving room and placed them on the dresser but he didn't pick up the menu card. Assuming he must want only a warming drink, she took her notepad and pencil from her apron and went over. 'Are you ready to order, sir?' That was better. She sounded truly polite and professional now.

'Do you serve chocolate?' he asked. 'To drink?'

'I'm afraid not. But we have coffee if you'd prefer it to tea?'

'I would. And might I have one of those scones? They look very English.'

Did that mean he wasn't English? He spoke the language like a native but if he were living abroad it would explain why he wasn't away at the war. On the other hand, he might simply be home on leave and craving a reminder of the country for

225

which he was fighting.

Lily wrote the order down and moved away to fulfil it.

He thanked her when she returned with his coffee and scone. 'Lily's Tea Room is new, is it not?' he asked.

'Fairly.'

'Lily isn't the baker I saw downstairs,' he guessed.

'I'm Lily,' she said, and he nodded as though her answer confirmed his expectations.

'Business is brisk?'

Lily looked around the empty room. 'It's early still, but I expect — ' She broke off, pleased to hear footsteps on the stairs. She wouldn't have liked him to think she was presiding over a failing enterprise.

'I mustn't keep you,' he said.

Soon there were customers sitting at several tables. Lily was kept busy but not too busy to be aware that, while he spent some time looking out at the street, at other times he watched her. Did he always have that gleam in his eyes?

He seemed to be in no hurry to leave. 'Might I trouble you for more coffee?' he asked, as she cleared the table next to his.

'Certainly.'

She fetched it quickly.

'This is a good situation for a business,' he commented. 'The street outside is busy.'

'The shops here are excellent.'

'So each shop draws customers to the others?'

'I think so.'

More customers were arriving. Others were

leaving. Lily sent the man a rueful smile and went about her day, glad of the slenderness and lightness of foot that meant she could glide easily between tables and chairs.

'My bill?' he requested, a few minutes later.

Lily gave it to him, took his money and counted his change, realising it would embarrass her if he left a tip but not quite understanding why.

'I've enjoyed my time in Lily's Tea Room,' he said.

'I'm glad,' Lily told him, aware of more warmth gathering in her cheeks.

'Excuse me!' another customer called.

The blue-eyed man nodded to show he understood she was working and Lily went to take an order for more cake.

By the time she'd served it he'd gone. Clearing his table, she took a moment to look through the window. He was on the street outside, taller than most men and more upright too. She watched him cross the road then turn and look up.

Was he looking up at the window where Lily stood?

Not wanting to be caught staring, she darted back. Only when she thought he must surely have gone did she move forward again and glance tentatively out of the window. Yes, he'd gone. She finished clearing the table and discovered a thruppeny tip under his saucer. For a moment she hesitated to pick it up. But it was only a tip and would come in useful for Elsie's next treat.

She had little leisure for daydreaming about blue-eyed strangers through the rest of the day but his visit had taught her that she wasn't as indifferent to all men as she'd thought. Not that it mattered. The stranger had gone and Lily had a business to run.

★ ★ ★

'You've grown even taller,' Lily observed when Artie returned for Christmas.

There was even a small moustache on his upper lip. Lily was tempted to tease him about it but decided to wait until she was sure it wouldn't make him feel self-conscious. After all, he was almost a grown man now.

She took him for his first look at the tea room now it was up and running.

'What do you think?' she asked, wanting very much for him to be proud of her achievement, modest as it was.

'It looks very nice, Lil, but I hope it doesn't mean you're working harder than ever.'

'I enjoy working.'

Just then Elsie arrived and all was bustle. The girls cooked a meal for Artie that first night and he was as charming as ever though she guessed that being surrounded by evidence of her hard work reinforced his guilt over the fact that she needed to earn her own bread while his was provided for him.

Not wanting him to feel any guilt at all, Lily spoke about how women across the country were working hard to keep things going at home. Phyllis needed no prompting to tell him how women were driving ambulances, issuing tickets on omnibuses and working in munitions factories where the smallest lapse of concentration could result in loss of life or limb. They'd served such women in the tea rooms and admired the chirpy attitude of the Canary Girls as they were called because their fingers, faces and hair were stained yellow from contact with chemicals.

'Obviously we want votes for women as much as ever,' Phyllis said, 'but campaigning is taking second place to the war just now.'

Artie smiled. 'I know women are every bit as clever as men, Phyll. How could I not know when I have a sister who's still much cleverer than me despite all my years at school?'

Lily didn't feel cleverer anymore. Probably Artie was just being kind.

'I wish I could join you for Christmas dinner but I'll be dining with Mr Alderton,' Artie told them. 'I can see you afterwards, though.'

'Come for the evening,' Lily urged. 'We're planning a jolly time.'

Mr Bax was cooking a turkey and bringing his sisters over in a taxi to join in the feast. The Tibbs sisters were coming too and staying in a guest house nearby.

Elsie had to work during the day but, like Artie, she'd come in the evening.

It was lovely to have everyone together. The turkey was a delicious treat and Mr Bax ensured that everyone found a silver sixpence in their portion of Christmas pudding. There was sherry to drink, games to play and small but thoughtful gifts to be exchanged.

Lily hugged the happiness close but sadness picked at its edges. Both Hilda and Marion were ageing rapidly. Beatrice and Betty Bax were getting no younger and even Mr Bax's jowls were hanging low in the candlelight.

In unguarded moments Lily saw Artie's smile faltering too and no wonder. In another week it would be 1917. Artie would turn eighteen in May and unless peace came he'd be required to fight.

21

'Good morning.'

Lily was clearing a table but turned at the sound of a voice. The man with the blue eyes was back, tiny drops of January drizzle sparkling in his black hair. She was clearing a table and hoped he'd attribute the sudden warmth in her cheeks to exertion rather than …

What? Pleasure, certainly, but mixed with self-consciousness. 'If you'd like to sit down, I'll take your order shortly,' she said, seeking refuge in brisk efficiency again.

'Thank you, Lily.'

He'd remembered her name! Lily felt a moment's delight followed by foolishness. Of course he'd remembered it. The tea room was named after her.

She took the tray into the serving room then returned, armed with pencil and pad.

'Still no chocolate?' he asked.

'I'm afraid not.'

'Then I'll have coffee with … ' He turned to look at the display on the dresser.

'A slice of fruitcake, please. And a happy New Year to you, Lily.'

'Thank you. To you as well.'

She escaped to the kitchen before she blushed again.

'Business is prospering still?' he asked on her return.

231

'We're not complaining.' The tea room was busy for mid-morning.

More customers arrived and Lily excused herself to serve them but she caught him watching her now and then. Each time he sent her a smile.

Eventually he glanced at his watch in a way that suggested he had an appointment to keep. He paid his bill then shrugged into his coat and walked to the door. 'You have a serving room through there, I suppose?' he asked, nodding towards it.

'We do.'

'For a moment I thought you were appearing and disappearing like a fairy.'

He was teasing her and, despite coping with all sorts of customers from flirts to dragons, Lily didn't know how to respond.

'Thank you,' he said, and, smiling, he set off downstairs. Lily was too busy to see if he looked up at the window, but when she finally cleared his table she found another thrupenny tip.

She'd thought he might be simply passing through the area the first time he'd come but this second visit made her wonder if he lived or worked nearby. It also made her wonder if he'd return another day. It was strange how one man's smile could affect her so differently from the smiles of other men.

But perhaps he smiled at all young women. Lily had no intention of becoming the sort of fool who daydreamed her life away. She had too much to keep her occupied in the real world.

She wasn't doing war work exactly but she still felt useful. Providing food and drink helped people to go about their daily business, whether that involved a job or looking after home and family. Providing *nice* food and drink helped to keep people cheerful in difficult times. And providing somewhere to sit helped people to rest, see friendly faces and talk with friends. Sometimes important news was shared and arrangements made for helping friends and neighbours.

Lily was particularly pleased when young men from the army, navy and even the Royal Flying Corps came in. How exhausted some of them looked! How strained around the eyes! She was glad to provide a haven where they could sit quietly to gather their thoughts and ease their tired bodies.

Artie wrote to say that, despite the appalling losses in last year's Somme campaign, there was cause for optimism about what this year might bring. Lily prayed he was right and hoped he was managing his nerves at the prospect of joining the fighting.

He wasn't the only young man to be worried. One day Lily served two women who were talking about the RA-BA-SA salts one of them had bought to send to her son. 'They're for shell shock and trench nerve,' she explained. 'Five shillings and ninepence, but worth the money if they help Percy. They go in the bath and there's enough salts in the box for seven baths. I only hope Percy can manage to keep his baths private because he doesn't want anyone else to know how he's feeling.'

The café had been open for three months and Mr Bax gave no sign of regretting his decision to let it go ahead. Quite the contrary, in fact. 'You've breathed new life into the place, Lily,' he told her

233

one morning. 'It's hard work running a café as well as a bakery but I'm actually enjoying it.'

Lily was delighted to know that her venture was giving him pleasure. It was earning money too. Not a fortune, and not yet enough to employ Elsie, but the signs were promising.

The following morning Lily overheard customers talking. 'I see they've got a buyer for the shop next door,' one said.

As soon as a breathing space opened up in the day's work Lily ran out into the street. Sure enough, a board outside the Sollifords' shop announced, *Sold Subject to Contract.*

The estate agents were Chambers & Sons, 16 Marley Row. That was only five minutes' walk away.

'Would you mind if I took a longer break today?' she asked Mr Bax and Phyllis.

She ran all the way to Marley Row where the estate agents had a ground-floor office.

The gentleman inside looked puzzled by the appearance of a young girl who could surely have no interest in purchasing or leasing property. 'May I be of assistance?' he asked.

'I'm enquiring about the Sollifords' haberdashery shop. I believe you've agreed a sale?'

'That is correct.'

'Is it going to continue as a haberdashery shop?'

'I believe the purchaser's interests don't run to haberdashery. Chocolate was mentioned. But I'm afraid I haven't understood the nature of your interest, Miss …'

'Tomkins. It's just that a friend of mine is looking for a position in the area and I wondered if the new owner might need staff.'

234

'I have no information about staffing require-ments.'

Lily nodded, disappointed but unsurprised. Then the word *chocolate* suddenly loomed large in Lily's mind. 'Do you mean the sort of chocolate people drink?'

'I'm afraid I don't know. And I'm not sure I should be discussing a client's private affairs.'

'Is your client a young gentleman?'

'Mr Goddard is in his middle twenties, I believe. Do you know him?'

'He isn't from around here?'

'From Switzerland, but — '

It was all the information Lily needed to iden-tify her blue-eyed customer as the Mr Goddard who was buying the shop. 'Thank you,' she said, anxious to leave now.

She stepped back outside, feeling the bite of the winter wind though it didn't feel half as bitter as her emotions. What a fool she'd been. He hadn't been interested in her. He'd come to her tea room only to study the street outside and ask questions that would help him decide whether the shop next door suited his ambitions — a café that sold warm chocolate drinks and doubtless more besides.

And when he'd stood outside looking up, he'd been staring at the building rather than at Lily.

Doubtless his café would have money behind it. The sort of money that could provide a place of comfort and sophistication, and soon entice cus-tomers away from Lily's homespun enterprise.

Mr Goddard hadn't lied to her. But he'd abused her friendly openness and trust, and that made her feel angry. Hurt too, and worried because if the tea room was driven out of business, Mr Bax wouldn't be able to sell it as a going concern. He might even decide to retire all the sooner without the tea room to interest him. That meant Phyllis and Lily would lose both their income and their home.

She'd been walking quickly as the thoughts circled in her head but now she slowed her steps. Perhaps she should wait until she had a clearer idea of what Goddard had in mind before she said anything to Mr Bax and Phyllis. There was no point in worrying them prematurely, especially as the sale was subject to contract. Anything might happen to stop it from becoming final.

She called in on the stationers and bought some card as an excuse for having been out. 'Got it,' she said, waving the card as she walked into the bakery.

Lily didn't like deceiving her friends. She went upstairs thinking harsh thoughts about Mr Goddard from Switzerland.

22

Lily looked up at the *Sold* board every day but weeks passed and it never changed back to *For Sale*. Lily had no idea how long it took for a property to change hands but various possibilities passed through her head:

1. The lawyers were simply taking time to do whatever lawyers did.

2. Mr Goddard had decided not to purchase the building after all but the estate agents hadn't got around to changing the board.

3. There was no need to change the board because another buyer had stepped into Mr Goddard's shoes.

'It's a nice little business, is haberdashery,' Mr Bax told a customer who asked if he knew what was happening next door. 'Someone might buy it as a going concern.'

'They might,' Phyllis agreed. 'I just hope they don't sell fish. Awful smell!'

It didn't appear to occur to either of them that a new business might be a rival business. Elsie was different. Lily was changing for the cinema one evening when Elsie stretched her long body across Lily's bed, put her hands behind her head and said, 'You know what they say about troubles.'

Lily was puzzled.

'A trouble shared is a trouble halved,' Elsie explained. 'It's nonsense really because a trou-

237

ble doesn't shrink just because you share it. But I suppose it means troubles aren't as heavy if two people carry them. I'm here if you want to talk. If you don't … ' Elsie shrugged her large shoulders to suggest she wouldn't push Lily to confide in her.

Lily stood undecided for a moment then sighed. Sitting on the edge of the bed, she told Elsie about Mr Goddard. The important points, that was. There was no need to mention his good looks.

'Hmm,' Elsie said. 'You'll just have to wait and see what he does.'

'I shouldn't tell Mr Bax or Phyllis?'

'I'd wait until there's definite news.'

Lily nodded, relieved to know that Elsie's thoughts mirrored her own.

More time passed and Lily began to feel a glimmer of hope that Mr Goddard's plans really had come to nothing. But towards the end of February a customer came in and said, 'I see the builders are starting work next door.'

Lily seized a quiet moment to slip out to investigate. The neighbouring door was open so she stepped inside to see tools and building materials piled on the floor. 'Hello?'

No one answered but she heard voices in the room behind the shop. 'Hello?' she called again, moving towards them only to back up swiftly as a man appeared, clearly not expecting to find his way blocked by a girl.

'You gave me a fright there, Miss. This place ain't safe, what with tools and such. What can I do for you?'

'I'm from Lily's Tea Room next door. Could

you tell me the name of the new owner of this place?'

'Your pa worried about noise, is he? Tell him we won't make more noise than can be helped but a man can't use a hammer without banging it and we've a lot of work on, what with fitting out a shop down here and sprucing up the living accommodation upstairs.'

'I just want to know the owner's plans for the shop.'

'Summat to do with sweets, I heard.'

'Sweets? Or chocolates?'

'I don't see as how it makes much difference, Miss.'

'Is the owner Mr Goddard? From Switzerland?'

'It's a Mr Goddard, all right, but I dunno about Switzerland. Now, if you don't mind … '

Lily took the hint and left.

Mr Bax and Phyllis had heard about the building works too. 'Well?' Mr Bax asked, on Lily's return.

'It's going to be some sort of confectionary shop. Sweets or … chocolate.'

Mr Bax and Phyllis looked at each other. 'Sugar mice and barley sugars might draw more customers to the street,' Mr Bax said.

Phyllis nodded. 'All the local businesses could benefit.'

Lily still said nothing about her suspicion that the chocolate would be the drinking kind, in direct competition to the tea and coffee available in the tea room. Of course, Lily could serve drinking chocolate too but she suspected Mr Goddard's chocolate would be much more luxurious than

239

anything she could provide.

'What do you think?' she asked Elsie later.

'I still think we need to find out more about this man Goddard's plans before we say anything to Mr B and Phyllis. Let's leave it for a day or two then I'll call in next door and say I'm looking for work.'

'If you could ask how long the work is likely to take, that would be helpful too,' Lily said. 'The builders are making a lot of noise so the tea room isn't quite the restful paradise it — ' She broke off suddenly.

'What?' Elsie asked.

'It just occurred to me that one way of drowning out noise would be with music.'

'A gramophone player?' Elsie was enthusiastic.

'I've no idea of cost but perhaps we could pick one up second-hand. We'd need records too.'

'It's my day off tomorrow. I'll investigate.'

'You're a fantastic friend, Elsie. I really do wish you could work here with us.'

'You'd employ me if you could. Besides, helping the tea room is fun.'

Clearly, that was more than could be said of Elsie's present job.

She arrived just after closing time on the following afternoon. Grimacing, she shook her head.

'I went next door but the builders couldn't tell me if staff are needed. All they'd say about the building work was that it would take a few weeks.'

'And the gramophone?'

'Too expensive.'

'What's too expensive?' Phyllis asked, coming in.

240

Lily shared her idea for music.

'What a shame we can't afford it,' Phyllis said.

Mr Bax had come in after her. 'There's no need to buy a gramophone because I already have one,' he said. 'Or rather Beatrice does. She inherited it from an old employer but never uses it. I'll ask her if I can bring it here.'

He brought it by taxi in the morning. 'Beatrice says we can borrow it with her blessing. These records too.' There were more than a dozen of them, from popular music to classical. 'Where do you want it?'

They settled it in the serving room from where the music could float into the tea room without interfering with the customers' conversations.

'Let's play this one,' suggested Elsie, who'd come round before work to see this exciting machine. 'It's got a terrific name — "The Egyptian Trot".'

It was a jolly ragtime number. 'I'm not sure this is the right background music for tea and scones but it's great for dancing,' Phyllis said, striking poses like ancient Egyptians she'd seen pictured in a book.

'I'm too old for dancing,' Mr Bax said, but Elsie grabbed his arm and made him dance with her.

'If I'm prepared to dance when I'm as graceful as a hippopotamus, I'm sure you can manage,' she told him.

She left him shuffling his feet and thrusting his arms about then pulled Lily into the dance as well.

They all danced together, giggling at each other's more outrageous movements, then Elsie remembered she had to get to work and the others remembered they had to open the shop.

241

The music not only helped to counter the noise from the builders but also received numerous compliments from customers. 'Even the customers who only called in for bread were humming and swaying in the queue,' Phyllis reported, for the music reached downstairs too.

The music ignited Lily's spirit of defiance. Whatever Mr Goddard had planned for next door, he'd find that Lily's Tea Room wasn't going down without a fight.

More weeks passed and Lily was able to put daffodils, tulips and primroses into her displays of greenery. The days were growing longer, the temperature was turning milder and lighter colours were making an appearance in the clothing customers wore.

Spring brought cheerfulness though it also brought challenges. With wheat being in short supply Mr Bax was required to use more raw wheat in his bread, together with maize, barley and even potatoes which he hated because mashing them and mixing them into the dough was a horribly messy process. The war bread didn't taste as good either so Lily made sure the tea room always had two kinds of soup available as well as baked potatoes and tarts.

She was clearing a table by the window one morning when a glance outside caused her heart to jolt. It was him. Mr Goddard. Crossing the road with a shorter, stockier, limping man at his side. Presumably he was on his way to inspect his building works.

The morning wore on with Lily taking and serving orders while using every spare moment to

242

wash and dry dishes ready for the lunchtime trade. Then lunchtime came and brought Mr Goddard and his stocky companion with it.

Lily's heart suffered another jolt at the sight of him, but when he sent a twinkling smile her way she burned with anger inside. Not that she intended to let him see that anger and neither did she intend to sulk like a petulant child.

Either response would pander to his vanity by suggesting he had power over her.

'Table for two?' she asked. 'We've only one vacant table, I'm afraid.'

It felt good to show him that her little business was thriving despite its shoestring budget.

She'd spoken politely but impersonally as if she'd never clapped eyes on him before and it pleased her to see his smile falter as though he couldn't quite believe she'd forgotten him. She waited for both men to sit then passed menu cards to them. 'Shall I give you a minute or two to make up your minds?'

'Yes, please,' Mr Goddard said, clearly puzzled by her coolness.

Lily went to see to some other customers but returned to his table soon, not wanting him to think she kept her customers waiting. Mr Goddard sat back in his chair to study her thoughtfully. When he asked for soup she wrote the order on her pad with a professional smile then turned to his companion.

He was older by as much as ten years and not half as handsome. In fact, his features were ugly when considered individually, his nose being too big, his mud-coloured eyes being hooded and his thin-lipped mouth being half-buried in a beard. But somehow his features added up to pleasantness. Niceness, even. He ordered soup too.

Lily brought their order with swift efficiency. 'I like the music,' Mr Goddard commented.

'Thank you. It's certainly proving popular.'

'Useful too,' he said wryly as he heard a bang from his builders. 'I'm sorry about the noise. It's my fault because I've bought the shop next door.'

'I heard it had been sold. It's going to be a sweet shop, isn't it? Or am I confusing your shop with someone else's?' She shrugged to suggest she wasn't interested enough to have bothered remembering.

'Mostly chocolates,' he said. 'I'm Luke Goddard. This is my cousin, Pierre Glasse. We've been working as chocolatiers in Switzerland where our family has a business.'

Chocolatiers? Lily hadn't heard the word for people who made chocolate before. 'When do you expect the building works to finish?' she asked, as though that were her only concern.

'In another week or so. Pierre is here to supervise the kitchen installation. We'll open in three weeks' time.'

Lily nodded, and was glad when another customer raised a hand to attract her attention. 'Excuse me,' she said, walking away.

The two men stayed no longer than it took to finish their meals. Mr Goddard gave her another considering look as he paid the bill but said nothing except to thank her for her service and compliment her on the soup. Lily declined to point out that, if his shop drove her out of business, he'd have to seek his lunch elsewhere.

He left a sixpenny tip under his saucer. Lily wanted to crush it with her heel but tips were to be shared so she tossed it into the tip jar.

Realising Mr Bax and Phyllis might think it odd if she kept quiet about his visit Lily mentioned it casually as they closed for the day. 'The chocolate shop men came in earlier.'

'Men?' Phyllis said.

'Two of them. They expect to open in around three weeks so we shouldn't have to suffer with the noise for much longer.'

'We'll continue with the music, though?' Phyllis asked. 'Customers like it.'

Lily looked at Mr Bax.

'I'm sure Beatrice will be happy for you to keep the gramophone,' he said. 'Nice chaps, are they? The sweet shop men?'

'I ... didn't have much time to talk to them. I was busy.'

'Let's hope that they make good neighbours.'

Elsie called round later to accompany Phyllis to a lecture on expeditions to the South Pole. 'The new neighbours came in,' Phyllis told her.

'Oh?'

'Lily can tell you about them while I fetch my coat.'

Elsie waited until Phyllis had left the room then raised an eyebrow at Lily.

'What did this Mr Goddard have to say? I'm surprised he had the gall to show his face.'

'I don't think he regards himself as our enemy exactly. But if the success of his shop means the death of the tea room I suspect he'll just shrug it off as being the way of things in business.'

'You'll have to fight him,' Elsie advised. 'I might try again to get a job there. I could feed information to you like a spy.'

'You'd be dismissed.'

'They'd have to catch me spying first.'

Phyllis returned, buttoning up her coat. 'Sure you don't want to come?' she asked Lily.

'Thanks, but I need to make new menu cards.'

After they'd left, Lily took card, pens and a small artist's painting set into the tea room. She also took her sewing box to experiment with little booklet menus that fastened up the side with ribbon.

She'd been working for only a few minutes when someone banged on the shop door downstairs. Had Phyllis returned for something she'd forgotten? Her key perhaps, given that she hadn't let herself in?

Lily went downstairs and came to a halt when she saw Mr Goddard through the glass panel in the door. Not wanting to appear naïve and awkward, she pressed on and opened it.

'I hope I'm not disturbing you but I wanted to give you these,' he said.

Only then did she realise he was holding a large bouquet of flowers.

'They're a peace offering,' he explained. 'For all the noise you've had to endure.'

'There's no need for a gift,' Lily told him.

'I'd *like* to give a gift.'

Even in the semi-darkness she could see the amusement was back in his eyes.

It annoyed her but, not wanting to appear churl-

246

ish, Lily took the flowers. 'Thank you.'

She expected him to wish her goodnight and leave but he simply stood watching her. 'Well,' Lily finally said. 'I'll bid you — '

'Might I have a few minutes of your time?'

Did he want to explain his plans and point out that there was no room for hard feelings in business?'

'Very well,' she said, then added a fib. 'Though I don't have long before my friend returns.'

'To do what?' he asked, smiling. 'Rescue you from the big bad neighbour who's imposing on your time?'

'Hardly.' Lily put coldness into her voice, not liking to be mocked.

He stepped into the shop then followed her up to the tea room. She gestured to an empty table but too late to stop him from walking to the table at which she'd been working. He picked up her experimental menu card. 'Pretty,' he observed, then looked around the room at the flowers, foliage, handwritten signs ...

'You're working hard to make this place successful.'

'I am.' Lily couldn't keep the sparks from her eyes.

'I've offended you,' he said. 'I realised it earlier. And I don't think it's because of my noisy builders.'

Why not be honest? 'Competition isn't personal. Is that what you think?' Lily asked. 'You're just doing the best for your business and I should accept it as a fair fight? I'm sorry but that isn't possible.'

247

It wasn't a fair fight for one thing. He appeared to have money while she had none. But more importantly, it was a question of decency. Luke Goddard was threatening livelihoods. 'This place doesn't just provide my friend, Phyllis, with a job,' she told him. 'It's also her home. And Mr Bax—'

'I've no idea what you're talking about.'

Lily stared at him.

He gestured to the table. 'Sit down and tell me what you mean.'

'This is *my* tea room,' Lily pointed out, bridling. 'It's for *me* to invite people to sit.'

Humour glinted in his eyes. 'So invite me.'

Lily hated to think she might be acting childishly. 'Very well. You can sit, though I can't imagine we have much to say to each other.'

'Thank you.' He sat but Lily remained standing.

That made her feel childish too so she pulled out a chair and sat opposite him.

'You're worried that my chocolate shop will be in competition with the tea room?' he asked.

'If you're selling hot chocolate drinks, how can it not be? I doubt that there's enough business for two cafés.'

'I'm not selling hot chocolate drinks. Or any other sort of drinks.'

Lily was bewildered. 'But you asked about hot chocolate drinks when you first came here.'

'I'm a chocolatier. All things chocolate interest me, but it doesn't follow that I'll be selling all things chocolate. My chocolates will come in boxes tied up with ribbons.'

Lily didn't know what to say. Her uppermost

248

feeling was relief but she also felt foolish.

'Let me tell you about myself so there are no more misunderstandings,' he said. 'I'm known as Luke Goddard but my full name is Jean-Luc Goddard. My father was English and I spent much of my childhood here. My mother was Swiss and moved the two of us to Switzerland after my father had an accident and needed to change jobs. I learned chocolate from my grandfather but I have uncles and cousins working in that business so it'll never be wholly mine. I've always wanted a business of my own and I also hankered to return to England so here I am.'

Luke paused as though to let his explanation sink in, then continued. 'There were three reasons for choosing Highbury rather than a smarter part of London. The first was the fact that my grandparents lived here and I've always liked it. The second was the practical consideration of being able to afford a property. And the third was about what I want to achieve. I'm not interested in bringing more luxury to people who already have plenty. I want to bring delicious chocolate to people for whom it'll be a treat. Everyone should taste the delights of this world.'

Lily was of the same opinion. Her tea room attracted all sorts of people from those who lived among Highbury's most pleasant streets to ordinary men and women for whom it was ... Yes, a treat. A delight.

Well, this was unexpected. Clearly, Lily needed to adjust her opinion of Luke Goddard but right now she needed to say something — anything — to stop herself from staring at him as though

249

she'd been struck dumb. 'Don't you need sugar for chocolate?' she asked.

'You're thinking the shortages mean I might not be able to get hold of enough?'

'Won't they?'

Luke shrugged. 'We plan to be inventive with other ingredients – nuts and fruits especially – to reduce the amount of sugar we need. Even if we keep our prices modest compared to some other chocolate shops, it's still a fairly expensive product so we won't need to sell huge quantities to make a living.'

'We?'

'Pierre is a distant cousin,' Luke explained. 'He had an English mother and a Swiss father. He worked in my grandfather's business and learned the craft — or should I say the art? — of chocolate too. He'll be running the shop when we first open.'

'Oh?' Was Luke returning to Switzerland?

'I won't pretend I wouldn't like to expand into other areas eventually — hot drinking chocolate even — but that won't be for a while and it might not be here, particularly if it threatens other businesses such as yours. We live in difficult times with this war raging and it's impossible to predict the future, especially as — '

There was a sudden commotion in the shop below and Elsie and Phyllis came upstairs, chattering. 'The lecture was cancelled due to the lecturer's lumbago,' Elsie announced, then came to a halt when she realised Lily wasn't alone.

Phyllis careered into the back of Elsie then she saw Luke too. 'We didn't mean to interrupt,' she said.

250

Luke got to his feet. 'I was just leaving anyway.'

'This is Mr Goddard from the shop next door,' Lily said. 'This is Elsie Davenport and this is Phyllis Beckett.'

He shook their hands. 'I'll be selling the sort of chocolates that come in pretty boxes,' he explained, as though to clear the air in case Elsie and Phyllis had shared Lily's suspicions.

'That should bring new customers to the street,' Phyllis approved, while Elsie sent Lily a sly look that showed she not only understood Lily had been wrong about this man but also wondered why nothing had been said about his rather impressive appearance.

'I'll let myself out,' he said, moving towards the stairs.

'Wait!' Elsie called.

He turned.

'Can I have a job in your shop?' she asked. 'Please?'

He laughed at her boldness.

'I believe in plain speaking,' she explained.

'So I see.'

'But I'm a hard worker.'

'Talk to my cousin, Pierre. I'm going to be away for a while.'

'Away?' Lily asked.

'I can't return to my homeland without doing what I can to defend it,' he explained. 'I've joined the army.'

23

'It was nice of him to bring flowers,' Phyllis said, when they'd heard the shop door close behind him. 'Being on good terms with neighbours is important.'

'Especially when they're good-looking,' Elsie added. 'Isn't that right, Lily?'

Lily wasn't thinking about his looks. Her thoughts were too busy with the fact that she'd jumped to conclusions and misjudged him. Now he was going off to the war with all its dangers and she'd lost the chance to apologise.

Or had she? Surely he wouldn't be going away immediately?

She became aware that her friends were waiting for her reply. 'Being on good terms with neighbours is certainly important.'

Elsie gave her another sly look but to Lily's relief said nothing more about the man from Switzerland's handsomeness. 'I hope this Pierre gives me a job,' Elsie said instead. 'Imagine being surrounded by chocolates all day.'

'You'd be selling them, not eating them,' Phyllis pointed out.

'I don't see why I can't do both, and working next door will be almost as good as working here. Wish me luck?'

'Of course!' Lily and Phyllis chorused.

Lily took a selection of cakes next door as a peace offering the following day but only Pierre was there, supervising the workmen in the big kitchen that was being installed behind the shop. Stocky and strong despite his limp, he was very much the man in charge. She introduced herself to him in case he didn't remember her then said casually, 'No Mr Goddard today?'

'He reported for duty. He's gone off to fight.'

'Already?' Lily was shocked.

'Luke doesn't waste time.'

'No, I imagine not. Still, I expect he'll be in training for a while so you'll see him before he's sent overseas.'

'I hope so.' Pierre's expression turned bleak.

It occurred to Lily then that a lesser man might have resented the fact that Mother Nature had given him a squat, lame body and plain features when it had given his cousin the sort of fine physique and features that made him stand out in a crowd. But Pierre was clearly too good a man for that. Love and concern for his cousin brooded in the mud-coloured eyes and Lily honoured him for it.

'Please pass on my good wishes,' she said.

'I'll be sure to. Not there!' Pierre roared impatiently at one of the workmen.

Obviously in the way, Lily retreated swiftly to the tea room.

At closing time Elsie burst in. 'Can't stop. I just wanted to tell you that I've got the job in the chocolate shop. I start in two weeks' time so I can help to get it ready for opening. Here's hoping I don't crush all the chocolates. Or eat them. Anyway, I just wanted to let you know. Got to dash now as my dragon of a housekeeper is expecting me to help prepare dinner. I can't wait to see her face when I give my notice in. She'll have to get someone else to do her reaching and peeling for her.'

With that Elsie rushed away again. Lily was delighted for her. Elsie was due some good fortune and it would be lovely to have her sharing their evenings and working close by at last.

There was another advantage to Elsie's new job. She'd be on hand to tell Lily if Luke called in on leave before he left for the war so Lily might still have her chance to apologise and wish him well.

Mr Bax refused to take rent from Elsie when she moved in above the bakery.

'You've been a great help to the tea room so it's only fair that you should have something in return.'

He insisted on buying a bed for her and they placed it in Phyllis's room because Phyllis wanted Lily to have a room to herself, being the boss.

'I may be the manager but we're all equal as people,' Lily pointed out, but Phyllis wouldn't budge.

Elsie was thrilled to have a new job. 'How do you get along with Pierre?' Lily asked curiously after the first few days, because the man she'd met was certainly no pushover.

'I can handle Pierre,' Elsie assured her. 'He might use French swear words but he doesn't scare me.'

'How do you know he's swearing if he's speaking in French?'

'I know because of the sighing, shrugging and eye-rolling that goes with it when I tell him I won't be bossed about.' Elsie grinned wickedly.

254

But she was excited about the chocolate shop opening and keen for it to be successful. 'Can you think of a way to make the opening special, Lily?' she asked. 'I'm not good with ideas.'

Lily was glad to help, not only for Elsie's sake but also as a way of making up to Luke for having misjudged him.

The outside woodwork of the shop had been painted a rich dark red with the name, *Goddard & Glasse, Chocolates* being announced in swirling gold lettering across the window. Inside there was more dark red and gold. Luxurious indeed.

Lily suggested that in the week before opening there should be nothing in the chocolate shop window except for a selection of chocolate boxes tied in gold ribbons and a sign to be changed each day to count down the time to the opening. *Seven days, six days, five days, four …*

She also suggested that on opening day Elsie should tie a ribbon to the door so it could be cut ceremoniously, with a free chocolate being offered to everyone who came to watch. Pierre was apparently happy to leave the ideas to Elsie so she wielded a large pair of scissors and cut the gold ribbon as a small crowd gathered outside and broke into applause.

Lily was one of the shop's first customers. She bought two boxes of chocolates, one to send to Hilda and Marion, and the other for Mr Bax to give to Beatrice and Betty. Both sets of sisters sent notes thanking her with so much warmth that Lily felt she couldn't have spent her hard-earned money better.

Easter brought Artie home but he had little

time to spend with Lily. 'Mr Alderton isn't well,' he confided when they snatched half an hour together.

'There's something wrong with his lungs and I'm afraid it might be serious. Sorry, Lil. I'd hoped we might have a day out together but it isn't looking likely.'

'Mr Alderton has been good to you. It's only fair that you're good to him.'

Lily meant every word but she was still dismayed because this holiday was their last chance to be together before he enlisted in the army after his final term at Camfordleigh.

At least there was good news from the war as America had finally decided to join in. 'Will it make a lot of difference?' she asked Artie.

'I certainly hope so.'

They managed to snatch only one more hour together before he returned to school. 'Mr Alderton's doctor doesn't think his life is in immediate danger anymore, but he isn't likely to linger long so he's putting his financial and legal affairs in order.'

'I'm sorry,' Lily said, pitying Mr Alderton while wondering what his death would mean for Artie.

'He's always made it clear that I'll have to earn my own living once I leave school and I wouldn't expect anything else,' Artie explained. 'I've been amazingly fortunate in the way he's paid for my education and now I need to put that education to good use. Well, not now exactly because of the war. But Mr Alderton wants me to have a job to come home to when the war is over.'

'Does he have something in mind?'

'He's giving me introductions to a number of possible employers. If one of them likes the look of me when I go for an interview, they might be willing to hold a job open for me while I'm away. Quite a few employers are holding jobs open for chaps who are fighting.'

'What about somewhere to live?'

'Mr Alderton is leaving most of his estate to his old school but there'll be a pension for Mrs Lawley so she can retire,' Artie told her. 'She'll keep the house in Hampstead running for another year so I'm not immediately homeless, though, and I'll receive a small sum to help me with lodgings or other accommodation after that.'

Perhaps then Lily would be reunited with him properly and they could live side by side again, sharing some of their evenings and days off too. Not that she wanted to be a financial burden to him. On the contrary, she wanted to pay her own way. But there was the war to survive first.

'How do you feel about all this?' she asked.

'I'll regret Mr Alderton's passing, of course. I can't pretend to feel love for him. In some ways I'm no closer to him now than on the day I met him. But I respect him and I'll always be immensely grateful to him. I only hope I haven't disappointed him.'

Not that again.

'He used to talk about the possibility of university for me but he stopped mentioning that some time ago,' Artie said.

Lily repeated what she'd told him before. 'He just wanted you to have better opportunities than would have come your way without an education.

If he isn't proud of you, he's a fool,' she added.

Artie smiled but wryly. 'I always hoped I'd be able to start helping you once I'd finished school. Instead I'm going into the army.'

'Can't be helped and I'm managing well anyway,' Lily insisted. 'Now, tell me about these interviews.'

'The first one is with a shipping company. Dad worked in shipping in his own way down at the docks so it feels sort of ... right to me.'

'I'm glad,' Lily said. 'Let me know what happens.'

She reached up to kiss his cheek, sensing his need to return to Mr Alderton. 'I hope he doesn't suffer.'

Lily wished she could slow down time over the following weeks. She prayed for peace so there'd be no need for Artie, Luke and thousands of other young men to risk life and limb in fighting which had brought little advantage to anyone as far as Lily could see. But she could only continue to do her best to give comfort and pleasure through her little tea room and make the most of her own life.

Artie wrote to tell her he hadn't warmed to the shipping company. Neither had he been inspired by an insurance company or a business that traded in precious metals. But he'd also been interviewed by a building company — Grover's — and felt much more enthused.

The building company is in Kentish Town, not far from Hampstead. It isn't as grand as the other businesses but it appealed to me a lot. The boss is Mr Grover. Apparently Mr Alderton played an important role in his education and that's why he's willing to grant a favour in return. I only hope I can do the job well. Mr Grover's wife happened to call in to the office on her way to the Oxford Street shops with her daughters. The daughters are Celia, who looks to be around our age, and Violet, who's a little younger. They were very smartly turned out but charming.

Lily was thrilled for him.

Elsie's happiness was another joy. It was lovely for all three girls to be back under the same roof, sharing jokes and laughter. Pierre became a friend too. He knew few people in London so the girls were glad to keep him company, especially as he was an excellent cook and proud to introduce them to dishes such as coq au vin when he could get hold of a chicken. He introduced them to wine too.

It amused Lily to see Pierre and Elsie together, the short man and the tall girl, bossing each other around and rolling their eyes when the other refused to be bossed. Arguing too in a good-natured way about everything from what should be displayed in the shop window to whether it would rain that day.

'Silly man,' Elsie called him when he suggested beef was best served with horseradish sauce. 'Everyone knows it's better with mustard.'

'Only those who don't know food,' Pierre retorted.

'I know food. I love food. That's why I'm bigger than you.'

'You're taller. I'm stronger.'

259

Elsie stuck her tongue out at him.

'Doesn't he mind the way you speak to him?' Phyllis asked later.

'Why should he?'

'Because he's your boss.'

'That doesn't make me his slave.'

'You're incorrigible, Elsie.'

'That's one of your big words, Phyll, and I'm not sure what it means. But it sounds about right for me.'

Artie returned to school towards the end of April but only to sit his examinations before travelling back to London to be with Mr Alderton. 'He likes me to read to him,' he wrote to Lily.

Artie had learned he was to be awarded prizes for cricket and cross-country running. 'No prizes for scholarship, I'm afraid,' he told Lily when they snatched a few brief minutes together.

'You've done Mr Alderton proud,' Lily insisted.

A week later Artie sent a note informing her that Mr Alderton had died with Artie at his side. Mr Grover, Artie's future boss, and a solicitor were executors of the Will and would help to make the funeral arrangements.

'Would you like me to come to the funeral?' Lily asked.

'You have your tea shop to look after,' Artie pointed out.

Besides, Mr Alderton had only ever been interested in Artie. Lily would still have gone to the funeral if Artie had needed her but, seeing that he'd cope without her, she was glad to stay home to work.

He had much to do to sort out the possessions Mr Alderton had left to various friends and colleagues, but for the first time since their Bermondsey days Artie managed to spend some time with Lily on their joint birthday. Mr Bax baked a cake decorated with eighteen candles which they blew out to cries of, 'Make a wish!'

Lily could have made many wishes but settled for: *I wish the war would end.*

Soon Artie would be one of thousands of young men serving in the forces and Lily wanted to keep them all safe.

Artie joined the Royal Norfolk regiment, his experience in the Camfordleigh Officers Training Corps leading to a junior officer commission as a second lieutenant. Between being measured up for his uniform, buying his kit and replying to letters of condolence sent by Mr Alderton's old friends and connections, Artie had little free time but managed a Sunday afternoon with Lily.

They spent it strolling in Kensington Gardens and Hyde Park. 'You'd never guess a war was raging,' Lily said, looking around at children playing with toy boats by the Serpentine and people strolling by in summer clothing — straw boaters and flannel trousers for the men; lace-edged blouses with big flowery hats for the women.

But just then a young man in khaki came into view. Artie was in uniform himself, 'To wear it in and get used to it,' he'd said, looking self-conscious about it.

Lily gestured to a bench. 'Let's sit.'

They sat side by side. Artie took off his cap to smooth his hair back and when his hand returned to his lap Lily reached out to squeeze it.

'I'm more afraid than ever,' Artie admitted. 'But I'll do my best for the men who serve under me. The OTC is meant to prepare junior officers but I'll be in charge of chaps who are a fair bit older than me. I hope they won't think they're risking their lives for an inexperienced idiot who jumps out of his skin at the first noise of battle.'

'They'll understand your fear because they'll be frightened too.'

Lily thought of Luke, who was seven or eight years Artie's senior. How would Luke feel about taking orders from a boy who just happened to have been to the right sort of school?

Luke would be kind, Lily decided. Boys like Artie might be giving the orders but it would be men like Luke who'd brace their young officers' courage and steady the troops, despite their own fear.

'You'll be going to a training camp before you're sent anywhere near a battle,' she reminded him.

'Of course I will.'

'I'd like to come to the station to see you off,' Lily said then. 'I'm sure Pierre won't mind coming out of the kitchen to mind the chocolate shop while Elsie takes my place in the tea room.'

'There's really no need. I'm only going off to camp.'

And perhaps he felt he had a better chance of keeping his nerves in check in front of other men if he was alone 'All right,' Lily conceded. 'But when you're sent overseas ... '

'That'll be different,' he agreed.

Lily clung to Artie when they parted but, not wishing to overwhelm him, she blinked back her

262

tears and released him. 'Write to me,' she pleaded.
'As often as I can.'

A week later Artie wrote to her from training camp. He wasn't the only Camfordleigh boy in the regiment so he had familiar faces around him and had met other good chaps too. Camp was hardly luxurious but he was sleeping and eating under cover. *In any case life at boarding school has prepared me for strict routine, substandard food and shared accommodation*, he wrote, *so you really shouldn't worry.*

Not worrying was easier said than done, but every day Artie was safe was a day to be treasured. Lily had read his letter quickly when it had been delivered then gone out for a walk later to read it more slowly. Despite being on her feet all day she often walked in the evenings. It helped to calm her after the bustle of the day's work.

Letting herself back in through the shop door, Lily heard voices up in the tea room on her return. Loud excited voices. Her ears identified Elsie's laugh, the low rumble of Pierre's voice and then another voice that made her breath catch in her throat. It couldn't be …

It was.

Lily quickened her pace but then slowed it again, taken aback by just how fast her heart was beating at the thought of seeing Luke again. She'd realised long ago that she found him attractive but even so this fizz of eagerness surprised her.

And it had little to do with her need to make her overdue apology.

She came to a halt, took a deep breath and climbed the stairs quietly, hoping that, if she saw

263

him before he saw her, she could use the moment to steady herself. The door to the tea room was ajar. Lily crept along the landing towards it. She saw Elsie, Phyllis, Pierre and yes, there was Luke.

He was telling a story, presumably about his experiences at training camp, but Lily only caught the end of it. ' … The next moment the poor chap was face down in the mud.'

There was more laughter then Luke's head turned as though instinct had alerted him to Lily's presence. He stared at her for a moment, his blue eyes pensive, then a slow smile curved his mouth and Lily's heart felt as though it were being flipped right over. 'Hello, Lily,' he said.

24

Lily prepared for bed that evening trying to decide if she was sorry or glad that the others had been present during Luke's visit. Their company had deprived her of the chance to get her apology off her chest but had also saved her from the awkwardness of being alone with him when she knew how she felt but didn't know if he felt the same. After all, Luke had smiles for everyone.

Perhaps it was the wrong time to think about romance anyway. Luke was going off to war while she was trying to make her mark on the world, however small that mark might be.

From the moment she'd seen him Lily had guessed he was home because he was about to be posted overseas. 'You're on embarkation leave?' she'd asked.

'I am, and I'm lucky. Most men are given only forty-eight hours' leave. I've been given more than twice that for some reason.'

Lily had heard customers complaining that leave wasn't always given consistently, some men being given more and an unlucky few receiving no leave at all before they were posted abroad. She searched Luke's face for signs of fear but encountered only another smile. 'I want to enjoy this leave because I've no idea when I'll be home again,' he'd said.

Or even *if* he'd be home again.

'I want to eat decent food because the food in

the camp has been grim and the food I'm likely to get at the front will be even worse. Tinned stew and biscuits hard enough to break teeth.'

'I'll cook your favourites,' Pierre promised.

'I want to taste normal life again, and work in the shop for a while too.'

'I'll show you the ropes,' Elsie offered. 'Seeing as I'm the boss and Pierre is just the kitchen skivvy.'

Pierre rolled his eyes and Elsie grinned.

'But I don't want to work *all* of the time,' Luke continued. 'I'd like to get out and about a bit, and I hope each of you will honour me with your company at least once.'

'I will,' Elsie confirmed. 'Especially if you're paying. I'm the incorrigible one, by the way. According to Phyllis.'

'Phyllis is right,' Luke said.

'I'm game for an adventure too,' Phyllis told him. 'The question is, are you?

There's a lecture on women's suffrage tomorrow, if you'd like to come? Women may have stopped chaining themselves to railings while the war is on but we shouldn't lose sight of the goal, especially as the work women are doing these days proves we're more than equal to men.'

'Phyllis loves all that Votes for Women stuff,' Elsie explained.

'Don't you want the right to vote?' Luke asked.

'Of course. But I'd rather leave the campaigning to Phyllis and spend my time enjoying a show or a meal.'

'Then that's what you and I will do,' Luke said. 'And yes, I'll pay.' He turned back to Phyllis. 'I'll

266

come to your lecture. I'm all in favour of votes for women.'

Phyllis nodded approvingly. 'Excellent.'

'What would you like to do, Lily?' Luke asked. 'Assuming you'll honour me with your company?'

'I'll be happy with a walk,' Lily said. It would give her the chance to apologise.

He spent the following day in the chocolate shop. 'I think I was able to teach him a thing or two,' Elsie said wickedly. 'By the way, Phyll, he'll call for you at seven. He says he's looking forward to it.'

Phyllis nodded. 'Luke Goddard has the makings of a sensible man.'

And like a sensible woman she was downstairs ready and waiting at seven so Lily didn't get to see him.

'He didn't nod off in the middle of the lecture?' Elsie asked on Phyllis's return.

'He was interested.'

'Here's hoping he'll be interested in tomorrow's variety show.'

Elsie had chosen a variety show because she liked to laugh. She too waited downstairs for Luke to collect her after another day in the chocolate shop and, again, Lily didn't see him.

'Luke paid for excellent seats,' Elsie enthused afterwards. 'There was singing, dancing, acrobatics, magic tricks... Oh, and a performing dog.'

The next evening Pierre cooked a meal for all of them, including Mr Bax and his sisters who came by omnibus and would travel home by taxi afterwards.

Pierre cooked in the bakery kitchen and they ate

267

upstairs in the tea room, pushing tables together to make one large table which seated all of them.

It was a lovely evening. Luke sat one seat along from Lily on the opposite side of the table so she could see him clearly as he smiled and laughed at Elsie's antics.

'I thought my hands might be too big for handling delicate chocolates but I've crushed hardly any,' she joked. 'Apart from rose creams which get crushed quite often so have to be eaten.'

'Rose creams are your favourites,' Phyllis pointed out.

'Isn't it strange how they're the ones that get crushed when I'm feeling peckish?'

Pierre shook his head despairingly.

Only occasionally did Lily catch Luke's cheerfulness giving way to something more wistful. He'd look around as though committing the evening to memory and she wondered if he were hoping that looking back on happy times would comfort him in the difficult days that lay ahead.

He noticed her watching and sent her a tiny nod. It felt intimate to Lily, a gesture of mutual understanding. Then Elsie drew them both back into the conversation with a comment about Luke's time helping in the chocolate shop.

'He did all right, but if he wants to know what really hard work looks like, he should spend some time with Lily in the tea room.'

Luke smiled then raised an eyebrow at Lily. 'How about it?'

'You're on leave. You shouldn't be working all the time,' Lily said.

'That sounds as though you don't think I'll

268

cope. I'll have to prove you wrong now.'

He arrived early the following morning. 'Private Goddard reporting for duty,' he said, saluting her.

She sent him down to the bakery to bring up freshly baked loaves and cakes then decided to clear the air between them. 'I never actually apologised for misjudging you over the drinking chocolate. Let me say now that I'm sorry.'

'I misled you. I should have realised what you must have thought when you heard I was setting up next door.' He smiled. 'There. We've both apologised. Now we can enjoy our day.'

'Of course.'

He was an excellent worker. He rolled his sleeves up to wash dishes, wiped tables, took orders and served food and drinks. For a tall man he was fast and surprisingly agile. He was careful and tidy too. And the customers loved him. He had friendly smiles for the younger women, winks for the dowagers, jokes and breezy chat for the men and gentleness for a soldier who looked exhausted. In short Luke Goddard had charm and Lily was just as affected by it as anyone else.

More perhaps. She only had to look at him to feel warmth spreading through her veins while his smile sent her heartbeat skittering. But how did he feel about her? Certainly, there was softness in those blue eyes when he looked at her but was it there when he looked at others too?

'It's been a good day,' he said at closing time.

Lily made tea and carried it to a table so they could relax for a moment before clearing up. Luke stretched his long legs out and grinned. 'Did I pass muster?'

'You didn't do too badly,' Lily said, but he knew she was teasing him.

'You work hard,' he said. 'Elsie's right about that.'

'I'm right about most things,' Elsie said, coming to join them. 'I don't think Pierre understands that yet. You should have a word with him, Luke.' She helped herself to tea. 'Was the work too much for you, Luke?'

'I enjoyed it.'

Elsie's face wore one of those smiles that suggested she was thinking private thoughts. About Luke and what he might mean to Lily?

Not wanting Luke to be embarrassed, Lily turned the conversation to the chocolate shop and as soon as the tea was drunk she got up to clear the tables.

Luke insisted on helping her, with Elsie supervising his every move. 'Haven't you got work to do next door?' he finally asked.

'It's time your cousin did some work,' she told him.

Once the tea room was pristine Lily walked Luke downstairs. 'Thank you for your help.'

'I enjoyed it, but I hope you don't think it takes the place of our walk?'

'I like to walk,' Lily assured him, her heart swelling with pleasure because he wanted to see her again.

She expected a short walk during the evening but Pierre agreed that Elsie could work in the tea room so Lily and Luke could take a whole afternoon. They decided to make Regent's Park their destination though it was some distance away. Luke took her arm as they crossed a road and seemed disinclined to release it again so Lily left it where it was. 'It won't be too far for you?' he asked.

'No, but if it's too much for you …?'

Luke smiled. 'I think I'll manage.'

'Do you miss Switzerland?' Lily asked after a while. 'I've only seen it in pictures – snow-covered mountains, lakes, valleys … It looks very beautiful.'

'It is. I love Switzerland, but there's something about London that feels like home. Have you travelled?'

'Only as far as the south coast. Hastings.' It was a journey of little more than fifty miles but still helped her to feel slightly less naïve.

'Perhaps one day you'll travel further.'

'Perhaps.' If she could afford it when the war was over.

Suspecting that war was the last topic of conversation Luke needed, Lily pointed across the road. 'There's a tea shop over there. Would you mind if I looked in the window?'

'Looking for ideas?'

'I like to see what others are doing, certainly.'

They crossed the road. 'Your tea room has much more charm than this place,' Luke said, and Lily glowed with satisfaction.

Regent's Park was lovely, a vast open space bordered by beautiful white-painted properties. 'Do you want to go into the zoo?' Luke asked.

'Do you?'

'I've seen it before but I'm perfectly willing to see it again.'

271

'Another time perhaps.' Lily did want to see the animals as she'd never seen anything more exotic than a parrot a sailor had once brought to Jessy Street, but she sensed that Luke would prefer to enjoy the peace that walking offered.

They followed the paths to the boating lake.

'I love being beside water,' Lily said. 'I suppose it comes from spending my early years by the Thames. Not that the river is anything like this lake. It's busy and dirty.'

'You were brought up in Bermondsey, weren't you?'

Elsie or Phyllis must have told him that. 'Yes. Artie and I lost our parents young so we lived with our grandmother. She was a wonderful person. Hardworking, brave, selfless... And very loving.'

'But then you lost her too and were separated from your brother.'

'Two blows in swift succession,' Lily confirmed. 'But Artie was offered an amazing opportunity and it would have been selfish of me to object.'

'Artie's benefactor was only interested in educating boys?'

'Mmm.' Lily smiled as a thought struck her. 'I doubt Phyllis could have persuaded Mr Alderton to go to a lecture on women's suffrage.'

'Men like that are fools. Everyone has potential. Male, female, rich, poor ...'

'That's how I see it.'

'You're ambitious, Lily.'

'For my little tea room, yes. While I've got it anyway.'

She explained about Mr Bax's plans for retirement in the not too distant future. 'I want to learn

272

all I can before then. Afterwards… Who knows? I'm not interested in growing rich or building an empire, but I do want to feel satisfaction in a job well done.'

'I understand,' he said.

'But enough of me.' Lily was suddenly self-conscious again. 'Tell me about your childhood.'

'It was a lot easier than yours.'

He was an only child brought up in a happy home. His father had been a carpenter, a craftsman who was much in demand until an accident cost him the strength in one of his arms. 'It wasn't practical for him to work with heavy wood after that so we moved to Switzerland where he learned chocolate. He was good at it too. He was never afraid of hard work and he valued perfection over speed.'

'Are your parents still alive?'

'No, but I was lucky as both of them lived until I reached adulthood. My father died five years ago when I was twenty. My mother lived two years longer. I lost my grandfather earlier this year. He'd been ill for a while and I promised to stay with him until he no longer needed me. It's thanks to the money he left me as well as my own savings that I've been able to set up the chocolate shop. Pierre refused to be my partner as he had little money to put into the business but I regard him as my partner in practice if not in law.'

'Which is why you called the shop Goddard & Glasse?'

'I insisted.'

Lily liked him for it.

'I expect it seems odd that I've opened a shop

273

when I'm going off to the war,' he said. 'I suppose I like the idea of there being a future waiting for me if I'm lucky enough to return. If I don't return... Well, Pierre will inherit the business so I'll have given him a chance to make something of himself. He's older than me. Strong as an ox in some ways but he was run over by a cart when he was a boy. His leg was badly broken and badly set by an incompetent doctor. It took Pierre a long time to recover. He was unlucky with his family too as his father was a drunk while his mother was one of those clinging, weeping women. They left Pierre with debts he felt honour-bound to clear even though it took him years. He deserves some good fortune.'

'He does,' Lily agreed. 'But does he deserve Elsie?' She smiled and Luke smiled with her.

'Your brother is in training at the moment, isn't he?' Luke asked then.

Lily nodded.

'You're worried about him. Is he worried about himself?'

'Yes, but that doesn't make him weak or cowardly.'

'Of course it doesn't. Only fools are unafraid.'

'It isn't just the thought of falling or being injured that troubles him. He's worried his fear will get the better of him and he'll let himself down. Let his men down too. He was in the Officers Training Corps at school so he's been made a junior officer even though he's never been near a battlefield.'

It seemed to Lily that Luke with more years and experiences behind him would make a more effective leader than an untried boy. Not that she doubted Artie's courage or ability. He was just so young. 'I wish he could have enlisted as an ordinary soldier so he wouldn't be under such pressure but it seemed to be expected that he'd become an officer.'

'The army needs junior officers and the OTC gives young men like Artie a head start with training and discipline,' Luke said. 'Compared to men who've never been near a parade ground, I mean.'

'I understand that, but it seems unfair to put boys who've only just left school in charge of men who are older and more experienced. Don't those older men resent it?'

'Some do,' Luke admitted, 'but others feel paternal towards their young officers.'

Lily smiled, grateful for Luke's kindness. But something else was troubling her. She didn't like to mention casualty lists, though. Not when Luke's own life was in danger.

'What is it?' he asked.

Lily opened her mouth to tell him she was fine but he raised an eyebrow in a way that suggested he wouldn't fall for anything less than the truth. Even then she hesitated.

'You're thinking of all the young officers who've lost their lives,' he guessed.

'Well...' The casualty lists in newspapers included a frightening number of them.

'It isn't easy being a junior officer,' Luke conceded. 'They don't sit on the side lines in battle but get out there and lead their men into the thick of it.'

Lily had even heard that the enemy deliberately

275

picked off officers so the men under their command would flounder. The thought made her wince.

'If Artie is anything like you, he'll find his courage somehow,' Luke said, and he gave a small nod that meant that Lily had to keep her courage high too.

He was right.

They looked in on another tea shop on the way home and this time went inside. 'Lily's Tea Room still wins my vote,' Luke said, looking around.

'Goodness. I must repay you for your compliment by treating you to your tea.'

'This is my treat. I wanted to enjoy my leave and thanks to Elsie, Phyllis and you I've enjoyed it a lot.'

Had he enjoyed their company equally, though? Lily had no way of knowing.

They walked home arm in arm but Luke drew her to a halt just before they reached the bakery. 'Thank you for a terrific afternoon, Lily. It's been lovelier than you can know.'

Bending forward, he kissed her cheek and Lily's heartbeat quickened. But then he straightened and looked down on her, thinking… If only she could tell.

'Look after yourself,' he said.

'You too.'

They walked the few steps to the bakery door and Lily went inside but she couldn't let him go without another word. She pulled the door open and leaned out. 'Take care!' she called to his retreating figure.

Luke turned and smiled. 'I will. I've a lot to live for.'

25

Lily didn't see him again before he left. Without him, the mood of both tea room and chocolate shop felt flat. 'What a grumpy old ogre Pierre can be,' Elsie reported.

'He's worried about Luke,' Phyllis said.

'Yes, but what good does moping do? Pierre will help Luke far more by building up the business.'

'Easier said than done,' Phyllis suggested.

Lily agreed with both of them. It was impossible to stop worrying but they had to press on with life.

Several days made no improvement to Pierre's mood but on the fourth day Elsie came in looking pleased. 'I've sorted out Pierre's temper,' she told them.

Lily and Phyllis exchanged glances. 'What did you do?' Lily asked.

'Stuck his head into a bowl of melted chocolate. I told him I'd do it again if he didn't pull himself together.'

'He didn't threaten to dismiss you?' Lily wondered.

'Or murder you?' Phyllis added.

Elsie snorted. ''Course not. Once he'd washed the chocolate out of his hair, he laughed and said I'd done him good.'

'I hope you'll never be tempted to do me good that way,' Phyllis said, but Elsie only grinned.

They were all glad when letters came from

Luke. One was addressed to Pierre and another to the three girls together. Did that mean they were equal in his affections? Just the thought of a soft look from Luke's gleaming eyes made Lily's breath catch, but either Luke felt differently or he was postponing any tenderness until after the war. Time would tell.

In the meantime Lily resolved to be thankful that Luke had been safe when he'd written and in good spirits too. In the weeks that followed he wrote more letters, often relating lively stories about the men who were serving with him.

The girls stored up funny stories to include in the letters they sent in return.

Lily wrote about seeing a carter's horse snatch the flowers off a passing woman's hat. Elsie wrote about a customer who thought chocolate was brown because it was made with milk from brown cows. And Phyllis wrote about a young man who'd rushed out of a women's suffrage meeting saying he was in the wrong room and his dad would kill him if he got involved with females who meddled in politics.

Lily admired Luke for putting a brave face on things in his letters but knew he must be suffering terrible sights and conditions.

'Another letter from Luke,' Elsie said, waving the envelope one morning. 'I'll read it first, shall I?'

'Just as you like,' Lily told her, but the all-seeing look was back in Elsie's eyes.

Had she guessed that Lily had more than ordinary feelings for Luke? At the very least she suspected it, Lily guessed, because Elsie handed the letter over with a knowing smile.

'Actually, I'd better get next door before Pierre starts doing his French swearing,' she said.

Lily could only hope she hadn't confirmed Elsie's suspicions by blushing.

★ ★ ★

Time went on and it was Artie's turn for embarkation leave, though he hadn't had long in training. He was pale but dignified when Lily saw him. 'I'm as ready as I'll ever be for whatever lies ahead,' he told her, then smiled wryly. 'Sorry, Lil. I'm always leaving you, aren't I? Perhaps one day I'll be able to fulfil my promise to help you.'

'It isn't your fault and I'm managing well so you've no need to worry about me.'

They were in the tea room alone, Elsie and Phyllis having gone to Pierre's to allow brother and sister time together. Mr Bax had insisted on making a steak pie for their dinner so Lily took it out of the oven and served it onto hot plates alongside vegetables. Artie produced a bottle of wine Mrs Lawley had found in Mr Alderton's cellar.

Lily had drunk wine with the dinners Pierre cooked so didn't feel totally unsophisticated. 'I wonder what Gran would make of us sitting here like this?' Lily asked. 'Mum and Dad too?'

'They'd think we'd come a long way from Jessy Street and they'd be proud. Especially of you, Lil. Your success is entirely down to your own efforts.'

'I've been lucky in other ways,' she said.

She wondered what Artie and Luke would

make of each other and decided that Artie would admire Luke's calm self-possession while Luke would feel kindly to such an open, eager-to-please young man as Artie.

Thoughts of Luke also reminded her of how he'd said he wanted to enjoy his leave. 'What would you like to do in your time off?' Lily asked Artie. 'I won't have to work all of the time because Pierre is going to serve in the chocolate shop while Elsie helps in here.'

'I'll have to spend a little time with Mrs Lawley,' Artie said. 'She's rattling around in Mr Alderton's house by herself these days. Mr Grover has asked me to spend some time in the office too. Apparently, his clerk left to work in a munitions factory so he's short-staffed. It won't hurt me to start learning the business anyway.'

'We'll still have a day out together?'

'Definitely. I'd like to look at London landmarks, if you don't mind?' Artie said. 'I've seen them before but I want to remind myself of them. I know I won't be fighting for landmarks exactly, but I suppose I see them as representing England.'

They travelled around London on foot and on buses, climbing the spiral staircases to the top decks to give themselves the best possible views.

Buckingham Palace, Westminster Abbey, the Houses of Parliament, Trafalgar Square...

'I haven't exhausted you?' Artie asked, and Lily laughed.

'Not at all.' Not when she spent most days on her feet, rushing around.

She didn't see him the following day as he went to Grover's but he arrived the day after looking

280

excited. 'I took some papers round to Mr Grover's house last night and he invited me to stay for their family dinner. So kind! Celia Grover had the most wonderful idea.'

Celia was the elder daughter, if memory served Lily correctly.

'She thinks I should have my photograph taken before I leave. I'd like a photograph of you too, Lil, so I can have it with me at the front.'

It was indeed a wonderful idea. Lily would be glad to have another photo of Artie to add to her small collection.

The visit to the photographer's studio was fun. The photographer posed Lily in a stiff-backed armchair then instructed her to hold very still while he went to the tripod that held his camera and took her picture. Artie went next, looking handsome and proud in his uniform. Then the photographer took a photograph of Lily sitting in the chair with Artie standing at her side.

The photographer promised to develop the photographs quickly and provide them in a number of sizes — larger ones for framing and smaller ones for carrying in wallets or purses. 'What an enjoyable way to spend a morning,' Lily told Artie.

'I must write to thank Celia for suggesting it,' he said, and there was a glow in his eyes that made Lily begin to suspect he rather admired Celia Grover.

Not wanting to embarrass him, Lily said nothing but her curiosity about the young woman was aroused.

Artie collected the photographs the following day and presented copies to Lily. 'I'm going to buy a frame for this one,' she said, admiring the larger picture of Artie. 'I'll keep it by my bed so I can see you last thing at night and first thing in the morning.'

'Are you sure you want to come to see me off at the station tomorrow?' Artie asked. 'Celia and her sister have said they'll see me off, so if you're busy...'

'I want to come,' Lily insisted.

As she approached Waterloo Station the following day she saw a taxi pull up.

Artie got out and so did two young women. Lily was too far away to see them clearly but both looked to be very smartly dressed. She quickened her pace, ready to meet them with a smile but they merely exchanged a few words with Artie then got back in the taxi and drove away. Artie stood waving to them.

'Lil!' he said, as she reached him. 'It's good of you to come.'

'Was that the Grover sisters?'

'They insisted on bringing me in a taxi.'

'That was kind. They couldn't stay?'

'They were being considerate and giving us time alone. Well, here goes.' He picked up his kit bag and another smaller bag which he held up. 'Gifts from the Grovers. A Fortnum's fruitcake, some gentleman's relish, and brandy.'

'You're going to have a lot to carry because I brought cake too, and some of Pierre's chocolates,' Lily said.

'I'm sure I'll manage.'

Inside the station crowds were surging this way and that as men in khaki were seen off by loved

282

ones. Lily accompanied Artie to his platform then clutched him close, not wanting to let him go. But it wasn't fair to make leaving awkward for him. She took a deep breath and released him, unable to keep the tears from her eyes but managing a wobbly smile. 'Don't be a hero,' she urged. 'Just do your best and come home.'

He bent to kiss her.

'And write,' she said. 'Write often.'

'I promise.' He stepped through the barrier and got on to the train. Moments later he leaned out of a window and waved. Lily waved back. Steam hissed, a whistle blew and the train lurched forward. Lily kept on waving long after the train was out of sight.

* * *

Both Artie and Luke wrote often and uncomplainingly though Lily had overheard enough customers talking to know that life in the trenches was truly dreadful — periods of relentless rain and mud, overflowing latrines, bad food, exhaustion and, of course, the terror of bullets, shells and evil gasses that burned from the inside out. Lice too.

'It's all very well getting our uniforms fumigated now and then,' Lily had heard one soldier say to another in the tea room. 'It doesn't touch the eggs the buggers lay in the creases and the moment a man works a sweat up, out they hatch and it starts all over again.'

'I pinch them out with my fingers,' the other man said.

'I try to burn them with a candle.'

'Mate of mine did that. Set fire to his uniform.'

It was impossible to avoid the dread of Artie or Luke being hurt — or worse — but they were being brave and Lily had to be brave too. At least they were in France so there was hope of seeing them on leave at some time in the future.

Some families hadn't seen their menfolk in more than a year because those men were serving far away in countries such as Egypt and their leave wasn't long enough for them to travel to Britain and back again.

June brought terrors to London too. Not just Zeppelins but German aeroplanes — Gothas — which dropped bombs from on high. The bakery had a cellar reached via a hatch in the kitchen floor but no one had been down there for years. The threat of the Gothas persuaded Mr Bax to clear it out one Sunday so it could be used as an air raid shelter. He rigged up a ladder people could use to get in and out, and took chairs, blankets, food stores and candles down there. He also filled buckets with sand and water and kept them behind the counter, to help put out a fire if the bakery should be struck.

August came and as usual Mr Bax shut up shop for a week. Lily spent a few days in Hastings with Hilda and Marion, touched by how pleased they were to see her. They'd mentioned in a letter that there'd been a fire on the pier. Walking along the beach one day Lily looked over at the blackened ruins and felt sad.

When she'd last walked here with Artie, the pavilion at the end had looked pretty and joyful. Lily could only hope that its destruction didn't symbolise the country's hopes in the war. Three years had passed since the war's beginning and still there was still no sign of peace.

Lily hugged Hilda and Marion close when she left them. 'Take care,' she urged, because neither of them looked particularly robust.

Life went on as usual then one day Phyllis had news for Lily and Elsie. 'I've enrolled on a book-keeping course.'

'You already know how to keep accounts,' Elsie pointed out, because Phyllis had been helping with the tea room and bakery accounts for months.

'Yes, but the diploma I'll receive for doing this course will *prove* I'm capable.'

'Are you bored with working here?' Lily asked.

'Not at all. I'm just thinking ahead. The course is an evening class — one evening each week — so I'll be working here as much as ever.'

Lily was relieved, but she knew Phyllis was being sensible in looking ahead to the future. It was time Lily did the same by speaking to Mr Bax about his retirement plans. After all, he'd agreed she could open the tea room for a year and that year was almost over. If he planned to retire soon there'd be no job or home here for Phyllis and Lily, and no home for Elsie either.

26

'I *have* been thinking about retirement,' Mr Bax admitted when Lily asked for a private word with him. 'My sisters were talking about it only last night.'

Lily fought down dismay but knew she had no right to feel disappointed. Mr Bax had kept to his end of the bargain and she had to do the same.

'I've enjoyed running the tea room so much,' she assured him. 'I'm sure the experience will hold me in good stead in the future, even if I have to go into a different sort of job for a while, and I'll always be grateful for the opportunity you gave me.'

'You're running ahead of yourself there, Lily. The thing is, I've enjoyed the tea room too. It's given me a new lease of life, having three lively girls around.'

'But your sisters...'

'They brought the subject up because they don't want me to retire without consulting them. They can see what a difference it's made to me, and the tea room gives them a lot of pleasure too. They love hearing about what you're doing and coming to visit. They want me to keep it going for a while.'

'They're not just saying that to be kind?'

'The kindness is all on your part for putting new life into old bones.'

'Another year, do you think?'

'I do.'

Lily kissed his cheek. 'Thank you so much! Please thank Beatrice and Betty too.' With that Lily rushed off to share the news with Elsie and Phyllis.

'I'd been wondering what was going to happen,' Elsie said, and Lily felt guilty that she hadn't spoken to Mr Bax before. 'I'll tell Pierre he's stuck with me for a while longer so he'd better watch his step,' Elsie added.

'Another year will be perfect,' Phyllis declared. 'It'll give me a chance to earn my diploma.'

She began her course three weeks later and came home looking deeply satisfied. 'It's going to suit me well as figures are where my talents lie. I'm not like you, Lily. You can imagine something and turn it into reality. I can never do that. The way I see it, a wise woman should be aware of her weaknesses while making the most of her strengths.'

'My only talent is being tall and strong,' Elsie said. 'I'll make the most of that by carrying those boxes of preserves upstairs.'

'You're helpful, hardworking and good at making people laugh,' Lily called after her. 'They're excellent talents.'

Phyllis's enthusiasm for her bookkeeping course didn't diminish. Every Wednesday evening she set out eagerly and returned looking pleased.

One Wednesday evening Lily sat in the tea room reading the latest letter from Artie who assured her he was well. There'd been dreadful loss of life in the fighting around Passchendaele so as ever Lily was hugely relieved to hear from both Artie and Luke.

Artie thanked her for the socks she'd sent him.

287

Socks are always welcome. I'm feeling spoilt because Celia also knitted me a pair, while her sister, Violet, sent handkerchiefs. They don't have brothers or cousins at the front so I seem to be the soldier they've nominated to benefit from their kindness.

Celia again. Artie mentioned her often. Lily smiled at the thought of him being a little bit in love. Whether Celia was the right person for him or just a passing tenderness, Lily hoped he'd find happiness in marriage one day. He had so much love to give.

'Well, this is interesting,' Elsie said from where she was standing by the window.

Lily put the letter down. 'What's interesting?'

'Phyllis is being walked home by someone who looks like her twin brother, right down to the spectacles.'

Lily got up to look.

'Too late,' Elsie reported. 'They're in the shop porch now.'

Lily heard the street door open and close. Moments later Phyllis came upstairs. 'Useful evening?' Elsie asked her casually.

'Very useful, thank you.'

'It must be nice to be walked home afterwards.'

Phyllis sighed.

'It isn't my fault I happened to be looking out of the window,' Elsie protested.

'A person is allowed to look out of a window, isn't she?'

'His name is Michael and he's taking the same bookkeeping course,' Phyllis told her. 'He walked

288

me home because he happens to live nearby.'

'That's all there is to it?' Elsie asked.

'Not that it's any of your business, but yes,' Phyllis told her.

Elsie winked at Lily behind Phyllis's back. Lily had spotted a faint tinge of pink in Phyllis's cheeks too. Not that Lily had any intention of embarrassing Phyllis with questions.

More weeks passed before Michael was mentioned again. 'Going alone?' Elsie asked innocently as Phyllis got ready to go to her women's suffrage group.

'If you must know, I'm going with Michael,' Phyllis admitted.

'It's raining,' Lily observed. 'You should invite him in instead of leaving him waiting outside.'

'I never keep people waiting.'

'Then perhaps you could invite him in for a cup of tea when he walks you home.' Phyllis looked accusingly at Elsie who put up her hands defensively. 'No teasing. I promise.'

'Hmm.'

Phyllis did invite Michael in for a cup of tea but sent Elsie a scowl that dared her to tease him at her peril.

He was just as Elsie had described him – uncannily similar to Phyllis, from his slim build and pale face to his straight dark hair and glasses. At first sight he looked to be a quiet, shy sort of man but that impression vanished the moment he stepped forward to be introduced, offering his hand without hesitation. 'Michael Picton,' he said. 'Pleased to meet you, Lily.'

His eyes were intelligent and eager. Of course

they were. Phyllis wouldn't be attracted to a fool.

Elsie behaved herself when she was introduced but sent Phyllis a grin when Michael's back was turned.

Over a cup of tea he told them he'd been invalided out of the war due to shrapnel wounds to his chest. 'My injuries are nothing compared to those many chaps have suffered but they've left me with a damaged lung so I can't do hard physical work anymore. I used to work in a warehouse. Now I do clerical work which suits me better, but I'm keen to improve my prospects so I'm learning bookkeeping alongside Phyll.'

'Michael would like to go into politics one day,' Phyllis told them.

'My spare time is limited at present, but yes,' he said, 'one day I'd like to go into politics to try to make Britain a better place for all of us.'

'I can see Phyllis in Parliament too,' Elsie said.

'Women need the right to vote first,' Phyllis pointed out.

'They'll get it,' Elsie predicted.

'Hopefully sooner rather than later,' Michael said. 'Depriving women of the vote is indefensible. All people should have a say in the running of their country.' Passion blazed in his eyes and in Phyllis's too though their expressions softened when they looked at each other. What a promising relationship this was.

Michael stayed long enough only to drink his tea. 'It's been a pleasure,' he said, 'but we all have work in the morning.'

Phyllis walked him downstairs. Another few minutes passed before she came back upstairs, looking self-conscious. 'No teasing,' she insisted, glaring in Elsie's direction.

'I was only going to say that Michael seems nice,' Elsie told her.

'He *is* nice. But we haven't known each other for long so don't start imagining ... Just don't start imagining anything.'

'Wouldn't dream of it,' Elsie said, smiling.

Christmas was approaching and they all worked hard to put together parcels for Artie and Luke. 'It'll be bitterly cold and wet in the trenches so socks, scarves and gloves are always welcome,' Michael advised, having spent a winter in France himself. 'So will some nice things to eat and a book of puzzles or a story or two. It's terrifying out there, but there are also times of boredom.'

Everybody contributed one way or another and the boxes became packed with fruitcake, tinned ham, chocolate, gloves, scarves, socks, soap, toothpaste, novels and puzzle books. Lily hoped they'd give both comfort and pleasure.

For those still at home Christmas Day was celebrated in the tea room again.

Mr Bax brought Beatrice and Betty, while Hilda and Marion came up from Hastings. Michael came too during the evening, having spent his day with his parents and brothers. Phyllis had spent the previous evening with Michael's family. 'But don't make anything of it,' she'd said, glowering at Elsie again.

'As if I would!'

They all drank a toast to Artie and Luke but kept other war talk out of the celebrations, not wanting to dampen spirits. Russia had left the war

291

shortly before Christmas and Pierre had taken a pessimistic view of what that might mean. 'If the Germans aren't fighting the Russians in the east, they'll have more men to fight our boys in the west,' he'd predicted.

Lily supposed that must be so, but as 1917 gave way to 1918 she refused to stop hoping for an end to the hostilities.

January brought biting cold and cruel winds. In a lull between customers Lily glanced out of the window at people scurrying along in the darkness of late afternoon as though keen to get inside to firesides and hot drinks. Were there any firesides and hot drinks for Artie and Luke right now?

She turned from the window and gasped. The tall man standing in the doorway was like an apparition. Unreal.

But then he smiled.

'Artie!' Lily ran and threw her arms around his neck, uncaring if the customers in the tea room disapproved of such a public show of affection.

'I'm sorry I didn't let you know I was coming, Lil. I didn't know I had leave until yesterday, and then I had to rush to catch the boat. I've come from the station in all my mess, I'm afraid.'

'I'm just so happy to see you.' Lily felt tears forming but blinked them away.

'Well, look who's here.' Elsie came upstairs, smiling. 'Phyllis told me you'd arrived, Artie. Take him away, Lily. I'll help in here.'

'Thanks.' Artie squeezed Elsie's shoulder then followed Lily into the serving room.

'Hungry?' she asked.

'Starving.'

She warmed soup and made a sandwich of cheese and pickle. Putting them on a tray, she carried them upstairs to her bedroom so he could eat undisturbed.

There was only the bed to sit on but they needed nothing more.

Lily let him eat, telling him about the bakery, the tea room, the chocolate shop and also Phyllis's Michael. Only once he'd finished eating did she say, 'Tell me about you. You're very thin.'

'This food is delicious compared to what we get over there. But I'm fine, Lil. I haven't disgraced myself.'

'I never thought you would.'

'That's because you're always so strong. I'm… not so strong, but I've managed to be strong enough. I won't pretend I haven't been terrified, though, especially when we're waiting to go over the top or someone thinks they can hear Germans tunnelling under our trenches to plant mines that'll blow us to smithereens. The fear is like a living thing that jumps around inside a man. But I haven't funked it, and that's such a relief.'

'I'm so proud of you, Artie. How much leave do you have?'

'Less than a week, allowing for travelling.'

'Then we should make the most of it. You must want a hot bath and shave next, though. You're welcome to stay here if Mrs Lawley hasn't had time to get the Hampstead house ready.'

'I telephoned her from the station and she said she'll be delighted to look after me. It may be her last chance to mother me before the house is sold. I'd better head off now but I'll see you again tomorrow, if that's all right?'

'I'll make sure it's all right.'

'I'm so glad we'll be spending some time together. I have to see Mr Grover too as he's keen for me to learn what I can about the business.'

A thought struck Lily. 'I imagine Mr Grover will be busy working, but why don't you bring the Grover sisters and their mother here for tea? It would be a way of thanking them for their kindness.'

'What a lovely idea.' He got to his feet. 'That was a delicious meal, Lil. Thank you.' He'd left his heavy pack in the serving room. Heaving it onto his shoulder, he said goodbye to Elsie then continued down to the bakery to take his farewell of Phyllis and Mr Bax.

'We'll see you again soon?' Phyllis asked.

'Hopefully tomorrow.'

He duly arrived the next day but came alone. 'Mrs Grover sends her apologies but she and the girls have a previous commitment,' he explained.

Was that true? Lily felt a revival of her old concerns about Artie's willingness to involve her in the life he lived when away from her. 'You're welcome to bring them another day.'

'I'll certainly try,' Artie said, without any obvious awkwardness.

'Don't feel you have to entertain me today,' he continued. 'I'll happily sit in the tea room and just watch the world go by. If I won't be in your way?'

He was clean and freshly shaven but the removal of dirt and stubble only exposed paleness and strain. She made him a cup of tea then sat him at a small table by a window while she went about the business of serving her customers.

'You work hard,' he observed, when she changed his empty tea pot for a full one.

'Yes, but I enjoy it.'

'You've always been a hard worker, Lil.'

After a while he got up and helped her to clear a table, carrying the tray into the serving room. 'You don't have to do that,' Lily told him.

'I want to do it. This place feels reassuringly normal. Dear old England, going about her business.'

He exchanged a few words with Mr Bax in the bakery kitchen and with Phyllis in the shop then went next door to see Elsie and Pierre. When he returned he was smiling. 'Poor Pierre. He seems like a decent chap but Elsie bosses him mercilessly.'

'She doesn't have everything her way. Pierre knows how to fight back.'

'He's worried about his cousin. The Luke you've mentioned in letters.'

It would have been odd not to mention him. Lily only hoped she hadn't given away her feelings for him. Luckily, there was nothing in Artie's expression to suggest she had.

'Mr Bax lent me an apron so I can help,' Artie said.

'You should rest.'

'I need a taste of normality.'

It was lovely to spend time with him and she was reminded of the day when Luke had helped. Artie was shyer but equally charming. Once again, she thought that the two men would like each other if they ever had a chance to meet.

Hopefully, one day...

'I've enjoyed it,' Artie said later. 'Perhaps I'll have time to help again but I'm promised to Mr Grover tomorrow. He says he doesn't want to tire me, but the more familiar I can become with the business the more easily I'll settle to it once I'm working there properly.'

'I'll see you before you return to France?'

'Of course.'

★ ★ ★

Two mornings later he called into the tea room. 'I'm taking Mrs Lawley to lunch today to thank her for looking after me over the years. This afternoon I'm bringing Celia here for tea, if that's all right?'

Pleasure gusted through Lily like a balmy breeze. It would be wonderful to meet the girl who'd clearly caught Artie's eye. 'Just Celia?'

'Apparently, Violet and her mother have another appointment.'

Was that true? Or had Celia manipulated the situation because she returned Artie's regard and wanted to keep him to herself?

Excitement fizzed inside Lily as she awaited their arrival. 'Your visitors,' Elsie finally announced, having agreed to bring them upstairs and help in the tea room so Lily could sit with Artie and Celia for a while.

Smoothing her apron, Lily turned from where she was clearing a table. Her eyes widened. She'd expected a pretty girl but Celia was lovely, a fair-haired, blue-eyed beauty who was dressed

296

fashionably and expensively in a cream skirt and jacket, frothy lace blouse and broad-brimmed hat trimmed with silk flowers.

No wonder she'd caught Artie's eye.

Lily smiled a welcome but Celia didn't notice because she was looking around. There was nothing wrong with taking an interest but Lily felt a faint stirring of unease because the expression on Celia's face was bewilderment, as though she couldn't quite believe such a homespun sort of place had anything to do with Artie. Oh, dear.

'This is Lily,' Artie said, and Celia roused herself to smile.

Lily roused herself too, responding warmly as she shook Celia's hand. How soft Celia's fingers were compared to her own. Lily's skin was work-worn. 'I hear you've been very kind to my brother,' Lily said. 'Your family too.'

'We're pleased to help.'

'I've saved a table by the window.' Lily led them towards it.

She'd made a special effort to make it look nice, dressing it in a new tablecloth and adding a specially made flower arrangement of ivy mixed with sprigs of yellow jasmine. Celia seemed not to notice. She sat down but with another glance around that made it clear that Lily's Tea Room fell well short of her usual standards.

Elsie brought over tea things and a tiered rack of sandwiches, scones and cakes.

Artie introduced Elsie as Lily's friend. 'Delighted to meet you,' Celia said politely, but her voice was flat.

'Enjoy your tea.' Elsie walked away without

297

meeting Lily's eyes.

'Shall I pour?' Lily asked.

'Oh, certainly.' Celia's delicate shoulders shrugged.

'I hope you enjoy afternoon tea?'

'Oh, yes. We have it at home, and Mother often takes us to tea when we're shopping. Fortnum and Mason is our favourite, but we also like Selfridges.'

'I can't say I've tried either,' Lily admitted.

'Really?' Celia sounded surprised.

'I don't go shopping much. I assume you enjoy shopping because your clothes are lovely.'

Celia looked pleased then seemed to decide that good manners required her to pay a compliment in return. She studied Lily's plain black dress, apron and cap, and floundered.

'I need to dress plainly for work,' Lily explained. 'It doesn't trouble me, though. I love my little tea room.'

'How nice.'

'You give the most wonderful teas, Lily,' Artie said. 'Do tuck in, Celia.'

She smiled up at him and Lily began to understand why he was so taken with her. It wasn't just because she was beautiful but because the smile she had for him was warm, feminine and ravishing.

'What do you suggest, Artie?' Celia asked.

'I think you might enjoy one of those cucumber sandwiches.'

She blinked her heavenly eyes at him then took a sandwich and nibbled the edge of it.

'You don't go out to work, I understand,' Lily said.

298

'Goodness, no. I don't know where I'd find the time even if I wanted to work. I rarely have time to feel bored. If we're not shopping or visiting, I have dress fittings and piano practice. I also help Mother by embroidering handkerchiefs to sell to raise funds for charity. Mother says it's important to be seen to help the poor and unfortunate.'

'I'm sure it is.'

Artie's sunny charm kept the conversation going for a while longer but eventually Celia studied her watch. 'Look at the time, Artie. Mother is expecting me at home.'

Artie pulled a sad face. 'We have to leave, Lil.'

They wouldn't see each other again before he returned to the front.

'I'll just say goodbye to Mr Bax and the others,' he said, and Lily suspected he wanted to leave her alone with Celia for a moment so they could get to know each other better.

An awkward silence followed. Lily tried to fill it by enquiring about Celia's sister but, not getting much of a response, decided to fill it with action instead of words. 'You must let me give you some cakes to take home to your family.'

'Oh, no! No, thank you. Not that your cakes aren't delicious but Mother doesn't know... She isn't expecting me to take cakes home today. They'd go to waste.'

Lily's instincts tingled. Celia had almost said something else before changing her mind. Mother doesn't know what, exactly? That Celia was out with Artie today? If so, what did that mean? That Mrs Grover didn't want Celia spending time with young men in general? Or that she didn't want Celia spending time with Artie in particular because he was almost penniless and just a member of her father's staff?

Lily hoped it wasn't the latter. She didn't want his heart to be bruised. Neither did she want Mr and Mrs Grover assuming he was seeing their daughter behind their backs.

Artie returned then and Celia jumped up with barely concealed relief.

They all walked towards the stairs. 'I've something for you,' Lily told Artie, slipping into the serving room for a box packed with food, socks and other things.

'Thanks, Lil. You really are the best sister a chap could have.'

Lily wrapped him in a hug. 'Look after yourself and come back safely.'

She turned to Celia. 'It was a pleasure to meet you.'

'A mutual pleasure,' Celia said.

Lily supposed both of them were lying. She saw Celia and Artie out then climbed back up the stairs to the tea room where Elsie sidled up to her. 'Well? Did you like the golden beauty?'

'Artie seems taken with her.'

'Isn't she rather grand for the likes of us?'

It certainly seemed so. Not that Celia had been hostile exactly. Lily wouldn't go that far. It was more that Celia had appeared to think that she and Lily lived on different planets, each being alien to the other. Lily couldn't see how she'd ever enjoy the old sort of closeness with Artie if he chose to live on Celia's planet.

'Mind you,' Elsie added, 'I suppose Artie's a fair

few steps above us on the grandness ladder too.'

Was he, though? After the bumpy start to his life at Camfordleigh, Lily had thought he'd gained acceptance among people like the Grovers but was that actually the case? Perhaps Celia was keeping her interest in him secret from her parents because his education had in fact left him in a sort of No Man's Land between social classes.

But he was going back to the war and many months would pass before he was next home on leave. His interest in Celia might wane just as her interest in him might wane. The important thing was that he stayed safe.

27

Celia very much enjoyed meeting you, Artie wrote a couple of weeks later.

Lily suspected the enjoyment had arisen more from spending time with Archie than with his sister, a girl whom Celia had obviously considered a strange creature. Still troubled by the suspicion that Celia had seen Artie in secret, Lily wondered if Celia was writing to him in secret too. Might his future job be at risk if Mr and Mrs Grover learned about it?

Lily considered mentioning her concerns when she wrote back to Artie but was afraid of worrying him when he needed all of his wits about him simply to stay alive. After all, there were enemy snipers on the watch.

She found herself wishing she could talk to Luke about the situation. Not only did he know what it was like to spend months away at the front, he was also in company with young and impressionable men like Artie all the time. He might have sensible advice to give about what, if anything, Lily should do.

But Luke had no expectation of being granted leave soon as far as she knew, and she was reluctant to write to him about personal matters anyway. It would be one thing to mention her concerns casually in conversation if it felt right at the time. Writing about them assumed a level of familiarity that she wasn't sure existed. Lily mentioned Art-

302

ie's visit in her next letter, but kept the tone light. Impersonal.

It wasn't until several weeks later that Pierre rushed into the bakery shop one morning shouting, 'Luke just telephoned. He's coming home! Merciful God, he's coming home!'

Luke arrived that afternoon. Dirty, unkempt but, judging from his smile, unbroken. 'I didn't want to walk past without saying hello,' he said, calling into the tea room on his way to his own shop next door.

Lily swallowed, fighting the urge to run to him. 'Hello, Luke.'

'I'm back as you can see, and in dire need of a bath.' He rubbed a hand along his unshaven jaw.

'You look like a pirate,' Lily said, smiling to hide his effect on her.

'You look like a flower of England.'

It sounded lovely but was it the sort of thing he'd have said to any English girl just then? Or was there a softer-hearted meaning behind the words aimed only at her?

'I still have no drinking chocolate, but if you'd like coffee...' she offered.

Luke shook his head. 'I'd drive your other customers away, looking like this. Besides, Pierre is expecting me.'

'Of course.'

'I'll see you again soon, I hope.'

'I hope so too.'

Elsie burst in a few minutes later. 'You're invited to a feast. Pierre is doing that French thing of throwing his hands in the air, kissing Luke's cheeks and promising a dinner fit for a king. Or

303

at least as fit for a king as he can make it, given rationing and food shortages. You'll all come?'

Certainly they'd all come. Michael was welcome too, Elsie said. The more, the merrier.

It was a lovely evening. Pooling their meat rations meant Pierre was able to get hold of a joint of beef which he cooked in wine with herbs, mushrooms and onions. He'd bought wine and beer to drink as well.

Luke had lost weight and gained fine lines at the corners of his eyes but he answered their questions about life at the front calmly, without dwelling on its tragedies. By unspoken agreement no one probed too deeply. It was a night for celebrating life instead and toasting the fact that women had been given the vote at last. 'Only if they're over thirty and have property, I understand, but it's a start,' Luke said. Then, 'How's the chocolate shop? How's the tea room?' he wanted to know, and so they told him, injecting humour and enthusiasm into their stories.

'And Artie's been home.' Luke turned to Lily.

'I was so pleased to see him,' she said, but Luke must have sensed that something was amiss because he stared at her for a moment then nodded as though to suggest they'd talk about it another time.

That time turned out to be later that evening when Luke invited Lily to go walking. 'Just a little stroll around,' he told her.

They said little at first, settling into a steady pace and absorbing the feel of the damp twilight air and relative quiet. Luke looked up at the dark sky occasionally.

At trees and building and gardens. Now and then he drew in deep breaths and let them out in sighs. 'Are you reminding yourself what you're fighting for?' she asked, remembering the way Artie had wanted to store up memories of London's landmarks.

'Mmm, though I suppose what I'm fighting for isn't just a place. Neither is it just about loyalty to King and country. It's about preserving freedom from aggression. Freedom for everyone, however humble.'

'You still don't regret leaving Switzerland?'

'Much as I love Switzerland, England is home. I don't regret joining the army either. Fighting is hellish but war brings out the best of humanity too — courage, self-sacrifice, the gentleness of soldiers caring for wounded comrades... How's Artie finding it?'

'He's managed well so far.'

'So you're anxious about him for another reason.'

Lily told him about Celia. 'I'm worried about what will happen to his job offer if her parents object to him courting their daughter.'

'And if they don't object?'

'I'm worried he might rush into proposing to her. I've heard of other young soldiers getting engaged or even married in an incredible rush.'

'The war seems to be making some people behave that way,' Luke admitted.

'I suppose it's about feeling alive and making every hour count when the future is so uncertain.'

'Would I sound like an interfering busybody if I said I think they need time to get to know each other before making any sort of commitment?'

Luke smiled. 'You'd sound like a sister who wants her brother to be happy.'

'I do. If I thought Celia would make him happy, I'd be glad for him even if I couldn't be part of his world.'

'But you're not convinced that Celia is the girl to make him so.'

'She's certainly beautiful and she might be a nice person too but I can't imagine her keeping house on a small budget or supporting Artie through life's ups and downs.' Lily *could* imagine Celia being expensive, demanding and easily discontented.

'Has Artie given even a hint that he intends to propose to her?' Luke asked.

'Do you think I'm foolish to worry about all this?'

'I just wonder if you're not getting a little too far ahead.'

'My grandmother used to say that worrying too soon is like inviting a trouble in when it might otherwise pass by.'

'Sensible woman. Artie's spent the last years cloistered in a boys' boarding school. It's hardly surprising if he's had his head turned by the first pretty girl to show an interest in him. But that doesn't mean he won't take the time to get to know her properly before making any sort of rash proposal.'

'I hope you're right.'

'If you want to know what I think, it's that you should trust Artie to figure things out for himself. He must realise it's unlikely Celia's parents will consent to their daughter rushing into a marriage or even a courtship with a man who's yet to establish himself in work let alone secure a home that's suitable for a wife.'

Luke paused then added, 'There's another reason why the Grovers might object to the relationship. Some men are returning home with terrible injuries and will never be the person they used to be, physically or any other way. Celia's parents might not wish their daughter to take the risk of being burdened with such a man for the rest of her life.'

Lily winced at the idea of darling Artie ever being considered a burden. But she was his twin. Her love for him was deep and enduring. Celia's affections might be shallower.

'It's an important consideration,' Luke continued. 'I'd never make any sort of commitment to a girl while I'm still fighting over there.'

He wasn't looking at Lily as he spoke but even so she wondered if he were sending her a message, warning her off because he'd guessed how much she liked him and either genuinely believed the time was wrong for romance or wanted to let her down gently as he didn't feel the same. She was aware of a blush rising but kept her voice steady as she said, 'Shall we cross the road to the bookshop? I'm always looking for books to send to Artie.'

If Luke had intended a hint, then she'd received it and would save them both from embarrassment by treating him as just one friend among many in future.

He gave no sign of wanting to avoid her in the

two days that followed. He worked beside her in the tea room for half a day, appeared happy for her to be included in shared meals and even invited her to walk out again on his last evening. Lily took pains to ensure she neither said nor did anything that crossed the line of friendship, but whether they were talking about the war or admiring London's buildings, it seemed to her that their thoughts and opinions sat comfortably together.

'I wish the war was over,' he said on that final walk.

Their gazes met and his expression looked tender to Lily's eyes but perhaps that was simply wishful thinking on her part. 'It has to end one day,' she said.

He nodded. The moment passed and they walked back home.

'Take care,' Lily urged, because he was returning to the front early the next morning.

'You too.'

He kissed her cheek and Lily closed her eyes momentarily to savour his touch.

But she opened them again as soon as his mouth left her cheek and even took a small step backwards as she smiled her final farewell.

Lily was in no doubt now that she was in love with Luke. It was unbearable.

But somehow she had to bear it just as she had to bear both Luke and Artie being in peril at the front.

One week later a telegram came.

28

It was Phyllis who brought the telegram upstairs. Phyllis who must have told Mr Bax of its arrival because he rushed up after her, bringing Elsie and Pierre from next door. They stood in the serving room as Lily tore the brown envelope open and scanned its contents with frightened eyes.

'Sit down,' Phyllis urged, pulling a chair forward because Lily's legs had gone weak. Then she took the telegram from Lily's trembling fingers and read it out loud.

'*Missing in Action*. That could mean anything,' Phyllis said.

'Lost in the confusion of battle,' Elsie suggested.

'Or captured,' offered Pierre.

'Or injured,' Mr Bax pointed out, adding quickly, 'Not necessarily badly, but he might be stuck in a field hospital somewhere.'

'It's much too soon to fear the worst,' Phyllis said.

Lily appreciated their efforts to console her but was much too distressed to speak. *Missing in Action* could also mean that Artie was… She shuddered.

It was sometimes said that a mystical connection between twins meant they'd sense instantly if the other were in trouble but Lily dug inside herself and felt no instinctive awareness of what had happened. She felt only fear and a pain so acute she wanted to slide off the chair and curl into a ball on the floor.

'We should close for the day,' Mr Bax said.

'No need for that,' Elsie told him. 'Pierre can manage next door so I'll take over here. If that's what Lily wants?'

Lily stared at her. Every thought was like a block of granite she had to drag into place. She managed a nod which she hoped would convey thanks as well as agreement and got to her feet.

'Do you want one of us to sit with you?' Phyllis asked.

Lily shook her head but squeezed Phyllis's arm to show she was grateful for her thoughtfulness. Upstairs in her room, Lily sat on her bed and studied the telegram again. *Missing. In action.* Groaning, Lily lay back.

Some time later Elsie tapped on the door then came in with tea and a small sandwich. 'Would it be stupid of me to ask how you're feeling?'

Lily sat up. 'Not stupid at all. Kind, in fact. But I think you know the answer.'

'It really would be stupid to tell you not to worry. But I *will* tell you to stay hopeful. From what I hear about this war, there's a lot of chaos over there.'

'I'm staying hopeful.'

'That's my girl. I'll leave you to your tea now.'

Lily sipped it slowly, surprised how welcome it was. She nibbled a little of the sandwich too though she hadn't much appetite. Crossing to the window, she stared out at the sky, praying for Artie still to be alive.

More time passed and Lily heard Elsie calling goodnight to departing customers. The tea room and shop were closing. Getting up, Lily headed downstairs.

'I can clear up,' Elsie assured her.

'I need to be busy.'

Elsie gave her a searching look. 'I suppose it's never been your way to give in, whatever life throws at you. All right. Help if you must, but don't feel you're being weak if you need to stop.'

Over the days that followed Lily worked as hard as ever though she slept little and her dozes were haunted by terrible dreams. Artie was in her thoughts constantly but to sit brooding was torment. Activity was much to be preferred.

Three days after the first one, another telegram arrived. Phyllis brought it up to the tea room, her face sombre. 'You should sit down,' she advised, but Lily couldn't delay a single second before she opened it.

She read it and swayed a little before she steadied herself, breathing out slowly as relief bathed her limbs in a feeling as soft as golden honey. 'He's alive. Artie's alive.'

'Thank God!' Phyllis ran to the top of the stairs and called the news down to Mr Bax who was pounding his way up with Elsie and Pierre following.

'Does it say what happened?' Elsie asked.

'Just that he's been wounded and he's in hospital. In England already.'

'Let's hope that means his wounds aren't bad,' Phyllis suggested.

'Which hospital?' Elsie wondered.

'A place called Elmsfield in Sussex.'

'Call it,' Elsie said. 'You can use our telephone.'

'*My* telephone,' Pierre corrected. 'But yes,

311

please use it to call.'

It took some time to be connected to a Matron who had information. Yes, Lieutenant Tomkins was there. Yes, he'd sustained a wound. A leg wound. No, he hadn't lost the leg and no, his life wasn't in immediate danger. Certainly, Lily could visit but it would be better if she waited and telephoned for more news tomorrow as Lieutenant Tomkins was still being assessed.

The Matron was unflustered but firm. Despite her eagerness to see Artie, Lily didn't insist on visiting earlier. The hospital staff needed to devote their time to looking after patients instead of being troubled by visitors.

'You must let me pay for the call,' Lily told Pierre.

Pierre wouldn't hear of it. Neither would he let her pay when she telephoned the hospital the next morning to be told that she might visit on the following afternoon. He gave her chocolates for Artie too, but Lily insisted on paying for others she hoped to give to the Tibbs sisters. Having learned that Elmsfield wasn't far from Hastings, Lily planned to call on them after seeing Artie, time permitting.

She walked from the station to the hospital, a distance of almost two miles but she was keen to save on taxi fares when possible. The hospital had been set up in an old mansion house and as she walked through the gardens Lily thought they'd be wonderfully soothing for patients to look out onto once they were sufficiently recovered. It was merely a passing thought, though. Lily was too worried about Artie to dwell on the future.

312

She was directed to a long ward that must once have been a gracious drawing-room. It had magnificent fireplaces at each end and several tall windows along the outside wall but now it was fitted-out with at least twenty beds arranged in two rows down the length of the room.

Lily was about to ask a white-aproned volunteer nurse for directions to Artie's bed when she saw him, halfway along the ward.

Emotions cascaded through her. Love. Anxiety. And then relief for, despite the cage that kept the blankets from touching his injured leg, he was sitting up, reading. Glancing round and seeing her, a smile of welcome dawned like sunshine on his beloved face. 'Lil!'

She hastened towards him then reached down and kissed him, wishing she could gather him up and hold him close. 'It's so good to see you!'

'It's good to see you too but I don't know why you're crying.'

Laughing, Lily dashed her tears away.

'I'd fetch a chair for you but I'm somewhat incapacitated so you'll have to fetch one yourself,' he said.

Looking round, Lily saw several chairs nearby. She brought one over and sat, unable to resist the urge to take Artie's hand. 'How are you?' she asked.

'They've saved the leg and they think I'll be able to walk well enough but running may be beyond me. I've been lucky to escape infection. Gangrene sets in with astonishing speed over there and — But enough of that.'

'What happened?'

313

'We were on a night raid of German trenches when a shell landed nearby. I was rescued the next day but a message to that effect got lost somehow.' He frowned. 'You didn't think that I was missing?'

'Only briefly,' Lily said, glossing over the agony of those three uncertain days. 'I soon heard that you'd been found. I'm sorry about your leg but at least you won't be going back to the fighting. Or so I assume?'

'I won't, and I'm thankful for it. But I can't help feeling bad for the chaps still over there.'

'You've played your part. You've no need to feel guilty.'

'No,' he agreed, but Lily could see he felt guilty anyway.

She could also see that, beneath his sweet smile, his face was wan. 'Have the doctors said how long you need to stay in here?' she asked.

'Not yet, but my impression is that it'll be weeks before they get me walking again.'

'Do you realise this place is only a couple of miles from Hastings? If you need to convalesce when you leave, perhaps Hilda and Marion will look after you.'

'Good idea,' Artie nodded. 'Now tell me some news. How are you, Lil? How is everyone else? How's the tea room?'

Lily laughed again. 'Give me a chance to answer!'

'Sorry. I just feel so … out of things.'

Lily told him about her friends and the businesses though she had nothing to say that she hadn't already mentioned in her letters.

'Have you heard from Luke?' he asked next.

314

Lily had been prepared for the question because it was natural for one soldier to be interested in another soldier's experiences, even if they'd never met. But her cheeks still felt warm as she answered. 'He always sounds in good spirits but I expect he feels grim much of the time.'

'All the chaps put on a show,' Artie said, then winced.

'You're in pain.'

'It's just a twinge.'

But he looked exhausted too. 'You need to rest.'

'It seems feeble for a chap to be tired when he's just lying in bed talking to his sister. Especially when she's come a long way to see him.'

'Can't be helped.' She got to her feet, returned the chair to its place against the wall and saw Artie was already drifting into sleep. 'I'll come again,' she said, kissing him.

She walked back into Hastings feeling immensely grateful that Artie was alive and likely to make a good recovery. He'd made no mention of Celia Grover.

Was that because one or both of them had lost interest in the relationship or because the Grovers had put a stop to it? Lily hadn't asked, not wanting to upset her brother when he was already low, but she hoped to find out as time went on.

Marion Tibbs answered the door to Lily's knock. 'What a lovely surprise! Come along in and I'll put the kettle on. Hilda's a little unwell as you'll see, but she'll be all the better for seeing you.'

Hilda did look unwell. She was sitting in an armchair, swathed in blankets, but her eyes glowed when Lily walked in. 'I'm so sorry you're ill,' Lily said, kissing her old friend's cheek.

'I'm just a bit badly in my chest but it's a real tonic to see you.'

Lily explained about Artie but made no mention of his convalescence.

Clearly, the sisters were in no fit state to look after anyone at the moment, though hopefully that might change.

Marion brought the tea and Lily spent an hour chatting about life in Highbury until she noticed Hilda starting to tire as Artie had done. 'I'll come again soon,' she told them, feeling a tug on her heart at Hilda's increasing frailty. 'You must both come to London too when you're well enough.'

'We will, we will,' they chorused, but Lily wondered if it might be too much for them. Even Marion looked tired.

Lily left them with hugs and sincere affection. Heading for the station she noticed a shop that sold flowers. Dashing in, she bought a bunch of daffodils and ran back to the sisters' house. 'I couldn't resist them,' she said, pushing them into Marion's hands.

'You already brought us chocolates!'

'You're two of my dearest friends,' Lily explained, and ran off to catch her train.

Back in Highbury, pleasure over Artie's good prognosis was tempered with concern for the Tibbs sister. 'I must visit them once I can persuade this slave driver to give me some time off,' Elsie said, scowling at Pierre who rolled his eyes.

'So must I,' Phyllis said.

'We'll close the tea shop occasionally if necessary,' Lily suggested. 'I know we need the income, but friends 'come first.'

She wrote to Artie that evening, mentioning Hilda's indisposition without dwelling on it as a serious concern. Artie had his own recovery to worry about.

She enclosed jokey notes from Elsie and Phyllis, knowing they'd cheer him up and also give him occupation in writing back. Two days later she received a reply in which Artie mentioned having received a parcel from Celia containing two issues of *Strand* magazine and a tin of Fortnum and Mason biscuits. *Wasn't that kind?* he wrote.

Lily wondered if Celia's parents knew of the parcel and, if so, whether they were aware of the attraction between Artie and their daughter. Again, Lily decided to wait and see what happened.

A letter also came from Luke. He'd got into the way of writing separate notes for each of them as he seemed to have decided that was the best way of feeding their interests. To Elsie he passed along jokes and funny stories. To Phyllis he wrote about the war and politics as far as was allowed when letters from the front were censored. To Lily he wrote about Artie, the cafés he managed to visit on rest periods, and his observations on anything from moonlit skies and forlorn flowers to the local children who'd only ever known life in a war.

In return Lily told him about the tea room, life in London and Artie's progress. She visited Artie for a second time a week later and was pleased to see he had more colour and sparkle. 'Have one of Celia's biscuits,' he suggested, nodding at the Fortnum's tin that stood on his bedside table as though in pride of place.

'Perhaps later,' Lily said.

Artie frowned. 'You do like Celia, don't you, Lil? She always speaks highly of you.'

For a moment Lily was unsure how to respond.

'She's such an angel,' Artie added.

'She looks exactly like an angel with that fair hair and those blue eyes,' Lily said, and was relieved to see Artie relax again.

She wondered if she should caution him against getting involved with Celia too quickly but remembered what Luke had said about trusting Artie to figure things out for himself. It was hard to break old ways of thinking but Artie wasn't her little brother running around the Bermondsey streets anymore. He was a grown man and might resent even well-meant interference. Besides, while he was injured and unwell he needed his spirits to be brought up instead of taken down.

She turned the conversation to Hilda and Marion. 'I'll look in on them before I leave,' she told him.

'You haven't actually asked if I might convalesce with them?'

'Not yet.'

'There's no need to put them to any trouble. It's been suggested I go to a convalescent home in Hampstead. I'll be closer to you, Lil. To the Grovers too.'

And especially to Celia. Had the suggestion been hers?

'I'll be able to start learning the business sooner,' he added.

'From your convalescent bed?'

'Mr Grover wants me to learn tenders, con-

318

tracts and schedules of work. I can do that easily from my bed as there's nothing wrong with my brain.'

'You'll need to rest.'

'Only some of the time.'

With that Lily had to be content.

She was glad to see Hilda looking a little better too, though nothing could take away the air of frailty that was creeping over both sisters despite the fact that neither was particularly old. Lily had brought more gifts — tinned pilchards, beef paste, marmalade, jam and tea as well as Mr Bax's bread and cakes. 'Just leftovers from the tea room,' she said, though that wasn't entirely true.

Worried that the sisters might be short of money as they were in no condition to take in paying guests, Lily had brought everything that could be spared from the bakery cupboards and trawled the shops for foodstuffs too.

'What a kind girl you are, Lily,' Marion said. 'You've always had a big heart.'

Lily took more supplies each time she visited though early in April Artie moved to the Hampstead convalescent home.

It had been agreed that Lily should be the one to visit the Tibbs sisters while Artie was in hospital but it was time to give the others a chance.

'I'm keen to visit,' Phyllis said. 'Now I have special news to share.'

'Special news?' Elsie asked.

Lily was puzzled too, but after a glance at Phyllis's deliciously happy face she looked down at Phyllis's left hand. 'You're engaged!' she cried, seeing a ring.

'Engaged?' Elsie questioned.

'To be married, of course,' Phyllis told her.

Elsie shrieked and threw her arms around her friend.

'You're crushing me!' Phyllis protested.

Lily joined in the hug. 'Congratulations, Phyll,' she said. 'I'm so happy for you. Michael is a lucky man.'

'I'm a lucky woman.'

'You're both lucky.' How lovely it must be to love someone and know you were loved in return.

Typically, Phyllis's ring was neat instead of fancy — a modest ruby with a modest diamond on each side. 'Very pretty,' Lily told her. 'That ruby suits you.'

'Red for a rebel,' Elsie agreed.

'I'm not a rebel exactly,' Phyllis said. 'I just like — '

'Fairness and justice,' Lily supplied.

'Exactly.'

'Pierre should cook a celebratory dinner,' Elsie said.

'You can't *ask* him to cook,' Phyllis protested. 'He might not want to bother.'

'I've no intention of *asking* him. I'm going to *tell* him.'

With that Elsie left, returning later to report that Pierre would cook dinner two nights later. 'Mr B and his sisters are coming. Is Artie well enough to come?'

'I doubt it, but I'll let him know he's invited,' Lily said.

Artie sent a note saying he couldn't be at the dinner in body but he'd be there in spirit. *I'll drink a toast to Phyllis and Michael from the comfort of my armchair with my gammy leg up on a stool,* he wrote, *even if the toast is only tea.*

It was a lovely evening but, despite being delighted by her friend's happiness, Lily woke the next morning struggling to catch hold of some happiness of her own. As always, she reminded herself of her blessings. Artie had survived the war. Luke was still alive as far as she knew. She had friends and work she enjoyed. Even so Lily's heart ached when she thought Luke might not love her and Artie might be heading for disappointment too.

But it did no good to brood and who knew what the future might hold? Lily got up and went about her day.

'You should take Artie some cake,' Phyllis suggested, for Mr Bax had baked a cake to celebrate her engagement.

Artie was delighted to receive it. 'You'll pass on my thanks to Phyllis and Michael?' he asked, then his attention was caught by someone coming into the lounge. Celia.

She looked exquisite though a little disconcerted to see Lily. Not that she let her manners slip, but there was awkwardness in her greeting as though she had no idea what she and Lily were going to find to talk about. 'I've brought more papers from my father, Artie,' she said.

'Excellent. I've finished with these ones.' He passed an envelope to her. 'Is Violet still unwell?'

'Another headache,' Celia said, but her cheeks turned a soft shade of pink and Lily guessed she was lying.

Violet had stayed behind because Celia wanted to be alone with Artie. The fact that the sisters had conspired about it suggested to Lily that Mr and Mrs Grover preferred Celia to be chaperoned when acting as messenger for the business. Was that because they wanted to impose a boundary with the boss's daughter on one side and the humble employee on the other? It wasn't as though Mr and Mrs Grover had visited Artie as friends might have done.

'Your father is busy, I expect,' Lily said.

'Yes, it's difficult to keep staff when there's a war on.'

'So I imagine. He's lucky he can ask you and your sister to carry messages for him.'

Celia nodded but another blush gave away the fact that she'd done the asking.

She turned back to Artie. 'Oh, Artie, I saw the sweetest little dog on the journey here. I'd love to have a dog one day. I'd have one now if dogs didn't make Mother sneeze.'

'I like dogs too,' Artie said, going on to tell Celia about the neighbour's dog he'd exercised when living with Mr Alderton as a boy.

'If I had a dog, it might eat all the food in the tea room,' Lily said.

'I can just picture Mr Bax running after it shaking a tea towel,' Artie said, smiling.

'How is your little tea room?' Celia asked. 'I thought it was very … quaint.'

'I enjoy working there very much.'

'How nice.' Clearly, it didn't sound at all nice to Celia.

322

Lily didn't stay much longer. 'I'll come again,' she told Artie, and left Celia with another compliment on her choice of hat, another delicious confection that boasted surprisingly realistic pink fabric roses.

Once again, Celia looked at Lily's clothes and settled for a smile.

'You won't forget to thank Phyllis and Michael for the cake?' Artie said.

'Such a happy event, an engagement.'

Celia smiled at him adoringly and Lily walked away with an anxious heart.

29

Towards the end of April Artie moved into lodgings in Kentish Town, not far from the Grover's office and building yard. Lily was allowed to visit and was pleased to find that, once his landlady had overcome her suspicion that Lily might not in fact be Artie's sister, she was strict but fair. She was also a believer in building young men up with as good food as could be managed in wartime.

Artie was using just a stick for support and keen to reach the moment when he wouldn't need any support at all.

'This is a new beginning,' he told Lily, eyes shining. 'I've had the best of good luck in receiving an education and surviving the war. Now it's time I made something of myself and also made good on my promise to help you.'

'You're a dear but don't feel you have to look after me. I'm just fine running the tea room.'

'You're an inspiration, Lil. But you should still be able to fall back on me.'

Was he thinking of the tea room closing when Mr Bax finally retired? Even then Lily hoped to be independent somehow. It gave her a sense of pride to stand on her own two feet. Besides, Artie might need all his resources for himself, especially if he actually married Celia.

Once again Lily longed to pour all her concerns into a letter to Luke but feared she'd be assuming an intimacy that didn't exist. She still felt her heartbeat quicken when Elsie came in the following day and announced, 'Letters from Luke.'

She passed one to Phyllis and another to Lily. 'I'll read mine later,' Lily said as though a note from Luke was pleasant but of no great significance.

She needn't have bothered. Elsie had that knowing look in her eyes again.

Lily turned away to avoid it. She tied an apron around her waist and slipped her feet into comfortable shoes. When she glanced around again Elsie was staring at her reflection in the small mirror they kept in the serving room so they could ensure they stayed neat and tidy through the day.

It wasn't like Elsie to look in mirrors. She stepped away quickly when she realised Lily had noticed. 'Just wondering if I should cut my hair,' she said.

'Any particular reason?' Lily asked.

Elsie shrugged. 'Maybe it's time for a change.'

'You have lovely hair. So thick and healthy.'

'So orange,' Elsie mocked.

'Distinctive.'

'Easy for you to say when your hair's dark and silky. Anyway, I suppose I'd better go and do some work before Pierre starts whining.'

'Pierre never — ' Lily began but Elsie had already left.

Artie's walking improved rapidly and it wasn't long before he stopped using the stick for all but the longest walks. 'Do you think you might be able to come over to me for a visit?' Lily asked. 'The others would love to see you.'

He came one May evening to celebrate his and

325

Lily's nineteenth birthdays.

'I'm enjoying the new job,' he told them enthusiastically. 'Grover's builds all over London but I'm based in the office at the moment. I'm meeting lots of interesting people, including members of the council as they give us some of our contracts.'

'It sounds an excellent opportunity,' Phyllis's Michael told him.

'Michael has a new job too,' Lily said, hoping to keep Artie off the subject of Celia. 'Michael and Phyll have their diplomas now.'

'Congratulations, both of you. You're keeping accounts for a furniture manufacturer, I believe?' Artie asked Michael.

'It's my first job in accounting. I'm keen to do well.'

'Of course, especially as you're going to marry Phyll.'

Did all roads lead back to marriage and Celia? 'Phyllis has taken on the chocolate shop accounts,' Lily said. 'That's in addition to the bakery and tea room.'

'I'll still be working in the bakery shop, though,' Phyllis said.

'Have you made plans for the wedding?' Artie wondered.

'We're busy saving,' Phyllis told him. 'Not for a fancy wedding. We'll be happy with a small occasion as long as we have the people we love around us. But we need to set up a home of our own as well.'

Artie nodded as though he too faced that challenge. Then he smiled. 'We're hardworking people.

There's no reason to think we won't succeed, is there?'

'None at all,' Michael agreed.

Their circumstances weren't the same, though. Phyllis would be content with a modest home but the same couldn't be said of Celia. As for Lily herself, she'd gladly live in a freezing garret with Luke.

★ ★ ★

More weeks passed. Artie was loving his job and developing a good working relationship with Mr Melling, who oversaw the actual building work. Mr Grover had declared himself pleased with Artie's progress though Lily had heard no mention of Artie being invited to the family home as a friend.

An awful sense of foreboding settled on her shoulders when she thought of Artie.

She was worried about the Tibbs sisters too. Both Phyllis and Elsie had visited and shared Lily's concerns about the sisters' health, particularly Hilda's. Lily returned to Hastings herself and what she saw upset her badly. Hilda was losing substance fast. Her frame looked lighter, her hair wispier and her skin felt thin to the touch.

Lily took Marion aside. 'Have you had a doctor in to see her? If you're worried about the fee, I can — '

'Bless you, Lily, but Hilda has seen a doctor. He said that none of us last forever and Hilda's time might be drawing near.'

'But why? What's wrong with her? Can't he help?'

'Hilda's health is simply declining. If it isn't one thing troubling her, it's another.'

Lily swallowed, the tears in her eyes feeling like needles. Marion took her hand and squeezed it. 'The doctor is right. None of us last forever and Hilda and I have lived longer than many, especially when you consider all the poor young men losing their lives in the war.'

But Hilda was barely sixty. Far too young to fade away. 'If I can't pay for a doctor, you must let me help in other ways,' Lily insisted.

'I won't deny that some help will be welcome. But you have a tea room to run. Please don't do more than you can reasonably manage.'

Lily took to visiting the sisters every week, travelling down on Saturday evenings once the tea room had closed and returning late on Sundays. She spent the time cleaning, shopping and cooking then reading to her friends from books or chatting with them about old times as well as Lily's life in London. She always took food supplies, including homemade soup, fruit and vegetables, to keep them going until her next visit.

Spending more time with them meant spending less time with Artie though Lily never missed a chance to see him no matter how weary she was. Artie had always been sweet-natured and that hadn't changed, but he was maturing before her eyes, bristling with ambition and purpose. If only Lily could be sure he wasn't heading for disappointment.

One day Celia accompanied him to the tea room again.

'Give me your honest opinions of her,' Lily

328

asked Elsie and Phyllis afterwards, needing to be sure that her own concerns were justified.

'Spoilt princess,' Elsie declared without hesitation.

'I agree,' Phyllis said. 'I don't think she has the sharpest brain in the universe either though perhaps that's only because she's never had to wake it up.'

Elsie stood, saying she had chocolate boxes to fill but she looked back when she reached the door. 'People don't choose who they love, Lily. Sometimes love just happens,' she said.

Was Elsie thinking of Luke and suggesting it was hypocritical of Lily to object to Artie falling in love when she'd done the same with Luke? But Luke was no Celia. Even if he didn't return Lily's regard, he was clever, shrewd and grounded in the world of hard work.

Lily couldn't write to Luke about Artie but it was a relief to be able to write to him about Hilda and Marion, *though perhaps I shouldn't burden you with troubles from home when you're faced with danger every day*, she wrote.

No, you should, Luke replied. *It helps me to know that the natural cycle of life continues at home. It's far from natural here. Try not to dwell on the fact that Hilda's light is fading but cherish the way she's enriched your life through love.*

Luke was right. Hilda was reaching her end naturally with many years of life behind her. Not that it made losing her easy to bear. Lily's heart crumpled every time she left the sisters, wondering if she'd ever see Hilda again.

Then one day Elsie came into the tea room

looking grave. 'Marion just telephoned. Hilda's taken a turn for the worse.'

'I'll go to her,' Lily said, unfastening her apron. 'I'll take over in here.'

'Thank you. But if we have to close the tea room, then that's what we'll do.'

Lily ran up to her room to pack some overnight things then raced down to the shop.

'Wait!' Mr Bax cried.

He gave her a bag of food supplies. 'Only what I had to hand but I hope they'll help.'

Lily hugged him but couldn't speak because her throat was too tight.

'Telephone Pierre's shop when there's news,' Mr Bax urged.

It was evening when she arrived in Hastings. Had she arrived too late to say goodbye to her old friend? Marion opened the door to her and Lily was dismayed to see how tired she looked. 'I'm so sorry,' Lily said, touching a hand to Marion's arm. 'Am I...?'

'You're in time. Come along in. Hilda is in bed. Go up while I make some tea.'

Lily went upstairs where Hilda lay looking small and faded. But she smiled when she saw Lily and raised a weak hand. Lily took it, kissing Hilda's cheek then sitting in the chair beside the bed to stroke the wasted fingers. 'It's so good of you to come,' Hilda said.

'Where else would I be when my precious friend needs me?'

Hilda died peacefully as the room was lightening to the pearly grey of morning, Lily sitting on one side of her and Marion sitting on the other.

330

They took turns to kiss Hilda's forehead then sat with her for a while longer, quietly shedding tears.

'Thank you for coming,' Marion finally said. 'It made Hilda's passing easier for her and you're a great support to me.'

Lily patted Hilda's arm and went downstairs, setting the kettle to boil then standing at the kitchen window watching the first birds venture into the small garden until more tears blurred her vision. Another era of her life was over, another beloved person gone, and the sadness was intense.

She didn't rush to make the tea, wanting to allow the sisters time alone. When Lily eventually returned upstairs, Marion turned a ravaged yet accepting face to her. 'I've been lucky,' she said. 'Some brothers and sisters find it hard to rub along together but I was blessed in having a sister like Hilda.'

Lily thought of Artie and felt another pang of worry but it wasn't the time to dwell on her own woes.

They drank their tea sitting beside Hilda as the world outside continued to stir into life. But there were arrangements to be made. Lily touched Marion's arm and they returned downstairs. 'The funeral,' Lily began. 'I'd consider it an honour if you'd let me help to pay for it.'

'It's kind of you, but Hilda and I have money put by for our funerals. I'd welcome your help with the arrangements, though. The undertakers are Collins & Sons. Could you call in and tell them we need them? I'd be grateful if you'd telephone the doctor too.'

Lily went out to see the undertakers and telephoned both the doctor and Pierre. 'I'm sorry,' Pierre said when he heard the news, his words sounding simple but heartfelt.

'Is Elsie there?' Lily asked.

'She's looking after the tea room again this morning. Phyllis will work in there this afternoon.'

'But that'll leave you and Mr Bax short of help.'

'We were all up early to prepare.'

How kind they were. Fresh tears sprang into Lily's eyes. She blinked and swallowed hard. 'I'll telephone again when I know more about the funeral.'

There was someone else she had to telephone — Artie. She called the Grover's office and was relieved to find him there. 'Give Marion my love,' he told her.

The doctor and funeral directors duly came and went about their business then Marion produced a wide ribbon of black crepe and tied it to the doorknocker.

'It's the ribbon our parents used when family members passed on,' she said.

'Tradition is good. Comforting.'

They kept the curtains drawn over the windows at the front of the house but open in the kitchen where they sat at the table. Lily warmed some of the soup she'd brought and encouraged Marion to eat as they talked about the funeral arrangements. 'It'll be a small affair with few mourners,' Marion explained.

'But those mourners loved your sister dearly. That's what matters.'

Marion smiled and they spent the afternoon reminiscing about Hilda's life — about how she'd

332

loved barley sugars but hated pear drops, about her amazement when she'd first seen Buckingham Palace and heard that Queen Victoria really lived behind all those windows, about her talent for cooking, and about how much she'd enjoyed hearing news of Lily's Tea Room.

Towards evening Marion reached for Lily's hand. 'I'll be glad of your company tonight, Lily. It's the first night without Hilda so it's bound to be hard. I'll be grateful if you'd stay in the morning too, to help me to write to the people who need to know what's happened. But then you should go home.'

Lily began to protest.

'You have a tea room to run. Hilda wouldn't like to think of you closing it on her account. And I need to begin adjusting to my changed circumstances.'

Marion needed time to grieve alone and, realising it, Lily nodded.

She spent a busy morning finalising arrangements with the undertakers, buying black-edged notepaper for Marion to use for her letters, and buying enough food to keep her going for a few days.

'You mustn't worry about the funeral tea,' Lily told her. 'I'll take care of that.'

'Thank you, dear. That's a weight off my mind.'

'I'll be back the night before the funeral to get everything ready, but don't hesitate to telephone Pierre if you want me to come sooner or just need to hear a friendly voice. And afterwards... You must come and stay with me for a while.'

Lily saw little of the countryside on the journey back to London. She sat beside a window but her vision was blurred by tears and her thoughts turned inwards. She shed more tears when she arrived home to be wrapped in the arms of both Phyllis and Elsie. But then she dried her eyes and blew her nose. 'I must get to work,' she said. 'It gave Hilda a lot of pleasure to think of me making a success of the tea room. Work feels a more fitting tribute to her than moping.'

Artie called in during the evening, holding Lily and stroking her hair as she sobbed again. 'I'll explain to Mr Grover that I really must have the time off for the funeral,' he said.

They decided to close both shops as well as the tea room on the day of the funeral. It was the only way they could all attend.

Lily travelled down the evening before and found Marion grieving but calm.

The next morning Lily set up the dining room with plates and cutlery ready for the cold meats and cakes she'd brought for the funeral tea. She set out glasses too as Mr Bax and Pierre were bringing sherry.

The weather kept fine for the church service and burial. Afterwards, they returned to the house for the food. 'Have you thought about coming to stay with me for a while?' Lily asked Marion.

'Bless you, Lily. Perhaps I'll come one day but just now I want to be near Hilda.'

'You'll look after yourself?'

'I shan't be foolish.'

Lily was worried all the same. Marion was composed — heroically so — but Lily wondered if she'd simply go through the motions of life until

334

she was reunited with her sister.

'You needn't worry about me,' Marion insisted. 'I feel my best years are behind me but at my age there's nothing wrong in that. I'll be perfectly content visiting Hilda's grave and hearing your news now and again.'

'I'll write often,' Lily promised.

They ensured Marion's house was spotless and her pantry well-stocked before setting out for London. Artie accompanied them all to Highbury but declined to come inside. 'I need to catch up on some paperwork.'

'Don't tire yourself.'

'I like to work. I need to work too if I'm to have a comfortable future.' He hesitated then added, 'You must know how I feel about Celia, Lil. I'm going to wait until I've proved myself to Mr Grover for a while longer then I'm going to speak to him about her. Obviously I'm not in a position to propose marriage yet, but I'd like his permission to court Celia formally. Wish me luck?'

30

Afterwards Lily felt grateful to the stranger who happened to be walking along the pavement towards them just then. His approach gave Lily an excuse to step aside to make room for him and in the process she made a supreme effort to hide her distress.

'There's nothing I want more than for you to be happy,' she told Artie, because that at least was true.

They parted and Lily went inside, climbing the stairs to the tea room on heavy feet. 'You look all-in,' Phyllis remarked.

'Artie's planning to ask Celia's father for permission to court her.'

'You don't think he'll get it?'

'Either way I'm worried for him. He'll be terribly disappointed if Mr Grover refuses and it might make it awkward for him to continue working for the family. But if Mr Grover consents, I'm worried Celia will make Artie unhappy after a while. Can you honestly see her settling down to the sort of modest life he can offer?'

'No,' Elsie said. 'But I can perfectly imagine that pretty mouth turning discontented.'

'So what's to be done?' Phyllis wondered.

'Lily will just have to be ready to comfort Artie when it all goes wrong,' Elsie said. 'Unless you have any better ideas?'

Phyllis hadn't.

Unable to resist writing to Luke about her worries, she wasn't surprised when he wrote back to say he agreed with Elsie.

It isn't for me to give advice, but my opinion (if you want it) is that interfering risks alienating Artie however things turn out. If he's rejected by the Grovers, he'll feel a fool once he knows you expected him to be rejected all along, while if he goes ahead and marries Celia, he'll know you have a poor opinion of his wife. Neither possibility will make for a comfortable relationship with you going forward.

Deciding Luke was right, Lily reconciled herself to waiting to see what happened though she felt as though a clock was ticking in a countdown to doom.

Meanwhile life went on and Pierre announced that he wanted to take them out to celebrate his birthday. 'You'll have to get a new dress,' Phyllis told Elsie.

'No one's going to notice a little scorch mark,' Elsie argued, having ruined her only decent dress with an iron.

'The scorch mark is huge,' Phyllis insisted.

Elsie went shopping a few days later but wasn't in the best of humours on her return. 'I don't know why I was persuaded to buy this dress.' She threw the box onto her bed. 'It's going straight back.'

'At least let us see it on you,' Phyllis pleaded.

Elsie resisted until Lily joined in the urging. 'Oh, for goodness' sake!' Elsie said then. 'I'll put

337

it on just to shut you up, but it's still going back.'

The dress was form-fitting and a deep forest green that complemented Elsie's red hair beautifully. 'You look incredible,' Lily declared.

'I look awful.'

'It's striking,' Phyllis argued.

'Precisely. There's no way I'm going to stand out in the crowd looking even more of an idiot than usual.'

'You could wear it again to my wedding.'

'Weddings!' Elsie rolled her eyes and stormed off to change.

She swapped the green dress for a mediocre brown one but seemed to be no happier with it. In fact, it gradually dawned on Lily that Elsie didn't appear to be happy with anything.

'Are you all right?' Lily finally asked.

'Why shouldn't I be all right?'

Goodness. It wasn't like Elsie to snap. 'I don't know. But if there's something troubling you, I — '

'Stop nagging me!'

Lily stared at her and saw Elsie's irritation give way to awkwardness.

'Sorry. That came out stronger than intended,' Elsie said. 'I suppose all the wedding talk is getting on my nerves. If it isn't Phyllis talking about her wedding, it's you worrying about Artie marrying Celia.'

Unfair! Phyllis only occasionally mentioned her wedding and Lily was trying hard not to keep mentioning Artie.

Elsie appeared to realise it because she sighed. 'I'm just not much of a person for weddings. It's not as though I'm ever going to have one.'

'You can't know that. Phyllis thought she'd never get married until she met Michael.'

'I'm not Phyllis.'

'But — '

'Let's make a bargain. I won't be grumpy about weddings if you stop fussing over me.'

With that Elsie walked off. In the days that followed she appeared to be making an effort to be more tolerant though she didn't seem to be quite herself and her riotousness at Pierre's birthday dinner in a West End restaurant came over to Lily as forced, as though Elsie were putting on an act.

But it was unreasonable to expect Elsie to be cheerful all the time. Lily wasn't particularly cheerful herself.

There seemed to be cause for worry every way she turned — Artie, Luke, Elsie, Mr Bax's inevitable retirement and also Marion.

Lily visited her again in Hastings. Marion looked both pleased to see her and at peace with the world but once again Lily felt that her friend was simply waiting patiently to be reunited with Hilda. Lily made tea and served the cake she'd brought. 'It's delicious,' Marion declared.

Worried about Marion, it didn't occur to Lily that Marion might also be worrying about her until, some while later, the older woman reached for her hand. 'It's an anxious time but it won't help anyone if you let your worries get on top of you. Get out there and achieve your dreams.'

Lily smiled. 'I'll certainly do my best.'

'Good. Now, if you won't think me rude, I'd welcome a little doze.'

'Of course,' Lily told her. 'I'll go for a walk.'

A stiff breeze was blowing when Lily made her way down to the seafront.

How invigorating it was. Breathing in the clean salty air, Lily made some resolutions:

She'd follow Luke's advice with regard to Artie so her brother would have no hesitation in leaning on her for support if he was rejected by the Grovers or if he married Celia and found himself unhappy. There'd be no, 'I told you so,' from Lily.

She'd continue to wait and see what happened with Luke while keeping a close guard on her feelings so he had no reason to feel embarrassed.

In the meantime she'd focus her energies on making a success of the tea room.

Mr Bax had assured her that he was still in no hurry to retire while Phyllis had said she had no intention of turning into a stay-at-home sort of wife when she married Michael. Phyllis was sure to want to move on to a better job in time, but until then she was happy to build her experience by looking after their own accounts.

Lily turned back to her friend's house feeling more purposeful. But Artie was waiting for her when she reached London and what she saw in his face made her heart beat fast with dread.

31

'I've been a fool,' Artie said, upstairs in Lily's room.

Not wanting to blunder into a wrong conclusion, she waited for him to say more

'I went to the Grovers' house today and asked Mr Grover for a private word in his study.' Artie's mouth twisted. 'It didn't go at all well.'

'I'm sorry.' It grieved Lily to see her darling brother in pain.

'Mostly, I've seen Celia when she's brought papers *to* the office or collected papers *from* the office. We've only actually walked out together a few times. I had no idea that Celia's parents thought she was with Violet or other friends on those occasions.'

'Celia lied to them?'

Artie winced. 'Little white lies, perhaps, but told with the best of intentions, I'm sure. I've been hoping to prove my worth to Mr Grover and I'm sure Celia was hoping for the same thing.'

'He doesn't think you're worthy of her?'

'He was angry. He accused me of being an upstart who'd taken advantage of my position – a position given to me out of charity – to ingratiate myself with Celia in the hope of ingratiating myself into her family's wealth as well.'

'You'd never do that, Artie.'

'Of course I wouldn't, but Celia's father scoffed when I told him I was motivated only by love. He

341

told me he wasn't born yesterday and he knew ambition when he saw it. And if I thought I was getting my feet under his table I was very much mistaken. I *am* ambitious, Lil, but not in the way he thinks.'

'I know that, Artie.'

'I told him that Celia loved me in return but he jeered at that too. He suggested I'd used my looks and charms to win over an impressionable girl but she'd soon realise her mistake once she knew what sort of life she'd have with me because he – Grover – had no intention of stumping up even a farthing. I argued that he was underestimating Celia because she wasn't that shallow but he said we'd soon see about that and called her in.'

'You saw her?'

'He repeated the insults he'd thrown at my head then asked her how she'd really feel about the life I could offer her. No fancy clothes, no fripperies, no Belsize Park elegance but only mean little rooms in some shabby part of London with no servants to help so Celia would have to cook and clean herself while making every penny count. No more moving in their social circle either, so no dinners or parties or charity balls. Just worries over how to pay the bills.'

'What did Celia say?'

'She cried. Don't judge her harshly, though. Mr Grover can be an overbearing man. I told her I knew I couldn't provide for her at present but had every intention of making something of myself if she could only be patient.'

'And?'

'At that point her father told me to get out of

342

his house before he kicked me out. And if I didn't keep to my place in future, he'd kick me out of my job as well.'

'He doesn't know how honourable you are.'

'No, he doesn't.'

Despite his hurt, Artie was full of fight. 'You know the worst thing Grover said? He said I may have a public school accent but I was a nobody from the back streets of Bermondsey with a sister who was just a waitress in a cheap tea shop. There's no *just* anything about you, Lil. You're the finest person I know. Grover may have riches, but you have courage, cleverness and kindness. You're worth ten of him.'

Lily was touched. She reached for Artie's hand and squeezed it.

'I was foolish in thinking he might have accepted me as a suitor for Celia but I'm not going to crawl away,' Artie said. 'I'm going to fight for the sort of life I think has value. I don't mean financial value particularly, though I hope not to be desperately poor, but satisfaction, challenge and fulfilment.'

'Good for you, Artie.'

'I expect Grover thinks I'm thanking my lucky stars I haven't been dismissed from my job but the fact is that I'm useful to him. I'm good at my job. I'm keen, organised and efficient, and I get on with the men. Melling, the foreman, has told me they respect me because I'm fair. I'll bide my time for the moment but I won't be at Grover's for long.'

'And Celia?'

'I told her I still loved her when I came away.

343

She couldn't answer through her tears but I won't lose faith in her. Not yet. She isn't like us, Lil. She's had luxury and position all her life. It's only natural for her to be scared about a future without them. A future with the wrath of her father hanging over her too.'

Lily made no answer. She was sad to see Artie brought low but filled with pride over his determination to make a life on his own terms. It was as though he were transforming from boy to man before her eyes.

Lily had to make a life on her terms too but the next morning fate threw down potential disaster in the form of an injury to Mr Bax. 'The stupidest thing,' he said, arriving with a bandaged hand. 'I dropped a glass last night and was clumsy picking up the pieces. It's quite a deep cut so heaven knows how I'm going to manage.'

A baker needed two hands for mixing, beating, stirring, decorating...

There was nothing for it but for Lily and Phyllis to pitch in and help, following his instructions as best they could so they had at least some bread and cakes to sell. Pierre came round to help too as his shop already had sufficient supplies to last for the morning if not longer. They managed to make enough baked goods to get them through that first day but the choice was limited and there'd barely been time to prepare the bakery shop or tea room properly.

'We need an extra pair of hands,' Lily said. Her thoughts touched upon Artie for a moment but a temporary job helping in a bakery wasn't what he needed.

344

Artie was on fire to make his own way in the world.

'I'm not sure I can offer my hands tomorrow,' Elsie said. 'I'll be needed in the chocolate shop while Pierre works in the kitchen to make up for missing most of today.'

Lily was struck by how miserable Elsie sounded and suspected there was more to it than sympathy for Mr Bax and his situation. 'Is something upsetting you?' Lily asked.

'Why should something have upset me?' Elsie was back to snapping.

Lily shrugged, waited for Elsie to leave the room then looked at Phyllis enquiringly.

'I don't know what's wrong with her,' Phyllis said. 'I've tried to get to the bottom of it but Elsie just snaps or walks away.'

'I'll talk to her,' Lily said.

'Choose your moment wisely,' Phyllis advised, then changed the subject. 'I wonder if Frankie might come and help Mr Bax?'

'Michael's little brother?'

'He's working in his uncle's glazing business at the moment but he doesn't enjoy fitting windows. He'd like to be a chef so he's thinking of applying for work as a kitchen boy though that wouldn't necessarily give him a chance to attempt actual cooking.'

Michael had brought Frankie to visit one day and Lily remembered him as a fresh-faced lad who'd been fascinated by the bakery. 'Helping Mr Bax wouldn't be a permanent job,' she pointed out.

'I'm sure Frankie's uncle will let him help out

345

here for a while. He'll probably be glad to get rid of him as Frankie isn't much of a glazier. Even a few days' work will give Frankie the chance to see what it's like to work in a kitchen and help him to decide if it's really what he wants. He won't expect to be paid much, if anything.'

Maybe so, but Lily didn't want the boy to be exploited. They'd have to pay him something even if it meant dipping into Lily's small savings. 'His uncle will take him back afterwards?'

'I'm confident he will.'

'In that case ...'

'I'll run round and tell him the good news.'

Frankie arrived the following morning, lanky and untidy but with a giant grin.

'I hope you're stronger than you look,' Mr Bax said.

'I'm a strong as a donkey,' Frankie assured him.

'I think you mean you're as strong as an ox.'

'Do I? Sorry. I'm not good with words.'

'Well, let's get started. Scrub your hands and forearms — not forgetting your fingernails — while I look out an apron and hat. We can't have that thatch of straw on top of your head flopping over the food.'

Frankie was a great success.

'The lad has a real feel for the job,' Mr Bax reported. 'And he never seems to tire.'

Mr Bax shook his head wonderingly and Lily guessed he was comparing Frankie's energy with his own depleting reserves. The thought reminded her that it was August already and the tea room would have been open for two years once they reached October.

346

It couldn't be much longer before Mr Bax retired. He had his health to consider and his sisters' wellbeing too. Beatrice and Betty came to the tea room often and always said how much they enjoyed it but neither of them was getting any younger. In the past months alone Beatrice had suffered an eye infection that took a long time to clear while Betty had strained her back.

Thinking about the tea room closing or continuing in someone else's hands brought a heavy feeling to Lily's stomach. It was so much more than a job to her, but she'd have to bear its loss bravely.

'I've decided to keep Frankie on,' Mr Bax said then.

Lily blinked. 'Permanently?'

'I've told him I can't promise him work forever but he says the same thing you've always said — that you want the experience anyway. Don't worry about his wages because I'll be settling them.' He paused then added, 'I'll give you fair warning when I finally decide to sell up.'

'Please don't keep going just for my sake.'

'I'm not. This tea room — and you young people — have given me a new lease of life. My sisters too. Even the problems we face remind us that we're still alive, and none of us want to waste our time staring at four walls at home.'

Lily was enormously relieved to be granted a reprieve for at least a few more months. She planned new menus and decorations with enthusiasm but continued to worry over Elsie. Unfortunately, Lily's attempts to get her to talk met only with irritation.

347

Lily spoke to Phyllis again.

'I wonder if she's feeling lonely?' Phyllis said. 'I know she's never seemed to care for the idea of a husband but perhaps she's changing her mind now she's seeing others beginning to settle down.'

'I'm not settling down with anyone,' Lily pointed out.

'Not yet. But I expect you soon will be.'

Had Phyllis guessed how Lily felt about Luke too? Lily's stomach gave a painful squeeze. Phyllis didn't know what Luke had said to Lily when he was home on leave, of course.

'I heard Elsie and Pierre bickering last week and it got rather sharp,' Phyllis continued. 'I don't think they were joking either.'

Lily cornered Elsie a few days later. 'Please talk to me. I know something's wrong.'

'Are you Lily the Mind Reader now? You should make a fortune on the stage instead of running yourself ragged serving people in a tea shop.'

'If you don't want to talk to me, perhaps you could talk to Phyllis.'

'And say what? That Lily the Mind Reader thinks … What do you think, Lily?'

'That you're not particularly happy.'

'This war's been going on for four long years with no end in sight. I'm tired of it all. Tired of hearing about death and injury, and all the people who'll spend the rest of their lives suffering in one way or another.'

'Are you worried that with so many young men losing their lives, there'll be none left for you to meet?'

'You think I want to meet a man?' Elsie looked

incredulous.

'It's a possibility.'

'Tall? Handsome? Gallant?'

Lily shrugged.

'Let me tell you, hand on heart, that meeting a tall, handsome, gallant stranger is the last thing I need.'

'I only — '

But Elsie had already walked away, shaking her head as though despairing at Lily's stupidity.

Lily reported the conversation to Phyllis. 'The war is terrible but I can't believe Elsie's been overcome by it,' Phyllis said. 'Elsie's strong. A fighter.'

'Will you try talking to her again?'

'Yes, but I doubt that I'll do any good.'

She was right. Phyllis got nowhere either.

Over the days that followed Elsie appeared to be making an effort to be more like her old self but the fact that it required effort meant it wasn't how she really felt. Lily supposed they'd just have to wait and see what Elsie did next.

One evening Lily sat down to read a letter from Luke. It was friendly.

Personal even in the way he described a walk he'd taken during a rest period. He wrote of the trees he'd seen, and how they were balm to the soul after the shattered stumps that were all that remained of trees on the battlefield. But he finished the letter the same way he finished his letters to Elsie and Phyllis: *Missing you all. Fond regards, Luke.*

Sighing, Lily set it aside only for her thoughts to settle on Artie. She'd been on her way to meet him for a walk the previous Sunday when she'd seen Celia emerging from a rather smart house arm in arm with a young man dressed in army uniform. A tall, good-looking man, as far as Lily could see. She'd hung back, watching as the couple approached a motor car that stood at the roadside.

The man opened the passenger door for Celia and she looked up, smiling, as he spoke to her. Then she laughed, a silvery sound that carried on the quiet, Sunday afternoon air. They'd driven away and soon were out of sight.

Lily wondered whether to mention what she'd seen to Artie but decided against it, not wanting to cause him pain or make him think she had a poor opinion of the girl he loved. He'd realise Celia had no love for him soon enough.

Hoping for a distraction from her thoughts, Lily looked around for the newspaper Elsie had picked up in the tea room after it had been left behind by a customer. A corner of it peeped out from under a cardigan Elsie had thrown onto a chair. Lily drew the newspaper out and saw it had been opened in the middle then folded over. Lily was unfolding it with a view to rearranging the pages when she noticed that circles had been drawn around some of the advertisements on the *Situations Vacant* page.

A cold feeling overtook her. Had Elsie drawn these circles?

Lily looked around as footsteps approached. Elsie entered but stopped when she saw Lily holding the newspaper. 'Ah,' she said.

'Elsie, are you looking for another job?'

'Thinking of it.' Elsie looked both defiant and

awkward.

'Aren't you happy working in the chocolate shop anymore?'

Elsie shrugged. 'It feels time for a change.'

351

32

'Aren't you happy working in the chocolate shop anymore?'
Elsie shrugged. 'It's time for a change.'

'That's what she told me too,' Phyllis said when she and Lily discussed it later.

'It's time for a change.'

'Do you believe her?' Lily asked.

'I don't think it's as simple as needing a new challenge.'

'Neither do I. She isn't bored. She's unhappy.'

But why? Lily had believed Elsie about not wanting a tall, handsome stranger in her life. It had to be something else.

Pierre had no light to shed on it. There'd been no upsetting incidents in the chocolate shop and no major disagreements either.

'Have you spoken to her about how she's feeling?' Lily asked.

Pierre gave her an incredulous look. 'And have her bite off my head like a crocodile?'

Poor Pierre. It couldn't be much fun working with Elsie at the moment.

Elsie continued to be both defiant and awkward in the days that followed.

'You think I'm letting you down,' she accused Lily.

'Not at all. I just want you to be happy.'

For some reason Elsie rolled her eyes at that.

'Elsie, if it's a change you want, I could work in the chocolate shop while you work in the bakery,' Phyllis suggested.

Clearly, it wasn't the sort of change Elsie wanted.

'Is it just your job you want to change, or living

here too?' Lily asked.

'A complete change would be better. It all depends on what sort of job I can get. If I can get one at all.'

'Of course you'll get a job. Any employer will be glad to — '

But Elsie had gone again.

★ ★ ★

1918 was proving to be a difficult year. Lily was glad they were shutting up shop for the usual week's holiday. The break might do them all some good. Lily planned on visiting Marion but on the last day of work a letter arrived. Opening it, Lily saw that it had been written from a nursing home. Oh, no.

> *Dearest Lily,*
>
> *As you may have guessed from the address at the top of this note I'm a little unwell at present but, even though I'm unable to play the hostess, I'd still consider it a great favour if you could visit me.*
>
> *Please don't worry. I'm perfectly comfortable here and the staff are all kindness.*
>
> *Fondest love,*
>
> *Marion x*

Poor Marion! The staff at the nursing home might well be kind, but the kindness of strangers

353

wasn't the same as the kindness of a loving friend. Of course Lily would visit.

She took the train to Hastings the very next day and made her way to the nursing home. She was shocked by Marion's frailty despite the warm smile she gave when she saw Lily approaching with her arms laden with roses.

'Aren't you the loveliest sight?' Marion said, as Lily kissed her cheek and tried to hide her dismay at the delicate feel of it.

'How are you?' Lily asked.

'Comfortable. Contented, even.'

And brave. So brave, because clearly she was fading out of life. 'Let me find a vase for these flowers,' Lily said, needing to escape for a moment to blink away tears.

A nurse fetched a vase filled with water. Lily arranged the flowers and placed them on the small cupboard next to Marion's bed.

'How beautiful,' Marion declared. 'I'll enjoy looking at them.'

'I've brought more gifts,' Lily said, bringing chocolates out of her bag. 'These are some of Pierre's finest creations.'

'Please tell him how much I appreciate them. I can't manage one now but perhaps later. Sit down, Lily. Tell me all your news.'

Lily sat down, held Marion's hand and talked about her life in London though, not wanting to worry her old friend, she skittered over her concerns about Artie and said nothing of Elsie's unhappiness.

'I want you to know how much your friendship has meant to me,' Marion said after a while. 'It was a lucky day when you came into my dear sister's life because that meant you came into mine too. It's given me more pleasure than you can know to see you and receive your letters. It's been a great comfort too, since Hilda died.'

Marion was visibly tiring. 'I'll let you rest for a while,' Lily said. 'But I'll still be here when you wake.'

'I don't want to be a trouble.'

'You're never that. The important thing is that you try to get well. You *are* trying, aren't you?'

'Bless you, Lily. I've never neglected myself.'

But was she fighting? Lily kissed the fragile cheek again and went in search of the nurse. 'Miss Tibbs,' she said. 'How is she?'

The nurse smiled, but sadly. 'Miss Tibbs is at peace with herself and with the world.'

In other words she was ready to meet her Maker calmly. 'Are you telling me she won't recover?'

'Patients can surprise us. But if I were you …'

Lily should prepare for the worst.

She walked in the grounds for a while, upset beyond words, but managed to greet Marion with a smile when the older woman surfaced from her doze. 'I'm going to stay in Hastings so I can visit you every day of my holiday,' Lily told her.

'That won't be much of a holiday for you.'

'It's what I want.'

Marion insisted that Lily should stay in the cottage and Lily was pleased to do so. It meant she could look after the place and say goodbye to it. She was glad Hilda and Marion had had a little time together in this small house by the sea but oh, what a shame they hadn't had longer.

Lily stayed the full week, visiting Marion each day to read to her and see to her comfort as best she could. Marion wouldn't hear of Lily staying longer. 'You have a tea room to run,' she insisted.

'I'll come next Sunday,' Lily promised, though she walked away wondering if she'd ever see her dear friend again.

Reaching home after a tedious train journey, Lily soon discovered that life in London hadn't stood still during her absence. Far from it.

33

I hope Marion is comfortable, Artie had written in a note he'd left for Lily. I'm afraid I found myself with no choice but to leave Grover's. Not because Celia chose to keep seeing me – no such luck – but for other reasons I'll explain when I see you, hopefully on Monday. I'll try to come to the tea room. Please don't worry about me. I have some money put by and I'm just as keen as before to carve a path for myself. Much love, Artie x

At work the next day questions about what had happened circulated in Lily's brain. She would have liked to think Artie had found a job elsewhere but he wouldn't have mentioned having money put by if he'd found another source of income. Worry over Artie and Marion made concentration difficult so it took her a moment to realise a man was hovering at the tea room door the following afternoon.

He was short and middle-aged with greying hair, a moustache and clothes that were neat but old and plain. 'May I show you to a table?' Lily asked.

'Actually, I'm looking for Mr Tomkins. I've arranged to meet him here. Am I right in thinking you're his sister?'

'I am.'

'I'm Mellings, Miss. The foreman at Grover's, though perhaps not for much longer.'

'Is the business in trouble?'

'Not exactly, Miss, but – ah, here's Mr Tomkins now.'

Artie bounded up the stairs, saw Lily and lost no time in hugging her. 'I'm so sorry about Marion,' he said.

Lily nodded. 'How are you? Your note didn't say very much.'

'I'll explain soon, but just now the customer in the corner is trying to attract your attention.'

Lily glanced around and saw he was right.

'Sam and I will find our own table. If you could bring us some tea, that would be wonderful. No rush, though.'

Lily attended to her corner customer then brought tea for Artie and Mr Melling. She couldn't linger because one set of customers was leaving and more customers were arriving. Lily didn't have a moment's pause, in fact, but glanced across at Artie and Mr Melling now and then, wondering what they were discussing so earnestly. They talked for more than an hour, Artie writing things down in a notebook and both of them looking at papers Mr Melling had brought.

Eventually, Mr Melling got to his feet and came towards Lily. 'Thank you for the tea, Miss. I'll wish you a good afternoon.'

He nodded and set off down the stairs. Lily glided across to Artie. 'Well?'

But the tea room was busy still and Lily was needed by her customers. 'Let me help you,' Artie said.

'There's no need for that.'

'I want to help and the sooner we get everything

358

cleared up, the sooner we'll be able to talk without interruption.'

He went downstairs to borrow an apron from Mr Bax then took off his jacket, rolled up his shirt sleeves and got to work washing dishes. When he was up to date with the dishes he helped in the tea room, delivering tea and serving food with a friendly charm that won him smiles from younger women and indulgent looks from mature matrons.

Lily was reminded of the times when Luke had helped and was struck again with the notion that Artie and Luke would find much to like in each other. Luke was still well as far as Lily knew but worry about him never left her and neither did the pang of hurt that squeezed her heart at the thought of her feelings for him going unreturned.

Perhaps she was foolish to write to him as she did, not with any sort of hint as to how she felt about him — or so she hoped — but still opening the window on her most private concerns about Artie, Marion, the tea room and the war. Their exchange of letters had created intimacy between them but it couldn't last.

When Luke returned from the war — and Lily couldn't bear to think that he might not return — he'd be a different person from the man who, distanced from home and friends, wrote letters from the trenches. He'd be purposeful, eager to make up for the time he'd lost by being away. Throwing himself into his business and perhaps finding a girl to love, he'd have no need for Lily's letters and she'd have no place in his life except as an acquaintance.

How unbearable that would be. Lily wasn't at

359

all sure she could stay to watch the man she loved building a new life with someone else. It might be better to move away and start afresh somewhere, perhaps even with Artie though that depended on his plans for the future.

Of course, it would be different if Luke loved her in return.

If.

Not knowing was torture. So too was allowing herself to hope because the higher her hopes soared the further they'd have to fall if they were to be dashed to the ground. As ever, Lily could only endure the uncertainty, pressing on with her work in the meantime.

That work was much lighter with Artie helping. After the tea room had closed they washed up, cleaned up and swept up in record time then spent another few minutes getting things ready for the morning.

'Enough,' Lily finally declared. 'Tell me what's been going on.'

Artie untied his apron, unrolled his sleeves and sat at a table where Lily joined him.

'I suppose you could say I saw Ernest Grover in his true colours,' Artie said.

'When I first started working for him I was grateful for the job and eager to please. Eager to prove myself too. And perhaps I wanted to like or at least respect him because he was Celia's father.'

A ripple of hurt crossed his face at the thought of Celia. Clearly, he hadn't even begun to get over her.

'Declaring my love for her changed all that. I realised then what an unpleasant snob he was. I

360

came to realise he was vindictive too. His manner changed towards me at work. He was rude and ungrateful, belittling everything I did and ordering me to do menial things to make me feel small. Only he didn't make me feel small. He made me see how petty a man *he* was instead. The final straw came when he knocked a bottle of ink over the contract I was studying at my desk. He told me to prepare a replacement but I told him he could prepare it himself because I was finished with him.'

Artie's mouth twisted in what Lily took to be a mix of ruefulness and humour.

'The worm had turned and he couldn't have been more shocked,' Artie said, 'especially as he needed the contract for a meeting that afternoon. He insisted I stay and replace it but I only smiled and told him I was leaving there and then.'

'Goodness.'

'It was impulsive to throw the job over before I'd found another position, but I can't regret it, Lil. It isn't as though I'd have earned a better reference by staying, and a man has to keep some pride.'

'What will you do? Why were you meeting with Mr Melling?'

'That's the exciting news. We're thinking of starting our own business.'

'A building business?'

'Are you worried I don't have the experience? I don't have much, it's true, but I've learned a lot over the past few months. Besides, Sam Melling has years of experience behind him when it comes to the actual building work. The idea is that he'll

361

supervise the work while I focus on finding clients, negotiating contracts, organising supplies and keeping all the papers and finances in order.'

'How will you find clients?'

'Hopefully, we'll start with recommendations from the architects and surveyors we know. We're not looking to operate on the scale of Grover's. At least not at the beginning. We aim to start small but become a company with a reputation for integrity.'

'Which Mr Grover lacks?'

'Sam has his suspicions about that. I don't mean large-scale fraud, but a bit of corner-cutting and the occasional bribe to someone in a position to award a contract. It's one of the reasons Sam wants to leave, the other reason being that he just doesn't have much respect for Grover as a person. Sam and I both believe that every man — every woman too — is worthy of respect, however humble their background. Grover doesn't, so Sam tells me some of the Grover's men will be only too glad to join us if we can offer them work.'

'Mr Melling sounds like a good person to have in your corner. But won't it cost a lot of money to set up a building business?'

'I still have the legacy Mr Alderton left me. My army gratuity too, and I've been putting money by ever since I started work. Sam has money to invest as well. The company will be a partnership.'

Lily could see how the idea thrilled Artie. 'I haven't forgotten my promise to help you, Lil,' he said. 'Money might be tight as the business gets going but in a year or two I hope it'll be on a stronger footing. I've always admired you, sis. I hope I can

362

make a success of a business the way you've made a success of your tea room.' He smiled and added, 'The Tomkins twins taking on the world.'

He had a tough road ahead of him. There was no doubt about that. Business might not materialise and money invested might all be lost. But this chance was what Artie needed. 'I couldn't be more proud of you,' Lily told him.

'Thanks, Lil. I only wish ... Well.'

Lily could guess what he was thinking. He only wished Celia felt the same.

'You'll stay to supper tonight?' Lily asked, wanting to cheer him.

'I'd love to.'

Pierre had announced that he was in a cooking mood so they all went next door for one of his casseroles laced with flavoursome red wine. Michael joined them and Artie shared his plans. Lily was delighted to see the goodwill in her friends' faces and hear them wishing him the best of luck.

'Nothing beats being your own boss,' Pierre declared.

Lily looked towards Elsie, expecting a quip about him being a terrible boss but she made no comment. She'd been as enthusiastic as anyone about Artie's news but her spirits were sinking already. What on earth was wrong with her?

'Michael and I have news too,' Phyllis said and Michael reached out to squeeze her hand. 'We've set a date for our wedding.'

The news was greeted with cries of delight. 'When is it going to be?' Lily asked.

'Next month. It won't be a big wedding. We'll marry in Christ Church and have a meal in the

George Tavern afterwards. All very simple.'

Phyllis looked anxious, clearly thinking of Artie's disappointment over Celia and Elsie's low mood, but both Artie and Elsie were too generous to resent the happiness of friends and congratulated the couple warmly.

Even so Lily detected hidden wistfulness in Artie's expression and as for Elsie...

Understanding suddenly slotted into place in Lily's mind. Of course!

34

After two days of keeping her eyes and ears open, Lily was sufficiently sure of her theory to share it with Phyllis who stared at her in wide-eyed astonishment.

'It never crossed my mind but it makes perfect sense,' Phyllis agreed.

'I don't think talking to Elsie will help, though.'

'Goodness, no. She'll bite your head off or take any job she can find just to escape an awkward conversation.'

'We need to find another way to help her,' Lily suggested.

It was going to take thought and ingenuity.

Artie was occupied for the rest of the week but called in at the tea room early on Friday afternoon. 'I know this is a busy time for you but I just wanted to say hello,' he said, taking a loaded tray from her and carrying it into the tea room.

'I'm glad you're here. Do you have any news about the business?'

'I've met with an architect and a surveyor and both seem willing to give us a chance when a suitable project arises. The architect already has one in mind. In the meantime I'm still working on budgets for the equipment we're likely to need. We'll have to buy some of it but I'm looking into hiring whenever possible, just to begin with. I'm also looking for a small yard we can rent. It'll need an office but a hut will do as long as we can put a telephone in there.'

'It sounds exciting. If you're not working on Sunday would you like to come to Hastings with me? I don't think Marion is well enough to see both of us but you could walk along the seafront while I'm in the nursing home and I could join you afterwards.'

'It's a lovely idea.'

'Don't worry about the cost of the fare. I'll pay for both of us.'

'I'll pay for myself, thank you, little sister. I'm not bankrupt yet.' Artie thought for a moment then smiled. 'I can call you little sister now but I remember when you were two inches taller.'

'That was years ago.'

'We've come a long way from Jessy Street, haven't we? But Mum, Dad and Gran... We'll never forget them.'

'Never,' Lily agreed. 'We've got a lot to thank them for, and I think they'd be proud of us.'

'They were good people. We were lucky to have them in our lives.'

'Lily?' Phyllis spoke from the open door.

Her face was sombre. She beckoned Lily to follow her into the serving room.

Heart beating fast Lily joined her quickly, Artie bringing up the rear.

'A telegram,' Phyllis said, handing it over.

It was from the nursing home. Marion had passed away.

The tea room was full so there was no question of closing it and Marion wouldn't have wanted it to close anyway. It was incredibly hard for Lily to serve up smiles and chatter when her throat was tight from the sobs she kept imprisoned inside her but Artie was magnificent. He borrowed Mr Bax's apron again and took charge so Lily could have occasional moments of respite in the serving room. He did so with charm so no one minded if he wasn't quite as knowledgeable as Lily.

As soon as the lunchtime crowd thinned he urged Lily to go next door to use Pierre's telephone to call the nursing home. She needed to know that her old friend had died peacefully and hadn't suffered.

'Miss Tibbs was perfectly comfortable, both in body and in mind,' the Matron assured Lily. 'She said more than once that she felt her life to be complete and she was looking forward to being reunited with her sister.'

Relieved, Lily asked about the funeral.

'All her affairs are in the hands of her solicitor. Let me give you his telephone number.'

Lily wrote it down, thanked the Matron for caring for Marion and then telephoned the solicitor, Mr Percival. 'My client was keen to save you from the trouble of arranging her funeral,' he told her. 'You're in business in London, I believe.'

'I run a tea room but I still want to come to the funeral.'

'Of course. I'll advise details in due course.'

Lily returned to the tea room, determined to get through the afternoon somehow. As soon as the last customer left, Artie took her into his arms and she sobbed against his chest. When she'd quietened a little he made her a cup of tea and insisted she should sit and drink it while he cleared up after the day's business.

'I'm calmer now,' she told him a little later. 'It just felt too much to lose Marion so soon after Hilda.'

'Of course it did.'

'Thank you for all your help but I'll be fine tomorrow.'

'Sure?'

'Marion and Hilda wouldn't want me to mope. They'd want me to get on with things.'

The following day was a Saturday. Lily was sad though able to cope, but when evening came she sat down to write to Luke about Marion, feeling the need for the closeness that existed through their letters even if it could go nowhere else.

She posted her letter on her way to walk with Artie on Hampstead Heath on Sunday. It was a fine, blowy day and some of the children were flying kites.

'Look how high that one is,' Artie said, pointing.

Lily began to follow the direction of his arm only to see a girl in the distance.

Celia.

She was with another girl – possibly her sister – and two young soldiers walked beside them. Was one of them the young man Lily had seen before?

Perhaps. It didn't matter. The important thing was to get Artie away quickly.

'Let's walk to those trees,' Lily suggested, nudging Artie onwards.

But he'd seen Celia too. He stared at her for a long moment then said, 'Yes, let's,' and headed for the trees.

'I'm sorry,' Lily said, when they were out of

danger of being spotted in return.

'Celia is a beautiful girl. It isn't surprising if she's caught the eyes of other men.'

He made an obvious effort to stay cheerful for the rest of the walk but it was as though clouds had drifted across the sun.

'Please don't worry about me,' he begged Lily, when they parted. 'I'm not the first man to have his heart bruised and I won't be the last. Hard work will be my salvation, just as it's been yours.'

Despite Artie's reassurance Lily felt reluctant to take forward the idea she'd had for helping Elsie. She spoke about it to Phyllis as they cleared up after work the next day.

'It's a great idea,' Phyllis said.

'I'm glad you agree but I think we should wait a week or two before attempting it.'

'We don't want to rub Artie's nose in unhappiness,' Phyllis said, nodding.

'Rub my nose in what?' Artie asked from behind them.

Both girls whirled around. 'We didn't hear you come in,' Lily said.

'Obviously not. But I'm here now and I'd like to know what you meant.'

Lily explained her thoughts. 'But the plan can wait a while.'

'If Elsie is unhappy, she needs to be helped now,' Artie said firmly. 'Tell me what I can do.'

'Well...' Lily began, and told him exactly how he could help.

The next morning Lily spoke to Elsie. 'I think we should all have supper together tomorrow.'

'Any particular reason?'

'We're going through difficult times. I think we should do something cheerful. All of us together.'

'All of us?'

'Mr Bax has a prior engagement but Phyllis, Pierre, Michael, Artie …'

'I suppose I'd better make myself available then,' Elsie said, though a cheerful evening looked like being the last thing she wanted.

Artie played his part very well by keeping Elsie and Pierre talking in the chocolate shop. It meant Lily and Phyllis had everything ready by the time Artie arrived in the tea room leading a glum-looking Elsie and an equally glum-looking Pierre.

Glasses of wine were handed round. 'What are we toasting?' Elsie asked.

'Life,' Lily told her. 'It seems to me that we should seize every chance to be happy. Even if it means taking risks.'

'Risks?'

'The risk of feeling foolish. The risk of feeling vulnerable …'

'You've been reading too many books,' Elsie said, pulling a face, but Lily had already seen that her words had struck a chord.

'What are we eating?' Elsie asked next, as though to move the conversation onto safer ground where no heart-searching was required.

She looked around the tea room then frowned when she saw that only two places had been laid on one of the smaller tables. 'What's this? We need a bigger table, don't we?'

'Why don't you get one ready?' Lily suggested.

Elsie put her drink down and walked over to a large table.

370

'Pierre, would you mind helping her?' Lily asked.

He looked reluctant to go anywhere near Elsie but squared his shoulders and went over, taking hold of the table without saying a word.

Lily and the others crept out of the room.

'Oi! What's going on?' Elsie demanded, as Lily closed the door.

Elsie's footsteps approached rapidly on the other side of it. She rattled the handle. 'Is this door locked?' she demanded.

'It is,' Lily called. 'And it's staying locked until you and Pierre have talked through how you feel about each other.'

'How we...? You've taken leave of your senses, Lily Tomkins.'

'There's food and the bottle of wine to finish. Take a risk, Elsie. Be brave. You too, Pierre. We're going next door so you can bang on this door as much as you like. We shan't come to open it.'

Ignoring the protests, Lily led Artie, Phyllis and Michael downstairs and into the chocolate shop.

'Let's hope Elsie and Pierre don't murder each other,' Lily said.

'Or join forces to murder us,' Phyllis added.

Two hours passed before Lily and the others returned to the tea room. 'Is it safe to open the door?' Lily called.

'You were preaching about taking risks earlier,' Elsie shouted back. 'Why don't you take a risk and find out?'

Lily unlocked the door and opened it cautiously, ready to duck if Elsie threw something at her. But there was no danger of that. Elsie and Pierre were sitting at the little table looking embarrassed but radiant too, and Elsie's scowl was clearly faked. 'All right, you can spare us the smugness, Tomkins. You were right.'

'*We* were right,' Lily pointed out, including the others in the compliment.

'All of you, then.'

Pierre reached across the table for Elsie's hand and kissed it before looking up at Lily. 'We would never have talked if you hadn't locked us in this room. This table...' He gestured to the flowers and paper hearts Lily had scattered across the cloth. 'We had to ask each other why you had made it so romantic.'

Lily imagined the conversation had started stiffly, with Elsie insisting she had no idea what was going on and dismissing the hearts and flowers as stupid.

Perhaps Pierre had said much the same. But two hours was a long time to be locked in a room. Eventually, they would have eaten the food and, with their tongues loosened by wine, inched their way towards confessing their love for each other.

'I never thought this magnificent girl would look at a man like me,' Pierre said. 'So short. So ugly.'

'You're not ugly!' everyone chorused, and Lily added, 'You have a very pleasant face actually.'

'But not a handsome one,' Pierre said.

'I never thought Pierre would look at me,' Elsie confessed. 'A female giant with hair like a ginger sweeping brush and big, clumsy hands.'

'It's love that's important,' Pierre told her, smiling tenderly. 'Soon I shall present a ring as a token of that love.'

'An engagement already?' Lily asked.

'We've wasted too much time being shy of each other,' Pierre said. 'We don't want to waste any more. And I want to get my wonderful Elsie along the aisle before she changes her mind.'

Lily was delighted. Hugging Elsie and then Pierre, she was pleased to see that Artie was generous with his congratulations too though the reminder of what he'd lost must be painful. She was aware of an ache in her own heart as well.

Would Luke ever look at her as tenderly as Pierre looked at Elsie?

But this wasn't the time for thinking of herself. It was a time for celebrating the happiness of two friends and honouring the life of another.

* * *

They closed both shops and the tea room for Marion's funeral. It was a small affair but there was no doubting the warm regard in which Marion had been held by those who were present. By arrangement with the solicitor, Mr Percival, Lily tied the Tibbs family's black crepe ribbon to the doorknocker of Marion's house so the tradition wouldn't be broken. 'Might I keep the ribbon afterwards?' she asked him.

'Certainly. Miss Tibbs wanted you to have these too.' He passed over a small, worn Bible and a silver necklace on which hung a gold ring. 'It was her mother's wedding ring.'

'How incredibly kind,' Lily said.

'Both sisters were very fond of you. I have a letter for you here which explains their thinking.' He took an envelope from his coat pocket and passed it over. 'I suggest you read it later.'

Lily put the envelope and gifts into her bag and retrieved the black ribbon once the funeral was over. She took the Bible out again on the train journey home, smiling fondly when she saw that someone — the sisters' father, perhaps — had recorded their births inside the cover. Lily decided she'd record their deaths there when she got home, adding words that made it clear how much they'd been valued. Hilda and Marion might not have left any family behind, but they'd left plenty of love.

The urge to make them proud of the way she lived her own life had Lily's thoughts turning to the future again. Blissfully happy now, Elsie would be running the chocolate shop with Pierre and in time Phyllis would doubtless look for work which would make the most of her excellent brain. Lily's future was less certain.

She still wasn't sure she could bear living next door to Luke, especially if he began courting someone else. Much as she loved her tea room, Mr Bax's retirement might be a cloud with a silver lining in giving her an excuse for moving away. She'd miss the tea room dreadfully, though. She'd miss her friends and she'd also miss Luke but sometimes a person had to put herself through pain in order to protect her long-term wellbeing.

'I've got a big pot of soup ready to be warmed if anyone's hungry,' Pierre said when they reached London.

Mr Bax decided to head home but Artie agreed

to come and share the soup.

'We need something warm,' he said, because it had begun to rain after they left Hastings and the air was unseasonably chilly.

They had to pass the bakery to reach the chocolate shop. 'Artie!' someone cried from the bakery porch.

'Celia!'

Bedraggled and thoroughly wet, she stumbled into Artie's arms.

35

Up in the serving room Lily filled the kettle with water and put it on the stove to boil, having agreed with Pierre that the soup would have to wait for a while.

Artie had taken a sobbing Celia into the tea room and Lily had closed the door to give them privacy though she was desperate to know what Celia intended by coming here.

Clearly, she still had some feelings for Artie, but was she here to tell him that she was sorry she could never be with him or to tell him she wanted to be with him despite her parents' disapproval? Lily supposed she'd know soon enough.

She arranged the tea things on a tray. Balancing it carefully, she knocked on the tea room door and Artie bade her enter.

He was sitting with his arms around Celia, comforting her as she sobbed. Lily put the tray on the table beside him. 'I'll be upstairs,' she told him. In other words she'd wait in her room in case he needed her.

'Thanks, Lil,' he said.

Phyllis had gone next door so Lily sat alone on her bed. Half an hour passed before Artie came up to talk to her. 'She loves me,' he declared simply.

'You're very loveable,' Lily told him. He deserved to be happy but could Celia make him so? Lily wished she felt more confident about it.

'Have her parents agreed she can continue seeing you?'

'They forbade it.' Artie came to sit on the bed.

'So she's here to say goodbye?'

'She's here because she's tried to forget me and live the life they want for her but it hasn't worked. She can't bear giving me up.'

'She wants to see you in secret?'

'Celia had a big row with her parents. They told her she had to choose between a comfortable life with them and a mean, sorry little life with me. She chose me.'

'She's left home?' Lily was shocked.

Did Celia expect him to marry her immediately? She was young so how would that be possible without her parents' consent? Even if they gave that consent to spare themselves the shame of having a daughter living with a man when unmarried, what would a rushed wedding mean for the couple's happiness when they hadn't had time to get to know each other properly? And what would it mean for Artie's dream of setting up in business?

'I'll admit I didn't expect this,' Artie said. 'But I love Celia so how could I be less than delighted? I'm not going to allow her to throw herself into marriage with me, though. She needs time to be sure she's made the right decision.'

'You can't be considering — '

'Living with her unwed? Of course not. If she changed her mind about me, her reputation would be in tatters. No, I'm going to find respectable lodgings for her.

I'll start looking tomorrow, but for tonight...'

'She can stay here,' Lily confirmed.

Artie squeezed her hand. 'Always the most generous sister.'

'You'll still be able to set up in business with Mr Melling?'

His face sobered. 'I don't know yet. Celia only has ten shillings in her purse.

Naturally, I'm glad to support her but it's bound to take a toll on my savings. I may need to look for a different job.'

'Oh, Artie.'

'A man can't have everything he wants, and knowing Celia loves me will make up for any disappointment over the business.'

He smiled but Lily could see that it would cost him a real pang to let the business idea drop. And what if Celia decided she didn't like what her parents had called a mean, sorry little life? Artie's money would have gone and his dreams with it.

'Celia can sleep in my bed,' Lily said. 'I'll make up a bed for me on the floor.'

'That won't be comfortable for you, Lil.'

'It'll be fine. I can lie on cushions.'

'Will you come and speak to Celia?'

'Of course.'

Celia got up when Lily entered the tea room. 'It's good of you to help me,' she said, calmer now though her lovely face was still ravaged by all the tears. 'I went to Artie's lodgings first but his landlady told me he wasn't in. She wouldn't allow me to wait for him inside so I came here. I hope you — '

She broke off at the sound of movement in the shop below. Elsie and Phyllis came upstairs. 'Sorry to interrupt,' Phyllis said. 'We brought some soup.'

She was holding a covered pot.

'Thank you,' Lily told her. 'Celia is staying here tonight.'

'How nice,' Phyllis said, though Lily could see she was concerned.

'Celia can have my bed,' Elsie offered. 'I can sleep next door so —'

'No, you can't,' Phyllis vetoed firmly.

'I can sleep in Luke's room.'

'You're not staying by yourself under the same roof as Pierre and that's that.'

Elsie rolled her eyes.

'Celia is having my bed. I'll sleep on the floor,' Lily explained.

'It sounds mad to me when there's a perfectly good bed lying empty next door but what do I know?' Elsie asked. 'At least I can go next door to borrow bedding.'

She returned with blankets, sheets and pillows. Phyllis warmed and served the soup then both girls withdrew upstairs.

Lily, Artie and Celia ate quietly. Shy but happy looks passed between Artie and Celia. Lily wished she could shake off the fear that the happiness wouldn't last.

It had been a sad and exhausting day so Artie left soon afterwards. 'I'll be back in the morning,' he said.

Lily went upstairs to prepare her makeshift bed and give them a chance to say a private goodbye.

The following morning Lily was carrying freshly baked bread and tarts up to the tea room when Celia appeared. The golden hair had been arranged with care but otherwise Celia looked subdued. Wary even.

'I hope you got some sleep,' Lily said.

'Plenty, thank you.'

Barely able to sleep herself, Lily had lain awake listening to Celia's soft breathing. 'Now, what would you like for breakfast?' Lily asked. 'Mornings are busy here but we try to snatch a few minutes before we open to eat something. Nothing grand, I'm afraid. Just bread and cheese, toast or porridge.'

'A little bread and cheese will be perfectly satisfactory, thank you. Perhaps with a cup of tea?'

Reaching the serving room, Lily put the tray of bread down and poured tea for Celia from the pot that she'd already filled.

'Potatoes!' Phyllis announced, entering with a basket of them.

She was followed by Frankie who'd brought up a big pot of soup that had been made in the kitchen that morning.

Celia darted out of his way.

Frankie gaped at her, doubtless thinking her lovely, then roused himself and returned to the bakery kitchen.

'Feel free to sit in the tea room,' Lily told her.

Celia duly moved away so Lily could get on with the morning's preparations.

As soon as she had a moment free Lily prepared slices of bread and cheese for

Celia and herself and took them into the tea room where Celia was sitting at a window table. 'Do you have plans for the day?' Lily asked, joining her.

'Artie is taking me to look for lodgings then

I need to go shopping. I didn't manage to pack anything from home.'

'We'll be open all day if you need to come back.'

'Thank you.'

Lily bolted her food and got back to work having told Celia she had no need to rush her meal.

'Has she offered to help?' Phyllis asked.

Lily gave her a cynical look.

'Quite the spoiled little madam, isn't she?'

'She loves Artie. That's a point in her favour,' Lily reasoned, but hours later she was appalled when Celia returned carrying several bags and a hat box. Two of the bags bore the Selfridges name. How much of Artie's money had she spent?

'Artie's gone to see that man who works for my father,' Celia reported. 'We found lodgings for me not far from here. It's a plain sort of place but it's only temporary and I'm treating it as an adventure. Tell me what you think of this hat.'

Celia took it out of the box and put it on. The hat was straw-coloured and decorated with cream flowers. 'You don't like it?' she asked.

'No, it's lovely. It's just… Excuse me. Those customers need serving. Do sit down, Celia. I'll bring you some tea.'

Celia sat but looked deflated. Would she complain to Artie that Lily had been unkind?

Artie gave no sign of having heard a complaint when he called in to collect Celia later though perhaps she'd save her grumbling for when they were alone.

'How was your meeting with Mr Melling?' Lily asked.

'We haven't cancelled our plans yet, but I've

warned him that my circumstances have changed. Thanks again for all you've done for Celia.'

Lily hugged him, placed a dutiful kiss on Celia's soft cheek and waved them off.

It wasn't until she was getting ready to sleep in her own bed again that Lily remembered the envelope Marion's solicitor had given her. With all that had happened since then, it had slipped her mind. Lily opened it, expecting nothing more than a note confirming Marion's gifts of the Bible and ring but was surprised to find two letters inside. One of them bore Marion's careful hand-writing so Lily began to read that one first.

Moments later she gasped.

36

Lily chose to keep Marion's letter to herself for the time being. Deciding what to do about it would require careful thought and Lily wanted neither to rush into a decision nor confuse herself with the opinions of her friends, however well meant they might be.

When morning came she went about the business of getting the tea room ready as usual, trying to clear her head by thinking of pleasant things. After all, amid all the uncertainty and worry there was much to appreciate. The tea shop was doing well, Phyllis and Michael's wedding was approaching swiftly, and Elsie and Pierre were blissfully happy.

Elsie soon brought more good news. 'I've got it!' she yelled, pounding up the stairs.

'Got what?' Phyllis asked, coming after her.

'My ring, of course. A messenger just delivered it from the jeweller. Look. Isn't it the most beautiful ring you ever saw?'

It was an emerald surrounded by diamonds. Elsie danced around the tea room with her hand in the air, admiring the way it sparkled. 'Me getting married,' she mused. 'Who'd have thought it?'

'We would,' Lily and Phyllis told her.

'It's a lovely ring,' Lily said.

'Gorgeous,' Phyllis agreed.

Elsie walked over the window to see how the

stones sparkled in the daylight.

'Are there no customers in the chocolate shop today?' Lily asked, winking at Phyllis.

'Pierre can look after them.'

'If you leave him with all the work, he might decide he wants his ring back,' Phyllis suggested.

'Tough. He can't have it. Anyway, I'm his fiancée now. He should be falling at my feet in gratitude. I'd better go and show Mr B and Frankie the ring or they'll be wondering what all the fuss is about.' Still holding her hand aloft, Elsie floated out of the room, murmuring to herself as she went. 'Me, a fiancée!'

Phyllis shook her head, smiling, then went down to the shop. Alone in the tea room Lily refused to contrast Elsie's happiness with her own uncertainty over Luke and Artie. She was thrilled for Elsie.

Customers came and went, keeping Lily busy all day long. Even so she couldn't stop her thoughts from returning to Marion's letter occasionally. She'd read it so many times last night that she knew the words by heart.

Dearest Lily,

I'm writing this while I'm still able to hold a pen because I suspect my remaining days on earth will be few. By the time you receive this letter they'll have passed but I don't want you to grieve for me. Neither Hilda nor I had the knack of making friends but we were blessed when you came into our lives because you opened up a whole new world of interest to us. We love you and we're

proud of you, and if we can help you on your way
through life then we wish to do so.

This brings me to the purpose of this letter because
it isn't just to thank you for your friendship. I
hope to do that in person before I'm recalled to my
Maker. It's to explain why Hilda and I are leav-
ing everything we own to you. It doesn't amount
to a fortune — mostly it's the house in Hastings
— but it's yours. Mr Percival will sell the house
and you can do as you choose with the proceeds.
We wish you well, Lily. You're the daughter of our
hearts if not our bodies and we love you.
Marion x

How amazingly kind of the sisters! Whatever
she did with the money, Lily would be eternally
grateful for their generosity.

Mr Percival's letter had confirmed that she was
to inherit the entire estate and asked for instructions on whether the house and contents should
be sold immediately. Lily had written back to
ask him to delay a sale until she'd had a chance
to decide which of the contents she might keep.
She'd sent the letter this morning, snatching a
moment to run to the post box across the street.

If Artie and Celia were to set up home together,
they might be in need of the furniture as well as the
pots and pans. Could Celia even cook, though? If
not, she'd just have to learn.

The tea shop was closing when Lily was startled
to realise Celia was hovering by the door. 'Sorry,'
Celia said. 'I didn't mean to make you jump.'

'You took me by surprise, that's all, but come
in. Sit down.'

'I don't want to get in your way but I do have something to say to you.'

'Oh?' Had she given up on Artie already?

'Can you spare me five minutes?'

'Of course.'

Lily put the tray down, sat at a clean table and gestured to Celia to join her.

'How can I help?'

'I want you to know I took most of the things I bought yesterday back to the shops.'

Lily hadn't expected that.

'You looked dismayed when you saw them and I gradually realised why. I was extravagant and Artie can't afford extravagance. I bought cheaper things instead and not many of those. I know I need to be more careful in future, especially if Artie is to set up in business with Mr Melling. I don't want his dreams to change because I've been impulsive.'

'I'm glad.'

'I may not be used to economy but I'll train myself. Artie is worth the sacrifice.'

Clearly, there was more to Celia than Lily had thought. She should have trusted Artie's judgement all along.

'I know you don't like me much, but I really do want to make Artie happy,' Celia said. 'Oh, you don't need to deny it,' she added, as Lily opened her mouth to reply, 'I've been horribly spoilt and selfish, and I know I've been a snob so I don't blame you for not liking me. I hope you'll give me a second chance, though. For Artie's sake, if not for mine.'

'Of course I will,' Lily said, smiling. 'Make Artie

386

happy and I might even come to love you.'

She was even more surprised when tears glistened in Celia's eyes. 'I'll certainly try. Well, I know you're busy so I won't keep you any longer.'

They walked to the door together. 'Goodbye,' Celia said, offering to shake hands.

'Oh, come here.' Lily drew Celia closer and kissed her cheek.

It was a weight off Lily's mind to know that Celia was neither shallow nor superior. It meant Artie had every hope of being happy. Phyllis, Elsie and now Artie happy. Which only left Lily. But she wasn't going to brood on that.

By the time she went to bed three possibilities had occurred to her about how she might use her inheritance:

She could look into buying the bakery and tea room from Mr Bax. He might be willing to let her pay the balance in instalments over time if she didn't have enough to pay him the total value all at once though she'd have to be careful not to embarrass him if he needed payment in full in order to house himself and his sisters. She also needed to decide if she could bear living next to Luke.

She could set up a tea room of her own in a place where property was cheaper.

Perhaps even in Hastings. That would take her away from Luke but would mean leaving her other friends behind. Artie and Celia too.

She could use the money to help Artie in his business. His savings wouldn't last forever, especially now he had Celia to maintain, and Lily's money might be the difference between the business succeeding or failing, particularly if it took some time to find clients.

To help her own dreams or to help Artie's? It was a terrible dilemma and Lily needed time to think her options through.

* * *

Rain threatened on the day of Phyllis and Michael's wedding but nothing could dampen the joy of the occasion. Phyllis wore a simple white dress that Michael's mother had made together with the veil and wax-flowered headdress Mrs Picton had worn at her own wedding.

Michael wore his best suit with a carnation pinned to the lapel. Frankie had bought a suit for the occasion too as he was to be his brother's best man. He looked smart but endearingly bashful.

The number of guests was small — just Michael's family and a handful of friends — but a warmer-hearted group of people would have been impossible to find. After the ceremony they walked to the upper room of the George Tavern for a modest but welcome meal. 'I want you all to be able to sit down and enjoy the day as guests,' Phyllis had said.

She had, however, accepted a cake, baked by Mr Bax and decorated with Pierre's help. It was a beautiful creation.

They all waved Phyllis and Michael off on a three-night honeymoon in a Brighton guest house then said their goodbyes.

Mr Bax and his sisters settled into taxis. So did Michael's family. Lily, Artie and Celia walked home with Elsie and Pierre walking behind them, bickering in the old good-natured way about what they wanted at their wedding.

'The best pastries for pudding,' Pierre suggested.

'I want trifle.'

'But — '

'You're in England now. That means trifle.'

'The English eat pastries too.'

'But they prefer trifle.'

They reached the chocolate shop. 'I'm going to sit with Pierre for a while,' Elsie announced.

'And I'm going to walk Celia home,' Artie said.

Celia looked as though she wanted to come into the tea room to talk. 'You don't need to rush off for my sake,' Lily said.

Celia hesitated, glanced at Artie then said, 'It's been a long day. Perhaps we'd better get on.'

'Goodnight, then,' Lily said.

She assumed Artie wanted to spend time alone with Celia, perhaps to talk about the wedding they'd have when they were in a position to marry, but Lily was curious about why Celia had wanted to stay.

Elsie arrived home half an hour later. 'Lovely wedding,' she declared, 'and who'd have guessed Celia would turn out to be human?'

'She's proved me wrong about her but I'm glad,' Lily said.

Luke had been right to advise caution.

Luke. The thought of him made Lily's heart feel hopelessly raw. But life went on.

The next morning brought Celia back to the tea room. She looked unsure of herself. 'I hope I

389

won't embarrass you by asking,' she began, then trailed off.

'Asking me what?' Lily prompted.

'It occurred to me that you must be short-staffed with Phyllis away on honeymoon.'

'Frankie is going to work in the shop but yes, it's going to be a challenge.'

'Might I help?'

Another surprise.

'Sorry,' Celia said, turning away. 'I shouldn't have asked. I won't — '

'Don't go! If you really want to help, I'll accept the offer gladly.'

'You don't need to pay me. I just want the experience because it might help me to get a job somewhere else. It isn't right that Artie should be paying for my lodgings. I'd like to earn enough to pay for them myself so Artie can use his money for the business.'

Lily found an apron and cap for Celia then set her to work preparing tables.

She was slow and clearly not yet at ease serving customers, but Lily could see that she was trying hard. Doubtless she'd soon loosen up, and quicken up too.

'Do you know, I'm shattered but feel oddly... satisfied,' Celia said, when they finally closed for the day.

'Perhaps that's because you've done something useful with your time,' Lily suggested.

'You're right. I feel ashamed of the sort of life I used to lead.'

'The important thing is that you've changed.'

'You're like Artie, Lily. Generous.'

390

Celia helped to make supper too and ate her meal hungrily. 'I've never had so much appetite,' she said.

'You've never worked so hard. Eat as much as you want,' Lily urged. 'You've earned it.'

The compliment won her a grateful smile.

Celia came the next day too. 'Don't feel you have to spend all of your time here,' Lily told her.

'I enjoy it. I like feeling useful.'

'You're very useful,' Lily told her. 'Quite a treasure, in fact.'

Celia laughed. 'I'll never have your knack of juggling six tasks while chatting to customers but I hope I'm good enough.'

Even after Phyllis returned from honeymoon Celia continued to help in either the tea room or the bakery shop. It freed Frankie to learn more of Mr Bax's baking skills. Lily, Phyllis and Mr Bax all agreed that Celia should be paid a wage and the first time she received her weekly pay packet she couldn't have been more pleased.

'Thank you so much for letting me work here, Lily,' Celia said, then smiled at what appeared to be a passing thought.

'What is it?' Lily asked.

'I was thinking about how I used to be afraid of you.'

'Afraid of me?' Lily was stunned.

'Perhaps fear isn't the right word. Awe might be better. Yes, I used to be in awe of you. Not that I understood what I was feeling then. It actually puzzled me. I thought I should have the upper hand because my family had money and status, but you always seemed so brave and capable. And

Artie thought the world of you. I suppose I was a little jealous.'

'Artie thinks the world of you too.'

'I know. I only hope I'm growing worthy of him.'

'You are,' Lily assured her.

October came and brought cause for celebration. Based in a small yard not far from the tea shop, Tomkins & Melling, Building Contractors, was hard at work on its first small project and had another in the pipeline. Artie had also proposed to Celia and been accepted joyfully. Lily had another ring to admire, this one a sapphire to match Celia's blue eyes.

'You can't get married before me,' Elsie protested to Celia.

Pierre was hoping Luke would be home for his wedding to Elsie and as the month wore on it began to look more and more possible. The talk in the tea shop and out on the street was of the war and this time it really did appear as though the end might be in sight.

Some customers heard the talk with ravaged faces because their loved ones had already fallen. Others heard it with expressions of desperate hope that peace would come before their loved ones suffered a similar fate. Lily felt that desperate hope for Luke. Whether he cared for her or not, she wanted fervently for him to survive.

Early in November they all thrilled to the news that the German ally, Austria-Hungary, was out of the war. Rumours circulated that Germany itself would soon seek peace.

Then one day a customer rushed up the stairs into the tea room to shout that an armistice had been signed. After four devastating years the bloody war was over, he said, and promptly burst into tears.

Some people rushed out to buy newspapers as though they'd believe it only when they read it in print. Others raced home to their families or joined crowds gathering in the street to cheer and sing and dance. Still others simply stared as though too numb to take it in.

Lily headed for the serving room where she sat down heavily. It had been several days since she'd last heard from Luke and the fighting had apparently continued to the last moment. It would be too cruel if he'd fallen in the last hours of the war.

'You've heard?' Mr Bax had come upstairs with Phyllis.

'It's wonderful news,' Lily said.

Pierre and Elsie ran up too. 'Our Luke is coming home!' Pierre raised his arms to heaven but of course Luke would only be coming home if he'd survived.

Three days passed before Elsie raced into the tea room with more news. 'He's alive!' she announced. 'Luke is alive.'

Thank God! Lily felt dizzy with relief. 'I'm so glad,' she said, but had Luke written only to Pierre or was there a letter to Lily caught up in the postal service somewhere between here and France? Post from the front had never been reliable.

Elsie gave her one of those all-seeing looks but thankfully kept her thoughts to herself.

Lily received a letter from Luke the following morning. He wrote that he was well and thankful that the war was over though mindful of the poor souls who'd lost their lives or would suffer from their injuries for the rest of their days. He was looking forward to coming home and seeing his friends but had no information yet about when this might be.

He made no mention of wanting to see Lily in particular. Not that there was necessarily any significance in that. A face-to-face conversation on his return would be much more appropriate if he had tender feelings for her.

If.

More news filtered through. Fordyce and some of Artie's other friends from Camfordleigh had survived. Customers also reported the survival of sons, brothers, husbands and nephews, though in the cruellest of blows the son of one customer had been killed on the very last day of fighting.

The peace was followed quickly by more good news. Another law had been passed allowing women to stand for Parliament.

'We'll see you there one day, Phyll,' Elsie predicted. 'You and Michael both.'

Luke wrote to say he was delighted by the news but he still had no idea when he'd be returning. There were rumours that men were being selected for return based on their occupation and usefulness at home. Luke wrote wryly that a man who made chocolate probably wasn't at the top of this list.

A week later Lily had a visitor. But it wasn't Luke. It was a woman.

37

Older than Lily by a handful of years, the woman was strikingly attractive, a vision of fair beauty dressed exquisitely in pale blue silk.

'Miss Tomkins?' Her voice was accented. French?

'Yes.'

'I am Hélène Moreau. You have heard my name before, perhaps?'

'I'm afraid I haven't.'

'I am the friend of Luke Goddard.' Miss Moreau announced the connection as though expecting Lily to be much impressed.

Instead Lily felt wary. *The* friend of Luke or *a* friend? It was hard to know if the visitor's words had been selected deliberately or resulted simply from awkwardness with the English language. 'I'm a friend of Luke's too,' Lily said, to test Hélène's response.

The visitor's smile left Lily in no doubt that Hélène believed the friendships involved very different degrees of intimacy. Lily's heart began to rattle against her ribs.

'Luke has been my friend – and the friend of my family — in Switzerland for many years,' Hélène continued. 'His absence has been hard to bear. *J'ai été* misérable sans lui. But still he is not returned?'

'Not yet.'

Hélène's lovely mouth made a moue of disappointment. 'I must bear the separation longer.

395

But now I will drink your English tea.'

Lily showed her to a table, conscious of the swish of Hélène's silk dress as she walked. 'Would you like cake as well?'

'*Gateau? Non.*' Hélène shuddered. 'Tea only, *s'il vous plaît.*'

Lily went to fetch it, preparing a tray with trembling fingers. She took a deep breath then returned to Hélène's table. 'Luke must have mentioned me if you know my name,' Lily suggested.

'The little English girl who serves tea in a café,' Hélène said, as though quoting him. 'Yes. He is fond of this café. To him it is... Oh, what is the word? Amusing? Yes, that is it.'

Lily winced.

'Luke and I have such hopes, but this war...' Hélène shook her head, pouring tea but adding no milk or sugar. 'Luke is a man of principle. Until he was certain he would return whole in his body and his mind, he would not... not...' She looked up at Lily. 'I know not the word.'

'Commit?' Lily said, and Hélène nodded.

He'd told Lily much the same thing. Had he got the idea for letting Lily down gently from having already used the argument to explain his feelings to his true love, Hélène? Or had he merely seized on a convenient way of disentangling himself from every woman who'd shown an interest in him? Either way, it was clear that he had no special feelings for Lily.

'Excuse me.' Forcing a smile, Lily retreated to the serving room to blink back tears. She'd never been sure of Luke's love. Not for a single moment. But to know he felt nothing more than friendship for her was crushing.

But there was work to be done and not for anything would Lily let Hélène see her distress. It was mortifying to think of her reporting it to Luke with a sympathetic but amused shake of her elegant head. 'That poor little girl must have imagined … So sweet but so sad.'

Lily blew her nose and returned to the tea room to show some new arrivals to a table. Discipline had ever been her friend and it helped her now though her heart felt ready to burst and she was desperate to be alone.

Hélène didn't stay long. Lily had just fetched a tray of tea for her new customers when she saw her visitor rise to her feet. 'My bill?' Hélène asked.

Lily wanted to tell her no payment was required but feared it might be taken as a sign of how upset she was. 'Of course,' she said, taking Hélène's money and bidding her goodbye with what she hoped was breezy indifference.

Clearing the table, Lily saw that Hélène had barely touched her cup. Clearly, English-style tea served by a little English girl in a quaint English tea room wasn't to her taste.

Doubtless Hélène had gone next door to see Pierre after she'd left the tea room. Perhaps she'd also identified herself downstairs in the bakery shop where Celia was helping Phyllis. Not wanting to be thought strange by keeping quiet about Hélène's visit, Lily mentioned it to them but received only blank looks in response. 'We were too busy to notice people going up to the tea room,' Phyllis explained, and Celia added, 'I was too terrified of giving the wrong change.'

Lily was even more surprised when Elsie gave her an equally blank look on her return from the chocolate shop. 'Pierre didn't have any visitors today.'

'She was a family friend of Luke's. I assumed she was a friend of Pierre's too but perhaps not.' Lily shrugged to suggest she hadn't been particularly interested.

'What did she want?'

'To say hello to Luke, if he'd been here.'

'She came all the way from Switzerland to say hello?'

'I imagine she was in London for other reasons. I didn't have much chance to talk to her.'

Lily hid her face by turning away to wash dishes. Elsie was floating on a cloud of happiness these days but hadn't lost her ability to look deep inside a person and see things that person preferred to keep locked away.

Lily yawned several times during the evening to give herself an excuse for going to her room early. She sat on her bed for a while then got under the covers and gave herself up to misery.

She was exhausted the following morning and a headache sat just above her eyes. Yet, despite the heartache, she was glad of Hélène's visit. If Lily's hopes had to be crushed, it was better for her to suffer sooner rather than later because she'd start to heal all the sooner. And this way she could pretend romance had never entered her thoughts and spare both Luke and herself from embarrassment.

Not that there was any sign of Luke returning soon. December was passing rapidly but he was still in France and rumours suggested it could

398

be many months before all of Britain's soldiers, sailors and airmen came home. So much for the promise of early discharge Lily had seen on recruiting posters at the beginning of the war.

She mentioned Hélène's visit in a letter to Luke but he said nothing about her in his reply. It didn't matter. The important thing was that he knew now that Lily was under no illusions about him.

She threw her energies into decorating the tea room with holly, fir cones and baubles, placing slices of dried oranges and cinnamon sticks into the foliage to scent the air with Christmas smells. She made new menus too, painting sprigs of holly at the tops.

Elsie and Frankie helped Mr Bax to haul sacks of holly and other greenery from home so they could decorate both shops. 'We've done our bit. We'll leave the artistic stuff to you three,' Elsie said, nodding at Lily, Phyllis and Celia.

It was sad to know that Hilda and Marion wouldn't be sharing Christmas with them this year. Luke would be absent too but everyone else would be here even if Phyllis, Michael and Frankie could only come during the evening.

'I never realised how much fun Christmas could be,' Celia said. 'We used to go to Selfridges and Fortnum and Mason for our shopping because it seemed important to buy gifts that would impress people with their cost. I see now that real joy lies in being inventive with very little money and giving people presents they'll really like.'

Lily smiled. Freed from the narrow snobbery of her parents, Celia had become as important to

Lily as Elsie and Phyllis.

With Celia helping in the tea room and bakery shop, there was more time for Christmas shopping. They'd all contributed to a parcel for Luke and sent it off to him in France, Lily giving a book — a Sherlock Holmes mystery — that she hoped he might find entertaining. Now she shopped for her other gifts.

Busy saving for their marriage, Artie and Celia had little money for new clothes so Lily bought a shirt for Artie and a blouse for Celia. Neither was expensive — and nowhere near as luxurious as Celia had enjoyed in the past — but Lily knew they'd be welcome all the same.

Shopping gave Lily time alone to think about the future. She couldn't delay the sale of the Hastings house indefinitely and wondered if she should appoint New Year as the deadline for reaching a decision. It would introduce some certainty into her life. Making plans of one sort or another might also help her to stop brooding. Lily was tired of feeling as though her heart were trailing along the floor behind her. Self-pity was awful and Gran would be ashamed if Lily gave in to it.

On Christmas Eve they set up the tea room for the morrow, laying the table, hanging paper chains across the ceiling and decorating the tree Frankie had carried in for them. Down in the bakery kitchen, a freshly-plucked turkey waited on a plate in the pantry alongside baskets of potatoes, carrots, parsnips and greens. A pudding and cake too. And bottles of sherry, wine and beer.

'I think we're ready,' Elsie announced, adding

her clumsily wrapped gifts to the pile under the tree. 'Pierre is making supper soon if you'd all like to come round and share it?'

'I'll join you later,' Lily said. 'I'd like a breath of fresh air first.'

She sat alone for a moment then put on her coat and went for a walk, needing quietness and solitude to give her the strength to make a good show of enjoying the festivities.

Lights were showing in windows now the threat from Zeppelins and Gothas had passed. Walking beside rows of houses, Lily caught the cosy gleam of gold from fires and Christmas tree candles while some windows framed scenes of families gathered together happily.

People passed her in the street. Purposeful people bearing shopping or hastening home to loved ones. All wished her a Merry Christmas and Lily wished them a Merry Christmas in return. She saw a group of carol singers, paused to listen to 'Silent Night' then walked on again.

Reaching Highbury Fields, she stepped in to sit on a frosty bench. Resisting the temptation to sigh, Lily counted her blessings instead. She was lucky. After all these years she was reunited with Artie at last. No longer were they snatching mere moments together. They were sharing their lives fully.

She had the best friends anyone could wish for too. A job she loved, and even the prospect of money once the Tibbs sisters' house was sold. She was grateful for all of it, yet the sigh escaped anyway.

'Is there room on there for me?'

Lily's head whipped round. 'Luke!'

'I saw you come in,' he said, sitting beside her and dumping his pack on the ground.

He hadn't shaved again and his jaw was dark with stubble. But when he smiled his teeth looked white and the light from a nearby streetlamp caught the familiar gleam in his eyes. Lily's heart skittered like a frightened sparrow's as she was torn between launching herself at his chest and running away because she was unprepared for this meeting and terrified of exposing how she felt.

For a moment she simply stared at Luke's beloved face. When she spoke her voice emerged huskily as if it hadn't been used in a while. 'This is unexpected.'

'I didn't know I was being discharged until yesterday. Luckily, I managed to get on a boat.'

'Just in time for Christmas.'

'Mmm.' His eyes were soft. So very soft.

Lily swallowed hard, cast around inside her head for something to say and finally sought escape in humour. 'I'm afraid the turkey might not stretch to include you as we didn't know you were coming. You might have to settle for a sandwich for your Christmas lunch.'

'Even a sandwich will be an improvement on army rations. Food isn't the only reason I'm glad to be back, though.'

Lily needed to swallow again. 'It must be wonderful to have all that fear behind you. To know you can wash and bathe, and wear your own clothes. To choose how to spend your time ... '

'I'm more excited at the thought of being with the people I care about.'

Was he thinking especially of Hélène? Was she waiting for him somewhere in London? Lily shied away from the answers.

'Did you receive the gifts we sent?' she asked instead.

'I did and they're in here.' He patted his pack. 'I haven't had time to buy gifts to give in return, though. Except for one gift, which I've been carrying close to my heart for a while.'

He dug under his greatcoat to the breast pocket of his uniform and pulled out a small leather pouch. Opening the drawstring, he tipped something wrapped in fabric into the palm of his hand. Unfolding it, he revealed a ring. A solitaire diamond on a gold band.

Lily's stomach lurched. There could be no doubt about it now. Luke loved Hélène. He held the ring up to the sky. 'I chose a diamond because it's like a star. I carried it with me all this time to remind myself of the brightest star in my firmament and the future I want to enjoy with her. I used to kiss the ring because I couldn't kiss her. It gave me comfort. Something to live for in those dark days in the trenches.'

Lily had to say something but what? How it was possible for a heart to hurt so much?

'Weren't you afraid of losing it?'

'I kept a note with it in case I fell.' He tugged a piece of paper out of the pouch and offered it to Lily.

She leaned away, horrified at the thought of reading a tribute to Hélène. 'I don't think I should read anything so personal.'

'I suppose it is rather personal. I'll read it then.

403

In the event of my death I wish this ring to be forwarded to the girl I love.'

Lily got to her feet. 'It's cold. We should be getting back.'

'I haven't finished.'

'I think you've read enough.' She set off down the path.

'*That girl is Lily Tomkins,*' he read.

A thrill of shock stopped Lily in her tracks. She turned slowly, searching Luke's face to try to make sense of what she'd heard. 'But I thought... I understood...'

'Hélène?'

Lily nodded.

Luke grimaced. 'It was obvious from the stiff way you wrote about her that she'd been making mischief. Hélène's father was my father's friend. He came to France and we met when I had a week in rest camp. Hélène came too and I took the opportunity to tell her about you. I've long known she has a partiality for me despite every discouragement on my part and I thought I was doing her a kindness by letting her know my heart belonged to you. It never crossed my mind that she'd go to London with the intention of driving a wedge between us.'

'She made it sound as though you shared an understanding, but wouldn't turn it into a commitment until you'd returned from the war safe and sound.'

'I'd told *you* I couldn't commit until I'd returned.'

'I thought it was your way of letting me down. I thought you'd got the idea from having already said it to her.'

404

'It was the other way round. Hélène knew I'd said it only to you, but obviously she used it to try to turn you against me.'

Doubtless to leave the field clear for her.

Luke smiled and held out a hand to invite Lily to return to the bench. Lily sat, her heart beating crazily.

'I'm in agony here,' Luke said then.

'Agony? Are you hurt?' She turned on the bench, searching him for signs of injury.

'I don't mean physical agony. But I've just bared my soul to you, Lily. I've told you I love you. How do you feel about me?'

Didn't he know? Could he not see it, sense it, feel it? 'I love you, of course.'

He breathed out slowly. 'Thank God!'

'I just never dreamt that...' She gestured to the ring. 'So soon!'

'We've known each other for more than a year, Lily.'

'But we've spent most of that time apart.'

'My feelings for you date from the first day we met and they've been growing ever since. We might not have spent much time together but we've spent long enough for me to know you're the woman I want to spend the rest of my life with. And we've written often. Letters that have spoken from one soul to another. So ...'

He moved off the bench and got down on one knee. 'Will you do me the honour of becoming my wife?'

She laughed at the deliciousness of life. 'Nothing could make me happier.'

'Nor me,' Luke said, grinning, and he slipped

the ring onto her finger.

'It fits!' she said.

'That's because I've looked at your dainty fingers often and imagined this moment. I've spent many an hour thinking of the future we might share too.' He sat beside her on the bench again. 'I'd like us to buy the bakery and tea room when Mr Bax is ready to sell them. Not with any intention of forcing him out, though. He could stay on as baker if he liked, choosing how many hours he worked and continuing to train the boy, Frankie, you've mentioned in your letters. If Frankie would like to stay on as well.'

'I'm sure he would.'

'I've got ideas for developing the tea room but only with your approval. The chocolate shop has a big room upstairs that sits right next to the tea room. If we knock both rooms together, we could expand into tea dances and perhaps evening entertainment too. Mark my words, Lily. The end of the war will rush in a new era. People are weary of misery. They'll want joy.'

'It's a wonderful idea,' Lily said, already excited about the new challenge.

'We'll have to look at the costs,' Luke cautioned. 'We'll have to speak to the bank about a loan as well, but —'

'I have some money.' Lily told him about the Hastings house.

'How incredibly kind of Hilda and Marion,' Luke said. 'I imagine nothing would please them more than for their gift to help you and your tea room.'

'True. Do you think we might ask Artie to do

the building work?'

'Of course.'

Lily glowed with pleasure. 'We're all happy now,' Lily said. 'Except for Hélène.'

'I could never have made Hélène happy because I neither love her nor share her taste for grandness,' Luke said. 'Now she knows I'm out of reach she'll soon find someone else. She isn't the sort of woman to sit at home pining, especially as I suspect her feelings for me are more about wanting me than loving me.'

Lily nodded thoughtfully then smiled. 'Let's go home. The others will be wondering where I am and I can't wait to see their faces when you walk in beside me. I can't wait for you to meet Artie either. You'll like each other, I'm sure.'

'I'm sure too, but there's something more urgent that requires our attention before we go home.'

He looked at her with darkening eyes that made Lily blush with pleasure. And with that they moved together for a kiss.

Acknowledgements

Heartfelt thanks are due to my lovely readers, my super agent, Kate Nash, and to everyone at Team Aria who has helped with this book including my wonderful editor, Rhea Kurien, my copy editor Dushi Horti, my proofreader Jay Dixon, my cover designer Cherie Chapman and Marketing manager, Vicky Joss. You're all fabulous.

We do hope that you have enjoyed
reading this large print book.

Did you know that all of our titles
are available for purchase?

We publish a wide range of high
quality large print books including:
Romances, Mysteries, Classics
General Fiction
Non Fiction and Westerns

Special interest titles available in
large print are:
The Little Oxford Dictionary
Music Book, Song Book
Hymn Book, Service Book

Also available from us courtesy of
Oxford University Press:
Young Readers' Dictionary
(large print edition)
Young Readers' Thesaurus
(large print edition)

For further information or a free
brochure, please contact us at:
Ulverscroft Large Print Books Ltd.,
The Green, Bradgate Road, Anstey,
Leicester, LE7 7FU, England.
Tel: (00 44) 0116 236 4325
Fax: (00 44) 0116 234 0205

Other titles published by Ulverscroft:

THE BRIGHTON GUEST HOUSE GIRLS

Lesley Eames

Thea's loathsome stepbrother is trying to trick her out of her inheritance of her parents' beautiful house in the seaside town of Brighton by means of a will which Thea believes to be forged. Anna is pregnant and grieving, her explorer fiancé lost at sea. Her violent father drives her from the family home in the backstreets of London's Bermondsey and her fiancé's upper-class relatives cruelly reject her. Daisy is in search of independence, running from a man she doesn't want to marry. Together the three girls set up Thea's home as a guest house and embark on a mission to outwit her stepbrother by proving his fraud.

A WIDOW'S VOW

Rachel Brimble

1851. After her merchant husband saved her from a life of prostitution, Louisa Hill was briefly happy as a housewife in Bristol. But then, her husband is found hanged in a Bath hotel room, a note and a key to a property in Bath the onlt things she has left of him. And now the debt collectors will come calling.

Left with no means of income, Louisa knows she has nothing to turn to but her old way of life. But this time, she'll do it on her own terms — by turning her home into a brothel for upper class gentlemen.

Enlisting the help of Jacob Jackson, a quiet but feared boxer, to watch over the house, Louisa is about to embark on a life she never envisaged. Can she find the courage to forge this new path?

THE WOMEN OF WATERLOO BRIDGE

Jan Casey

London, 1940. After her fiancé breaks off their engagement, Evelyn decides to do her part for the war effort by signing up for construction work on Waterloo Bridge. She begins to realise that there could be so much more to her life than anything she'd ever dared to dream of.

Grieving after her little boy dies in an air raid, Gwen is completely lost when her husband sends their younger children to the countryside for safety. Enlisting as a construction worker, she is partnered with cheerful Evelyn. The two women strike up a heartwarming friendship.

Musical prodigy Joan's life has always been dictated by her controlling mother. When an affair nearly ends in scandal, Joan finally takes her life into her own hands. She soon finds work at Waterloo Bridge. Yet there are other troubles for her to overcome ...